A Dance in the Dark

ISBN-13: 9798819546093

Map design: Pyetro dos Santos

To all readers who wish to escape the real world for a few hours (because they hate this world).

And to all the people who, like me, are passionate about reading stories.

I dedicate this book to you.

Attention:

This book is for those who ENJOY reading and are seeking a different reality to escape for a few hours. You won't find perfect characters or a perfect plot. This is not a perfect book so please, read with no expectations and with an open mind.

1. Before anyone is in doubt, her name is pronounced like the wine rosé.
2. Those who have read this book have said that it gets better from chapter 11, in case you think about giving up.
3. This is a contemporary fantasy novel, but it's set in a palace. Does it fully make sense? Probably not, but don't judge me for that. 21st century novel in a palace. That's it.
4. There's a list of the characters at the end in case you get lost because I might have created too many characters. Sorry!
5. You'll find more messages like this in the middle of the story, and it'll be me commenting. Deal with this and let's interact :)

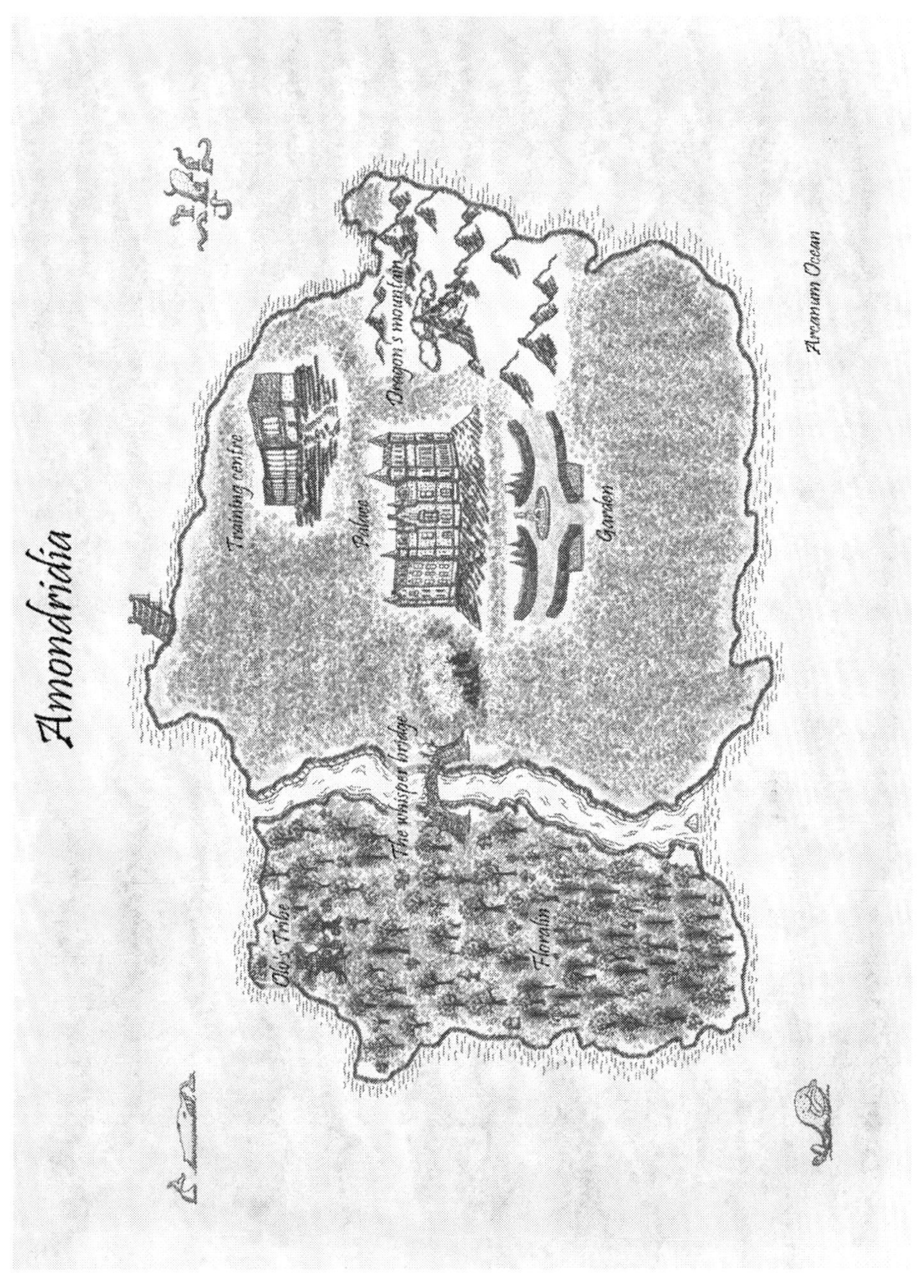
Amondridia
Training centre
Palace
Dragon's mountain
Garden
Arcanum Ocean
The whisper bridge
Olo's Tribe
Floralin

Chapter 1

One day I read that sometimes, in real-life fairy tales, the princess needs to befriend the dragon and kill the prince.

We all grow up hearing how the prince always appears to save the princess. How a simple kiss saves their lives after they spent years being the prisoner in a tower or in a deep sleep (well, that part I don't judge because it's a divine gift), bites the poisoned apple, needs to kiss a frog, is mistreated by the stepmother and *blah blah blah.*

I love these stories. They're melodramatic. They make me believe in magic. In the supernatural. A supposedly true love.

It's a lot of people's childhoods.

The principle of magic and fantasy.

Classics.

I've lost count of how many times I've watched, read, or heard these stories.

Okay, you don't necessarily have to kill the prince. He can be useful. But a princess doesn't always need a prince, or a crown or a dress. Sometimes she uses a rifle, other brushes, maybe a sword or even hands (~~an AK-47~~ ~~ops, you did not read this).~~

The problem with these stories is that they focus a lot on love and forget that after the princess marries the prince and takes the queen's throne, she finds herself trapped in a castle again, controlled by rules and conducts that no one dares to mention, not to mention the daily problems we all deal with.

Too bad this story doesn't technically take place in the real world, but it's a little more real than the fairy tales we read and hear.

Here we start with the conflict, then we explain the conflict.

But remember one thing: not everyone has a happy ending in the story so beware of the character you decide to love (or hate), maybe he/she won't survive at the end of the story after, or maybe he/she isn't the villain.

<3

Rosé's pov.

Cursed child, you shouldn't have been born. No? No. Poor thing. Lonely. Why are you so quiet? Is everything all right, darling? Stop. What? No. Look at her. Poor. She should have died. She shouldn't have been born. I love you; I love you. Rosé. Rosé. Rosé. Sleep, honey, you're going to have a long day. Stop. No. No. No? Protect. She's a secret. Protect her. Daughter. Solitary. Nobody likes you. They're going hunting, bunch of dickheads. Scream louder. Die.

There were concrete walls surrounding me.

I've spent a lot of time there.

When looking up, there was no roof. Nothing to cover me from the drops that fall on my face, mixing with my tears and soaking my sweater. It was cold. I couldn't feel my hands anymore or my feet. My teeth were shaking. My hands were covering my ears, hoping not to hear the voices, but they seemed to get louder and louder.

Damn child. How is she still alive? Powerful, but cursed. Alone. Without anyone. Why are you going to abandon me? Nobody likes you. Rosé. Cursed. Protect? Never. Why is that?

I tried to get up, but I was too weak. My lungs burned in pain. Every attempt to breathe was like filling my lungs with ice. I could smell the salty taste of my tears on my trembling, probably cold lips.

There were days when I could get up. Scream louder. Fight the voices. Against what was there. I was stronger. In control. Sometimes I almost broke the hard walls. Sometimes I could make the rain stop. But I was getting weaker and weaker. Vulnerable. No willpower.

I felt in a bathtub full of overflowing water where someone was pulling me down in the hope that I would drown in my own despair and chaos. In others, inside a closed box, without light, without air, without life.

I'd ask the voices to stop, but my voice came out like a whisper. Too weak to be heard. No one was there to save me. No one would come. No one ever comes.

Looking at my body it was almost purple. *Stupid child.* Maybe I was.

<3

"Rosé, are you still alive?" Eliot's voice flooded my ears, bringing me back to reality. "Is everything all right?" *No,* I wanted to answer.

No, I'm not.

"Yes, I'm fine." That's what came out of my mouth.

Chapter 2

Seven years ago

"You're crazy!" says a female voice, almost screaming.

Both were in the kitchen but on opposite sides.

"Crazy? Isn't there anything different to call me? I've lost count of how many times you've called me that in the last few months," asked the man in a normal-level voice, wiping a glass.

"Oh no? Taking Rosé to another country is not crazy," she replies with a sarcastic laugh, stopping to look at him and then returning to the pile of dishes in front of her. "Sorry dear, my mistake." Pure irony. She could feel her face burn and her hands trembled. Rosé was her most precious possession, her daughter, she could not just let her go. Not when she knew the danger Rosé was in. She couldn't go back to London. She knew how painful this would be for everyone. It always was. "Tom, she's staying, and if you want to go, that's fine. I understand it's your country and you miss it, but Rosé stays. This discussion is over," she argues as calmly as possible, abandoning what she was doing and heading to the living room.

She couldn't stand to be there anymore. Her anger and sadness were strong. She knew that if she held another glass or something, she would break it.

"Come back here, we haven't finished this conversation." He follows her.

"That's the problem, we never finish this conversation." Her voice was weak. She turned to look at him, finding his brown eyes already on her.

Everything went well between them. Rosé, the couple's daughter, was already thirteen years old, and their lives were perfect. The two of them worked in the area they liked the most. They received a salary that kept them well in Brazil despite the country's economic crises and the corrupt government, until Tom decided to return to England. The problem began to get serious when the conversations passed the walls of the apartment. The neighbours had already knocked on the door asking if everything was okay. Looks in the hallways and elevator were no longer discreet. The daughter of the couple who previously doubted the gossip that ran through the building now tried to spend less time at home.

Before, the discussions occurred when she was not at home, but then Rosé noticed the looks between the two.

"If you want, I can remind you why we left England," she says. Her mouth pressed together, forming a straight line, almost difficult to see. Her arms were crossed, and her gaze was on Tom once more, who did not keep eye contact.

Coward, she thought. *You can't stand an exchange of looks.*

"You don't have to," he says, adjusting his square glasses.

"Great."

"Helena—" he began.

"Don't come to me with 'Helena' – I made a promise, Tom, and I'll keep it." She pauses for a second. "This has nothing to do with Brazil, this has to do with Rosé. She's okay here and happy. She has friends and family. You can't just come to me, and even her, after all these years and say you want to go back. Well. London is not safe, and you know it very well. By the way, you know what it's like to leave your country and move to another. I don't want it for her." Her face was burning again. She had raised her tone of voice and had only noticed when silence prevailed again.

"Hele—" begins Tom once more but is interrupted again.

"We spent thirteen years living a quiet life here. Far from it all, Tom.

Everything. Controlling. We're fine. If we go back, you know that …" Her voice was no longer of anger, but of despair. Tears flowed down her hot face. Burning her ocean eyes. She tried to stop them from coming. She tried to clean them, but others followed in their place.

She held her hair in a ponytail. The anger was making her sweat.

Tom stood still for a second or two. Thinking about what to do. Thinking of something that could stop all this. He went to his wife and held her hands. They were hot and sweaty. "She needs to go back," he says, taking one of his hands to Helena's face, trying to dry her tears.

"Look at me. This here," he says, making a pointing gesture with one of his arms, "this is not us. As you said, it was thirteen years, Helena, *thirteen years.*"

"No," she whispered. She couldn't do that. Helena couldn't think of the possibility of her daughter away from her. The cute little baby she had raised. All the fear and suffering that she had endured would be in vain if she let Rosé go.

"We'll go in a month," he says letting go of her hand and walking away. Tom took his hands to his black hair and left.

"Why don't you go first? Look at the situation in London. Talk to Prinze. Then I'll send Rosé," she says with a fake smile.

"Do you think I'm an idiot? That I don't know that when I get on that fucking plane, you're not going to disappear with her? As you said, I'm old and I don't fall for that fucking trick of yours." Tom tried to get his breath back and laced his tie.

Those were his last words before he put his head down and walked further away from her.

The air in the apartment was heavy. Hot. Making it difficult for them both to breathe. The noise of cars and horns could be heard from afar. Most lights out.

"SO YOU'RE GOING TO ABANDON ME?" Helena screams behind his back. Tom just stops, but he doesn't turn around. He didn't want to look at her face. He knew if he did, he'd regret it. He would see Helena's face, her red cheeks of anger, her tears standing out in the light tone of her skin. He knew that her expression would make him give up what he had planned for days, because, after all, Tom loved her very much and to see her so, it hurt in his heart, but he needed to control his emotions. "After all I have done for you and for her? Where I am in your flawless plan? Where's your love for me? Is it gone? Evaporated? You know I can't go back there."

Tom understood why she was acting like this. He knew the promise she had made years ago; he didn't need anyone to remind him, but things had changed. Thirteen years had passed since the decision they had made. It was different now, he was sure of that. He had to. Maybe it was his pride that was talking louder. Maybe he was wrong, but he needed to come back and Rosé needed to come back with him.

A long silence dominated the place. The room was still dark. No one had bothered with turning on the light. Helena looked at Tom's back, still waiting for an answer. She waited for him to turn around and tell her he wouldn't leave. That he was going to stay with her in Brazil. She expected an apology or something. An answer that would put an end to this discussion that had made her lose many hours of sleep.

But nothing.

He didn't say anything.

"Where is your daughter?" Helena asked, recovering. There were no more tears in her eyes. Her voice was firm again. Chin raised. "Hm?" Silence. Tom didn't take any steps or make any other sign.

"Exactly. It's almost 8:00 p.m. Your daughter is not home yet, and you don't know where she is." Fists formed on the side of her body. "This is not the first time. When you take her, are you going to do that? Abandon her as you did me? Stop worrying? Every moment she leaves this house until she comes back my heart aches, thinking she might not return."

The silence continued for a while.

"You. Will. Not. Take her." Helena wanted to scream, but she remained in place, back straight.

"We'll be leaving in a month," he repeated and headed towards the corridor.

"You know what? FUCK YOU. FUCK YOU. TAKE YOUR OPINION AND…" Helena stops short in a bid to control herself; she lets out a loud sigh. Helena couldn't catch Tom's eye. "What's your problem? What have I done to you? Answer me!" she ordered, taking her hand to her face, drying her tears. She didn't know what to do with her hands or how to act. She was tired of this conversation. Tired of Tom's behaviour. She was, on some level, relieved at his going, but remembering Rosé, her blood boiled, and anger took over her body.

Rosé was all she had.

"You have done nothing wrong. I just need you to understand that this is for her sake. She has a right to know," he says, turning to her, prepared to face Helena once again.

Helena let out a sarcastic laugh. "Know? Know what exactly? What are you referring to? Tell me. Hm?" There was a cruel smile on her face. Tom looked away, he nervously shuffled his hands from his waist up to his face, anxiously stroking his beard. "Exactly. Sometimes you surprise me, you know that. You haven't told her until today and probably won't until someone almost kills her."

"You are impossible," he complains, breathing hard, trying not to freak out. "Me?"

"Stop acting crazy." Regret came even before the last word left his mouth.

"Crazy? Maybe I am. No … actually, I'm sure. I'm crazy and you … freaked out, sick, ignorant, and proud. You look like a saint. People look at you and think you're fucking shy, but let's tell the truth, Tom, you're not like that. All you think about is yourself. You think it's all about you. Look at these last 20 years. Look at everything that happened and think to yourself how many things could have been avoided if you had an ounce of consideration for the people on your side. You put yourself in a maze with no beginning or end and you brought with you every single person around you."

Silence. Helena knew that those words had hurt Tom, but the expression on his face remained neutral.

"You want to take Rosé? Fine. Take her at once and take her to that place. Do what you want, Tom, but if I find you've crossed any established limit," she says, raising her finger, "you are dead. If she tells me you faltered, Tom, the last thing you're going to see is going to be—" The last words of her sentence were lost in the air when the couple's daughter entered the room. She had almond-shaped eyes, and light brown hair, like Helena's.

Her cheeks were wet. Her fists were clenched on the side of her body. Both Tom and Helena exchanged glances without knowing what to do or say. It wasn't the first time Rosé had seen them fighting. She couldn't stand the screaming and the fights; she knew Rosé couldn't stand to have to answer to the neighbours, pretend that it was nothing and that she was fine. Helena knew Rosé couldn't take it anymore.

Chapter 3

"I could hear it from far away." That's the only thing Rosé could say. She dropped her bag on the living room floor and went to her room in silence, passing her speechless parents.

She closed the door hard, making a loud bang, and just stood there, leaning against the door for a few seconds until she retreated to her bed. The tears running down her face.

She stayed there until she had no more energy or tears to cry.

The sleeves of her blouse were soaked from trying to dry her face. She couldn't take it anymore. Rosé wanted to pack her bags and run away, but she had nowhere else to go.

Whispers were only heard from the room. Rosé got up and headed toward her dressing table. Her eyes were red and swollen. Her flushed cheek and the sides of her hair stuck to her face. She wanted to scream.

There were lots of pictures and souvenirs hanging around the mirror. Photos with her friends at school, in the park and at parties. There were pictures of her parents and her mother's family, since her father's family was in England. There were movie tickets and magazine clippings, but what she liked most was a specific photo. Probably the most spontaneous photo taken of her parents. They were dancing at her ninth birthday party, and she was behind, admiring them in her princess dress and a crown. Her mouth was dirty with chocolate cake, and she held her favourite stuffed animal. A dragon she called Sasa.

Her mother had chosen that name.

That night Rosé could hear her mother's low cry in the living room that soon blended with hers. After that day the house was empty, and not because there was no one in the house, but because no one dared to talk if it wasn't important.

The house was cold and, with time, empty, with full suitcases.

Before she left, Rosé entered her room for the last time. It was almost empty, with only a few pieces of furniture that were already from the apartment. She said goodbye to the place where she has spent much of life. She remembered every time that place was her shelter on bad days, the sleepovers, the lazy days, and everything in between. Finally, she said goodbye.

She knew she'd never go back there.

"You're going to be fine," Helena says from the door. She went to Rosé and hugged her, stroking her hair for a while. "Look at me," says Helena, holding Rosé's cheeks and raising her head. "Pay attention. Never. Never put your head down for life. It is too cruel, and if you lower it, things are only going to get worse. Even though the crown is heavy, a princess never drops it."

"I'm going to miss you," Rosé replies with a voice made hoarse from crying. She hugged her mother for the last time.

"Me too, angel. Don't forget to call me every day and tell me everything, like, everything. I mean it. I love you so much and no matter what they say about me, I will always love you." Rosé knew her mother was trying to hold back her tears.

"I love you too."

<3

Her grandmother called her over and delivered an amulet decorated with a thick red line and a pendant with a spiked symbol – greater than and less than combined and one line in the middle and another two with a rose and a wolf.

Rosé joined her father so they could leave for the airport. Tom noticed the object on Rosé's wrist but said nothing. Rosé didn't look back, that would be stupid, and she knew that if she looked, she wouldn't be able to contain her tears.

Rosé never took off that amulet.

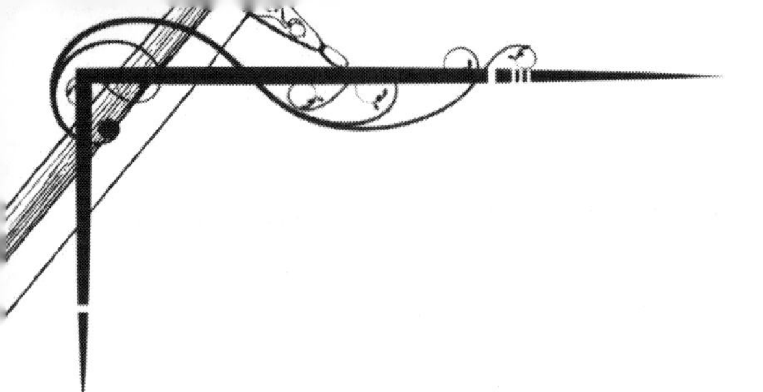

Chapter 4

Present

"How's your week been since our last meeting?" asked the middle-aged man, looking over his round glasses. His hair was greyish, as was his beard. His face was wrinkled and had a huge scar on one side that went through the corner of his eye and down to his jaw. Rosé always wanted to ask about it, but never found the courage to do it.

"It was the same old thing. Home, university, work, home," she says, looking out the window. It was a beautiful day outside even though it was cold. The sun was shining in the sky. "I don't know why you're still asking."

"I'm your psychologist," he commented. "Still having the same dream?"

"I had it last night."

"Want to talk about it?"

"No."

"The reason you're here is so we can talk."

"We've talked about it countless times and it keeps coming back almost every night. And well, I'm still alive."

"That's good to know."

Much had changed since Rosé had left Brazil. Despite practicing English with her father, it had not been enough to get along at first. There were several things she didn't understand.

Countless times a day she felt like someone was holding her heart and squeezing it. Like the air in her lungs had been stolen. Maybe that's why she felt a hole in her chest. She remembered the nights clearly. The endless crying and the desire to end it all. To break everything around her. The desire to end the pain. She remembered the sheets of paper ripped apart by her pen because words were no longer enough to express her feelings. The blurry reflection in the mirror that she no longer recognized.

She felt like she had no identity anymore. The incessant pain. The urge to scream stuck in the middle of her throat. The voices in her head reminding her of her insufficiency. The anger, the hate and the pain never went away, but they chased her no matter where she went.

A full mind inside and an empty girl on the outside.

Some said it was just her being dramatic. Sometimes even she thought so, when her little breakdown ended and she wondered why she was suffering from something so small, but when the world fell apart, she realized that what was small at the time seemed bigger than ever.

The pain never went away, Rosé just learned to deal with it.

Despite preferring a quieter place, her father continued living in London when Rosé moved to the university campus. And despite all these years, she was still upset with him.

Moving into adulthood wasn't easy. She was practically alone. But that's what Rosé always wanted: to be independent. She started working at a local store to pay for her expenses. She lived on campus and shared a house with four other people.

The adaptation was a little complicated from the beginning and, at the request of her father, she began to go to a psychologist who was an old friend of his.

And there she was, one more day.

The room wasn't very big, but it was cozy. It smelled like an old book, mixed with the smell of lavender and men's cologne. There were two sofas facing each other, a desk full of papers, family photos, a woman and what she deduced to be six grandchildren (no father?), and framed psychology certificates. Some plants and bookshelves full of books. Rosé could not understand why Mr Watson had so many books. She once tried to count how many he had, but it was useless.

She always got lost and then gave up.

Rosé had been in that same office for a few months now. Her father had hired him after an anxiety crisis about moving to university.

Even after so long, the office hadn't changed much.

Maybe one piece of furniture or the colour of the walls.

Despite her curiosity, she had never gone to the trouble of asking why he had so many books. How could anyone read so many? She had read some books when she was younger. It was a way, she thought, of running away from reality, but with time she lost interest. School occupied much of her time and she began to see them as a waste of time.

"Do you want some to borrow?" asks Mr Watson, realising that Rosé was more interested in the books that were behind him than in the question he had asked. "I have something in nearly every genre.

You can choose."

"I don't waste my time reading books anymore," she says.

Mr Watson lets out a laugh.

"Wasting time? Reading books is not a waste of time, Miss Johnson," he says, putting his clipboard next to him and getting up, heading towards the bookcase. "Books are a door to another dimension. A place where you live another life. You have different experiences in a world totally parallel to yours. Books …" he takes a book from the shelf and opens it, "they are a way to escape the real world for a few hours." *Dramatic.*

"I know. I used to read when I was a kid. I thought it was magical how you could forget you were reading and be completely immersed in a different place, living a different life. But then when you woke up from a trance and find yourself in the real world, it just hurt you because you know that no matter how much you dream, you'll never be able to live the damn lives of the protagonists. So, I appreciate the offer, but I'm still not interested." Rosé let out a long sigh, as if she had forgotten to breathe during her comment and sank further into the couch.

"Well, you don't have to apologize for giving a sincere opinion. I like your mind."

"Is that supposed to be a compliment?"

"Yes. Maybe. There are people with minds which are, let's say … not very interesting and very monotonous. They live based on other people's thoughts. They have no original thoughts of their own. Deep, if you know

what I mean. Their minds are very simple," he says, looking over his glasses, "and ordinary."

"Why the fuck does every old man do that? Aren't the glasses supposed to be there so you can see better?" Realising the audacity of her question, Rosé responded, "I'm sorry! I didn't mean to be so rude."

"I've said you don't have to apologise, and too bad you don't want a book to borrow," he replies while arranging his glasses. "You know what? What I'm going to tell you is just a theory, but maybe, Rosé, that's what you're missing in your life. Maybe it is—" "Books?" she interrupts him.

"Perhaps. Or maybe to just get out of reality a little bit. Do something different," he says, looking over his glasses again which seemed to add wisdom to his comment. "Get out of your … comfort zone. Is there anything you'd like to do?"

There were a lot of things. Walking down the street at dawn with her friends. Lively parties and dances. Walk on the beach. Sunset or sunrise. A trip somewhere or even get drunk with her friends and laugh at stupid things. Walk barefoot on the ground in a place surrounded by trees. Dancing in the rain, parading …

"A lot of things," is what she said. "But …"

"But? What's to stop you from doing them? Courage?" Rosé didn't answer, she just stared at him, and he got the message. "Right."

Among so many things that have happened in her life since arriving in England, one thing she could never forget was the first time she met Mr Watson.

Life must have been hard for him during these last few months because, for Rosé, he had aged a lot in such a short time. To her, when she remembered the first time, she had seen him, he looked a little younger. With fewer wrinkles.

Although her life had not changed much after the sessions began, Rosé enjoyed attending and talking to him. It was a time when she could just stay and argue about what was going on in her life. It was like a break in the middle of the day. He was quiet. His soft voice and calm personality passed this impression. The session with Mr Watson was over and Rosé was returning to campus again. It was a kind of long journey, as the office was in central London and her campus was in the West.

London was always full of tourists. You could hear people speaking countless different languages and despite being in a country whose official language was English, that was the language you least heard. They were people walking over each other in every direction. Conversations mixing, people screaming, old people grumbling, people trying to get to their destinations, lost people, car horns, people pushing you, children in uniforms, the smell of tobacco and urine in the air, and people dressed as cartoon characters to make money.

Welcome to London. Well, at least central London.

The nearest tube entrance passed through one of the busiest parts of London, Piccadilly Circus. It was full of people and Rosé had not had time to get her earphones to distract herself and would not risk getting them in amongst this amount of people.

There were people protesting and talking about the importance of taking care of the environment. Others were trying to take pictures and complaining that there were people passing in front.

Until she managed to get on the subway, Rosé bumped into a man with almost shaved hair who cursed her, and she cursed him back, stepped on something strange on the floor and passed some musicians. With each escalator the air was getting denser and warmer. In cold times, like the ones that they were in now, that was good. But when it got hot, you often remembered that you're sharing limited air with multiple people. The smell of urine rose again, it made her cover her nose with her scarf which was flooded with smell of perfume.

She had a great taste for perfumes and that was indisputable.

The underground was not full, and she managed to find a place to sit and that's when she could finally get access to her headphones. When the music began to play, a sense of relief ran through her body. She couldn't hear anything above the singer's voice. The world seemed calmer, but of course it only lasted when she was inside the underground because when she was walking, she needed to keep the volume of the music down.

A woman's life. Welcome.

A few stops later, Rosé went out and headed to the next platform and waited until the tube arrived. She had missed the last one and now had to wait five minutes for the next. The music had changed to a more exiting beat. It was very hot down there and sweat started taking over some parts of her body. That station was even less crowded, which sometimes scared her. She was still a five-foot woman in a big city. Alone. And a slight shiver went down her spine when a strange man stared at her on the other side of the tracks. Rosé looked away, thinking he would do the same, but when she looked again, the slightly blond-haired man kept staring.

He was dressed in clothes that looked old and dark in shades as if he hadn't washed them for days. His hair was careless, and this was visible from afar. She thanked him for not being on that side of the tracks and looked away once more.

Despite the temptation to check if he was still looking at her, she didn't want to risk it.

The tube arrived and she once again found a place to sit. Although the station was not full, the tube was and two stops later she ended up giving her place to a mother, who thanked her. She had a baby on her lap and a little girl who looked five years old. The girl was staring Rosé all the way while drinking her juice, and it disturbed her a little.

Why were people staring at her?

Rosé could see her reflection in the glass. She looked tired. She needed a hot bath. Her legs were tender, and she realised that, in fact, she needed some serious hydration. She didn't need a good reflection to see her tired look and deep dark circles. She didn't like what she saw, and she realised she needed to stop eating so much and lose a few pounds. But she gave up. Fuck it. She knew she would eat more than usual if she wanted and would not be able to continue on an exercise routine for long.

There's only one bus left to get home, she recalled. The path this time was not long, but the wind was biting for those who were not well dressed. She couldn't feel her hands anymore.

<3

When she arrived, she was greeted by Eliot in the kitchen. He was one of the boys she shared the apartment with and was the only person she could trust.

"Rosélina," Eliot says, humming. "How was your day?"

"I've burned several neurons." Lectures that lasted almost two hours. Lunch alone. A good walk to the office. She didn't need much effort to burn neurons, they seemed to do it themselves.

"I know what that's like," he replied, letting out a laugh. "I had a fucking exam today. I don't know if I can think anymore."

Eliot was one of her favourite roommates, apart from Hanna. She considered him more of a colleague than a friend. Sometimes they went out to eat or go somewhere, but that was it. Nothing too special.

Eliot was tall with fire-coloured hair and a face full of freckles. He was a drama student, which made him spontaneous and theatrical. Rosé loved his good humour, but sometimes she wanted to throw him out the window.

(Let's be real, there is no remorse in that thought.)

"What are you cooking?" asked Rosé, grabbing a bottle of water from the fridge. The smell was amazing.

"Pasta a la Carbonara," he replied in an Italian accent, making the famous Italian sign, which made Rosé laugh.

"It looks nice, but I'll pass, I need to go to sleep. I'm dead," she said, heading to her room.

"Who said I was doing it for you?" He seemed outraged, but Rosé knew he wasn't. Eliot had never been like this with her, but he'd already had grand fights with many people.

"Me."

"Ha poor thing," comments Eliot with a smile on his face, not taking his eyes off the pan. "Goodnight, Rosélina."

"Goodnight and call me Rosé," she challenged him, taking one last look at Eliot before entering her room. Rosé took a quick shower, even though she had little energy for it, and put on the first t-shirt she saw and some shorts. Who in the 21st century wears pyjamas? And with the last of the last strength she had, she crawled into her bed.

Priorities. Tomorrow was another day and maybe she'd organize the room.

In a few minutes, she fell asleep. She couldn't remember what time it was when she got home, or when she last ate, or if she had something to send the next day. She just wanted to sleep and forget about her problems. The rest she would solve in despair and under pressure. Typical Rosé.

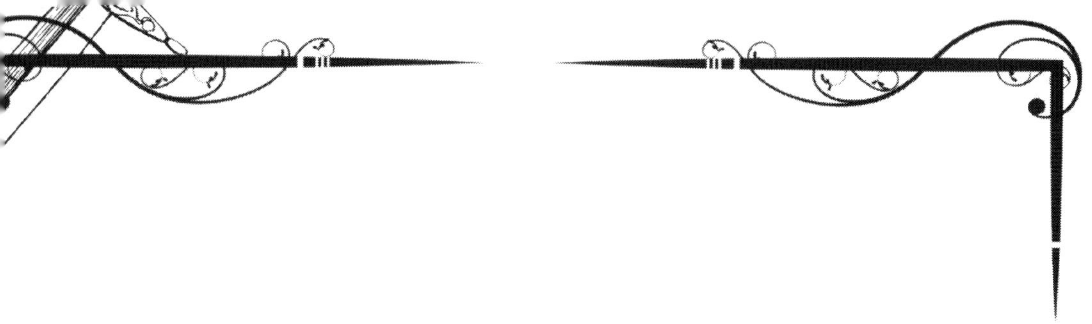

Chapter 5

Rosé woke up the next day with rays of light on her face. She curled up in the bed for a bit longer, looking at nothing, thinking about nothing. She then went to the bathroom and almost died stumbling over one of her trainers. *Girl dies after tripping over her shoe because she did not have the decency to put it in place,* she thought to herself.

When she came back, Rosé went straight to her phone. It was five in the morning. She didn't mind waking up early, besides, who knows what time she went to sleep last night.

Her phone was full of unread messages. Her mother asking how her day was and if she was okay. The kind of brief, monotonous message. *Hi, my day was great and I'm fine. What about you?* The other message was from Eliot asking if she was going to sleep on an empty stomach as she hadn't come back to the kitchen to eat anything after she arrived and complaining that he had to have dinner alone because the rest of them were busy or had already eaten.

Rosé thought not to answer but decide to send a text anyway: *Sorry. I was tired.* The rest of the messages were from groups she didn't even participate in, so she decided to ignore them.

There was a particular someone who hadn't sent her a message: her father. Rosé hadn't received any messages from him in a few weeks. She knew he worked hard and was always busy, but always had time for her. At least she thought he did. She didn't even remember the last time she saw him.

Maybe it was two or three months ago.

She knew that university and her adult life had kept her busy all this time and that he also had a busy life. Besides, they were in London, a city that never stops and the more you work, the better, but it didn't cost anything to say hi or at least answer his own daughter's messages.

She missed her loving father who always paid attention to her. Despite family and adapting to their new life, he always showed great support at first when they moved to England. He had always cared about her, and he had always made a point of being there, ready for whatever comes and goes.

He worked hard to raise her, and Rosé always recognized that.

When they were still living together, she always saw him at night and in the morning and was greeted with a kiss on the forehead. He wondered what her day was like and if she needed anything. He was a good listener and Rosé was grateful for that. Luckily, she always had a good relationship with her father, even though she didn't always agree with his decisions.

However, in recent months he stayed farther away until he stopped answering her messages altogether. Not even a *Hi, I'm well, my love, and busy, I hope you're okay, I'll call you later.*

He never called.

Her thoughts were interrupted by a new message. It was Eliot.

Eliot – Sleeping Beauty woke up early.

Rosé – I went to bed early.

Eliot – Did you sleep well?

Rosé – Fainted.

Eliot – Did you dream about me?

Rosé – Hmm, no?

Eliot – So you didn't sleep well. Do you want to go out for breakfast?

Rosé – Are you lonely?

Eliot – Never alone, but also never badly accompanied. 8 a.m.?

Rosé – Fine.

Brief and direct conversation.

Chapter 6

Rosé and Eliot's trip to the café

had been quick. He didn't have much time left before his class.

He spent most of the time talking about the play they were preparing for, how it was starting in a few days' time and how he was overexcited about it. He also mentioned an audition he was planning for an action movie involving a stunt he had seen on the internet on a website they called 'dubious but with the possibility of being safe.'

This is the good part of being with Eliot: he would speak for him and you.

Rosé loved his personality and his funny way of expressing himself. His exaggerated comments, changing his voice and shaking his hands, it made Rosé laugh and almost choke on the coffee countless times. It was a random 'friendship' where they didn't have much in common, but they always had a subject.

He would always make her day.

But Rosé was the opposite of Eliot.

She's always been alone. A quiet girl, but not necessarily shy. If she had to deal with it, she'd figure it out, but she always avoided contact with human beings. She didn't like arguing, but she would if necessary and, when she was in a good mood, she would just ignore it and let the person talk alone. She loved to hit with words. The ones that hurt the soul. If she got hurt, she'd hurt twice as bad.

She wouldn't put her head down to anyone. The crown couldn't fall.

Rosé didn't like to draw attention, unlike Eliot. Of course, his exaggerated manner drew a lot of attention when they walked the streets. When they went to walk through the park on the way back to university, Rosé didn't know what to do other than hide her face when he almost hit a passing old woman.

"Why are you always like this? Frowny?" he asked, taking a sip of coffee.

"I'm not frowny," she protested. "I just don't like getting attention, like you and you know it."

He passed one of his long arms over Rosé's shoulder and pulled her closer to him, she felt his hot, hard body on her side. "So you're walking with the wrong person." Of course she was. Often Eliot made her feel ashamed, but sometimes she thought she needed it. Someone to cheer her up and get her out of her comfort zone. She needed adventures and Eliot was perfect for it.

"Oh seriously? I didn't realise it," she replied ironically. "And you're always like that? Stupid?"

"Rude," he disputes, making a sad face. Rosé squeezed his cheek too hard. "For fuck's sake, you look like my grandmother when she sees me. You just have to start speaking Irish," he says placing his hand on his cheek. Rosé began to laugh but stopped when she noticed a slight insult there.

"Wait, are you calling me old?"

"My grandmother looks young on your side." Rosé pushed him and unintentionally dropped her own coffee on the floor, almost wetting them both. Eliot looked at her, trying to hold back the laughter. She lifted her finger in warning, but it didn't help, he started laughing and took the cup and the lid, throwing them in the bin. "Well done. It was much more than deserved. Now, besides my amazing, wonderful, and perfect person, are you seeing someone else?" he asked.

Eliot had very large legs and sometimes Rosé had to run a little to reach him. "Has anyone ever won your heart? You can tell me. I like good gossip."

"Why the fuck does everybody ask me that?" Eliot and Mr Watson weren't the only ones. When she spoke to her mother a few days ago she asked the same question. "As if I needed someone to be happy. Me. Well. Alone."

"You are always alone. It's sad sometimes to see you as this and Hanna agrees," he comments, walking backwards. He looked at Rosé and took one more sip of his coffee which was still intact, making a noise with his mouth at the end so she would feel jealous, and he succeeded. She was in need of good coffee and got annoyed, taking his coffee and throwing it on the grass. Well, she meant to, but this just happened inside her head.

Eliot had one more sip.

"You need someone to sexually cheer you up, kiss, hug." `he took another sip of coffee and she just followed the movement once again. "I can't do this for you, and seriously, I've never seen you kiss anyone."

Sexually cheer you up. The fact that she had to get naked for someone and be vulnerable, scared her.

"Is that why you're my friend?" she asked with an angry tone. "Out of pity? Because if it is, you can leave." She crossed her arms in front of her chest and turned her face from him. She didn't care about people feeling angry with her, but pity?

Pity was the worst feeling in existence.

"No, no, no," he said, lifting a finger. "Have I said no? Of course not. I don't feel sorry for you," he defended himself. "I like being with you, you're different. Mysterious and … dangerous," he whispered the last part.

Rosé let out a laugh. "Dangerous?" she asked without understanding.

"Yes, you know. You don't depend on people, like, emotionally or to live, you know?" he says, frowning. "I don't know if I could live alone for long. Besides, you're a little aggressive sometimes. I wouldn't be surprised if one day you came to me and tell me you killed a man." Rosé bit his arm and he shrieked. "For the whore who gave birth to you, I hope she takes you back. Stop biting me."

There was one thing she'd learned these past few years. People are not permanent, and we should not get attached to them. She liked to be alone, on her own, and when she needed someone to go out with or talk to, she would go after someone. It's not pure interest, it's being alone, but not lonely. It's not giving too much of yourself to someone who might not be who they say they are.

No argument.

No attachment.

Without sharing too much of life.

And yet, creating great memories.

"You left a mark on me," he remarked, lifting his sleeve and analysing the mark of her teeth embedded in his skin. "Thank you."

"If you complain, I'll bite again."

"I would very much like my sexual partner to say this to me someday, but from you, no thanks," he commented and walked away as someone who was afraid of being bitten again, but soon returned to her side. "Going back to the boys—"

"Eliot, get lost."

"Come on, Rosélina. We only live once," he argues, holding up one with his fingers. "Once. Will you really live like this? Look around, there's so much to do and experience." He points at a man a few feet away. She rolled her eyes and kept walking. "Beyond the countless things to appreciate—" And that's when he bumped into an old lady.

"Watch out for that long arm of yours, stupid boy," she grumbled.

"Okay, there are some things that we don't need to appreciate," he comments, showing his middle finger to the woman, not before certifying first that she was not looking, making Rosé laugh. "I thought she was totally arrogant. She put herself in front of my arm. Besides, my arm's not that big," he says. "Or is it?" Rosé just denied it.

"What does your argument have to do with my friendships?"

"You're afraid to take a chance."

Rosé didn't say anything else. Eliot wore a white social shirt with a sweatshirt over the top, making both t-shirts look tight on his body which marked his thinness. He was much taller than her which intimidated her a little.

"How are you going to get someone if you don't have a social life?" he asked. She could feel his gaze on her, waiting for an answer.

"I don't need anyone."

"There's a lot of beautiful Brits out there. And I can say that." Rosé started laughing. Of course he paid a lot of attention to them.

"So, you're going to stay with them, take as many as you want, and leave me alone on this subject. Now …" Rosé looks at the schedule on her phone, "you have class."

"Are you going to campus?" he asked. "My class starts in fifteen minutes; I can accompany you and maybe until then I will introduce you to someone."

"If I were you, I'd run away before I take this fucking coffee and throw it at you and no. I think I'm going to stick around for a while. I need to relax before I begin my 5,000-word essay for Mrs Evans." She wanted some time alone. No Eliot. No company. With no one to talk to.

Alone.

"Okay, until later," he said, but by the time Rosé went to answer it was too late, he was already running. She laughed.

He had really taken the comment seriously.

<3(This thing looks like a butt. Nothing is greater than a butt.)

The sky was beautiful. Cloudless. Despite the strong sun shining in the sky, it was still very cold. The wind was so fucking cold again. Rosé found an empty bench to sit on, she put on a song to play and admired the view. It was a huge green space and to Rosé's surprise, the park was full for the time. It wasn't even 10 in the morning.

There were some little kids playing and running from side to side and some in the recreation part. Dogs running behind toys. Adults doing still exercises and others running around the park. There were elderly couples walking around and another having a picnic. University students taking advantage of the free classes to relax, read a book or have their prep done outdoors. Couples showing affection and so on.

She looked at her phone, waiting for some message from her father, but nothing. She turned off the screen and let a tear run.

Rosé stood there admiring, maybe Eliot was right, there's a lot to admire.

"Today is beautiful, don't you think?" Despite the music on her phone, Rosé was able to hear. An old lady had sat on the other side of the bench. Her hair was greyish, and her body was small despite the heavy robes. They were in the winter, almost spring.

"Still too cold," Rosé commented, looking up at the sky and then at a group of children running not far from them.

"I love sunny and cold days," she commented. "It's the junction of good and bad. The beautiful and the unpleasant." She looked at Rosé who observed her eyes more closely.

Heterochromia. One of her eyes was blue as the sky and the other brown.

"I love your eyes," commented Rosé. She couldn't help herself. They really were beautiful.

"I think someone was undecided on what colour to put and ended up putting the two colours," the woman remarked, letting out a shy smile. "Who was your best friend you were with just now? The skinny one, with sun-coloured hair," she asked, interested. Rosé wanted to laugh at the description but held back the laughter.

"Eliot, and he's not my best friend, just one of my flat mates," Rosé replied with a neutral tone. She never thought of Eliot as her best friend, she didn't consider him that close.

"University student?"

"Yes."

"To me he seemed like your best friend or boyfriend. The way you were laughing and talking. You weren't strangers."

"We just went out for some coffee. It was no big deal," she commented, rubbing her wrist near where the amulet was. "I don't make friends," said Rosé, looking forward, trying to avoid the woman's gaze. She was embarrassed. "I'm very good at pushing people away from me. Friendships are sometimes too complicated."

The white-haired woman let out a slight laugh. "What do you mean you don't make friends? You're missing the best part of your life. Friends. They're the ones who brighten our lives. They're our family at heart. Brothers of other mothers. Those responsible for creating your character and those responsible for the stupidest shit of your life. *I don't make friends,"* she repeated, laughing. "Do yourself a favour and go live." Silence.

Old people and their speeches about life, she thought.

"Fear," Rosé responded. She didn't know why she was opening up to that woman. Maybe it was because she was weird and would never see her again. "I'm afraid of clinging to someone or being hurt." Rosé wasn't lying, but she wasn't telling the truth. She wasn't just afraid of being hurt; she was afraid of hurting someone. Afraid of emotional dependency or someone just using her. She knew this was a silly fear, yet she was afraid. Rosé was afraid to be like Eliot.

The lady got up and picked up a rose that was near the bench where they were and returned to sit, delivering the rose to Rosé, which she took care so as not to be pierced.

"Squeeze the rose," the lady challenged her, seeing Rosé's care. "Really hold the rose stem," she repeated. "The stem and the petals. Tighten both parts."

"No!" protested Rosé. "The thorns will pierce me. It is going to hurt!" *Strange old woman.*

"I didn't ask for your opinion, I know they're going to hurt you, I wasn't born yesterday. Just squeeze it. With your right hand the stem and with your left, the petals." Rosé did not contest the woman and squeezed. She did as the woman asked. She could feel the pain of the thorns piercing her right hand and the hot blood dripping. She knew this would happen, just as the lady next to her knew, what Rosé didn't know was why she had accepted this challenge. "Ouch," complained Rosé.

The lady let out a gentle laugh. "Young. This is life, sometimes we embrace people we know will hurt us," she commented, taking the hand of Rosé who was bleeding and with a tissue begins to clean the blood and take out the thorns that have become trapped, "and over time our body heals. That's human," she continued. "Sometimes we find people who will only hurt us and when we realize that, we will leave them, just as you did with the rose and the thorns. They teach us not to do that anymore. But in the meantime, however, we choose people who will do us good, like the petals in your hand. They're both going to leave marks." Rosé looked at her left hand and saw it was red, but not with blood, the petals had dropped a reddish paint on her hands. "That's always going to happen. Sometimes we're going to be the rose in someone's life or the thorn and vice versa. Do yourself a favour and live. Make friends, meet people, because you have the power to decide whether they are part of your life or not."

She picked up her cane. "What do you have to lose?" She took a pause before continuing. "Reflect on it the next time you're going to do something. If your life is shit, what do you have to lose?"

Rosé didn't know what to answer. She stared at her hand and reflected on what the lady said. "Thank you for the speech." The woman moved beside her. "Were you listening to our conversation?" asked Rosé, turning her gaze to the lady and their eyes met.

She approached Rosé and said, "I may be old and full of wrinkles, but I love gossip and listening to a conversation with other people, just like your friend." They both let out a loud laugh. They stood there in silence, watching the world pass before their eyes. Rosé sometimes looked back at her. There was something about her that caught Rosé's imagination.

Finally, she said goodbye. "Oh. If shit happens, I didn't tell you any of that," the lady stated then continued her walk.

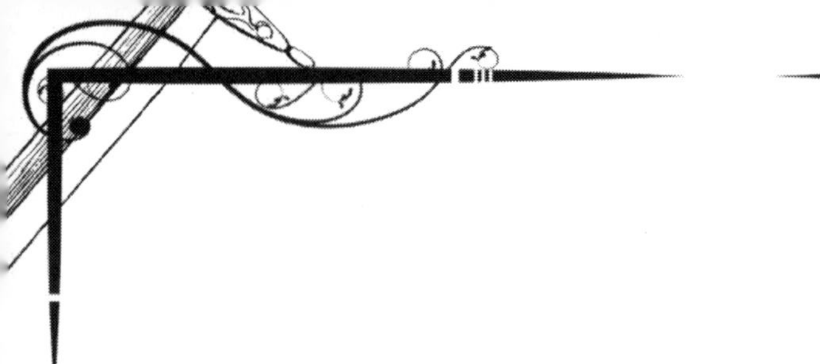

Chapter 7

Some days had passed since the park and the rose. The days were still cold, the sun was more present, It was a post-Christmas holiday; New Year and new plans, including University exams to everyone's (non) happiness.

Rosé no longer saw Eliot as often because he was always busy with exams and his plays. From time-to-time Rosé would meet him in the kitchen where he would ask her to help him with the lines.

Hanna had spent more time in the art studio than at the flat, she didn't come back until night-time.

Today by some miracle the three of them were at home.

"You did great," Rosé praised him after he recited his part without any mistakes.

"Seriously, I think he was terrible," Hanna commented, putting a spoonful of cereal in her mouth. "Could have done better." Eliot cast her a look of anger and then turned to Rosé.

"You were horrible," Hanna continued. "Could show more animation. If I didn't know you, I'd say you didn't want to be here or help me, but since I'm an amazing person and I know you, I know that's just Rosé being Rosélina."

Rosé smiled. "Thank you, thank you! I'm going to take that as a compliment. Maybe I'll be worse next time."

"Impossible. If that happens, I'll be very worried about you and send you to a psychiatrist," Hanna said while Eliot took the script from her hand, putting it in the bag. "What about your exams?"

"They're fine, I guess."

"Okay, you're a fucking liar. Nobody does well on these exams. I don't think there's anyone who does well on any exam," Hanna argued, pointing the spoon at Rosé and then going back to her food.

"If you don't do well in your exams, it's not my fault and it doesn't mean I'm doing badly too," she challenged.

"Sorry, nerd," said Eliot, raising his hands in a sign of surrender, followed by Hanna. "You're a kind of ironic person, did you know?" he remarked, leaning on the bench that divided the two and looking at Rosé with a deep look as if accusing her of something.

"Hmm, why?" she asked, doing the same thing as Eliot.

"You think reading is a waste of time, but you study writing at university. A little ironic, don't you think?" he commented, making a face of someone who was reflecting on something deep and taking his hand to the chin, exaggerating his facial expression.

"Not at all." She leaned further over the table, getting closer to him. "I know a lot of people who love to read but hate writing and a lot of people who love to write but don't like to read. Maybe it's ironic. Life is ironic."

"A great irony," Eliot and Hanna said together. "Jinx."

"So American," Rosé rolled her eyes.

Hanna got up, putting things in the sink, and getting ready to leave, trying not to be noticed, but Eliot grabbed her arms. "You'll wash it. I can't wash your shit anymore." Hanna snorted like a spoiled child but washed it. "You guys are going to my play Friday night, right?" asked Eliot, this time serious, waiting for the answer from the two as if it were important. "I want you two bitches to be there."

"Wow Eliot, you are so respectful," commented Hanna ironically. "Teach me."

"Shush."

Although Rosé was not a big fan of this kind of thing, where it involves a place full of people, she had to go. She had to support her friend. "Yes, of course I will." He had been talking about this play for days. It was the least she could do for him. "Bitch."

"I am," he answered, posing.

You don't have to communicate with anyone.

Just sit down.

And watch.

"Great. Now, I have to go. Bye Rosé and Hanna Boo."

Hanna left not long after him, giving Rosé a hug. "I'll be back late, don't wait for me." She was alone.

It was impossible not to know when someone wasn't home. Hanna listened to loud music and walked around her room. James spent all his time cursing at the people he played online games with, they often had to knock on his door so he would stop cursing, and Jessica spent most of her days at the other party's house, or her boyfriend's, and sometimes came back to sleep when they had fought. And Eliot was always in the kitchen or in the living room.

She was off duty. By some miracle, she didn't know why her boss messaged saying she wouldn't need Rosé for the next two days.

Rosé had nothing more to do that day, as she had already done one of her exams in the morning. She thought she did reasonably enough but knew she could have done better if she had read the question thoroughly at the beginning.

She was completely alone, and she liked it. She'd put on loud music and do whatever she wanted. Sometimes she would decide to clean the room and the house. Or she'd take advantage of the empty living room to watch her series on the huge television.

But somehow, that day, she didn't want to spend all day at her house alone, so she decided she was going to visit her father.

He had moved to an area almost in central London in a shared house near Mr Watson's office, another reason that made her go visit him.

Later she'd have an appointment with him.

But her journey could basically be summarized as: he was not home, and a weird man answered the door.

<3

"Earth calling Rosé," Mr Watson called again. Rosé wasn't paying much attention to what he was saying. She was distracted thinking about her father and how he had just stopped talking to her. Not to mention the fact that a man lives with him. She knew it was a shared house, but that man was familiar. She had seen him before.

She pushed those thoughts away.

"I'm sorry."

"How was the moon?" He held the same old clipboard. "That's where you were, isn't it?"

"No. The moon is a mess, I managed to destroy it too. Now I'm on Jupiter," she joked with a shy smile to add a little humour to the comment. Or maybe not.

Rosé had already attended a few more sessions with Mr Watson and talked about the rose and the old woman in which he said nothing, although did not fully agree with what she said. Rosé's father had not sent any sign of life for months, not even answering any of her messages which worried her. She had even thought of returning to the house again some other day. The man had confirmed that her father lived there, but on realising that going to that house again meant seeing the stranger, she gave up.

"You seem a little upset, Miss Johnson," Mr Watson noted, worried. "Did something happen?"

A lot of stuff. Countless things are happening. "No. Yes. Maybe the exams or the fact that I have to wake up every day and live. It's exhausting," another half-truth. That's how she had come to answer people. She felt that way, but it wasn't why she was behaving strangely. Her father wasn't the only reason she was acting like this, and she didn't want to talk about it.

"Pleasure. People try to seek the pleasure of life. They're so desperate to find it, that they get blind. You don't seek pleasure. You feel it. When we kiss, we close our eyes. When we pray, we close our eyes. When we sleep, we close our eyes. The pleasures of life are not seen but sensed. When walking, close your eyes and take a deep breath, smell the place. Feel the breeze hitting your face. When bathing, feel the hot water touching your body. Listen to the world around you. Pay attention to the world. When you do that, you'll find the meaning of life. Or maybe not. Maybe I just was too dramatic once again."

"You're not dramatic," she lied, "thoughtful, I'd say."

"Don't lie to me, Miss Johnson and alright, my daughter tells me this all the time." Rosé looked at the picture. "Our time has ended."

She looked at him for a few seconds before getting up and heading to the door. There was something wrong there and she couldn't tell what it was.

"Mr Watson?" asked Rosé before leaving the office, still at the door.

"Yes?" he replied, turning around and looking at her with some books and papers in his hand. For a second Rosé gave up asking him why it seemed silly to ask a stranger, someone who wasn't family, about his father. She as a daughter should know. He should get in touch with his family before his friends. Yet Rosé moved on with the conversation.

"My father said that he was very close to you," commented Rosé, looking at the amulet on her arm.

"Well, we're still very close," he replied, turning his focus to the books in his hand and putting them on the desk. "Why?"

"You ... Did you happen to hear from him recently?" She felt stupid asking that.

Mr Watson began putting some books back on the shelves, interspersing his focus between the books and Rosé. "Your father's been having complicated and very stressful days. A grown man's life is much more complicated than you might think, especially your father's."

"But did he have to leave his daughter?" Her tone was angry again. He didn't answer. "Weird."

"What exactly is weird?" he asked as he directed himself to the papers on the desk

"You know more about my father than I do," Rosé replied with hatred in her tone.

"I'm his psychologist too, Rosé. I know more about you than your father knows and vice versa. That's my job. I can talk to him if you want."

Rosé waved.

"Until the next session." He did not say any more, just gave a smile. Rosé took two steps out into the hallway and the door of the office closed behind her.

Rosé took a deep breath. She observed the place around her, trying to process all the information she was given in the latest hour. Her brain was not working properly that day; until she saw a Chinese restaurant and stopped for lunch.

Chapter 8

She went straight to her phone and joined the flat group chat. It was midnight when Rosé woke up after hearing some moans and explicit noises.

Rosé: Who's the son of a bitch doing this?

Eliot: I was going to ask the same question.

Jessica: What's going on?

Eliot: Someone's having a great night. I thought it was you. Jessica: I don't do it at home Hahaha Rosé: It's not funny.

Eliot: Rosé, just enjoy the sound haha Rosé: Really?

Rosé: Where's Hanna?

It took someone a while to answer.

Eliot: I have my hypothesis.

Jessica: James didn't show up either.

Eliot: I also have my hypothesis about it.

Rosé: Is anyone going to knock on the door?

Jessica: I'm not home.

Rosé: Eliot?

Eliot: No fucking way.

"HANNA. JAMES," she screamed from her room.

"LEAVE THEM!" Eliot screamed back. She could hear him laughing loudly.

"FUCK YOU, ELIOT."

"I THINK THERE'S ALREADY TOO MANY PEOPLE FUCKING AROUND HERE, DON'T YOU THINK?"

Rosé laughed and put down her phone. She covered her ears and tried to sleep.

They had a long night.

Chapter 9

"You were amazing," Hanna almost screamed as they left the theatre. She hugged Eliot so tightly that Rosé almost saw his eyes pop out of place. Today it had been the university play and most of the students had been in attendance. At least those who had great taste in life and loved art.

That year, the play had been about *Alice in Wonderland* and Eliot had played the role of one of the main characters, the Mad Hatter. It was part of the second-year drama students' grades.

"You look like him," said Rosé, making them all laugh.

"I'm sorry, Eliot, but I agree with Rosé," Hanna confessed, putting her arms around Rosé and Eliot's neck and pulling them down.

It was late when they left the theatre and decided they would celebrate Eliot's incredible performance, stopping at the convenience store for some beers and other drinks, and, after much discussion, agreed that they would order a pizza when they arrived at the flat.

"In fact, Eliot is the most annoying version of the Mad Hatter. If that's possible," added James, letting out a laugh and running away when Eliot set off on him. He tried to use Hanna and Rosé as a shield, but it didn't work out, so he ran away.

"You ass, motherfucker." Eliot's long legs gave him a huge advantage as he could take longer steps and get to James faster.

Hanna anchored herself next to Rosé. Her hair swaying from side to side. Hanna had a smiley piercing. Not to mention one in the nose and several in the ear.

"Go Eliot, take this bastard and knock him to the ground. I wouldn't let anyone talk about me like that."

When he reached James, he knocked him to the ground, but James was quick and pulled him together and the two fell.

Hanna, still with her arms around Rosé's neck, turned to face her. "Idiots. They look like two immature children fighting." Her face was blushing and there was a different glow in her eyes.

Hanna kept smiling and Rosé was jealous of it.

"Sometimes I doubt their age," added Rosé before running over to them both and pushing them to the ground once again and running away when they both started hunting her. Rosé didn't know why she had done it, but she felt something in her heart and reacted impulsively. Her mind spoke: *What if…* and she did.

Rosé could hear them laughing behind her. "Come back here, you'll pay for that," protested Eliot.

"You're like them," argued Hanna, her voice hoarse because she was also running.

They were all there and Rosé was ahead. The cold wind pounding against her face. It didn't take them long to catch up.

"Cut off her head," shouted Hanna doing a different accent and raising her hand as a sign of power. Eliot made her squat and James made a razor noise, cutting off the air, followed by the gesture of cutting a real head. Rosé got into the joke and muttered "Bluéh", closed her eyes, and showed her tongue.

The group's laughter echoed in the streets.

Four idiots in the middle of the street.

Four idiots acting like kids.

<3

"Where did you order this pizza from? It is horrible," protested James. He wasn't wrong. The pizza was too salty and the chicken almost raw, not to mention the horrible dough.

"From 'Pizzeria Zoo'," Rosé informed them, turning the lid to read the name. "I've never heard about them. It's Eliot's fault, he ordered," she said with her mouth full. The pizza was bad, but the hunger spoke louder.

"It was the one with the worst evaluation," he said, laughing.

"And why did you order it?" asked Hanna, throwing the piece of pizza back in the box, as did Rosé and James. "Fuck you, Eliot." Hanna got up and went to get another beer from the fridge and on opening it with her teeth, she took a huge sip. "Just to get that horrible taste out of my mouth."

James got up and went to his room and came back with a sound box. "Someone forgot the song."

"You," said Eliot with his mouth full of pizza.

Rosé made a disgusted face, wrinkling her nose. "Are you really going to eat this shit? I found hair on mine."

"One," he began, signalling with his finger, "I paid for it. Two, it's not even that bad, you guys are annoying. We have to give morale to the pizzeria, poor people."

"Poor is from my palate and stomach." James turned on the sound box and a hectic song began to play, one that Rosé did not recognize. James began to shake his head back and forth and Eliot followed him. Hanna, who was already standing, started jumping back and forth, shaking her hair, and soon involved Rosé by pulling her by the arms. "Let's go, Rosélina."

The music changed to *A Thousand Miles*. Rosé took the phone, Hanna and James a bottle of beer, and Eliot utilised the TV remote control as a microphone, and they all began singing along. Everyone was drunk. Rosé could feel her body heating up. Sweat dripping off her skin, her eyes getting heavy from the alcohol but she didn't care about that.

The music changed once again, this time to a slow song and from there they made pairs. Eliot and Rosé, Hanna and James dancing, almost falling drunk and laughing like idiots. Rosé felt something she hadn't felt in a long time: peace, love, and tranquillity. She was feeling free. They danced a little more and sang. They drank the rest of the beers.

But that didn't last long.

A melancholy hit her in the chest. Her heart grieved. She started to feel guilty. Why were you happy? She had no reason to. Soon it was going to be over. Tomorrow she'd wake up and start another day. She had to solve other problems. Her father didn't text. She had checked her phone several times that day.

Eliot noticed the mood swing in Rosé.

"Hey, alright? Did something happen?" he asked with a concern tone, looking directly in her eyes.

"No," she lied. "I'm just tired. I think I'm going to go to sleep," she said, dropping his hand and picking up her things in the chair. She could feel Eliot's eyes on her back, watching her leave the kitchen. As she went to her room she turned to the group of friends. Hanna and James were still dancing, but Eliot stared at her. "Congratulations, once again. You were amazing." She smiled at him.

"Thank you." Eliot opened his mouth to say something else, but he closed it. Rosé said goodbye and went back to her room. She hated it when it happened. That pain. The melancholy that appeared out of nowhere and dominated her whole body. Her mind. She was so happy, but she felt guilty about it. Like she doesn't deserve to be happy.

Chapter 10

Her room was still a mess because she didn't bother to tidy it up. *In less than a day it'll be messed up again.*

There were trainers scattered around. (Detail: the trainers that made her stumble a few mornings ago were still in place). Clothes were on the floor and on the bed. Papers and pens were vying for space with even more clothes on the desk. Laptop on the bed. Food, paper …

Looking at the phone screen, it was midnight and her stomach hurt. That pizza didn't go down so well. Rosé hated using the kitchen because she doubted the cleanliness. She had never been one to share things with people, and she wasn't going to start now. She usually bought something from the market and ate in her room alone or passed by a coffee shop or restaurant, but today had been a different day.

After a while of sitting in the only free space of the bed, staring at nothing, thinking about everything, she began to roll over her room more than it was already. She found the summary of her last lesson; her favourite pen that she blamed Hanna for stealing; found the charger of her Nintendo, more food packages, supermarket notes from months ago, many other random university papers and, to her surprise, a beautiful spider appeared when she lifted one of her bras which made her give a loud and sharp scream and drop it on the floor again.

Rosé hate spiders, of all types and sizes, since a very young girl. In one of the corners of the living room where she lived there was a spider that had been there since they arrived, and she had asked several times to kill it. *She's been in there a long time. She even pays rent, we can't just kill her*, Eliot joked once.

It didn't take long for James to show up at her door.

"What happened? Did anyone die?" he asked, agitatedly opening the door.

"There's a spider under my bra." Rosé at that point was already on the bed pointing to her lace bra on the floor.

James approached and with his fingertips lifted the bra. They both blushed. *A bra? It could be anything else, but no, it had to be under the bra. Stupid, wicked spider,*

Rosé thought. "It's a tiny spider, Rosé. Come on," he said, mocking her and taking the spider in his hand. "Look how cute, maybe it's Grace's daughter," he commented, letting out a laugh.

"Who?" asked Rosé.

"Grace, the living room spider."

"Did you give that thing a name?" asked Rosé, incredulous.

"Of course, everyone needs a name, besides, Rosé, she's been living here a long time and not everyone is heartless like you," he said, showing his tongue. Before leaving the room, he looked it over. "I think your room is slightly messy. I thought it was more organized. What a disappointment."

Rosé gives a debauched laugh and showed him the middle finger. "Get out of here."

"And you won't thank me? I don't mind dropping her in your room again," he said, threatening to put her down.

"NO," she cried. "Thank you so much for your help, now take this far away from my room." James let out a loud laugh, throwing his head back.

"I'll take it to Grace, right baby?" said James to the spider, putting on a baby voice.

"I hope she attacks it and they die together."

"How aggressive," protested James, making his way to the door. Rosé could see a smile on his face. "Pretty bra." James winked before leaving the room. Rosé made an obscene gesture again and blushed. That was her sexiest bra, but she had never worn it for any occasion.

It was a Friday ritual that the flat debated on what to eat and put on loud music, just like they did today. Rosé enjoyed their company and always joined in, but after what happened, she didn't relish looking at James' face so early so she decided she stay in her room. Besides, after the spider, she decided she would tidy up and finish writing for Monday's class, to get a free conscience. Just before she started tidying up she heard them all chattering in the living room and the music playing.

They were probably drinking, and they were going to stay awake until they couldn't take it anymore. It's been that way since the first week. It was all fun and games though and sometimes she'd be thankful for getting lucky with her housemates. She had already heard horrible stories from other people.

Rosé put on her headphones and started cleaning.

It took less time than she expected.

When she turned off the music and took off her headphones, she realized that the house was very quiet. Too quiet for a Saturday morning.

Several things have gone through her head.

Rosé stood still for a while, waiting to hear some noise, a laugh, or any movement. Something to prove they were alive, but nothing. No one had said anything, either cursed or laughed or had made any noise. She could feel the beats of her heart racing at every moment as if it were coming out of her chest. Someone could have entered the house, and murdered her friends and she was the only survivor and would have to face whoever had entered.

Or maybe they were playing a prank. Maybe the fire alarm went off and everyone left, abandoning her, but that didn't make sense because the alarm would still be ringing and they wouldn't leave her, would they? Other possibilities began to emerge, but for some reason she could not move. Her eyes turned to the door. Maybe she was just getting paranoid, something that had happened before, too.

She began to wonder whether she had locked the door or not until she was surprised by the noise of footsteps.

The steps came from the kitchen and were moving towards the rooms. To her room. They were subtle like they didn't want to be heard. They were shuffling, which made Rosé even more apprehensive. She couldn't move in any way. Her throat went dry, and she knew that whoever was there could hear the beats of her heart, even her wrists were burning. Her body had stopped working.

The steps were approaching, just as her heart beat faster and faster. In a few seconds or minutes, she no longer knew, the steps stopped in front of her door.

Rosé had her answer ready about not locking the door. The doorknob turned and a figure with fire-coloured hair appeared. Eliot.

"Rosé? Is everything all right?" he asked with half his face poking into the room. The air had already returned to Rosé's lungs.

"You scared me," she complained as she went towards her bed, sitting down. Her breathing was still irregular, and she could feel the sweat still present. "I thought something had happened. Everything was silent."

"Like what? Someone invaded the house, killing everyone and showing up in your room with a knife to kill you?" he said, laughing. "I think you would have heard screaming."

"Something like that," she confessed.

Eliot laughed once again, entering the room and sitting on the desk chair. "Well, no one was murdered, Rosé. The people just left."

"At this hour?" Rosé looked at her phone screen. *1:30 AM*

"They must have gone to some motel," he said, looking around, "after the incident." Eliot looked at her. There was something intense in his eyes. "We're alone." There was a malicious look there. Rosé just laughed, slightly desperately, trying to get into the joke.

There was a different look in Eliot and Rosé couldn't identify exactly what it was. Maybe it was his hair that was different and not all messy like usual or his style of clothing. Eliot had changed his clothes; she had never seen him wearing it. His style was more dramatic and nerdier, and now he was dressed like a fuckboy.

"Fuckboy doesn't suit you," she remarked, looking at his outfit.

"What?" he asked, a little confused. "Fuckboy?"

"It's a style. By the way, why did you change your clothes? Totally unnecessary." It was too late, and he wouldn't leave. Unless Hanna and James had let him go, yet it didn't give him any reason to change his clothes again.

"I didn't ask for your opinion on how I shouldn't dress," he said in a tone of anger, his jaw clenched.

"I'm sorry!" Rosé raised her arms in the form of surrender. Maybe Eliot had too much to drink. "I have something for uni to finish." Rosé wasn't lying, but she also knew that if Eliot left her room, she probably wouldn't do anything, but she wasn't feeling well. The fear she had just experienced had left her with a headache and dizziness, she was feeling weak.

Pizza and beer didn't help.

"Have I told you about the play I'm going to premiere in two weeks?" Rosé confirmed she had. "I thought it was hilarious. How could anyone write something as amazing as that? Rich people are being evacuated to Mars and other nearby planets while others are dying on earth because they supposedly have a man with a nose so big that he is stealing all the oxygen from the earth," he says, beginning to rummage at everything.

(I don't think I'll ever forget this story. The boy who wrote this in a philosophy class, I won't call you genius, because I don't want to feed your ego, but that was great.)

Rosé was not paying much attention to what he was talking about.

"Your mother, Helena, is getting married, right? Is the man cool at least?" he asked, stopping and looking at things, picking up a pencil and starting to spin it between his fingers.

"I haven't talked to him much, but he seems to be cool," she said. For her mother to be with him, he was probably nice. She had to admit that her mother was good with men, unlike Rosé.

"Cool," he commented with a lack of enthusiasm.

Rosé still didn't feel well so decided to go to the bathroom to wash her face. She turned on the tap and took the cold water to her face, relieving the headache a little and causing her body to awaken. She towel-dried her face slowly. When looking in the mirror, she realized that her eyes were red and her pupils were dilated, overshadowing the honey tone of her eyes.

It was the only thing she liked about her body. The clear tone of her eyes.

Her vision was a little blurred.

She could barely see the fine lines of her thunder tattoo that went from her neck down to her shoulder and collarbone. One of her biggest regrets.

"I don't think I'm feeling very well," she said to Eliot. "I'm feeling a little weird."

"You are an interesting person, Rosé," his voice was a little drowned out by the distance. "I'd like to get to know you better." What did that have to do with what she just said? And what did he mean to get to know her better? They already knew each other very well. Interesting? Eliot had always found her a little dull.

Rosé continued to look at her reflection. Her hands resting on the edge of the sink. That didn't look like the Eliot she knew. He would never say that to her, not because he's gay, but because he's a little shy about love. He had been like this for a long time, since he had fallen in love with a boy in his drama class. Eliot was funnier than that and was always moving his arms when he spoke and crossed and uncrossed his legs all the time.

Rosé remained silent and Eliot was still sitting in the chair. She couldn't see, but knew he was there by his breathing and hearing the noises of the chair as he adjusted himself.

"Are you okay?" he asked, breaking the silence.

"I am," she lied. "I'm just a little dizzy," and the silence came back. The dizziness had passed, but she needed some time to reason.

Rosé stayed there for a while longer thinking, but it was hard. It seemed like her brain wasn't working well. There was something wrong. When she was helping Eliot practice his lines, there was nothing talking about space travel and someone stealing the world's oxygen with their nose. Wasn't yesterday's play the last of this school year? That didn't make sense, just like he knew her mother was named Helena and that she was getting married.

She had never commented on her personal life to anyone, even Eliot. No one knew she had lived in Brazil and that she moved to London a few years ago. Rosé had never commented on her parents or their separation and not even that her father had not been in contact in a long time.

"Eliot?" she asked. "What is the name of the play you will present? I forgot the name."

"Um, I don't remember to tell the truth." Eliot always knew the name of the pieces he was going to present, as well as the authors and the year they were published, where they were performed at the beginning and bizarre curiosities about them. He loved the history of the most important pieces and knew all about his plays and the characters that he would present.

But that didn't make sense. The man in her room was Eliot. Same face, same fire-coloured hair, same height, same voice. That was Eliot. Her friend and roommate. Unless he had a twin who was impersonating him.

Rosé went to her room again and saw him sitting there again, this time fiddling with his phone. "How do you know about my parents?" she asked, trying to look normal when her heart was racing again.

His gaze turned to her again. If that wasn't Eliot, it was someone very much like him. He dropped his phone on his lap and crossed his arms.

"Stalking. That's how you find out about people's lives recently. Going into their social media," he said, not taking his eyes off her. "Why?" He had a great point. Too good, but her mother didn't have social networks.

"Nothing. I just didn't remember talking about it," she said in an almost inaudible voice.

"I'm surprised," he said.

"W-with what?" her voice failed.

"That you were paying attention to what you were talking about," he commented, letting a smile escape. What did he mean by that? Did he know she was too bad to put together what he was talking about?

"What do you mean? Of course, I was paying attention, Eliot," she lied once again. She had already lost count of how many times she had done this just that day. Her heart was still beating fast. Her hands began to get sweaty again. She could feel it under her arms too.

"Are you nervous, Rosé?" he asked, making a baby voice like James had done earlier. He got up and headed towards her.

"No, why would I be afraid?"

"It's not good to lie, Rosé." She wasn't understanding what was happening and the fear was probably already evident on her face. That wasn't Eliot. She didn't know how, but it wasn't him.

"Okay, that's enough. This isn't funny, Eliot," she said in anger. "I know you love acting, but it is better for you to go to sleep."

"Act?" A shy smile appeared on his face. "I can feel your fear from here as well as your heart beating so fast that it could come out of your chest if it wasn't properly connected to your body." His eyes were fixed on Rosé's. Neither of them looked away and the silence prevailed until in a snap she turned toward the door and ran as fast as possible, but when she reached it, the door closed by itself, as if a strong wind had pushed it, making a loud noise.

She tried to open the door, pulling and pulling again, but it seemed to be locked. "You can try, my love, but it won't work out too well," a different voice said and let out a laugh. The voice was no longer Eliot's, it was thicker and more adult. As she turned around, Rosé came across a familiar face.

It was the same man on the underground and the one she found at her father's house. The same man in dark, disgusting clothes and careless hair.

"Surprise!" he said, making a gesture with his hands of something bursting. "And did you like it?"

"What do you want? And how did you do that?" she said. This time she wasn't afraid, but angry.

"Well, hmmm," he said, making a strange gesture with his hands. "Where to start. It was very hard to find you, with so much … protection, so to speak. How was Brazil? Entertaining? Boring?" He expected an answer, but Rosé remained quiet. "Well, actually I told you while I was trapped in that ordinary man's body, but you're not prepared for it. You're an interesting person, you know? And I'd really like to get to know you better. Do you know?"

"No." The answer was simple and cold. "Get out of my room. Now."

"No," answered the man, serious, imitating Rosé and then laughing again. "As I said, it was hard to find you. You're not paying attention."

"And what do you want with me?" Rosé's sweaty hand was still on the door handle, squeezing it and giving light pulls in the hope that it would open.

"Stupid bitch, didn't you hear what I just said?"

"I've already answered you; do you want me to say it again? Because I think it was you who didn't listen to me right."

"Bold," he said as he approached her. "Daring. This reminds me of someone hmm," he said, taking a picture off the wall above her desk. It was one with her parents, dancing on her birthday years ago. "So beautiful together. Helena? Isn't it?" The blond-haired man asked, and Rosé just nodded. "They never loved each other. Not really."

"Yes, they loved each other, but their love was short-term," she protested.

"So foolish. Helena never loved Tom. Their relationship was nothing more than business," he said, staring at the photo.

"Liar."

"No, no, no, You're the only liar here, pretty girl," he said, tearing the photo in two and Rosé's heart together. That was the only picture she had of the three of them happy together. The others had been lost or burned. *I don't want any evidence of this relationship,* they both said.

"Weak," he said, "sentimental and weak. You're attached to the worst things that can exist, especially love. Love makes you weak, Rosé, learn that. Your father's been out of touch with you for months. Not a call or message," he commented, his jaw contracted, face showing disgust and repulsion. "Where's your father, Rosé? Isn't that what you're waiting for? An answer from Dad? What about Mom? On the other side of the world, marrying another man and forgetting you, waiting for the next baby to arrive," he said, getting closer and closer to her. "Didn't you ever think they got tired of you? Didn't you ever think you were a problem for them? That they didn't want you?" Each question was a punch in her stomach.

"Stop." Her voice was almost an inaudible whisper. Tears were running down her face.

"I'm sorry, I didn't hear you.".

"I said stop," she cried. "GET OUT OF MY ROOM". That could not be happening with her. She was always so careful and fuck! Not her.

"I'm sorry, Rosé, like I said, I need you," he said, holding Rosé's arm. He squeezed it with too much force, every effort to get rid of him was useless. He was stronger than her. He opened the door, pulling her out, but stopped.

"Surprise," someone said. "I'm sorry, but you can't have her."

(Our hero arrived)

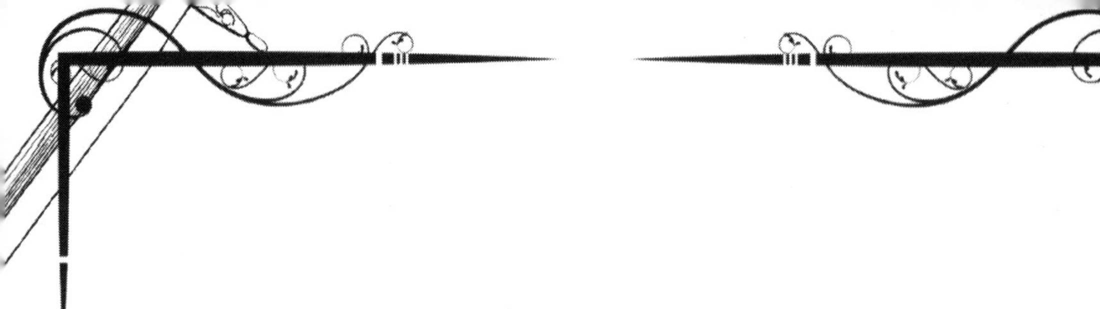

Chapter 11

Rosé couldn't see anything at all. She was trying to force her eyes to open, but they didn't follow the command.

She tried again, but nothing.

She was in a lot of pain. Her eyelids were heavy. She didn't know if she was lying somewhere or sitting down. She couldn't remember what happened before the blackout.

A horrible pain was running through her body. She felt something on her back that kept her from moving. The beats of her heart were accelerated, she could hear them as if someone had ripped her heart out of her chest and put it near her ears. She was weak and powerless.

Gradually the pain became bearable. Rosé's head didn't hurt like it used to. She felt something warm touching her skin which seemed to ease the pain a little and allowed her to open her eyes.

Rosé took a while to finally sit up. Her vision was still half blurry. Overshadowed by sunlight. The world seemed to be spinning. She could hear the sounds of birds singing and something damp on the floor. She took her hands to her head which still hurt a little. She rubbed her eyes with the expectation to see better.

When she opened them again, she realized she was in a forest. There were trees everywhere (don't tell me, shocked!), their tops prevented light from entering due to the amount of them and colourful flowers gave life to the place; huge branches were lying on the ground. There were mushrooms larger than expected, and the sound of running water in the background.

(Calm down, Rosé is fine, she hasn't smoked/eaten one and won't even eat a giant mushroom. She is not Mario.)

"I died," murmured Rosé.

Still sitting, looking around, she could see that the flowers were larger than normal. Not much, but bigger than she remembered. Maybe she was delirious for hitting her head too hard, or the fact that Rosé had never spent much time in nature.

In recent years, the only contact she had with it was in the parks of London. She didn't have time for these things.

For a moment she thought her lungs were so used to the pollution that clean air ended up affecting her brain.

She was so focused on her thoughts and trying to understand all that had happened until amid them she realized that she had no idea how she got there. She searched through her memories for what could have led her to this place, but nothing. She didn't remember going to some forest or even leaving her house.

It was then that she decided to retrace her day.

She remembered the unbearable noise of the alarm clock. She got up, bathed, and put on an outfit to go to class; she remembered making her coffee and leaving home in a hurry because, as always, she was late. Later she had to go to the session with Mr Watson. She remembered the crowded London Underground, the sounds of street singers and their instruments, she remembered going to work and assisting an unbearable person. She remembered her throbbing foot being in pain after wearing high heels.

She remembered Mr Watson greeted her when she arrived at the office, and he asked why she arrived late and Rosé gave the same usual excuse: underground. She remembered having lunch at the diner around the corner, whose quality she doubts a little. She remembered coming home and taking off those damn shoes and whispering all the bad words she knew when she saw the damn bubbles on her foot. She remembered she went to the bathroom and looked at her destroyed reflection in the mirror of another day in the life of being an adult, something Rosé still doubted she was.

No. Didn't that happen last week?

Rosé closed her eyes.

Exams and more exams, her father not responding, Mr Watson, Eliot and his play, the strange man in her father's house. Rosé could hear a snap in her mind.

Rosé recalled that before the mirror there was Eliot who was not Eliot, but the underground man in her room and that it was the same one that was at her father's house, who had forgotten to comment. The memories were mixing. She had not worn high heels that day, the bubbles were from the party that had gone to weeks before and a strange man wearing black had stolen her drink. Her head began to ache again, and a beep banging sounded in her ears, causing Rosé to take both hands them.

The noise was interrupted by something in the woods. Rosé was too immense in her thoughts and pain to have paid attention to what was around her. She got up quickly, still with a sore body. She tried to pinch her arm. A few slaps in the face, but nothing.

(Hehe, reading this again and imagining her doing this is kind of weird, a person hitting herself and everything.)

It was still in the same forest, surrounded by bushes and trees. She had no idea where to go, and it was then that she realised she should have paid more attention to those survival programs and not criticised them for possibly being fake.

Rosé started rummaging in her pockets to see if she could find her phone, but nothing. She looked round on the ground, between the leaves and the flowers, but no sign. Great. "A paranoid young woman lost in a forest, without food, water, or phone. That's how I imagined my life," she complained to herself. Rosé had no choice but to start looking for food or something useful.

After a few minutes of walking, she heard something that seemed to have come from behind her. Her body just froze. She looked around but didn't see anything. Rosé decided to take a few more steps, but again heard the noise of something moving through the bushes and plants, as well as branches being broken.

Maybe it was in her head. Not just the noises, but everything.

That didn't make any sense.

Looking around, Rosé returned to paying attention to the flowers and their vivid colours. They seemed to shine among the green leaves and there were plants she had never seen before. Their shapes were unusual and when she tried to touch one of the plants, it closed quickly, causing Rosé to take a frightened step back.

Maybe it's not a good idea to touch unknown flowers.

Rosé decided to walk a little further when she came across an empty area. An area without trees, without flowers, without shrubs. Just grass. She decided to sit down to rest and think about what she would do. Rosé had already walked a lot, she had tried to follow the noise of running water, but despite her efforts she had found nothing.

There was something in the air, like little floating balls. At first, she thought it was pollen, but they weren't the right shape, or maybe some animal she'd never seen before, but they seemed to have no life at all. They moved according to the slight breeze in the air.

The feeling of being observed had not quieted, but she did not care anymore. Rosé knew that she was delirious and that maybe it was a false alarm, all coming from her head.

She even thought she was reacting to drugs, but she ruled it out, she'd never come close to anything like that, even at university. Maybe she'd had something to drink that was modified, but she remembered she hadn't been to any parties in the last week. She prefers a sofa, pizza, and Netflix. Her father used to say that it makes her look older than she was.

Something interrupted her, returning her to the 'real world' once again. Something growled behind her. She rose in a snap and slowly turned, but nothing, just plants. She heard it again, behind her, but when she turned around there was nothing there.

She began to feel more anger at that moment than fear, but she didn't know what exactly she was angry about. Her mind? The mysterious sound? To have no idea where she was?

Despite the anger, fear was still visible on her face. Rosé looked around. She was looking for signs. Maybe it was just a helpless animal or maybe the wind, or maybe something from her imagination. One more to add to this place's list of weird things. She started hearing other noises. They seemed closer and closer to her. Gradually the sound began to get louder and was coming from all sides, until, in the middle of the plants, two huge yellow eyes appeared, a black animal possessed them.

It was like a wolf, maybe a little bigger than one. Its fur was dark, black as night. Huge honey-coloured eyes, like hers. They were glowing even though it was still day. She stopped and looked. She admired it until her body instinctively began to run. She ran as if her life depended on it.

She could feel the branches hitting her body. Scratching her skin. She didn't know where she was going. The earth seemed to tremble at every step of the animal behind it. Adrenaline had taken over her body. Her mouth went dry, and her lungs burned from shortness of breath.

Every time she looked back at the animal, it seemed ever closer. Rosé did not know where she was going and, in her despair, she stumbled upon something. The world seemed to have passed in slow motion, until she collided with the hard and wet ground.

Rosé looked back and the beast was a few feet away from her.

She thought about getting up and running a little longer but couldn't. Her body was screaming for help. It was all sore. And what was the point of running? She hadn't found anything since she got there. Nobody.

The creature was much bigger than her. Faster and stronger. She was at a loss.

She watched it approach her, step by step, cautiously. Rosé couldn't stop looking into the big eyes. However, she was forced to look away for a second after hearing another noise on her right side, and that's when she realized there were more.

More wolves surrounded her. They were the same; large and black. Rosé didn't know what to look at exactly. Their size, their eyes, or maybe their white, sharp teeth. As she watched them more closely, she realized that there was something different about them. They were gold stripes all over their bodies. They weren't like normal wolves, they were more intimidating, and they seemed more ferocious.

The first one started surrounding her without taking his eyes off her as if he too was analysing her. Maybe deciding how he'd kill her. Her body was motionless, and the pain she felt stopped. Her heart felt like it was going to come out of her chest. Sweat was running down her forehead. Her hands were wet and dirty. The sun no longer felt warm, even though it was burning in the sky.

Rosé didn't know what to do. Maybe because she didn't have anything else to do. She just wanted to wake up. Wake up from this nightmare in her room. She wanted her bed and phone. She wanted her mother and the warm hugs that made her feel safe, some things came into her head, but they left when she felt a burning in her arm.

The bracelet that was on her wrist began to burn on her skin. The urge was to scream, but she couldn't. In a sudden move to try to get it out, the wolf got startled, which in turn made it growl louder than the other times, which showed his white and huge teeth. He positioned himself into an attacking position.

The wolf continued to surround her, while the others only watched. There was no escape, they formed a circle. He was the only one to show any reaction. He stopped in front of her. She looked at it again. His growl broke the silence between them and this time he was ready to attack, and Rosé knew it. The last thing she saw before closing her eyes and waiting for death was him coming towards her and after that, a scream.

For a moment, Rosé thought it was hers, but maybe she was wrong.

She could feel the creature's warm breath next to her face. She knew there was something right there, in front of her. She kept her eyes closed, didn't want to look. She wasn't ready.

Rosé still felt her body intact and didn't feel any pain, only the adrenaline in her veins after what had happened. She moved one finger, then the other to check if they still had any movements. Then she tried her whole hand.

Everything seemed under control. Silence hung. Maybe it was all over, and she could go back to her house. She took courage and opened her eyes. The huge creature was still looking, but it was further away.

Below it was marks that gave the impression that he had been pulled back.

A few seconds passed and the creature withdrew a few more paces, and behind it a tall woman appeared.

Her body was covered with golden lines that stood out against her dark skin. They looked like they were drawn with paint. Her hair was blacker than her skin, short and curly, hidden in the hood she on her head. Her eyes were as golden as the drawings on her face. She wore white clothing, which also highlighted the tone of her skin, and on top was a navy-blue cape and hood.

She looked at the wolf that had almost attacked Rosé and said something Rosé could not identify, and soon he sat next to her, quiet and watching her closely. The woman turned to Rosé again and began to get closer, staring at her, analysing every detail.

Rosé could feel her body burning, she had never felt so intimidated. The woman looked at her from top to bottom several times.

Despite the attempt to approach, the woman was still in a position of defence in case something happened. Rosé didn't judge her for that.

"Who are you? And what are you?" she asked calmly, with a strong foreign accent. She was confused. Her eyebrows showed that. They were almost together. Her mouth was ajar, breathing with difficulty.

"R-Rosé," she responded with a trembling voice. "Rosélina." She didn't answer the second question.

"A human being? Perhaps."

For a second, Rosé thought to ask her the same. Ask her where she was and how she got there. She wanted to ask her why the drawings on her face and what these giant animals were. Were they really wolves? Rosé had many questions, but little courage.

She could live without answers, she just wanted to stay alive.

The woman's gaze was still on Rosé. She seemed lost and confused. For a moment, Rosé seemed to have seen fear in them. She was still in a defensive position, one leg forward and the other behind. Crouched. Positioned. *Totally unnecessary,* thought Rosé. She was alone and the hooded woman had her wolves with sharp, huge teeth. The woman seemed to reflect. Like Rosé, she seemed to try to understand what was going on. Both were motionless, staring at each other, until, in a sudden motion, she straightened up and raised one of her arms, picking something up in the air.

It was a pink envelope.

Rosé didn't remember seeing it at any time.

The envelope was light pink and was wrapped in a ribbon of a slightly darker shade of pink. It was delicate and small.

With her free hand, she snapped her fingers, and the envelope was suspended in the air at the height of her shoulders. The tape that used to wrap it up was now coming loose on its own and a letter came out from the inside. She read it, without even touching it.

At this point, Rosé had given up thinking too much and was just accepting the situation.

Realising that her mouth was open due to the astonishment she had just seen, Rosé quickly shut it, feeling a little stupid.

The woman looked around at the wolves and said something to them that Rosé could not decipher. It certainly wasn't English. Rosé had met people from all over the world and was interested in languages, but that one she had never heard in her life. Within seconds the wolves were gone and only Rosé and the curly-haired woman remained.

"Let's go," she said, breaking the silence between them by stretching her hand to help Rosé get up and then making a gesture to follow her. Rosé didn't hesitate. She didn't know what that woman could do, and at that moment, she was her only hope to get out of there.

They started walking through the woods. Her body was still sore, but bearable. She couldn't hide the pain at times, but the woman just ignored her.

For Rosé, those flowers definitely weren't a normal size, not even the mushrooms. She wanted to touch them again. She'd never seen anything like it. She tried to take her hand to a huge black flower but was quickly stopped.

The woman held her hand hard and pulled it away.

"Don't you dare! They are beautiful, but they can kill with one touch," she said. Rosé couldn't help but notice her strong accent again. This led her to think that maybe she wasn't in England anymore. Or was she?

"Dandara. My name is Dandara. Nice to meet you, *heres.*"

She still seemed apprehensive and afraid. She watched Rosé from the corner of her eye.

Chapter 12

In front of her, there were only trunks and plants which formed an old and narrow passage, like a ladder, made by Mother Nature herself years ago. Everything was covered in moss and some logs were no longer well connected, as perhaps they were one day. There was no other way out and Dandara had abandoned her there.

Rosé began to climb the small steps and gradually the path became narrower and narrower than before, where she could barely fit on it.

Where the fuck did that woman send me? It was slippery because of the moss and moisture in the air. Rosé almost slipped countless times. Her nails were stuck in the wet wood and her arms had already begun to hurt with the strain she put on them.

Further on, she happened upon a bridge made of the same material as the rest of the ladder. This made her stop and watch for a few seconds.

Rosé didn't know if she could trust the bridge, it seemed to be falling apart. It appeared so old that if Rosé put a little more weight on it, it would fall apart, but she had no other option. The forest behind was dense and she could easily get lost. In her mind, she kept remembering that it was just a dream, that if something happened, she would just wake up. She put her right foot first, testing whether it was firm enough to support her weight. Her hands touched the cold, moist trunk on the sides and with every step, her heart accelerated more. She wasn't acting rationally anymore.

She was tired of feeling her heart racing, there were times when she wanted to take her heart and throw it far away from her so she couldn't hear it beat, but she couldn't. She needed it inside her chest. She needed to stay alive.

Did she have to stay alive?

That's funny, because she hasn't wanted this and it's been a long time, but … every time she imagined the pain of the people who were going to stay. Her mother and father would not overcome their grief and would feel guilty for the rest of their lives. Would it be selfish to end it all? Would it be wrong to stop thinking about people for a moment and think about what you think is best for yourself? Would your choice be the best option you had? Did she really want this?

Rosé had several questions, but, as always, had no answer for them.

Almost halfway, Rosé could hear the sound of running water once again.

She couldn't give up now, not when she was already halfway there. The smell of fresh plants entered her lungs, which seemed relieved after years of pollution in the city. The water had scared her. She didn't know how deep it could be or what could be lurking in there. Rosé remembered Dandara talking about how fatal the black flower could be and wondered if there were more plants like that or other things.

Further on the bridge, there was a long space between the trunks, as if they had fallen or been torn off.

Despair took hold of her again.

How many times has that happened since she woke up the morning of Eliot's performance?

As she approached, Rosé looked down: Running water. Crystalline in a bluish tone that she had never seen in her life.

Not in person anyway.

The space between the trunks was too large for Rosé's legs. Even if she jumped, she wouldn't make it. It was almost two meters apart. Her hands were sweaty and the damp trunks around her were not helping. She looked around and the only options would be to move on or go back into the dense forest, but she couldn't. Rosé took a step back which made her stumble and almost fall. She crouched, her hands still holding firmly on the sides of the bridge.

"Okay, I'm going to be okay," she sighed, closing her eyes. "Think, just think what the best solution is." Her voice was weak. *Give up? Jump? Risk? Go back? Pinch my arm?*

Perhaps you should trust nature – a voice hummed in the air, scaring her – *one foot at a time.*

"What?" Rosé asked, voice rising. *Okay, people with pointy ears who turn into … whatever they are, poisoned flowers, broken bridge that is close to killing, now … voices from beyond?*

Voices from beyond? Like real? Died. That's it. I'm dead. Congratulations, Rosé, you finally got it all figured out.

You heard me. Trust nature and put one foot out at a time. For a moment Rosé thought it was something from her head. There was no one else there. On one side, plants, on the other, plants, up, an incredibly blue sky, down, deadly water prepared to drown, back, no one, just the path she had made.

Rosé laughed nervously, trying to keep her cool and sanity. "Who are you? And where are you?"

I'm everywhere. Trust me. The voice was calm and with each sentence, it came out as a melody that calmed Rosé's heart more and more. *Talking to the beyond, I get it.*

"Do you want me to put my foot in the abyss?" she asked, pointing to the hole.

There will be no abyss if you trust me.

Rosé let out another nervous laugh. "How am I supposed to trust someone I can't see?" she said.

You have no other way. They're waiting for you. It was like a whisper in her ears. All the hairs on her body stood up. Whatever it is, it wasn't lying. She had no other way. Rosé approached the hole. Hands clinging to the logs.

"Who? Who's waiting for me?" she asked, trying to distract herself.

There was no answer. Just a slight breeze that carried with it the cute, little, whitish animals she had seen before.

"One step at a time?"

One step at a time, repeated the voice

She could be unconscious somewhere or sick. She had seen strange things happen since she arrived, and she had worse dreams than that. People turning into wolves, huge, deadly flowers, maybe that thing was right. *It's just a dream. Trust. One step at a time,* Rosé repeated in her head. If she fell, she'd just wake up from the dream. She wasn't going to die.

Perhaps you'll feel more comfortable closing your eyes, the mysterious voice whispered again. A breeze tickled Rosé's neck.

Rosé stopped. "You have got to be kidding me."

It's better when you don't see it. Trust is blind. You don't see it. Win over time and lose it in just one second.

Rosé wouldn't argue, especially since it was a voice that came from beyond.

She decided only to obey. She closed her eyes and began to walk. She didn't know why she was doing it, but the same thought persisted in her mind: *you have nowhere to go.* She kept walking, waiting to fall and dive into the waters, but the moment never came.

Was the voice correct?

When she gathered courage again, she opened her eyes and realized that she was no longer on the bridge and the small abyss was still in the same place behind her. She didn't stop to think, she had already done a lot of it today and needed the neurons to rest in her brain to get to whoever was waiting for her.

Now all she had to do was go down the stairs made of the same material as the bridge.

Rosé continued to look at where she was stepping, afraid to put her foot where she should not. Maybe there was another abyss, or a piece of trunk cut off which could hurt her. Or her foot could get stuck somewhere. Her shoes were all dirty and muddy and she was stinking. Whoever was waiting for her would have to deal with the smell.

"You're late." When looking forward, a tall young man was leaning against a carriage. He had honey-coloured hair and wore black sweatpants and a light grey sweatshirt. "From what I remember the bridge is not that long. Got lost on the way?" he mocked, laughing and pulling away from the carriage to go and meet Rosé. "Aiden, nice to meet you." Rosé stretched out her hand to meet his.

"Rosé, you too." A relief took hold of Rosé. She was alive and with someone who seemed normal, but before she could reach his hands, she fell to her knees and the world seemed to tremble beneath her.

Her body was exhausted. The countless thoughts and near-death experiences had left her tired. Fear and anxiety seemed to be working together, finding a way to bring her down. Everything in her body hurt and she only realized it when she fell to her knees, weak.

Soon Aiden was already by her side helping her up, one hand holding her hand and the other on her back. "Are you alright?" Rosé just nodded. She leaned on him and soon was standing up.

Aiden walked away, watching her, perhaps expecting any reaction that Rosé could have. "I'm just a little tired." Mentally and physically.

"Let's go," he said, helping Rosé slowly to the carriage. Rosé realised that he tried covertly to clean his hands which had touched Rosé, but too late, she had already noticed.

Rosé didn't judge him. She was filthy. Nature likes to make its mark. "Sorry for the hands, and are you sure you want me to get in the carriage? It looks too clean and I'm …" Rosé looked at her dirty clothes, "disgusting and stinking." She had soiled herself on her way to the bridge and during it.

Paying more attention to the carriage, Rosé realised that it was of a pearly white tone and had details in gold with a huge coat of arms divided diagonally, the upper side was dominated by a howling wolf and the lower part by a crown and flowers, and the entire side of the coat of arms and around the two images was covered constellations.

Nunc et Semper. That's what was written below it.

She has never seen anything like this before. Well, she's never seen anything like this whole place before.

"I'm sure and don't worry, I can't smell it if it makes you worried," Aiden commented, letting a smile slip away.

"Where are we going?" she asked, following him. The ground was muddy and for the thousandth time Rosé almost fell to the ground. *Incredible, now I'm going to go ahead of the boy I just met. Something I've always dreamed of.* She thought to herself.

"You'll see. There's someone waiting for you there." Aiden opened the door of the carriage; Rosé had only now noticed there was no horse on either side. She looked at both sides one more time, only to make sure she wasn't hallucinating.

"You'll find out there. She asked me not to give you too much information. She thinks if we do this, we're just going to scare you. I'm just doing my job." Work. He wasn't helping a disgusting, stinky girl who had just gotten there. He was working, getting paid for it.

She asked not to give too much information.

Maybe that's what was written in the letter. Nobody cared about her there. Why did she think anyone would?

"How … how will the carriage move? It doesn't have …"

"Horses?" he said, letting out a shy smile. "Magic."

Rosé laughed, but her voice failed and became hoarse. She was incredibly weak, but soon she realised Aiden wasn't kidding. "Shall we go?" She recalled him reaching out to her, helping her in.

The carriage wasn't too big. There was white upholstery on both sides. *Damn white upholstery. They're going to turn brown quickly.* There were some details in gold that followed the same design as outside the carriage. Aiden sat on the opposite side of her and as he snapped his finger the carriage began to move through the trees, following a single available path.

"This doesn't look anything like a pumpkin," she said, looking around.

"You're not Cinderella."

Aiden handed her a sandwich and water. She started eating immediately. She was starving.

"What is this place?" she asked, looking out of the carriage.

"Well, according to the instructions I was given, I couldn't give you much information, because, as I said, there's someone in the palace waiting for you, but—"

"Palace?" Rosé interrupted him and took another bite of the sandwich, taking care that her hand did not touch it too much. Her gaze returned to Aiden. Were they going to a palace?

"It's … like that. It's not really a palace, but it looks like one," he said, putting both hands behind his head and putting his feet on the seat, next to where Rosé was sitting. *Lazy,* she thought.

"So, it's a palace?" asked Rosé, a little confused.

"Maybe."

"You're confusing me."

"And you're asking too many questions," he said, looking at his nails and turning to look at her. Both were silent, but Rosé's brain was processing many thoughts at the same time. Why didn't anyone answer the fucking questions she asked? Was it that hard? Rosé tried to fix some of her clothes that were crumpled, but it wouldn't do any good. Her legs kept moving and she couldn't keep her hands still for long.

"I asked you a question," she said sullenly.

"You asked more than one," he commented.

"I asked more than one because you can't explain things," replied Rosé, pressing her lips together in indignation.

"I felt offended."

"Are you one of them?" she let loose, waiting for a response. Aiden looked nothing like them, but at this point, Rosé didn't doubt anything else. Everything seemed possible in that place. Aiden did not have pointed ears and did not have the same chocolate skin tone and the drawings scattered around the body.

"Who?" he asked, his eyes closed, his body still in the same spacious and loose position.

"The werewolves." Rosé wasn't sure if that was the right thing to call them.

Aiden let out a smile on the corner of his lips. "They're not werewolves. They're called Olvs. And no."

"What are you then?" she asked him, waiting for an interesting explanation. Her anxiety needed that. It needed to be fed.

"If I were you, I wouldn't go out asking what people are in this place. It's kind of offensive," he said, opening his eyes to look at her again. "Well, I'm an Elementri."

"What's that?"

"Elementri are people connected to some element of the earth. Water, earth, fire, and air. In my case, fire," he explained. Rosé could feel pride in his voice. She wanted to roll her eyes, but he would notice it, so kept she her face as neutral as possible.

"One. How do I know what the person is? Two. I doubt you're what you just said." After that, a huge question came into her head: Where had all this come from?

Aiden looked at her from the corner of his eyes and then rolled them over and sat up in the seat before answering her.

"One. When the person presents himself, he usually speaks what he is, unless it is obvious. Two …" Aiden closed his hand with his palm facing up and, when opening, a flame of fire burst out of his hand. Rosé stared at the flame until he closed it again and the fire disappeared. His hand was black, like coal. "You can close your mouth now."

Maybe Rosé had become too distracted.

"You didn't tell me what you were when you greeted me," she disputed. Where was that boldness coming from? She's never acted like this with strangers before. By that point she had already finished the sandwich.

"My mistake, I'm sorry."

"Is that what you do? A flame of fire comes out of your hand?" she said, mocking his abilities once again. She could feel envy in her heart. She wanted to do what he does.

"No. I can do much more than that, but we are inside a carriage and a totally helpless girl is inside it, I cannot risk anything." The feeling of envy was exchanged for anger. He was also subtly bragging of his abilities. *Bold. I like that.*

"Do you have anything else interesting to share?"

"You're kind of deaf," he said, playing with a flame in his palm. His jaw clenched. He was getting frustrated, and Rosé was having fun with it. "I can't answer many of your questions because there's someone waiting for you in the palace, and they will answer your annoying questions. You probably have a lot of them."

"I'm sorry, for lots of questions, I don't know if you noticed, but I just got to a fucking magical place I don't know, where I've seen wolves turn into human beings, a fucking magic bridge that almost killed me, and now I'm in a carriage with an arrogant Mr Little Flame going to a stupid palace, where I'm going to meet someone I've never seen in my life, but I'm sorry for my curiosity." There was more than annoyance in her voice. Pain. Maybe fear. Rosé crossed her arms and turned to look at the landscape.

It was the only thing she could see. She didn't want to look anymore. *I'm angry even from the trees, how did I get so far in life?*

"Mr Little Flame?" he asked, taking his feet off the bench and sitting with his spine straight.

"Isn't that what you are?" asked Rosé, looking angry. Their eyes met and a strange feeling arose on her chest, and she could feel his eyes burn. Aiden didn't answer. Rosé looked away at her lap where her hands rested. Her amulet was no longer there. It had been a gift from her grandmother. And because of this stupid place, she'd lost it. Fresh pain overcame her and she had to hold on to tears so she wouldn't cry.

She'd never taken it off before. Never.

I miss her.

"Do yourself a favour and look the other way," Aiden commented after a while. Before looking to the side, Rosé let out one last look of anger at Aiden, who reciprocated. By obeying him, still with a sullen face, Rosé realised that the green trees that once dominated the view were replaced by dawns and white flowers.

"It snowed and I didn't notice? What happened here?"

"This is the entrance of Amondridia. White means peace, and whoever founded this place thought they were magnificent and wanted peace," he commented, standing by her side.

"Ammon what?" Aiden looked at Rosé from the corner of his eye and she could see anger in his eyes for a second, but there was something else there, something she couldn't decipher.

"Welcome, Rosé, to *Amondridia,"* he said the name of the place slowly, "but that's not all." He pressed a button on a small panel. The carriage obeyed. Now there were windows where there had been a wall. In front of him, there was a wide path that housed a huge, white, rectangular construction full of towers, with details in gold, the same as in the carriage.

On the left side, Rosé observed a huge space with another magnificent structure further away. On the other, there were plantations and flowers that formed walls. Behind the main structure, the palace, there were enormous mountains that were lost in the clouds.

The place was surrounded by gardens.

"Before you ask me, the structure on the left is the training camp and kind of a school sometimes, and to your right are the mazes that have in its centre one of the most beautiful fountains in this place, also known as the source of the magic of Amondridia."

Chapter 13

It didn't take them long to get to the big structure.

Aiden was the first to exit the carriage, offering his hand to help her exit too.

As they walked along, Rosé came across a bridge, with a watercourse underneath. There was a greyish stone wall with small sources of water that, when falling, formed a small and shallow pond on each side. There was also a set of stone stairs leading up to a large gate that would take them inside. All this was decorated with colourful flowers and sculptures.

Both headed to the huge gates that were already open. "I'll lead you to her. Follow me, please." Just after the entrance hall there were two corridors. Aiden took the left path.

Everything inside the palace seemed to be made of white marble and details in gold.

"The person liked white and gold," commented Rosé, looking around. Everything followed the same pattern.

"Obviously," he said coldly.

"Why are you being so arrogant with me?" protested Rosé.

"You're the one who started it. I was being nice, but Miss Perfection decided to make fun of my skills when you don't have any that you can show me, or do you?" Aiden didn't stop.

Rosé let out a faint and ironic smile, almost showing her tongue to him. "I'm not Miss Perfection and it seemed like an illusion, Mr Fragile Ego," lied Rosé without having any other excuse.

They looked like two kids fighting.

"Illusion? Honey, I'm not a fake magician from the Outer World, okay? And watch your words or you'll end up dying in seconds in this place." He finally turned around so he could face her. There were almost invisible red lines appearing on his body, like veins.

"Are you going to kill me with your stupid little flame?" Rosé mocked.

"I'm seriously thinking about it."

"Go on. Go ahead, do everyone a favour and kill me. That's what everyone's been trying to do since I got here. Why don't you take my heart and burn it? I'm tired of this world." She defiantly stopped where she was and crossed her arms. Rosé's words came out more sincere than she had expected, but she was tired of people treating her like walking trash. She was just curious and scared and tired of how she had been treated since she got here. "Kill me, Go on. I. Don't. Give. A. Fuck."

She was acting like a child. And she knew that very well.

"I'm not going to waste my time killing a stupid, spoiled girl with my stupid little flame. And just so you know, we're late, and if I don't deliver you in time then I'm fucked. So you'd better start moving both your fucking legs before you force me to carry you," he said, raising his voice.

"First, you tone it down, burning candle, and if you do a lousy job, it's not my fault. You should treat people better, and I'm not a dumb object to be delivered with a time mark, you stupid—" A noise interrupted her last sentence, causing the two to turn to the side where a man not much older than them was eating a snack. His hair was almost all shaved and his eyes were focused on them both. He wore a black tank top, exposing numerous tattoos on his arms and upper chest.

Rosé hadn't noticed him there.

"Why did you stop? The discussion was interesting," he said with his mouth full. He took another snack to his mouth.

"Seriously Gustav? Don't you have anything else to do?" asked Aiden.

"No," Gustav answered. "Now what were you saying?" He frowned, making his eyebrow move and consequently the piercing on it as well. "Little Flame, I think I'll start calling you that." Rosé observed him even more and realized that he had another piercing below the lips and a tattoo above the eyebrow, which Rosé deduced to be part of the Mandarin alphabet.

Rosé made an obscene gesture that drew a laugh from Gustav who continued to eat his snack. "In fact, I do have something to do," he said, standing up and heading towards the bin to throw away the empty snack bag. "Good luck with the girl there, Little Flame, she seems to be pretty bossy."

"Bossy is your fucking ass," Rosé reacted. She was sick of that place. "Are you all like that?" They both looked at her.

"Like you?" asked Aiden. "Less bad."

"You're the one who's yelling, princess. Also, if you'll let me say, I'm Gustav." A smile appeared on his face, showing the pointy fangs. A vampire? But he was eating human food. "Gustav Maximillian."

"Rosélina," she said in a dry tone. "For you it is Rosélina."

"Of course, it is," he said, taking another sip of his juice. They kept eye contact until he finished drinking.

Rosé's eyes went from the juice box to him again. "I thought people like you only drank blood."

"Continue reading your fairy tales, but that's not going to take you far," he said, walking away. "I'd like to stand here arguing with you, *Rosélina.* It would be something very interesting, but … I have more to do. Curious for our next meeting, *Rosélina,"* he announced and walked away.

Rosé watched him disappear at the end of the hall. "Now, is there any chance you could take to whoever this person is?"

"That's what I was trying to do."

They walked for a few more minutes until Aiden stopped in front of a white door and knocked twice. "Come in!" said a female voice on the other side. Aiden obeyed by entering first and holding the door so that Rosé could enter as well. Half the room was closed, and the other was a huge greenhouse.

There were numerous plants of all species, sizes, and colours. Rosé also noticed that on one side there were bookshelves full of books and jars with liquids and things Rosé had never seen in her life. Occupying a large part of the space was a huge grey marble countertop.

"I did what you asked me to do." A woman appeared from behind some plants on the countertop. She was not much taller than Rosé, her hair was baby pink and long which made her pale skin stand out. She removed her white lab coat and eyeglasses.

"I'm not an order," Rosé complained in a lower tone so that only Aiden could hear. She didn't mean to look rude in front of the woman.

"Oh, yes. Thank you." Her voice was sweet and calm. Before leaving, Aiden took one last look at Rosé and left.

"Rosé dear, it's so nice to be able to meet you in person," she said, dropping her glasses on the countertop and going towards her, hugging her so tightly that Rosé couldn't breathe properly. She kept a sweet smile on her face. "How you grew up," she said, squeezing Rosé's arms and looking her up and down. "I have photos of you as a baby, helpless and …"

She wrinkled her nose. "Oh dear, you're horribly smelly." The woman moved her hands and something light pink wrapped her hands. A shiver passed through Rosé's body and as she looked down, her clothes were clean again and there were no scratches or blood.

"I'm sorry, I don't mean to sound rude, but … do we know each other? How do you know my name?"

"You just met meta-elves, talked to a voice that comes from beyond, according to your words," she began, counting off the facts with her fingers, "argued with an Elementri and a vampire, saw me use magic, and that's the first thing you ask me? Curious." Rosé did not answer but fully agreed with everything the woman had said. "Anyway, I'm Ariady. Ariady Prinze. A mage."

(Pronunciation of her name is more beautiful in English. But anyway.)

"Mage, like a witch?"

"Mage, like a mage." Ariady smiled lightly. "We are alike, but not the same."

"What is this place?" asked Rosé in the hope that this time someone would respond properly.

With a twinkle in her eye, she replied. "Home. This is your home, Rosé. The place you never should have left," she smiled. "But nooo, they had to take you away," she complained.

The place you never should have left.

"Obviously I knew you'd have a lot of questions and …" The pink-haired woman took Rosé by the hand, as if she were a child, and directed Rosé to the huge counter, pushing things to make room. Her touch was soft and almost impossible to feel, like a bird feather on the skin. "Of course, I was preparing. Tea?" Rosé accepted. "And … well, it's a bit complicated, so let's go little by little."

Rosé took a sip of the tea and groaned. "This is good, what is it?"

"Ashy Tea"

"Ash-y tea?"

"Don't worry, it is a plant, when it dies it looks like ashes." Rosé could not describe the taste. She had never drunk a good tea like that. "It is basically hot orange juice with honey and an ashy plant." AKA her new favourite drink.

Ariady placed a small set-up on the table and at the push of the button a holographic map appeared. "First of all, you're in Amondridia." The same name Aiden had spoken to her when they were still in the carriage. "Amondridia is the name of this area of the map." She points out the right island on the map.

The river was not a river, but an ocean. "The other side is the forest of Olvs, the people who welcomed you, also known as meta-elves." She pointed her to the side of the map where there were only trees. "You can call this area Floralin too."

"What are …" began Rosé.

"Olvs are human-sized elves who have the ability to change from their almost human appearance to an animal. Each tribe turns into a different animal and gets a different name. Here, they turn into Olvs, also known as abyssal wolves. They no longer exist in the Outer World where you lived," she said, turning to the map. "Amondridia and the forest are part of a Lys, also known as Refuges for Creatures with Any Extraordinary Manifest. Nothings to do with Lys, but okay.

"Lyses are like parallel words inside the Outer World. Imagine a whole world inside a shoe box, for example, Lyses are something like this." This place was getting weirder every second.

"Why am I here?"

"First, I want to give you this," she said, handing over a phone. "I can't give it back for security reasons, so here's everyone's number and it's a normal phone like any other." Rosé kept it in her pocket and turned her attention to Ari. "I needed to give it to you before I forgot. Indispensable today."

"Thank you," Rosé replied, somewhat confused.

"About you being here, this is where things begin to get complicated, Rosé." *Complicated.* Her life was complicated enough, nothing else could shake her.

"Why, exactly?"

Ari let a long, loud sigh slip away. "Sit down," she said, pulling a chair out for Rosé and then one for her, they sat facing each other. "Can I ask you something?" Her gaze showed concern, and her voice was low and quiet. She contracted her lips and Rosé realized that Ari's body was tense.

"You're scaring me."

"It wasn't my intention. What I'll tell you now, it's not easy, and I don't expect you to understand at first, but please promise me that you will try your best to try to understand?" she asked, looking at her shaking hands and then at Rosé. "I think I can."

"Every creature—" Ari began.

The door opened with a loud bang, causing both to jump. "Ariady Elisa Prinze, how dare you to bring an Ordinary into Amondridia." Her voice was loud and authoritative.

"This is a private place, Li; you have no authority to enter without asking." Ari's feature had gone from concern to troubled. She straightened her spine and got up. "And second, she's not an Ordinary, now please retire." Her voice was calm and clear. She hadn't hesitated, not even once. The white-haired woman crossed her arms and took another step forward.

"What is she then? A witch? Elementri? Stupid?"

"Leave. We'll talk later."

"I do not follow orders," Li commented in a tone of disdain.

"But follow the rules." There was tension growing in the environment.

The woman made to turn from Ariady, the noise of her heels making her presence noticeable at every step. Rosé didn't dare look at her. "Is this the most important mission you had? The one you left me out of for months?"

"We didn't need a lot of people." Li approached Rosé, looking down. Her long fingers touched Rosé's chin.

"Look at me, thing," Li commands. Rosé didn't hesitate to do what she said. Just as Ari's expression had suddenly changed, so did Li's. Disgusted to surprised. She held Rosé's chin high with her index finger, analysing her features, and then she turned suddenly to Ariady. "Impossible. You intended to hide it from me for how long?"

"Leave," asked Ari once again, looking forward. "There is the door."

("There is the door, bitch." I'm sorry. I got excited.)

Her lips became a straight line and she elevated her head more. In seconds she was no longer in the greenhouse and the door was closed once more.

Ari sighed and went to the other bench, serving herself a little whiskey, drinking it in one sip. She then turned to Rosé once more. "Sorry about that." Rosé didn't know what to say or how to react. *What would be impossible?*

"Where were we? Yes, I'm … the creatures in this world are somehow connected with power or magic, often coming from the very nature of the world in which we live, thus making one creature stronger than the other. Our world has existed for many centuries and just as in the Outer World, theories and tales have spread and been created over time." Ari turns her focus to the table and where there was a map, a family showed up. "Among the most famous tales, there was the Lysion family. The Tale of Lysion."

She sighed and then looked at Rosé. "Maybe we should leave that for later," she commented. "Maybe it would be more interesting if I showed Amondridia to you first."

"I'm curious. Keep going, please," commented Rosé. She had started the story and now she had to finish it. Rosé didn't want to stay there. The sooner she knew why she was there, the faster she could get out.

"Curiosity is dangerous, and—"

"I don't care if it's complicated. I can handle it." "I hope you can." She lowered her gaze.

Rosé sat in the chair, waiting.

"People believed that the Lysion family was presented by gods with powers never seen before. A perfect combination of magic and power. Few believed this story. It was just a tale told from generation to generation. But one day, a group of sorcerers killed a supposed Lysion and the person responsible for the murder received the magic of this man.

"A very powerful magic. One that according to legend would be able to dominate the world if mastered properly. From there, chaos began. The Lysion family was hunted for years, as were all who had any blood connection with them. Even though they were powerful, they couldn't always escape death. Few survived. Twenty-one years ago, the last Lysion was killed by a man called Oldo Blake, ending the family's legacy, but …" she breathed hard and moved the ring on her finger before the last sentence, "but what they didn't know is that this last woman gave birth to a baby before her death. An heir. You."

Rosé observed her without any reaction. Her brain took a while to process what was going on. Lysion. Woman. Power. Lies. Gods.

"No, you must be mistaken. My mother didn't die. She's in Brazil, you got the wrong girl. I'm no Lion, or whatever you just said," she said, laughing. *The drug they used on me was good. Really good.* These people were crazy, and she needed to get out of there. They had probably eaten some of those fungi, or she had done it and hadn't necessarily noticed.

"Rosé."

"This is a dream." Rosé laughed again. "You must be confused; I don't have this fucking magic and my mother is in Brazil," she repeated, her voice trembling.

"Helena, isn't it?"

Fuck. The smile on Rosé's face disappeared.

"She was a close friend" Ari held out what appeared to be a picture of the two of them. "Your father, Tom, moved in with her when your real mother died. They swore to protect you and never come back. Helena made a promise to your mother, saying that she would never step foot on Amondridia or anywhere else and that she would raise you as far away from this world as possible so that no one would know about you. So, no one could hunt you down."

"So you're telling me my life was a lie?" She didn't know how to react. Usually, within herself, there were countless emotions sitting on her chest, but at that moment she could not feel anything. It was as if time had stopped, but her brain was processing a thousand things a minute.

"Rosé, breathe." She did. She took a deep breath. One. Two. Three. "It wasn't entirely a lie, but …"

She didn't want to believe it, but for some reason it made sense. Like how Helena had not come with them to England and said that one day she would understand. Like Tom never referring to Helena as Rosé's mother. How things happened so fast in their house and so slow elsewhere. *I'm a great magician.* He wasn't lying about it. Countless memories began to flood her head.

She didn't like to cry in front of other people.

She could deny it over and over in her head, but it somehow made so much sense. It was as if the thousands of questions she had, had been answered at once.

She had to get out of there. She had to go somewhere else. Rosé needed some time to reason. A little time alone. She went to the door, but she couldn't open it. Tears flowed from her face. Despair took over her body.

"I'm sorry, but I can't let you go." Ari's voice came out like a whisper. Perhaps Ari realised Rosé didn't want to hear anything else. So, she stopped there. Ari would leave the rest of the story for later. Let her absorb and understand what had happened. Ari went towards Rosé and sat next to her at the door and hugged her as the tears fell onto Rosé's face. Rosé felt the warmth of Ari's body on hers and, for a second, she felt peace and love.

She couldn't remember the last time anyone had hugged her. And that was very comforting but agonising. She had never let anyone she didn't know to touch her body and she wasn't much of an affectionate person, but at that moment, she didn't protest.

"Does my father know I'm here?" she asked amid tears and sobs.

"Yes."

Silence.

"I don't belong here."

"This is your home, Rosélina, and you will learn this over time. You may hate it here at first, but this place has more to do with you than you think." Ari was stroking Rosé's hair, calming her.

"How do you know that?"

"I met your mother, and your father said you guys are alike. Besides, nobody hates you here."

"Aiden hates me." More tears flowed down Rosé's face.

"You should give it another chance. You started the wrong way."

"And magic?"

"That's something we'll discuss another time." Ari kept stroking her hair. "I think for today you've experienced a lot. I'll take you to your room." Ari took Rosé by the hand and helped her up, with the other, she opened the door and began to walk her through the halls. Rosé couldn't think of anything. She just followed Ariady, her body seemed to be on auto-pilot. Her eyelids were heavy and her body was sore.

After a good walk through the palace, they finally arrived at Rosé's room. Ariady helped her sit on the bed. It was soft and cosy. Rosé had never had a bed this soft before.

"Are you hungry? Maybe a bath? Hmm … sleep?"

"I want to sleep," she murmured. Her voice, hoarse. "I want to rest."

"All right, darling." When Rosé looked at her outfit again, they had already been swapped for light pyjamas. As she laid her head on the pillows her brain shut down and the last thing she heard was Ari wishing her sweet dreams and the click of the door closing.

<3

"Really? There was no better way to tell her?"

"I was direct, what do you expect me to do? Wait until she found out alone? They stole the truth from her for almost twenty-one years," she whispered.

"Unbelievable."

"I could have come to her and said: 'Hi, your dad lied to you. Your mum is not your mum. You have power oppressed by a lucky charm until today and there are people hunting you, wanting you dead, now you are stuck here with magical creatures. Basically, you are fucked up'," Ari exclaimed with a fake smile.

"You did good."

"Do your job and I'll do mine, asshole."

Chapter 14

She was going to be hunted forever.

Her lungs woke her up. They searched and fought for air.

That had already become normal.

It took a while to remember where she was and how she got there. She was being hunted. People wanted her, not her, but her magic. Something inside her turned around. Her body was still processing the information and what had happened in the last twenty-four hours.

She didn't know how long she'd been there, looking at nothing, trying to figure it all out. The smell of good food penetrated her nostrils. She got out of bed half disoriented and found the light switch. She didn't pay much attention to the room.

She wanted the food.

On a desk in the corner was a tray of pasta and a glass of juice. Her belly complained and could not hold on, devouring it within minutes. She was grateful for being alone. That must not have been a very pretty scene to see.

When her belly was full, she went back to bed. There was no need to turn off the light. Her body was too tired, and she could sleep with the light on.

She lay down and closed her eyes.

'Okay, there are people trying to kill me, but … I'm in a safe place. But my life was a lie. Helena is not my mother. She never was, but that doesn't mean she wasn't my mother by heart. Okay, I'm going to go … That doesn't change anything. She's still my mother, but … My real mother is dead, and I don't even know who she was.' Rosé cried. 'How I don't know my mother's name? The tears dried up. But it's okay. I'll ask Ari tomorrow. There's someone chasing me.' She cried even more. Fear.

'Okay, I'm not going to let you … you what? What I am saying. My life's always been crap. Always excluded and afraid. Living, but not living. Maybe that's cool.' She yawned. 'How is being persecuted cool? Madwoman. But it's something different, a different experience with magic. FUCK I'M IN A

MAGICAL WORLD. No, I'm delirious. I need to get some sleep. I think I'm going crazy.' *What do you have to lose?*

What do you have to lose?

What do you have to lose?

What do you have to lose?

Nothing

She opened her eyes, and it was dark.

She closed them again and fell asleep.

The next two days she spent in bed sleeping, crying, and thinking. When she would wake up, the food was on the desk.

She just got up to go to the bathroom and eat, but everything seemed distorted. When she woke up on the third day, she only remembered glimpses of previous ones.

If your life sucks, what do you have to lose?

Get out of your comfort zone.

But someone's after me. They want me *dead.*

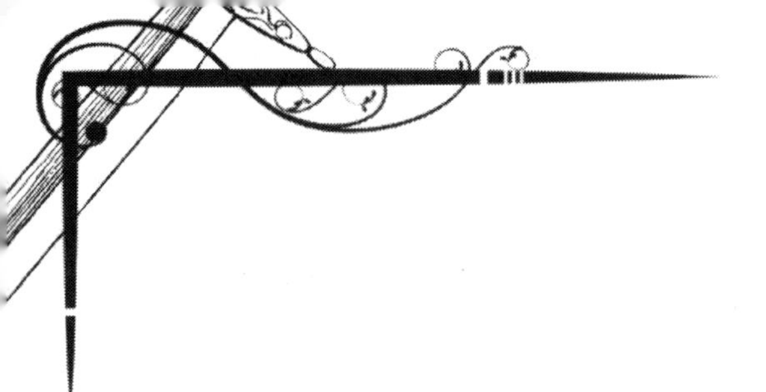

Chapter 15

Rosé woke up the next day with sunlight on her face again.

With her eyes still closed she tried to search for her phone on the bedside table but found nothing. She hit her hand in several places. She turned around once. Twice. *Since when was the bed that big? And where's the fucking table?* Rosé opened her eyes gradually, realising that she was almost at the edge of the bed and that she was not in her room on the university campus.

She quickly sat up, which made the world spin, and when everything returned to normal, she began to look around. That room, supposed to be hers, was huge. "No, no, no. This can't be real," she murmured to herself, closing her eyes once more and burying her face in her hands. Everything she had heard the day before, Ari, Aiden, Dandara, Gustav … all that was real. It wasn't a nightmare. Unless you sleep, dream, and wake up inside multiple times.

Rosé tried to get out of bed once more which made her dizzy again. The digital clock on the wall marked 5.37 a.m. Her stomach hurt; she couldn't remember the last time she ate. It was probably that bad pizza.

No.

She had woken up sometime at night to eat. She had had noodles. She tried to look for the tray, but when she looked around, there was nothing. Or was that three days ago?

How long has she been there?

How would she get food?

She didn't know how she was going to leave the room. Rosé didn't know that place. She didn't even know where she was.

On the left side of the bed were huge windows. Rosé went to it and opened them, noticing a slight tear in the white curtain. The window looked out onto the training camp. In front of the windows was a large, white dressing table.

As she approached it, Rosé realised that all her products that were in her old room were perfectly arranged on the dressing table. All her makeup and brushes, products, nail polish, and hairbrush.

All separate.

Heading to the huge wardrobe leaning against the wall opposite the bed, Rosé opened the door and to her surprise, all her clothes were there, folded and separated by style. Blouse with blouse, shorts with shorts, socks and even her panties, which made Rosé blush. *Who had put their hands on my panties?* Despite having many laces or 'unacceptable' panties, she still had panties from years ago that were comfortable but were destroyed and with holes in some places.

She had never bothered to get rid of them before.

The bedroom had two doors. One was closed, which caused Rosé to deduce that it was the door leading to the hallway, and the other was ajar next to the bed.

Upon entering the room, Rosé came across a reasonably large bathroom. There was a bathtub with a shower, toilet, and a huge sink, where once again several of her products were there, tidy.

Rosé did not remember taking a bath or brushing her teeth the day before or in the days before that, which made her feel disgusted with herself, especially when she looked in the huge mirror on the wall.

She took some clothes from the wardrobe and went looking for clean towels that she found in one of the bathroom cabinets. Relief flooded her body when in contact with hot water. She didn't want to take too long.

She washed her hair and body more than once and got out of the bath. She brushed her teeth and dried her hair.

When she got out of the bathroom there was a knock on the door.

Thanks! Someone to help me.

To her surprise, Aiden appeared carrying a tray of food. A wide smile appeared on her face; she couldn't help it.

"Is that smile for me? Or for the food?" he asked her, smiling. "Where can I put this?" Rosé felt relief when she heard humour in his voice. She thought he'd be in a bad mood after the argument they had had before.

"Do I have to answer? The food, of course. And you can put it on the bed. I hope it doesn't fall." Rosé put the towel on the chair and turned to him.

"Thank you."

"No problem." He carefully placed the tray on the bed, then he sat down. "You must be hungry. I came last night and every other day to see if you wanted to go get something to eat, but you were already asleep," he commented. "You were even snoring. It wasn't a nice thing to see." Rosé took one of the pillows and threw it at his head.

"I'm kidding, I didn't go into your room. I'm not allowed to. Rule number one living here, you can't go into someone's room without permission. But I knocked on your door and since no one answered I deduced that you were already asleep or didn't want company. Or maybe you'd run away somewhere." At that point, Rosé was already devouring the croissant with cheese and ham, and juice.

"Did you really come here?" Rosé asked with her mouth full, feeling something strange in her heart and relief in her stomach. She was surprised at his consideration for her and worried about her being hungry or not, but soon remembered that he might just be there on business.

"Of course."

There's a silence between them.

Maybe this was the time.

"I'm sorry," said Rosé, lowering her head. "I'm sorry for how I treated you and I'm sorry I'm crying right now, usually it doesn't happen, I ..." she said, drying some tears that flowed.

"Hey, no problem," he said, approaching Rosé. He took his hands up to her and then removed them, they seemed to be shaking. The tears were overshadowing her vision "Okay, I don't know how to react to this." He walked away.

Rosé started laughing. "Haven't you ever seen a girl cry?" she asked, taking another bite of the croissant. Crying could wait, food was the priority at the time.

"No. When I'm alone in a room with a girl, usually other things happen." He let out a smile from ear to ear. If she had another pillow on her side, she'd attack him.

"Idiot." The two of them started laughing. "If it wasn't you who left all those foods in my room these past few days, who was it?"

"It was probably someone from the Elite, they don't necessarily follow the rules. They are 'immune' to some of them for everyone's safety," he commented, watching her eat. Rosé offered but he denied it, saying he would soon join his friends.

Obviously. He had friends. Was that jealousy?

"What is the Elite?"

"They are the people assigned to take care of Amondridia, like a small Government. Ari is one of them. They're much older and well trained to take care of here. Many of them were mafia members and similar things. Assassins, warriors, soldiers and stuff there, but today they're on our side in the magical world and serve as security guards or something. There are people who still call them Legendary," he explained, lying down. "Gustav is also one of them." "The walking comic?" asked Rosé with her mouth full.

Aiden just laughed.

"Yes, the walking comic," he repeated. "I don't know how you're still alive. Don't play with them. Not everyone is as humorous as he is." Gustav did not seem to be a threat to her.

They were silent. Rosé finished eating.

Another chance.

"How are you? I don't know how much Ari told you about your wonderful story."

"Well, to the point where someone wants me dead and that my life has been a lie this whole time. That my parents lied to me. That whoever I thought was my mother is not my mother. That I'm supposed to be here because I need protection. In short: I'm more fucked up than I thought," she summed up in a matter-of-fact way. She's supposed to be freaking out, right?

"You seem calm for someone who is fucked."

"I'm desperate," she claimed, playing with her hands, "but I'm good at hiding and controlling certain feelings. And anyway, my life was shit for a long time, I think I needed a little adventure. She said she would tell me more about it another day, when I was better, and I had these days to think." She didn't know how many days she had stayed in that situation.

"Amondridia is a safe place, trust me. Well, it's supposed to be safe. At least you're in a magical place, so stop being those stupid girls on film and enjoy it. There's a lot of cool and sinister stuff. No one here is going to kill you or anything. Magic and power, dear."

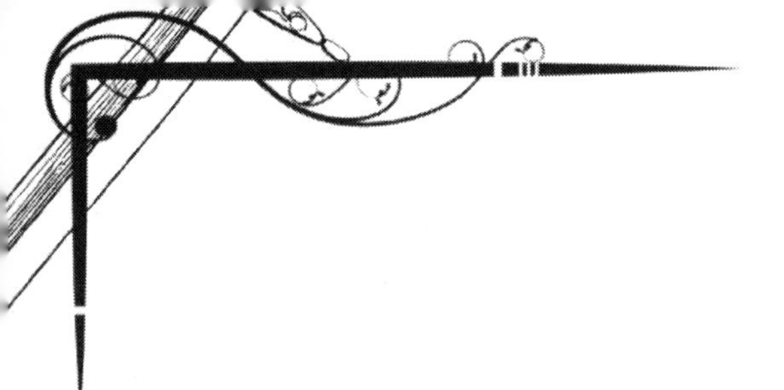

Chapter 16

Rosé followed him into the halls. She had agreed to meet Aiden's friends. She was willing to give the place and chance and there was no escape. And crying wouldn't change the fact that she would have to face whatever was coming after her. Meeting new people might help her get through all this.

What do you have to lose?

Nothing. She had nothing to lose.

She had not seen this part of the palace yet. The corridors were a little different but followed the same colours as the rest, white and gold with long, red carpets. It was full of paintings and drawings that seemed to have been hand-painted, not to mention those that had been painted directly on the wall or ceiling. The corridor was illuminated by chandeliers of all sizes.

"This place is huge; don't you get lost?"

"At first yes. I used to end up in totally different places, but over time you memorize them. I'm glad you asked me that, it reminded me of something," he said, taking something out of his pocket. It was an almost transparent cloth. "It's called a star guide. You tell it where you want to go, and it takes you. For example: guide us to the canteen." The cloth lit lightly and began to float in the air, directing them.

"You simply need to say the keyword, GUIDE, and where you want to go. To turn it off you just need to take it in your hand again and if by chance you say the keyword unintentionally, it will stop, and you just need to say 'proceed' or give another command."

Rosé observed the little shining cloth floating in the air.

"Thank you."

"Well, I don't think so. It wasn't quite my present," he commented, rubbing the back of his neck. "It was in my room with a note asking me to give it to you, but I wish I had the idea."

"I think I'm going to feel kind of stupid for using this. It's going to look like I'm lost."

"Of course, it won't. This place is huge, bigger than you think. Bigger than you see on the outside. It has expansion enchantments. Some people have lived here a long time and still use it, you'll see it's normal. Besides, one day you will know this place super well."

"Are things so far away?" she asked, realising that they had been walking for a long time. They both exchanged glances. "I still have many questions ahead. Just deal with it."

Aiden sighed, passing one of his arms over Rosé's shoulders, pulling her closer to him. "Of course, you have, I don't know why I'm surprised at this." Rosé looked at him and smiled. It was nice to know he was taking it all in his stride. Maybe he'd become her friend.

She heard something mumble behind her, she turned to look but saw nothing.

Her gaze turned to Aiden when he started talking.

"It was designed for this, the founder said it would help people move more if they leave places away from each other." "Smart but inconvenient."

<3

"We've arrived." When looking forward, Rosé came across an immense canteen, like the ones that could be seen in American high school movies. The middle of it consisted of numerous tables and chairs. The ceiling was mostly glass, showing a sunny sky.

There were plants hanging in some places and the same for the walls. The pillars were perfectly built and detailed, and on the left side of the canteen, was the food. This was the only part Rosé was really interested in.

As usual.

"Hey, Aiden." A woman waved at one of the first tables. Aiden moved away from Rosé and went to her, but first plucked the guiding star from the air and returned it to Rosé. Rosé just followed him. "You're late."

"I went to pay a visit," he said, pointing to Rosé. "Guys, this is Rosé. Rosé this is Misty Ortiz," he said, pointing to the chubby girl who waved at him. She had dark skin and chocolate-coloured eyes. Her hair appeared to have been perfectly drawn in black curls. She left her place and came to give Rosé a tight hug, who was surprised but reciprocated the

embrace. Her hair smelled like vanilla.

"She's an Elementri. Air, being more specific." Misty sat back in her seat. "This is Theo. Terran actually, but we all call him Theo Watson." Aiden pointed to a brown-haired man. He had whitish locks, blonder in certain areas. "Earth." Theo reached out for a handshake.

"Very pleased." Rosé just nodded. Theo's hand was warm compared to hers. *It is called vitiligo* said in his two-coloured skin. She had almost not realized.

"And lastly this is Nixie Watson. Water." Nixie was pale with short greyish blonde hair. Her ocean-coloured eyes lived up to her element. Nixie hesitated a little but reached out for a handshake just like Theo.

"Pleasure," she said, and her face was dominated by an indifferent look. Maybe she wasn't too much of a conversationalist.

"She is new to our world, right?" Misty asked. "O.M.G, you have to try the Moaning Cookies. You never tried, right? Is this an 'our world thing'? and bluns? Dragon eggs cake?" She smiled and closed her eyes. Aiden had to call her name so she would stop to breath for a second. "We should take her to Devils and the Snake Nut Head pub and—"

"She can't right now," Theo interrupted.

"Oh." Her smile faded. "Right, sorry." She buried herself in the chair.

Rosé felt bad for them both. "Maybe one day. What are those things you said?" Rosé asked with the expectation to make her smile again and give both some hope.

"M. Cookie is just THE best cookie ever; it makes you moan. No discussion." she informed. "Bluns are little white insects, but in food terms, they are little balls of different fruity flavours and when eaten they seem to bloom in your mouth."

"That sounded kind of sexual, Misty," Theo commented.

"Oh, shut up," she complained. "Dragon egg cake is not made from real eggs, but they look like them and have an amazing taste, they have Ashy plant on it."

"And the other places are in the Open Lys, they're pubs and nightclubs." Everything seemed amazing. Rosé just agreed with them. She didn't know how to react, she wanted to visit those places.

They started to talk about things Rosé didn't know and it wasn't directed to her so she got out her phone and started going through it.

She also watched them talk for a while. She had nothing to say. It wasn't the first time this had happened, staying out of the conversation. In the meantime, Aiden had gone out to get food and they had been talking for a long time. Rosé looked around, taking in her surroundings and coming to terms with the magical place she now found herself.

She was falling in love with it gradually, she started to forget the reasons for being there.

At some tables in front of her was a small group of people.

In another, there were people eating without even using their hands. The conversations got mixed up.

Her look turned to a table further in front of her and left where she could find a baby-pink-haired woman. Ari. She was with a group of people who looked older than her. Their looks met and she winked.

"Hey, how old is Ari?" she asked Aiden.

"I don't know how old she is. None of them usually say, but you can find it in books. I just know she's a lot older than she looks."

"Books? Is she in some history books?" Rosé couldn't hide the surprise.

"She is famous," remarked Misty. She was playing with a small, almost transparent bird that surrounded her and would stop in her hand.

They continued the conversation and Rosé returned to looking around until her gaze met with a man. He held her gaze and Rosé didn't dare break it either. She'd say his eyes were blue, but she was a little too far away from identifying them correctly. He was on Gustav's side. She had seen him before.

If it wasn't for her phone vibrating in her pocket, she wouldn't have looked away. *I hope you're okay xxx.* It was Ariady. *Meet me in the greenhouse when you're done.* She had nothing to finish, but she would wait for them to be able to leave.

Rosé spent time on the phone, trying to add apps, but didn't know half of them. They weren't like in her world. In her world, people don't use magic. Outer World, as they called. She thought about asking, but when she exchanged eyes with Nixie, she gave up.

"For all the blood that is precious, aren't you seeing that she is being set aside? Bloody children of nature." The comment came from a blindingly white woman. Rosé wondered if there was any kind of melanin in that skin. Her eyes were reddish brown, almost covered by bangs. Her hair was black and long. She wore a snake tiara and her whole outfit was also dark, reinforcing the lack of colour of her skin covered by random tattoos.

Behind her, there were two other men, the same one who stared at her and Gustav. "Ruby Browen, pleasure." She didn't stretch her hand, nor did she show any interest in hugging her. "I heard you arrived three days ago. Gossip spreads very fast down the halls," she warned, giving a forced smile, showing her fangs. "Welcome. That's Kay," she said, pointing to one of the men with fully tattooed arms and dark brown hair, almost black. "And that's Gustav," she said, pointing to the other with shaved hair and tanned skin, the man she met on her arrival. All three were covered in tattoos.

"I think we can introduce ourselves, Ruby, and we've met," commented Gustav. "Rosélina, the mad girl." Rosé cast a look of anger at him. "You see?"

Ruby rolled her eyes, muttered a strange word, "Rwvka", and left, followed by Gustav, who was smiling, showing off his fangs. The other man stared over for a moment. His eyes were actually a greyish blue. He approached and took Rosé's hand, depositing a gentle kiss.

She did not outwardly react, but her heart missed a beat.

He let a corner smile escape, exposing his dimple, and left.

As she looked, Rosé realised that almost everyone had turned their eyes away. "I hate them. They're so full of themselves," commented Nixie. "Makes me want to vomit."

"Don't even tell me," said Aiden, relaxing in the chair. "And what the fuck was that with Kay? It looked like he was eating you with his eyes." Rosé thought no one had heard Aiden's last comment, but, by the facial expressions, maybe they had just ignored him.

"What is rwvka?" (Pronounced as ruvka)

"What Ruby is, a bitch," Nixie answered, and everyone continued with their conversation.

Sometimes she exchanged looks with one of the groups and they seemed bothered by her presence there, they were no longer as excited as when she had arrived. Well, they didn't necessarily show any disdain, but there was something wrong there.

"I … I think I'll be going," remarked Rosé, rising. She didn't want to stay in a place where she wasn't welcome. "I have to meet Ariady."

"Is everything alright?" Aiden asked, quite worried. Rosé just waved and left, heading towards the exit.

Out of sight of the others, she took the cloth out of her pocket and requested directions for the greenhouses.

Rosé has never seen such a beautiful, white place in her life. For a moment she thought she was dead and was in heaven, but she remembered that heaven wouldn't have creatures like those.

There were numerous paintings hanging on the walls, as well as carpets and different objects, among them a white sword with silver details and blue stones, in which a white snake surrounded it.

Rosé was drawn to it, blinded by its beauty and details. Every moment her hand came closer, the energy grew between them. Something she couldn't explain. Rosé was nearby, just inches away, until a greyish mist stopped her, and a strong hand squeezed hers.

"If I were you, I wouldn't touch it," commented a serious voice behind her. *If there are countless things that can't be touched in this place, why do they leave them out?* Rosé turned and found the same tall man with greyish eyes. Kay. "It's too powerful for someone as Ordinary as you." Their looks were connected once more. His hand still squeezing Rosé's, not strong to hurt, but still hard to let go.

Ordinary, that was the third time someone had called her that, did he know who she was? Rosé recalled what Ariady had said about being a powerful creature, coming from a family whose power was greater than many other creatures and all those things she had heard, plus the deductions she had made.

She hadn't decided whether she believed it or not, but she was there for some reason.

"I know I'm incredibly beautiful and I'd like to stare at myself too, but it's bothering me a little bit," he said, passing one hand through his hair. Rosé rolled her eyes and, when she looked at him again, she tried not to laugh, but couldn't avoid the smile.

"I'm not admiring you, you idiot. I'm waiting for you to let go of my hand if you don't mind." Rosé pointed to their hands, still in the air. Connected. Kay looked at their hands together and then looked back at look Rosé.

"And risk you putting your hand on an object that can kill everyone in seconds without much effort if they fall into the wrong hands? I don't think so. Also, you should take a look at your health, your hands are cold," he said, letting her go and wiping his hand on the side of his hip.

"That was rude, did you know?" she protested, witnessing the act. "What exactly?"

"Wiping your hand after you touch someone." She straightened her back and crossed her arms. "You should not do it in front of the person." Aiden had done the same, but he was different. She had soiled his hand from the ground.

"Hygiene. I don't want to get infected," he said, sticking his hands in his pocket.

"Why are you still here?"

"I told you, to make sure you don't kill us, Ordinary."

"Stop calling me that."

"Do you prefer Smurf? Nugget? Pixie?" he asked, inching closer to her. "You're short, they fit you," he said, taking one hand out of his pocket and swinging it just above Rosé's head.

"How about I call you a proud narcissist?"

"Oh," he teased, taking his hand to the centre of his chest, "you hurt my feelings, Smurf."

"I didn't know you had such a fragile heart, pretty face."

Kay approached her and whispered, "Harder than stone. And … do you think I have a pretty face?" His eyebrows rose in surprise. Rosé swallowed. He was beautiful, yes. She couldn't deny his captivating eyes and how his face was perfectly sculpted. Not to mention his size and the damn ring in the corner of the lower lip that moved with each tremble of his lips.

"Yes, I think. I've noticed a lot of people here are beautiful, but … too bad few have something in here," she said, pointing to her head. "Including you." Rosé approached him, getting on the tips of her foot to get closer to his face. "Beauty is not everything, heart of stone." She gave a slight punch to his chest and stood back.

If his heart wasn't stone, his chest was.

His eyes were still fixed on Rosé, he moved closer to her. Their lips were almost touching each other. A malicious smile popped up on his face. She tried to walk away, but he kept getting closer. Rosé's gaze dropped to his lips, paying attention to the two dimples that formed. She could feel her breath quickening.

They were like that for some time.

"Maybe one day I'll show you I'm not just a pretty face, beautiful thing" When he moved backward, Rosé realised that he had taken the guiding star, he was stroking the soft tissue with his fingers. "It's been a long time since I've seen one of these. Are you a little lost?"

"For someone, I should be careful about, you seem very self-centred and stupid."

"I can turn your life into what your ordinary people call hell."

"I'm curious."

"You shouldn't be."

"How can you be such an asshole?" she says, picking up the cloth from his hands.

He made a sad face and then smiled. "I wouldn't say asshole. I would say tasty and funny and very intimidating, and huge." Rosé let out a loud and hysterical laugh, but, when trying to breathe, she ended up making a snorting noise, scaring her. She stopped laughing immediately as she took her hand to her mouth. She could feel her face burning.

Rosé turned and walked briskly away, her eyes wide and her hand still in front of her mouth. Something like this always happened; she always found a way to be ashamed.

Chapter 17

"Can I take him by the hair and rub him on the asphalt?" Rosé asked about Kay.

"No."

Ariady and Rosé were moving some plants out of place. According to Ari, they were already large enough to be taken to the main greenhouses.

Ever since she got there, Rosé had complained about Kay and how people seemed not to care about her. Even though she hit back and was rude to Kay, it didn't count, he had started it. She also mentioned that the Elementri didn't seem to like her and tried to convince Ari to let her go.

"I've told you I can't let you out. Do you forget who you are? And two, you're already home," was her excuse.

They spent the rest of the day talking about Rosé and everything that had happened in the last few years. The oath to take her away as her mother had been found dead. How Rosé needed to be a secret, but, of course, now many already knew about her existence. She also tried to explain why her mother did what she did, but there was something wrong with that story, because even Ari didn't know exactly what she was talking about.

"What are those pink bubbles on the table?" Rosé asked, touching the strange bubble that got stuck in her hands. "Ariiii," she cried.

Ari rolled her eyes, wet her hand, and grabbed it from Rosé's hand. "Sorry." She definitely should stop touching things.

"Pop Gums. They stick to you and do not leave for a while. Just water helps."

"You should keep mortiferous things out of people's way," she complained, following Ari again.

Ari's intentions for Rosé and how things would happen from now on was another topic of their discussion, including training and practices.

"Amondridia will always be here to protect you and you will be trained to be able to do the same for yourself and for us," Ari commented, lifting another vase, and taking it away. "That's the dilemma," she cried from the other greenhouse. "Amondridia is our kingdom, and we fight for it. Now and forever."

Rosé took another vase and went after her. "You mentioned training. Everyone here is trained?" she asked, putting the vase in the right place. They were too heavy. Sometimes she had to stop to catch her breath and flex her tender hands.

"Yes, from a very young age," she remarked.

"Don't children study?"

Ari had already returned with another vase. "Of course, they study, but in a different way. We do not use the same method of study as the other Lyses, much less that of the Outer World. Children have a tutor for the time that would be at primary, and they develop communication, trust, and other skills essential for the future. Personal growth. They learn to control their anger and feelings. They learn about diversity and dealing with their powers and magic, as well as learning to read, write, and basic mathematics.

"During the time they would be in high school they are taught about potions and first aid. They learn about accounting and how they can make money and how to manage it. They learn a little basic science and a little bit of our history. Just the parts relevant to them. They are trained according to their powers and learn martial fighting in case something happens to their powers and magic. Something important to keep them alive.

"They are encouraged to spend time in unpaid work to gain experience and find their passions, in addition to being advised to seek extra knowledge for themselves in books and the Internet. They also have some extra subjects involved. Over the years they are exposed to situations at more unlikely times and their skills are tested in practice and not in exams."

"Don't they have exams?"

"To cheat in? To stress over? Develop something that can be deadly to them and to us while they learn nothing? No. This is not the education system that we have, moreover, they do not study more than the basics of coexistence and life. For the rest of your education, you're alone. They are told every year how their decisions affect their future and how their lack of interest can result in a miserable life. When they reach a certain age, they go to a 'college' outside of Lys called the C.A.E, Centre of Advanced Education, and study subjects according to the professions they want to perform."

Ari mumbled something and the plants began to move from where they were and align perfectly on each other's side. Rosé couldn't believe what she was seeing. All the effort she had made all this time, had been in vain. All her effort and sweat.

Rosé was outraged.

"Why didn't you do this before?" She was not only outraged, but shocked. Angry.

Ari positioned them all before turning to Rosé and answering her question.

"Stop being lazy, besides, you need to exercise more and create some muscles because …" she said, snapping her fingers and a screen appeared in the air, "the person who was taking care of you in London described you as 'incredibly unhealthy, with a bad diet, unable to understand and lazy. No kind of exercise in recent months'," she read aloud and soon the monitor disappeared. "Really?"

"Responsible for me? I had a babysitter, and no one told me?" She looked up in exasperation. "This is totally unbelievable."

"Some," replied Ari, turning her back to Rosé, focusing on the plants.

"Who? Specifically, who wrote this because that's a big …" she stopped to think. It was all true. Shit. She hadn't really practiced exercise or anything like that for months, maybe years and her diet was horrible. "…lie," she meekly finished. How had anyone dared to write or report something like that? She was big enough to take care of herself.

"They're confidential, I can't give you much information. Not at the moment," Ari remarked, tying her hair in a ponytail and going inside, disappearing.

"I didn't like it." She followed Ariady.

"What exactly? Because you don't like a lot of things and I'm starting to lose count, child," she commented, picking up a bag of seeds and throwing it at other plants. They were large, the tips of the flowers and their leaves were black.

Rosé helped her.

"Child? And I didn't like having a babysitter looking after me like I was a kid." She was incredibly and absurdly disgusted.

"I'm sorry, *adult*, but if it wasn't for them, you would have been dead a long time ago. They're not babysitters, they're protectors, bodyguards, I don't give a fuck what you want to call it, but they saved you from what you can't even imagine. Usually, we call them Guardians and you have just one," she commented. She was starting to lose her temper.

"It's still ridiculous. This is all ridiculous. You stole the truth from me."

"For fuck's sake, Rosé, stop being ungrateful and complaining about everything and don't put me on that list. I told them that taking you away from here was not a good idea," she argued, she had a shovel in her hand and was aiming it at Rosé, if she hadn't dodged, she would have been hit in the face.

Rosé stopped planting what looked like seeds and looked at her. "What about my supposed magic?"

"One. We are still deciding what your training will be like, and two, you have already demonstrated some of your magic."

"I didn't show it."

"Yes, you did."

"No, I didn't."

Ari stopped and looked at her. "You're definitely not ready for this conversation." She returned to what she was doing, and Rosé returned the seeds back to the bag. Everyone was aware that they knew more than she knew about herself. They omitted information and hoped she would simply understand it all. They hoped that after years she would simply understand everything and accept it with grace.

"You're right, I'm not prepared for this conversation." She headed for the door, leaving Ari behind to do all the work. *She's got magic, she might as well do all this on her own. She doesn't need my human efforts for these things.*

"Rosé," she shouted. "Rosé come back here."

"I need to pee."

"Liar."

"You'll see I'm very good at it."

<3

Rosé was walking back to her room. Quiet and alone. She was thinking of everything but wanting to think of nothing. She wanted to forget these last few days and go back to her shitty and lonely life in London where there was no one behind her. Where she could lock herself in her room and stay there forever. She thought about Eliot and Hanna and what they'd be doing.

Maybe they were wondering why she was missing or maybe they hadn't even noticed. Maybe these people would have erased their memories. A tear ran when she thought of it. She'd never seen them as friends until now. Until that very moment. But they had been everything to her. They had treated her very well all these years and had cared about her.

She dried up the tears that flowed and composed herself. *Control your emotions,* that's what her father would tell her if he was there. If he had the decency to show up to talk to her. If he cared about her, but obviously she wasn't his priority. She was just a stupid child. A consequence of sex. A weight on his back.

She wasn't something he'd have to worry about anymore.

Or maybe he didn't even bother to worry.

Sometimes she wanted to suffer from amnesia and forget everything. Getting in a coma didn't seem like a bad thing and who knows, maybe she'd die. No one would miss her if that happened. Everyone would eventually get over it and get on with their lives. They'd be fine.

She straightened up. She tied her hair in a bun and headed for her room. More tears fell. There were people walking past her, looking curious, and worried. She could feel their fucking pity and she didn't like it.

You're definitely not ready for this conversation.

She smiled.

No.

She laughed.

Like one day I was ready for something.

She was passing through one of the busy corridors when she suddenly felt something being pulled from her hair, then she felt her hair falling on her shoulders. Kay passed by her faster than she would be able to keep up. He had her rubber band, putting it on his wrist.

He didn't look back and she didn't stop.

She wasn't after him.

Maybe that's what he expected.

She wouldn't waste her time.

She turned the corner where he supposedly turned, but it wasn't there anymore.

She didn't want to fight. She didn't mean to argue. She didn't want to talk to anyone.

Chapter 18

Rosé woke up the next day to a message from Ari.

"I hope you slept well. I'm waiting for you at the Morfeus Library. Use the guide star if you need it. When you arrive, knock on the door xxx"

Rosé took a quick shower and got dressed, she picked up her star guide and headed to the library. "Guide me to the Morfeus Library," she commanded. On the way Rosé passed numerous people she had not met yet, including a girl with purple hair tied in two ponytails, and a bald man.

She didn't stop to speak to them.

The guiding star stopped in front of an imposing door with several inscriptions written in an alphabet that Rosé did not recognise. She put away her star and knocked on the door that soon opened itself. When Rosé entered, she came face to face with an extensive library, with full bookshelves stretching from the floor to the ceiling. Further, into the room, there was a staircase that led to other floors.

She could not see the ending.

Most of the library was white, but there were many intricate details in light brown wood.

"Up here," said a voice that Rosé soon recognized. Rosé went toward the ladder, looking around. There were pictures of people, places, and objects everywhere, some on the floor and some hung alone on the wall. One painting was of a skull with smoke coming out of it. Others were jewels with bright pears and many other things.

"Well, everyone in Amondridia has something to do and I didn't want you to be alone. You have access to this library whenever you want. Also, these books will give you the answers to all your questions, with more details than the internet can give. Have a great day," and in the blink of an eye Ari was no longer there.

Rosé walked all over the library, looking at the titles of the books. *Vampire Anatomy, Fae's Anatomy, What To Do If You Come Into Contact With Certain Plants,*

Level 1 Potions, Level 2 Potions, Forbidden Potions, What's the Best Weapon For You, The danger of raw magic, Origins and so on. There were countless books there. She wondered if anyone had ever read them all.

Who was she trying to trick? She knew a lot of people who bought books and didn't read half of them, but they loved the covers. There is no better medicine in this world to cure a reader, than buying books.

Each section of the library had a unique decorative theme. Upon arriving at the history part, the library consisted of old maps and letters, as well as people she deduced to be important. The astronomy part was composed of stars and planets.

In addition to galaxies painted everywhere, there were also marbles of lights of different colours floating around. Science and anatomy featured bodies and romance had several drawings with the names of the book's authors and other exaggerated decorations of love.

She got a novel and start reading but was interrupted when an orange cat appeared beside her. He was passing quietly in front of Rosé, he stopped and watched her then went his way. "Psiu, Psiu," said Rosé to get his attention.

"Please don't give me 'psiu psiu'. I'm not a stupid cat." Rosé got a fright when she realised the voice was coming from the cat. She watched him in shock. Maybe this place wasn't doing her any good.

"What the fuck is that? Do you talk?" she asked with her mouth open. She could only be dreaming.

"Honey, it doesn't even look like you grew up in this world." He stopped and watched her more closely. "Unless you haven't grown up. Rosé-lina, no?"

"Call me Rosé."

"Rosélina. I've heard a lot about you. Since before your birth," he commented raising his paw and looking at his nails. Was the cat really analysing this? "Sometimes people forget or don't realise I'm there. The powerful, cursed girl. Show me what you can do."

"I can't do anything."

"What do you mean you can't do anything?" he asked indignantly. "You're a Lysion, you can do anything," he remarked, climbing up at a nearby table and sitting down. Rosé marked the page that she was on and closed the book, letting it rest on her lap.

"I haven't figured out how to do that yet," she said embarrassedly. At some point she'd have to learn how to do something.

"You better hurry, stupid girl, your world and life is in danger and, if you can't control it, we'll all die." Rosé felt a grip on her heart. She knew everyone was after her. She looked confused.

"What do you mean?"

"Your magic is very powerful, and if they fall into the wrong hands, they can multiply your powers and distribute it around. Power in the wrong hands creates irreversible chaos. And you really think these people aren't going to come after the ones who protected you with their lives?"

"With their lives?"

"You know very little about this world," he commented. Rosé watched him until he got close to a mirror.

"Can you also fly, curse, and disappear?"

"You're confusing the stories, honey." He raised his head and started smelling something in the air. "Do you feel it?"

"What?"

"That smell. It smells like shit," and so a fart sound echoed in the library. He sighed, relieved. "Oh yes baby." Then he went to a mirror that was on the floor and looked at himself. "I think I've lost a few pounds. Look at this, I'm even thinner." He kept admiring himself. "You wouldn't believe how much my belly was hurting."

Rosé was incredulous about what she had just experienced. The smell of rotten fish began to dominate the place. "For my nose's sake, fuck you," she cursed, she needed to leave as soon as possible, abandoning the book.

"Not stupid cat," he cried. "Mr. Bebbols and there isn't any female cat for me too."

"I should put something on your butthole."

"I put my tongue and it is good. You should try it sometimes."

Rosé left the library, heading towards her room, still not believing what she had just witnessed.

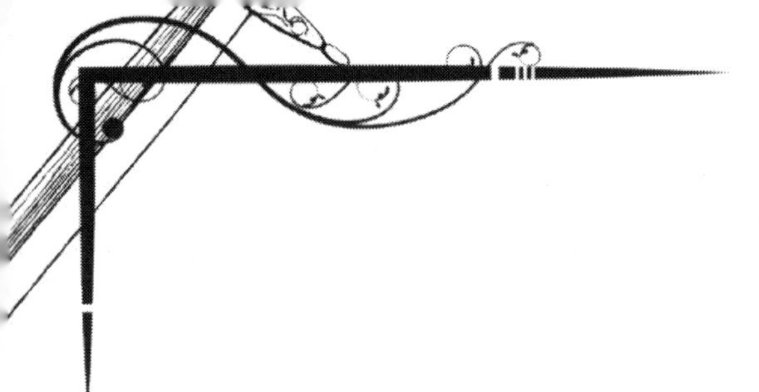

Chapter 19

Rosé had already lost count of how many days had passed since her arrival in Amondridia.

A lot had changed, but it still seemed like a dream.

She knew other people would love that dream. Magic, castle, potions, wands, wizard books, and famous creatures marked history. But, at that moment, these thoughts wouldn't let her sleep. How could she trust these people? Aren't there cameras watching her, like a reality show?

Rosé got up and turned on the light and then went to the desk. It had been a long time since she looked in the mirror. One day she was Rosé, a girl who went unnoticed, and the next she was a different Rosé, the most desired girl, and not even in a good way.

She had greeted Aiden in the hallway and had stopped to talk for a while, but no big deal. He had texted if she would join them to eat, but she asked Ari if she could eat in her room alone for a while.

In all her years, Rosé never imagined that she would find someone like that, loving and with a lot of patience, like Ari. She got angry sometimes, of course, but she sure had more patience than anyone there. These days patience has become something envied. The world does not stop and everyone here was always so busy. Ari didn't look much older than her, she guessed her to be 29 at most. It was impossible not to be jealous of her appearance. Her skin was flawless, not to mention her body was beautiful, almost as though it was sculpted.

Walking over to the wardrobe and peering into the large white mirror which hung next to it, Rosé came face to face with her image. This time she saw it in more detail. There were some scars left by pimples, dark circles under her eyes, indicative of sleepless nights, hairs to be shaved, accumulated fat in the belly and waist, the ends of her hair were dry …

Rosé didn't remember seeing Ari with any body hair other than her pink hair.

As she turned away, she saw that there was a dress hanging and a message alongside it.

'We're having a party in a few days. Xxx'

Below the dress was a pair of cream high heels, covered in glitter.

The light of the moon entered through the thin curtains. Rosé closed the wardrobe and approached the windows. She wasn't sleepy yet and she didn't intend to go back to bed. Rosé opened the curtains gently. It was a full moon. There were countless stars shining in the sky. More than Rosé had ever seen in her entire life.

She didn't want to stay in the room. She wanted to explore what was out there. Rosé hadn't been to many places since she arrived and was always accompanied. She put on her slippers and took a black fur jacket that she had in her wardrobe and left.

When she opened the door, she accidently made a loud noise. "Shit," whispered Rosé. The corridor didn't have much lighting which made her think about going back to her room and staying there, or maybe looking for something that would illuminate her path, but she gave up on the idea and went anyway. Her room was the last of the corridor on the west side of the palace.

Turning onto another corridor, Rosé came across a boy, around fifteen or older. He was way latter than her. One of his eyes was honey-coloured, as if there was a sun shining on his face, while the other was as white as the full moon. His expressions were delicate. His skin was perfect, and his curly hair was blacker than any night.

There was something different about him. His face seemed to disappear. In fact, his whole body seemed to be a malfunctioning projector. At one point he was there, perfectly intact and in high quality, and the next his body seemed almost invisible.

They exchanged a long look. Maybe she should have strayed from him. Passed him by and continued on her way or turn around and find another way. She didn't know who he was or what he was. There were many human things in him, but many abnormal.

There was something about him. Something Rosé couldn't identify.

He looked away and took something out of his pocket.

With a notepad and a pen, he began writing something on it. He looked at Rosé and approached her, delivering the notepad into her hands. She was confused at first. Maybe it was past time, and her brain wasn't working perfectly anymore. She took the notebook carefully and before looking at it, the child took a step back, waiting for her to read.

'You should not be out of bed', the note said. She knew that. She didn't need him reminding her about breaking the rules of this place. It was not recommended that you walk through the palace at night, for everyone's safety. Ariady had imposed this law for everyone.

"And neither should you," replied Rosé.

He took the notebook out of her hand and wrote 'I can't hear you. I'm deaf.' When she read it, something inside her broke and another part was overwhelmed by shame for not realising it. Rosé asked for the pen and wrote 'You are also out of bed.'

He took the notebook and read it, smiling.

'Fair enough,' he wrote in response, 'but I could defend myself if something happened to me.' She decided to ignore that last comment. Rosé wouldn't fight, she'd write peacefully. Rosé took the notebook one more time.

'What's your name?'

He takes the notebook.

'Nikko.'

'Rosélina.'

'I know. Everyone knows,' retorted Nikko, walking up to one of the windows and sitting on an elevation. He looked at Rosé while she was reading. Rosé went to him and sat next to him. She wanted someone different to talk to and Nikko was her best option.

'What do you mean everyone knows?' It hadn't been a long time since she had been here. As far as she was aware, no one really knew her. *Gossip running down the halls* – wasn't what Ruby said on her second day here?

Nikko took the notebook and wrote in response. He took longer than usual, as if he were thinking about what to write.

'Everyone knows when a threat comes to the palace.' That was like a kick in her stomach.

"Threat?" Rosé spoke aloud and made an angry face at Nikko who probably managed to read her lips and responded, laughing. His laugh was low and cute. Sometimes she forgot that deaf people are not mute.

'Threat? Is that how people see me?' she wrote angrily, putting strength on the page. It was weird talking like that. By writing. It was a silence conversation and yet there was a lot going on.

'Some of them do. There are many rumours about you spreading through the Lys, you know." He wrote quickly.

'No.' She was still confused. Rosé had noticed some looks but had not taken them seriously. She knew she was a rookie, and that people were talking about her, threats and rumours had never gone through her head. She didn't know how much of her story people knew.

'People think you're a Lysion, because of the Lysion's tale and the rumours and gossip are rife. Are you one?' he wrote. Rosé read and looked at him. The sun and the moon in his curious eyes were waiting for her answer. She didn't know if she could give him a sincere answer.

'What do you think?'

'I think people here keep many secrets,' he writes and when Rosé's gaze turns to him, she agrees with a nod of her head and a smile. Maybe that was one of the first times she'd smiled since she got there. An unwilling smile. 'But it's okay, there are things I'd rather not know, and I don't go after gossip. There are things that are best left unsaid, much less learned,' he warned. He was right.

Intelligent.

Rosé was going to write something in the notebook, but the sound of a door opening interrupted her.

"By which—" a man began, but when looking at the two he stopped and started again. This time making signs. "What waste of clove were you two doing outside of your rooms?" asks the old man who had apparently just woken up.

Nikko responds in sign language, causing Rosé not to understand what was happening. He turned to her and picked up the notebook: 'Good night.' He hugged her and ran away. Rosé just watched him leave and turned to the old man.

"And you, young lady?" he asked, looking at Rosé again.

"I'm going back to my room. Good night," she lied and continued her path. Looking back, he was no longer there, and the door was closed. Trust was everything. If it was in school or neighbourhood, that man would have watched her until she was out of the hallway and a little more.

Rosé went her way, still sleepless and with no plan to return to her room. Through the windows it was possible to see the flat part of the castle and the two towers at each end and further on the forest where everything had begun.

She went by old paintings with people dressed in black tunics and pointy hats. Some held trophies or certificates. All serious. Including a picture of a woman with long brown hair like chocolate, as were her eyes. Rosé hadn't paid much attention to them. For her, they were just a bunch of people in strange clothes *S. G.* was written under it.

She passed murals with warnings, floating brooms that cleaned the floor, a red and white cat wandering around and another black one running after a mouse that was definitely much faster than him.

She happened upon some stairs and climbed them, she wanted to get to the stars. Something particularly strange to think about but she wanted to get to the tallest tower, which did not take long.

In one of the towers there was no ceiling. It was a huge, uncovered, dirty area, in which Rosé, without fear of getting dirty, got down on the floor and lay there, thinking.

Silence. That's all she needed at the time.

A lot had passed in the time that she had been left alone. People. Places. Conversations she had. Aiden. Eliot. Hanna. Theo. Nikko. She had loved Nikko. There was something about that kid that was different. Maybe it was his honesty or his charisma or maybe he just somehow seemed to understand. She remembered his multi-coloured eyes and, how similar one was to the moon she now gazed on.

Looking forward, seeing the light of the moon reflect on the infinite sea, she wondered where she was. In what part of the world that island was and how no one had yet found or attacked it. Rosé wondered how she had gotten there and whether time was going on there as in the normal world. Outer World, as everyone seemed to refer to.

She was lying there watching the sky and the moon, not caring about the dirt on the ground, when she felt someone there, who soon lay next to her.

From the corner of her eye, Rosé could see who it was. Ariady. Her hair announced her.

"It seems to me that two warnings were not enough," she commented, looking at Rosé and then at the sky. Ari smelled of blackberry or some similar wild fruit. It was a sweet smell.

"I couldn't sleep," whispered Rosé.

"I understand."

"How did you know I'd be here?" Rosé asked. She didn't see anyone following her. This palace was too big to find someone that easy.

"I couldn't sleep either and I got the message from Mr Smith saying that he had seen you and Nikko in the hallway and that you were going to the opposite side of your room," she replied. They were both silent. There were people giving her away to Ari, like she was her mother or something. "Your mother used to come here," Ari adds. "That's why I came here first. Cielo Tower. In the moments she'd like to be silent and think, she used to come here and look at the stars. That's how she described heaven. The paradise of the stars. Cielo." A nice name for the tower.

"My mother?" she asks.

"I don't think I ever told you, her name. Sarah. Sarah Lysion." Something happened inside her stomach. "She's the founder of this Lys," she sighed. "Amondridia. I told you that Floralin was one part and that Amondridia was another, but actually … originally all this Lys was called Amondridia. Your mother adhered to the tribe of Joseph, the King of Olvs, when he needed it. So, she expanded and divided." *Sarah Lysion.*

She's the founder of this Lys.

Nice name.

Sarah.

Sarah.

Sarah.

"The woman on the portrait? S.G?"

"Your mother. Sarah Gracelin Lysion."

Tears ran down her cheeks. She closed her eyes and tried to remember the woman in the painting. That was her mother. That's why it was familiar. Because she had parts of Rosé that reminded her of herself.

It was still hard to believe that story. She had spent her entire life believing that Helena was her mother. They had so much in common. Sometimes she would get caught reflecting on the fact that people said they had nothing to do with each other and that Rosé was more like her father. Now things made more sense.

"Sarah was an amazing woman. Half Brazilian. Helena and Sarah were half-sisters by their father's side" Ari commented. Rosé lay in silence. Ari looked at her again and then to heaven. "When I told you about your family," she paused for a second, "I thought you already knew. At least some of it. I thought you knew Helena wasn't your real mother. I shouldn't have been the one to tell you and I'm sorry about that."

Rosé remained steadfast in her silence. She needed time to process everything.

"Don't let me talk to myself … please." Her voice came out low and sad. Ariady raised her hand to the sky and moved it gently and another constellation appeared. "They are false," she stated. They both looked at each other until Rosé turned to the sky again. Fake? "The sky, the stars, the sun, the clouds, the rain. They're fake. All kept by magic. Do you want to see snow?" In a touch of magic, it was snowing. Ari moved again and the snow stopped.

Rosé began to observe in more detail. They still looked real. "Why?" she asked. Ari smiled, she knew Rosé would be interested, just as her mother Sarah was captivated by the stars.

"Lys was raised a long time ago as a refuge. A haven for magical creatures," she explained. Rosé looked at her and could see a tear dripping down the corner of her eye. "You know, I think you've heard about us in the Outer World. When there weren't much technology things were different, but still complicated. Many of us have had horrible fates. Burned alive. Left to starve to death. Exposed to the heat of the sun without any protection, and more. They believed we were bad. Freaks. In fact, there are many who went to the dark side of magic.

"Even so, we were tales and legends for many. There was no way we could prove our existence but by memories," Ari paused. "In the old days, if someone saw us doing something 'supernatural' and told others they didn't believe it, but now … now they can remember record. Have proof."

Ariady had a hoarse voice.

"I'm sorry," it was the only thing Rosé said. She didn't know if it was the right thing to say, but she really was sorry. She had read several stories and watched films that talked about it but had never believed it, moreover, it was always fairy tales, and imagination. It wasn't real until a few days ago.

It wasn't something that was supposed to be real.

"Thank you," she answered, drying her tears with the back of her hand.

"Is that why you live here?"

"Yes. We were forced to find refuge out of the reach of the eyes of the Ordinary. The Olvs fled deforestation, as did other forest creatures. Mermaids were not very different; sea creatures, even endangered animals, were taken to other kingdoms. Other lyses. Far from the ignorance and pride of the Ordinary Man."

"Wait!" said Rosé, shocked. "Are there other places like this?" She felt a little stupid for asking that question.

"Of course. Countless scattered throughout London. England. The world. The UNOM sought some places that were safe and divided us into groups that could live in harmony and have a place to be who we really are."

"What is UNOM?" Rosé interrupted.

"United Nation of Magic," responded Ari. "They are responsible for the harmony between the magical world, based in New York, with the UN. Of course, many creatures did not want this and preferred to live in the Outer World. Isolated or like a normal human. They don't necessarily follow the rules."

"Can you leave?"

"You have the full right to this, no one is holding you here. Well, you're being held here for security reasons, but the consequences can be horrible if you or anyone else does something stupid," Ari said, sitting with her back against the marble wall.

"Where did you live?"

"I lived in Oxford for a while. I liked it there. It was a quiet town. Then I moved to London and lived like an Ordinary. I worked in a restaurant as a waitress and lived in a rented room in East London, but I couldn't take it, I needed a place to be free to do my thing. To be me. Ariady." Rosé was beginning to understand what many creatures had to go through. They were no longer as free as they used to be, their privacy had run out over time. "Do you know what? A lot has changed since then. Before, people saw us and it was soon forgotten. Today people see and can keep evidence for the rest of their lives, with fucking phones and cameras."

"I'm sorry."

"I appreciate it, but your pity won't change anything, I don't want it. It just makes me feel worse." She sighed. "A few decades ago, I met a man where I worked, David Dornfest. I found out he was a wizard when he accidentally chipped one of the mugs and restored it. When I commented that I was looking for a quiet Lys to live, he told me about Amondridia, and that's when I met your mother."

Rosé didn't know what to say. So, she just listened, she liked to listen to people, more than talk. Sometimes it seemed like other people's lives were much more interesting than hers.

"Do you like it here?" Rosé asked, unsure if she should.

"I think there's a feeling of love and hate between me and Lys," she said, raising her palms one after the other, changing the stars. "I hate the fact that it's all an illusion, false; but I like the great freedom that this place gives me."

Rosé still didn't know how she felt about this place. It was still hard to believe all this. Looking at Ari, her expression was sad. She seemed to have immersed herself in a deep ocean within her own mind. The light of the moon illuminated her face and Rosé could see that it was wet. She didn't know how to react. She didn't know what to say.

It's always been like this.

She never knew what to say to people. She didn't know how to take care of people, because she never had someone to look after.

Ari got up and cleaned her clothes.

"It's okay if you want to stay here, just don't wander around at night. Good night, Rosé."

"Good night," she whispered back. She didn't expect her to hear it. Rosé heard Ari go down the stairs until everything fell into complete silence again.

She kept looking at the stars. The constellation Ariady had formed in the sky shortly before was still there, shining. Her father had told her once that when someone dies if that person was good on earth, she becomes a star in heaven. Even though she didn't believe that she watched them regardless and Rosé wondered which star she would be.

Which one was her mother?

Still, at the top of the tower, Rosé decided not to return to her room and fell asleep there, thinking about the stars and Sarah. When the first rays of light began to break, she woke up with a sore body. She got up and went back to her room.

Chapter 20

Back in her room, Rosé lay on the bed, burying her face in her hands. This place was weirder than she could imagine. She took a deep breath. Rosé could do that. She could survive another day. That's what she'd always done, for as long as she could remember.

Survive another five minutes. An hour. A day. A week. Two. A month, and so on.

She thought about what had happened and smiled. Something spontaneous. This place was too weird. Stupid cat. Stupid tower. Stupid Lys.

But …

The chest pain was raw. There was a weight in her heart, a pressure to know everything she'd have to do. Expectations about her. How people were expecting her to act. She managed to ignore it for a while, the last five days had gone well. She was alive. But there would come a time when she couldn't do it anymore. There was a heavy burden on her back. Something she didn't expect.

She took a deep breath once more. She'd go down and eat with people. She'd try again to make friends.

She'd try and if it went wrong … then she'd have a reason. A reason to collapse.

She wouldn't cry. She closed her eyes that were already wet and opened them, avoiding the tears. A smile. Not spontaneous, just a simple weak smile.

She'd get over it.

Rosé went to take a shower before going down for lunch. To see if she could get those thoughts out of her head.

She was almost ready to take one last look in the dressing table mirror when she heard a horrible sound. Fire? No one had taught her about it or what she should do. When she was near the door, almost touching the doorknob, the door just disappeared. Rosé started banging on the wall where the door had once been and started screaming for help. But nothing happened. Panic dominated her again.

She looked out the window, but there was no one there.

The siren stopped ringing, but the place where the door was remained empty. Rosé didn't know what to do. She was in despair. Were they there to take her?

She tried. She really tried.

Control your emotions, she thought. But she had lost this battle. Her emotions were controlling her.

It's been a long time since she had a panic attack.

<3

Rosé didn't know how long she had been in the same position. Tears running down her face. Her heart was racing. Sweat running down her body. She felt inside the concrete walls again. Rain touching her face and body. She could feel the icy air touching her skin. She couldn't breathe. She tried, but every attempt seemed harder. The difference between that dream or sensation, was that she could not open her eyes.

Fear was taking over her.

A scream escaped her lips.

<3

Rosé heard the knocks on the door, but she didn't care. She heard one more try, but she ignored it again. It seemed like the person was going to break down the door. They were there to take her.

She was broken once more. Sweaty. Crying. It wasn't a vision she'd like people to see. Weak. Sensitive. Destroyed. Insufficient. A complete nothing. Without the ability to defend herself.

The door opened with a loud bang and footsteps began to approach Rosé, but she dared not take her hand off her face. She must have looked awful, her face swollen and red. She's seen herself crying in the mirror. Everyone must have seen her by now. She knew. She was the most horrible thing she'd ever seen in her life.

"Get out," she ordered with a weak voice. "I want to be alone. I did nothing."

"Rosé. Calm down, it's alright." Rosé recognized the voice. Kay. "I need to get you out of here. You scared me when you didn't answer the fucking door." He touched her. His hand was hot on her sensitive skin "Hey, look at me. What happened?" he asked, his voice showing concern. He showed no pride or superiority as she had heard the other times she had spoken to him. Kay tried to take her hands that still covered her face. But she kept denying him, holding them as tight as possible against herself. “Look at me. Give me one of your hands at least.” Rosé obeyed. Kay placed it on his chest, over his heart, until Rosé could feel his heartbeat, it was racing. "I'm here for you"

She calmed down a little bit.

She raised her face, and her gaze met his. He had a cut on his face.

At that moment she forgot about herself and her own pain. She forgot she had just come out of her own black hole, that she had gone into one of the deepest holes within herself.

“What happened to your face?” she asked, her voice faint. Still sobbing. She took one of her hands to his face, near the cut. They were trembling and wet with her tears. She tried to wipe it with her own finger, preventing a drop of blood from dripping down his cheek.

She didn’t know why she cared about him.

Maybe she was too vulnerable.

It was instinct and he didn’t stop her.

He didn’t say anything, he just watched her clean his wound. “I asked you first,” he said, letting go of her hand. Where did that intimacy come from? He was right there in front of her, worried. She was glad that her face was hot and red from crying so much that he must not have realised that for a slight moment she had blushed for him.

“I had a panic attack … I think …” Rosé dried up the rest of her tears and felt her body relax a little. “I didn’t know what was going on.” Kay frowned and helped her up. He held her tightly so she wouldn’t fall, noticing her weak body.

Rosé stood up and stared at him. “What’s up?”

“What do you mean? You didn’t know what was going on? Aiden didn’t tell you?” He stopped and crossed his arms over his chest. There was anger in his eyes. They were darker.

“Did he tell me what?” She was confused. Was there anything Aiden should have warned her about? He had told her many things.

“That son of a bitch only had one mission,” Kay almost shouted. His teeth clenched.

“What mission? What’s going on?” He ran his hands through his hair.

“Was your door gone?” He stopped to look at her. “Yes, and I was like a madwoman screaming for help.” He took a deep breath.

“Lys has been invaded, love,” he began. Her heart jumped when he referred to her as *love* but knew that it was probably just something he called everyone.

"Amondridia is very well equipped when it happens. When the siren rings, selected people need to go after the one who broke in and fight, as well as take care of those who are away from their rooms and help them find the secret passages to hide. Rooms that have children, older people, or unqualified people, have their doors removed so that no one can have access to the rooms until the threat comes out or is defeated. Didn't he tell you that?"

Rosé lied, "Maybe he forgot or commented on it, and I did not pay attention. He said a lot." Kay still had an expression of anger. A muscle tightened in his jaw. "Does this happen often?"

"If you're trying to defend him, don't even think about it." Rosé didn't want to show her weakness. She couldn't cry again in front of him. She stood still, looking at him, and he repaid the look. She passed him, picking up a tissue on her dressing table. "And no. It doesn't happen often. I just hope it is not because of you."

"You said we needed to go and you're bleeding," Rosé said, cleaning his face and watching the tissue going red. She threw it away and headed towards the door. "And second, watch your tone. I'm not a big fan of people who yell at me for no reason. Where do we need to go?" She tried to keep her face and voice neutral.

"Canteen."

Kay just followed her.

"Why you?" He just looked at her from the corner of his eyes. "Of all the people, why did you come to me?"

"Does it matter?"

"Yes. You are annoying. I don't like you. You don't like me. You are a fucking asshole. There is a thousand people in this fucking place. Why you?" she asked one more time. Kay was the last person she wanted to know how vulnerable she was.

He took a while to answer. "I'm your Guardian. You are my responsibility."

Him? Of all people, Kay is my Guardian? Fuck. I am fucked up.

(Reminder time: drink water)

The canteen was crowded with people. The majority of the people were intact but the rest had several injuries, one woman was taking care of them all.

Ariady came to meet her, giving Rosé a tight hug again. She was shaking, and her arm was bleeding. Behind her came Aiden and Misty. "What took you so long?" she asked, looking at Kay.

"Because I had to explain to her what was going on, because our friend Flames wasn't able to do the only thing he had been asked to do," he said, going towards Aiden and grabbing him by the collar of his shirt. In defence, Aiden burned Kay's arm.

"Don't touch me, or …" Aiden puffed out his chest.

"Or what? Are you going to burn me again? Come on, little fire, let's play. I'm all fucked up anyway," he said. He closed his fist, showing his veiny arms. "Let's see if you're really a man." Aiden's body began to create lines of fire. His eyes shone in a bright shade of red. Kay positioned himself too, the white part of his eyes fused into one black colour and his black fog began to emerge, but before they could do anything, Ariady took a huge jar of water and threw it over them both.

"Okay, I'm not going to thank you for demonstrating how to be two idiots. Now it's enough." Ari turned to Aiden. "Did you really forget to warn her about one of the crucial parts of this place?" she said in a calm voice.

She was waiting for Aiden's voice, but it was Kay who spoke.

"Seriously, is this how you're going to treat him, with that calm voice? You yell at me."

Ari signalled him to be quiet. "Aiden."

"I must have forgotten. I'm sorry," he said, lowering his head.

"Of course you forgot," said Kay, crossing her arms.

"Didn't you hear you were supposed to be quiet?" asked Rosé, taking a step forward and crossing her arms as well. Her blood was boiling. No one would talk about Aiden like that. Hadn't the scene he started been enough?

"Rosé is alright," Aiden said, coming to her and putting his hands on her shoulder. "It's fine." No, it wasn't. Aiden made a mistake but Kay didn't have to make such a scene because of it.

But he wanted to fight.

"Do you care about him?" Kay asked in a wicked tone, getting even closer to her "Do you care about the little fire?" The nickname became a thing now. He sounded almost as if he was jealous.

"Yes, does your old age means you're incapable of caring about someone other than yourself?"

"You don't—"

Am I lying?

Gustav, who was standing behind Kay, was holding back laughter. Kay just turned around and exchanged glances, which didn't help at all. Gustav tried to apologize, but it didn't do any good, because he started laughing even more.

"Who do you think you are to humiliate me like that?"

"Who do you think you are to humiliate Aiden?" she asked as she took another step forward. She didn't think about how he could kill her right there, in the blink of an eye. She wouldn't be quiet. She didn't care how old he was. "You talk about training and all that stupid stuff, 'you learn from mistakes', how can you learn from mistakes if you don't let people make them?"

Kay got a little closer to her. His jaw tightened one more time. His gaze was locked on hers. "If you do this one more time, I'll finish you off before your heart has finished its last beat," he whispered near her face. "And honestly, I don't think you're that interested."

Rosé started laughing in his face then stopped abruptly. "You're late, darling. I've got a lot of people coming after me, and you know it very well. Try a new threat next time." She wanted to cry because that wasn't a joke, but at the moment she just wanted to shut him up.

Rosé took one last look at Kay and winked. She could see Gustav laughing in the corner of her eye. She turned around and addressed

Aiden, directing him to the table. "I'm starving."

"Beautiful thing," he remarked behind her back, "but incredibly stupid."

"I have nothing to lose, unlike you."

Ariady let out a loud sigh. "You," she said, pointing to Kay, "in my office at seven. Now let's eat. Sabrina." She turned to the food area, and, in a snap of her fingers, all the tables were full of ready-made food kits. "Thank you so much."

Ariady teamed up with another group of people who looked older. Kay joined his vampire friends who had also fought during the invasion. Misty gave Rosé a slight smile when they sat at the table where Nixie, Aiden, and Theo were sitting.

"I'm sorry," Aiden said with his gaze down.

"It's okay."

"No, it's not okay. Of all the things I told you, this was the most important thing. They are after ..." Aiden stopped in the middle of the sentence. His hand was shaking. His eyes looked like coal. There was no light, no fire, only pain.

"After me. I know," she said, putting her hand on his to see if he would stop shaking but was forced to take it off soon after because it was too hot. "Oh."

"I'm sorry. I'm stressed." Aiden lifted a glass of water, but it exploded in his hand, scaring everyone. He left the table and headed for the door.

"Aiden," Rosé called, rising, but a strong handheld her back.

"Leave him," Theo said, pulling her back to the table.

Rosé sat down again and looked at Kay at a few tables ahead and their eyes met. They held it there, but soon he went back to his food. "I'm not hungry." The most obvious lie she had ever told and just like Aiden she left the table. For a moment she thought about going to her room, but she needed to talk to Aiden.

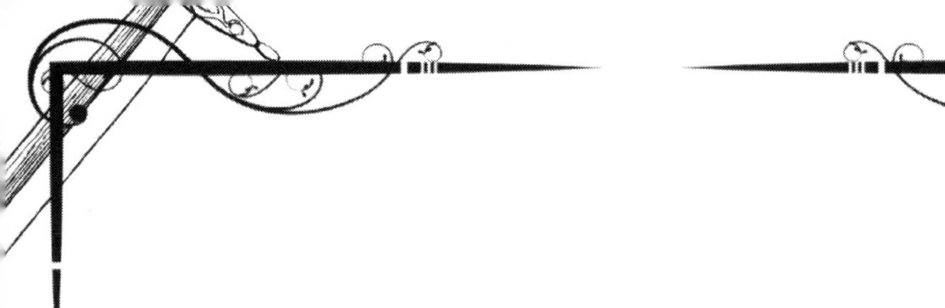

Chapter 21

Rosé took a while to find him.

She saw Aiden through a palace window. He was in a seat in front of a magnificent tree. As she approached him, Rosé said nothing, she just sat by his side and stared at the infinite-finite sea in front of them.

"You didn't see Ariady's face of disappointment," he commented, still looking forward. "I just forgot to warn you about—"

"Stop. I didn't come here to judge you or anything like that, I forgive you," she said, resting her head on his shoulder. Rosé had never done this to anyone before, but she needed to repay everything he did for her. He had been the one trying to get close even after everything she did.

"I—"

"Aiden?" interrupted Rosé.

"Yes?"

"Fuck them. We're friends, aren't we? We take care of each other. Always." Aiden nodded and rested his head on Rosé's. Her heart warmed. They were friends. Aiden had nodded. She had a real friend who saw her in the same way.

"The two of us against them?"

"Both of us against the world."

"We're fucked."

"Aiden?"

"Um?"

"Shut up," Rosé replied with a smile.

"Very unaggressive."

"Sometimes I'm aggressive with the people I care about, just accept it."

Silence.

"Thank you for defending me. No one had done that for me."

"That's what friendship is. In health, in sickness—"

"In poverty, in wealth."

"In stupid and illusion."

"Single or married."

"On bad days and happy days."

"In war and peace."

"In amnesia to remember friends about—" Aiden elbowed Rosé's ribs and they both started laughing. "Until death does us part," she said, extending her little finger.

"Until death does us part," he repeated, extending his pinky and squeezing it against Rosé's.

"You're fucked for agreeing."

"I say the same."

"Let's see who's the most fucked up." They both laughed once more.

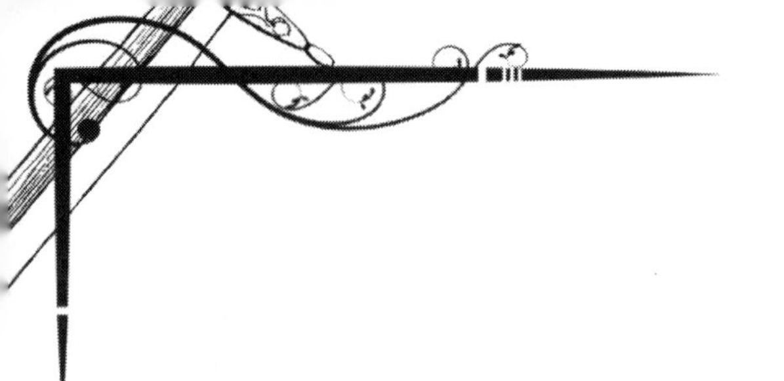

Chapter 22

That morning, Ariady had met a tall, black-haired man in the palace's grand library. The man's beard covered the entire bottom of his face. He wore thin, square glasses. His eyes were chocolate coloured. He wore formal clothes. Seemed to have come out of a work meeting. Black social pants, a white polo shirt, and a tie full of guns and patterned knives.

The library wasn't the only place reserved in the palace. Ari liked the privacy. The palace was full of passageways, rooms locked not only by keys, but by little-known magic. Cabinets of ingredients were forbidden to the variety of creatures that lived there. Potion rooms, gardens, greenhouses … Of course, it was no surprise the theories that the locals created.

The library was full of books. Shelves upon shelves. If someone said they could see the end of it, they were lying. There were not only books, but also paintings scattered on the walls, carpets with numerous symbols, and maps of different places. Trophies, chandeliers, vases of all shapes and colours. Tables, stairs that led to other areas of the room. Spiders, globes, floating planets or weights on wires, admirable windows, huge clocks, scrolls, and candles. Shiny crystals, dust dusters that moved by themselves, brooms, more stairs, piles of cards, dumpsters. Stacks and stacks of books on some tables that defied the law of gravity. Photos, collages, handwritten letters, pens, and notebooks. Everything and more in one room.

"Do you really think Rosé may not be … do you know …?" Ariady asked the man, sounding suspicious. Numerous theories had been created around the tale. Some exaggerated that only an idiot would believe in such great stupidity and others made sense.

"I don't think the Moridons-Blake would have done such damage to the magical world if they weren't at least sure, nor the Quintuple."

"Do you think the Quintuple is involved in these murders?"

"Of course, they are."

Ari searched for Lysion books in the library.

"These are all the books. Each, written by a different author, all related to the Tale of Lysions. Origin of the name, theories, first reports, opinions, surnames," Ari said, queuing them up. "This one," she said, pointing to one of the books. Its cover was worn. The pages turned yellow by time. It was earth brown with some twigs and leaves drawn in green. Its title was in Latin. "Lysions' tale, the Origin of Magic," translated Ari, perceiving the man's confused look. "It was written by Robert Kouris, he was the first to record the story in a book. He claims to be the nephew of David Kouris, the First Assassin."

The man took the book and began to flip through it, but it was all in Latin. There were other notes and underlined words. In a snap of his fingers, the text was translated into English. "It comments that it is hereditary, but that it only passes to one of the children. Rosé is the only daughter Sarah has had."

Ariady had spent a lot of time reading and studying all the books, taken notes, researched, compared with others, travelled from one country to another, talking to older wizards. She knew the books very well.

Her hair was no longer light pink, as usual, it was blond. Opaque. She seemed lifeless. She was worried, afraid of what might happen.

After a few minutes, Ari pointed to another book, this time light blue with black edges. "Nicole Brown," she announced. "A Sentiment. Very clever in my opinion. She only talks about what we know," she said when seeing the man flipping through the pages. That one had more notes than the others. Photos had been placed in half of the pages with annotations on the back.

"Who is he?" Tom asked, holding the photo of an Asian man. The photo was in black and white. The man in the photo wore a jacket, his beard was long, but he was bald.

"Klahan," she replied. "I never knew his last name. I met him when I went to Thailand in search of some answers. Sarah was still alive."

"Did you get the answers?"

"Not many. He was too old; he didn't remember much anymore. Besides, it was a long time ago. Thirty? Thirty-five years? He passed away a week after our conversation and I'm not going to take it as a mere accident, because you know very well it wasn't."

"I get it."

Nicole Brown, the author of the book, was well known among the magical creatures. She had a very different point of view of magic and the power that each inherited from their parents. It saved many wizards from being burned or something similar for centuries past. Everyone knew about her, there wasn't anyone who didn't know her name. She was an activist and one of the first women to write a book that was highly recognized.

"Brown died fighting a Moredom. They say they tortured her until she begged for death. She killed herself," Ari said, feeling a grip on her heart. "Tom?" called Ari.

The man raised his head. "Yes?"

"Do you think history will repeat itself?" she asked. "What happened years and years ago. The Hunt? A second Magical War? She's not ready for that. And it's her, against … fuck, a lot of people."

"For now, we only care about the people from Wysez. They are the ones attacking. You told her about them?"

"Yes."

Tom lowered his head, looking at one of the books he held. It was black with peculiar symbols on the cover. "I heard that a lot of people moved to Wysez. Not only a few remaining Moridom-Blakes, but some Dagons, Bloddshelfs, and others. Kay doesn't know that. The Death Mansion must be full of people. A prison if we consider what it keeps. A herd of creatures reuniting," Tom said, putting the book back on the table. He looked at the huge map of Lys hanging from one of the walls. "A wizard I met in Bristol said the Quintuples are entering the Obscure, recruiting lost ones." Tom didn't seem surprised. There was neither fear nor happiness in his tone, he seemed carefree, neutral.

"Obscure? No one who enters can leave. How are they doing this?"

"I don't know."

After an agonising silence, Tom walked toward Ari who was standing with her arms folded, looking at the ground. "We're going to make it, I promise you."

Ari loosened up and walked over to a desk. "You shouldn't make that kind of promise," she said. "I think we're done with it, now we need to…" she's interrupted by a noise at the door. The two immediately look at her.

Rosé.

<3

Rosé hadn't seen her father in a long time. Not since before she ended up in Lys. It had been months since he had called or texted her. He just disappeared. No sign of life. He had abandoned her.

At that moment she didn't know if she was happy to see him or angry. He had never spoken of Amondridia or his mother, or that she had a bunch of people chasing her.

Anyone who saw them together would know they were father and daughter.

Her eyes went from her father to Ari and from Ari to his father. A feeling of surprise and fear burned in her chest. Anger. Anger at his absence. Anger at the lies and everything he hid. The room seemed tighter than before. She wanted to hit him. To take whatever she saw in front of her. To get revenge for every moment he made her feel abandoned.

She wanted her father. Not that mage.

"Rosé, breathe," is what Ari said. She didn't realize she'd stopped breathing. She looked at her hands and there was something different about them. They were shining and dropping little sparks, until suddenly they stopped.

Fuck. She felt like she hadn't seen him in years. It looked like he'd abandoned her a long time ago. Maybe he did, but she didn't notice. Why is that? That's what was echoing in her mind. Her eyes didn't deviate from her father. He was the same and different. She could see the same features. The same man she trusted with her whole life but who had lied to her since her birth. He looked like a stranger. A man she'd never seen in her life.

"I missed you." Rosé did not move. He stood with open arms, waiting for her to forget everything and hug him. When there was no reaction, Tom nodded. "I understand if you don't want to talk to me."

Anger began to grow in her body. Her breathing failed. Disappointment. Hate. Pain. Relief. How could she feel relief? The man who lied to her and who was now in front of her as if nothing had happened.

I missed you. Have you?

She was still in the same position. Ari was pretending that nothing was happening and started messing with old scrolls and humming so the situation wouldn't get any worse and headed to the stairs. Their eyes turned to her, which made her lift her gaze and look at them as well. "I'm sorry, but I'm not a family psychologist, okay?"

"You lied," Rosé whispered.

"I never lied to you. I omitted the truth from you," Tom corrected. How dare he say that?

"You never told me about this place, about Helena not being my mother, about you …" she started breathing deeply and trying to keep her voice down. "Look at you, I don't even know who you are." Tears flowed down her cheeks.

Tom tried to approach but stopped when Rosé retreated. "Where were you?" she asked with a tone of anger. Despair. "Where have you been all this time? I didn't see you for months. You didn't even answer my messages or calls. You abandoned me."

"I never left you."

"Never?" she asked, laughing. "Helena was more present than you and she's not even here. She texts me every day. She used to," she corrected herself.

"Daughter, I—"

"Daughter? Now I'm your daughter?"

"You've always been my daughter."

"Have I? Biologically. Because until a while ago I believed Helena was my mother. But she's not, right?" She properly entered the library and closed the door. She slammed it, to be more specific. She could feel her face warm. The salty tears on her lips.

"Poor door," commented Ari. "I love it." They both looked at her and then turned their gaze at each other.

(Sorry, this came into my mind, and I had to put it in.)

"I'm absolutely sure of that. Have you looked in the mirror?" he said, proudly.

"They say I'm more like my mother. That's what gave me away to Oldo Blake," she says, remembering the man who chased her.

She has been saving that anger for a long time. She didn't want to scream, and she wasn't going to. "You know what? Forget it." That was the last thing she said before she went to the door again. The door Ari loved. (Okay, I will stop.) She didn't want to talk to him.

She didn't want to look at his face.

Her thoughts were interrupted when she heard a laugh behind her, it was Ariady who in seconds had climbed the stairs to escape what would be a long conversation.

"Really?" he protested, turning around and watching her coldly climb the stairs. How could she find humour in all this? Ari took a while to stop laughing and apologised repeatedly.

"Oh dear, I'm sorry. I'm a champion at laughing at the wrong time." She stopped and saw the look of contempt on her face.

Rosé was about to leave when the door closed with a bang that echoed throughout the library. Ari didn't say anything about the door.

"We haven't finished this conversation."

"I don't want to talk to you," Rosé said, still not looking at him.

"But I want to."

"You said it was okay if I didn't want to," she countered, turning around and staring at his chocolate eyes again. He put his glasses on and sat on the stairs. They were a few feet away, watching each other.

"I changed my mind."

"What do you want to talk about, Dad?" she asked with a sarcastic tone. "About you lying? Abandoning me? Forgetting to tell me my life was in danger? That I have magic I can barely control? That I—"

"That's enough. I got the message." He straightened his beard.

"Why?" she asked.

"To protect you."

"To protect me? Is that what comes into your mind? To protect me?" Rosé took a step back and then surged forward. "Give me a better excuse, because that didn't convince me," she said, raising one of her fingers at him. "An excuse that is true. One that convinces me to stay here and listen to you."

"Do you want to know the truth? The hard and cruel truth?" he asked, his voice like a whisper.

"I beg for it."

(Dramatic? Not at all.)

"Do you know who I am?" he asked, getting up and moving a little closer to her.

"At the moment? No. A while ago I knew you as my father who was married to what was supposed to be my mother. My hero. The one that told me to raise my head and control my emotions. The one that protected me. That was the man I knew," she spat the words out.

"One: Helena remains your mother—"

"She. Is. Not"

"She raised you. She was a better mother than I was a father. You must respect her for caring and giving her life for you." He had a great point. Helena did not deserve the hatred that should be directed at her father. "I didn't come here to talk about your mother. I came to talk about you. You are my priority at the moment."

"What a surprise. Wow. Shocked by it." Silence consumed the place. Rosé had found an armchair to sit in. Her body was tired, as well as her mind. As she sat in the armchair her body eased and became tense at the same time. "You were gone. You abandoned me as if I were nothing to you." Her mind was troubled. Tired. Rosé wanted to close her eyes and wake up in her bed, like she did when she was little. One minute she was on the couch watching TV and the next she woke up in her bed. She always thought it was magic, but one day she found out it was her father.

"You said you wanted the truth," he began. Tom ran his hands through his hair and then fixed his glasses.

"I don't want a story."

Tom let out a long sigh. Maybe just like her, he wanted to get something on Rosé. "Do you know how many people I've killed in my fucking life? I'm a killer. Before the Elite, I was an assassin. I was part of the mobs. I was paid to kill people and I'm not talking about wars. I am not talking about huge conflicts where we have an obligation to serve our glorious country. I'm talking about killing without knowing the person. With no personal reason. I've killed men, women, and even chil..." his voice failed. Rosé could see his muscles tense.

"And then … then I met your mother. The mighty Sarah Lysion. A woman whose gods supposedly gave a supernatural magic. I chased your mother for years. I was paid to kill her. I approached to find out if the rumours were real and then the unexpected happened and my whole plan went down the drain. The theories were true, and she really was what the whispers said, but by the time I realized, I was already in love with her.

"Honestly, I never wanted you. Not even in my deepest dreams did I wish for a child. After you kill countless people, a child is not something that comes into your head. But she wanted to. She was desperate for a baby. A child who could carry the Lysion lineage. I didn't want the responsibility. She knew what was ahead, yet she continued with the pregnancy and during all this it was planned what would happen. I was furious that besides a stupid baby I'd have to have a fucking responsibility—"

"Thank you for your consideration, Dad."

"Let me finish the story," he commanded. "Sarah gave birth to you during a cold day. You were already past the recommended time. She called you a lazy baby," he commented, letting out a smile. "Her eyes shone every moment she talked about you and that was the most beautiful thing I had ever seen. Then you were born, and she gave you to me. Our eyes met and you stopped crying and stared at me. Like I was your hero. A good man.

"You were a foolish, innocent, helpless baby and I was a murderer. A maniac who loved to kill people. Cold-blooded. But you were my baby. You carried my genes and, at that moment, when you were in my arms, I felt something I hadn't felt for a long time. It wasn't passion like I felt for your mother or another woman. It was a different love. A feeling very different from what I imagined being able to feel. But that didn't take away from the fact that I was still a killer. A torturer. Someone who took lives for entertainment.

"That day, I swore with my life and to the world, that I would not let anyone touch you, because if anyone dared to break your heart, I would torture them until they begged for death. Those were my thoughts and believe me they haven't changed much. And I ask you how you expect me to be that man and your father? I should be an example to you and not a monster. I don't know how to be a father. I was never a good father, but all I wanted in this world was for you to have a great life and that's where Helena comes into the story. I'm not a hero like you've always seen me, and I hope to make that clear." Rosé didn't answer.

"Say something."

"You shouldn't have abandoned me," she said. "You should have told me before I hated you so much."

"I know, I know. I made a mistake and I'm going to keep making mistakes. But I always knew where you were and that you were okay," he informed her. "Always. Every moment. Even when you came to visit me in that house."

"I was looking for you, how do you know that?" she asked, approaching him, but not hugging him. None of them were fans of hugs.

"I have always kept my eyes on you. Not mine, but I kept them. Mr Watson, Kay … I have always protected you and will always protect my little me, feminine and sensitive version."

Mr Watson she already suspected a little. She knew he might be passing information to him.

"Kay is my Guardian, right??"

"Yes." Tom sat in an armchair, and a glass of whiskey appeared in his hands. He had a sip. He sat with almost crossed legs. One of his arms rested on the arm of the armchair.

Like a king sitting on his throne.

"Honestly, daughter." Her stomach wrapped up. The word 'daughter' seemed to sound different this time. "Kaydan Dagon was the only person I truly trusted for this job." Ari cleared her throat. Rosé had forgotten that she was there. "The only person who was available for this," he added, increasing his volume. "I've known Kay a long time. I knew that he would not forget or lose sight of you, like Gustav would do or sell you to the first creature that appeared offering money, as Ruby possibly would do." He stopped and reflected. "No, I don't think money would work on her. But anyway, there aren't many left, and honestly, there are few I trust, especially about you, my daughter, and a woman, if you know what I mean. I know he wouldn't dare lay a finger on you without permission. And as someone who carries something very powerful inside of you, he was the perfect option.

"I don't know if you've noticed, but Kay is arrogant and very proud. His ego is exhaustively large and, when given a mission, he does not like to return defeated. He likes to brag about his great deeds, and I knew that when I asked him to do it, he would feel important …" He drank another sip of the liquid in his hands. "He would put effort into everything to go well. Besides, honey," he said, burrowing more into the chair, "he's the kind of person I'd like to keep around. He's determined. It's cold-blooded and may well be a threat if you go back to the other side."

Throughout his speech, 'go back to the other side' and 'keep close' had been the phrases she had paid the most attention to. She had already been told that he had a different past. Obscure and sinister, but Rosé found it hard to believe, because even though he was a killer, at the same time he had also proved to be not a bit intimidating or a threat.

"How long ago?" The question came out harsher than she expected.

"Since you moved from my house" Rosé stared him in the eye. "Oh please dear, don't look at me like that. Besides, from what I hear, he did more than his job, protecting you even from those ordinary idiots." She raised an eyebrow. "I heard you were very good at getting into a situation … let's say it's complicated. Parties, drinks, arguments. I'm surprised you didn't smoke or try any drugs."

"First, I didn't go to many parties. Second. Who taught me not to bow my head to any piece of shit?" He nodded in acknowledgment. "And what is the point in experiencing something that you know is addictive? I do not do drugs."

"Drugs and drinks make you forget your problems," he argued, returning the empty glass to the table.

"Are you trying to convince me to do drugs?"

"No, no, no."

"Great."

He watched her. "You may have your mother's perfect face, but we can't deny that you have too much of my personality in you."

"Is that supposed to be a compliment?" she asked.

"Not at all … perhaps. You are the fruit of a cursed angel and a merciless demon. A powerful mixture I would say."

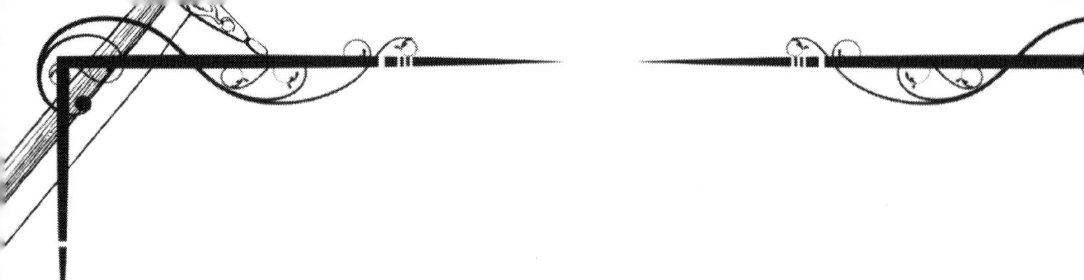

Chapter 23

It was after midnight when Rosé heard a knock on the door. As she called out for the person to enter, Aiden appeared behind her.

She was on a stool organizing things up in her wardrobe. Since she had arrived, she had never bothered tidying up her room or rearranging it to her style, so she had spent a good part of her day doing just that.

It wasn't the way she wanted it yet, but she was still in the process of fixing it. She had changed the placement of some things and hung paintings on the wall.

She was also reflecting on the conversation she had had with her father this morning. He had come by later that day to deliver her food and talked a little about his life before Lys and encouraged her to give this place a chance. He didn't mention Sarah and Rosé didn't push it. Maybe even she wasn't ready to talk about it.

She couldn't deny that she missed those moments together.

Aiden sat on the floor in front of the bed, dropping a huge bag on the side. "Do you need help?" he asked. Rosé declined, but inside she was cursing herself as she could really use his help.

She could see him watching her suffer. "Your room is much cosier." He had only been there once since she had arrived.

"Do you think?"

"Uhum."

"I still intend to change some things. I don't think it's to my style yet. Besides, is it not too late for you to be here? I thought the fire princess needed her hot beauty sleep," she commented, standing on tiptoes to pick up one of the boxes that someone had placed on the highest shelf.

Aiden laughed. "I thought the same of you."

"What are you doing here? Not that I don't want you here, but your visit was quite random." Rosé finally took the box and threw it on the floor without any delicacy and came down from the stool, scaring Aiden, who dropped his phone.

"Why don't you break it more?" he complained sarcastically. Rosé gave him a mad look. "And I came because I thought you wanted some company. Someone to talk to. We swear friendship and we barely know each other. How can you be my 8 this way?" Rosé opened the box and saw that there was nothing very interesting but some pictures there. She pushed the box into the corner of the room and sat next to him on the floor.

She'd take care of the box another time.

"What is an 8?"

"A way to call a forever friendship. Your forever person."

"It looks like a couple thing."

"It could be as well."

"So, we are 8s?"

"Technically."

She hadn't thought much of it when she made the promise. There was something about him that was different. They just connected, like they've known each other for years. Rosé looked at the bag and then at him again. "What's in there?"

"Curious?"

"Always."

"Food," he said, lifting the bag and taking some pots out of it. "One thing I've found out about you is your sense of hunger and also lack of it sometimes, but I think that's pure laziness." A delicious smell of pizza and cake hung in the air. "The last time I brought you food, you devoured it in a way I've never seen before."

Rosé elbowed him. "Can I?" she said, pointing to one of the pots with a piece of pizza inside.

"No, I brought the pizzas for decoration. I didn't sneak into the kitchen and steal some food for noth—" he commented sarcastically again, but Rosé bit his arm lightly and he pulled away, giving up on finishing the sentence. She laughed and took a huge bite of the pizza. "You are definitely a rwvka," he began, rubbing his arm. "Your full name?"

"Rosélina Alicia Johnson. Well, that's how I grew up, but apparently, it's Rosélina Alicia Johnson Lysion," she said, full-mouthed. That pizza was delicious, better than the one Eliot had bought. "What about yours?"

"Aiden Moore."

Rosé stopped chewing. "That's all? Aiden Moore?" She was outraged by it. His name was tiny.

"Are you going to complain about my name too?" Aiden questioned, devouring some waffles.

"No. I wish I had a small name like yours." She wanted a lot of things Aiden had, apparently. Rosé got up and went to a minifridge she had asked for a while ago from Ariady, she had also asked for her laptop back.

She took two bottles of water.

Aiden got up and took one hand to his chest and thrust the other into the air. "A very important question that will define our friendship." Rosé was nervous but smiled. "Who do you hate the most here?" Rosé began to laugh, but when trying to breathe, she made a snorting noise. "Great, I have a friendship with a pig," he said, sitting next to her, laughing.

"I ..." she said, trying to get her breath back. "The walking comic."

"Gustav?"

"No, the other one."

"Kay?" Rosé confirmed it. She hated him in so many ways. Starting with his voice, he was someone who thinks they know everything and finds himself the most special and strongest person in the whole world. Not to mention that she hates his face because he knows he is perfect in appearance, making him even more arrogant.

"So we're officially friends."

"Just like that? So simple?"

"Prin, hatred for people creates good friendships."

"New vocab?"

"Prin is short for princess. An 8 needs a special name."

"Well, I like Aiden, so ..."

They fell into silence, admiring the food. She had overeaten. Rosé took her hands up to her belly and noticed how bloated she was. She seemed pregnant. One thing she had to admit was that the food in

Amondridia was much better than she had ever eaten before in her life.

Rosé took her hand to Aiden's belly. She was not met by hard abs. "Ohh. You also have a food baby." Aiden looked at her for some seconds, reading her.

"Are you drunk?" Rosé took some time to answer him. No, she wasn't, and now she didn't have an excuse to give for her stupidity.

"I am going to call her Pooh," he commented when Rosé didn't answer. "Like the bear, you know?" And it was at that moment she discovered that Aiden was her forever person. Her 8. She discovered someone worse than her.

They both laughed.

"What would be the title of the most important chapters of your biography?" asked Rosé, breaking the silence, taking a sip of her water.

"'The birth of the most beautiful man', 'The fire that never stops burning', 'Aiden Moore, the god of fire' and 'The childhood of burning fire'," he declares, proud of his choices. "Where did you get that question?"

"A website."

Rosé looked at the piece of pizza in her hands. She felt sorry for her belly who would have to digest everything she was eating.

"Why don't you sit with us in the canteen anymore?"

"Because your friends hate me," was her quick response. She didn't have much to think about. She would never forget the looks they cast her and how they seemed to be very uncomfortable with her presence. She could live in love and hate with herself, but she would never be in a place she didn't feel welcome. It's cruel for both parties.

"Well, they get upset that you only go on the phone when we were together." Rosé felt like a click in her brain. Is that why they hated her? She had imagined countless things as usual. Worst-case scenarios. And of course, none of them involved being on her phone and not being communicative.

"Usually, people excluded me from conversations and so I always stayed on my phone, so I didn't look like an idiot, and nobody said anything, so ... Do they know who I am?" Aiden nodded.

Silence.

"Aiden?"

"Yes, Prin?"

"Where were you born? Do you have a family?"

"Cautyash, a Lys in Manchester just for Elementris of fire," he said, looking forward. "My parents still live there with my two older brothers." He didn't seem at all excited about talking about his family. Rosé looked at his profile, his gaze was low.

"Why did you leave?"

"They were kind of toxic. They wanted to decide everything in my life. I couldn't do anything I wanted, and I was barely alone." Rosé could see the pain in his eyes. "I had thoughts I shouldn't have. Thoughts that were not normal for a child like me. Until I heard about this Lys and, when I turned sixteen, I ran away here and was very welcomed."

"Do you miss them?" She should have stopped at the first question.

"I didn't stop loving them, I just learned to live without them. I'm not comparing them to dead people or anything. I'm grateful they're still alive. Sometimes I go back there and watch them from afar." He put the last piece of pizza in his mouth.

"They know?"

"You like to poke," he remarked, lowering his head and laughing.

"I'm just curious. Sorry. I am having parenting problems as well," Rosé reported. She got up and climbed on to her bed. Her ass was sore from sitting on the floor. She thought she was the only one with problems with her parents or her life.

"Perhaps. Once my mother saw me and we exchanged looks for a long time. Even though I was far away, I could see tears coming out of her eyes." Rosé lay on the bed, leaving her head on the edge, watching him upside down.

"Have you been talking to her?" Aiden looked at her and she got the message. "I'm sorry."

"No. I think it's best if we don't get any closer. They're happy without me and, unlike them, I like to see them like this. At the end of the day, I still love them, but I'm right to stay here. On the darkest days I miss them, but … today I have another family. I don't feel like running after the pain. The wound has already healed, and I want to leave it like this."

"Your biggest dream?" she asked, lying face down.

"Survive. Well, we are all survivors, fighting for life every moment we open our eyes in the morning." This hit Rosé in the heart, it was just a bad reality that they all had to face every day. "Favourite band?"

"I don't have one."

Aiden got up abruptly. "What do you mean, you don't have one?" Rosé shrugged. "Have you ever heard of Full Nappies?" Rosé blinked once. A lot of things went through her head at that moment, but nothing musical. "Promise me they'll be the next band you listen to."

"Okay. Don't you want to get up on the bed? The floor is too fucking uncomfortable." He agreed and climbed up next to her. "You don't know what I found out." Aiden straightened up in bed, curiosity taking over. He seemed restless.

"The walking comic is my Guardian." Aiden joined his eyebrows. "From what I understand he's taking care of me and making sure I stay alive." She looked down, playing with the tip of her t-shirt.

"Okay." He stopped and looked at her in amazement. "Kay can be an idiot and a fucking arrogant bastard. So annoying that he makes me want to cut my ears off, but he's amazing when it comes to fighting. It is not random that he's in command of all the training that happens here. He's one of the best. He was even on the cover of magazines, Incantus and J.H Cupid, two of the biggest and most prestigious magazines in our world."

"But I don't want to be watched all the time. How do I know he's not doing it now?" she asked, lying down again, letting the soft mattress wrap her up. Where was her privacy now? What has Kay seen her do? Countless moments flooded her mind. Did he …? No, of course not.

"I think you are fine, but it sucks."

There was silence between the two.

"Hey what party are we having in a few days?" she asked. "I got a dress and a note saying that in a few days we're going to have a party." Aiden was on his phone, just like her. He had spoken to her about Monstra, their social media, and she was still getting used to how to use it.

"It's a party that happens every year. Just a stupid tradition where you go in gala clothes and dance to classical songs. Half the people go to drink and go crazy, and it was Misty who made your dress."

"Misty?"

"Yes, she takes a fashion course at C.A.E. Her room consists of mannequins and fabrics and more fabrics and threads and fuck knows what else. Sometimes I get scared by those mannequins, she takes their arms or heads off and leaves them randomly around the room. Seriously, problematic sometimes." Rosé laughed. She knew exactly what that was like. Hanna kept leaving pieces of mannequins scattered around the house. "But she focuses more on the plus size. The outfit she was wearing the first time you met was one she made."

"She's talented," commented Rosé, recalling her face and ochre yellow skirt and colourful cropped top.

"Talented?" Aiden laughed. "She's a goddess. The fucking goddess of fashion. You should go to her room one day. It has countless amazing pieces. At least someone needs to have a future."

They spent the rest of Aiden's time there talking about the future and how neither had the slightest idea of what they wanted to do in life. Aiden commented that he intended to join C.A.E in the coming years if all went well but was still choosing a course. She commented on what her university was like and how she missed her old life a little. Aiden introduced her to the band Full Nappies and helped her download some apps.

Chapter 24

(Warning: Sensible content)

Aiden left before two in the morning.

Rosé woke up feeling unwell and tired. She had the same stupid dreams as many other nights. In one of them she made the rain stop, in another she had managed to break a wall with her own fist. With each dream, it was different, but the same scenario and today there was someone in a corner of the room. She couldn't see its face or get close.

Her conversation with Aiden had stayed in her head, just like the argument with her father. There wasn't a conversation she didn't think about over and over again. There were a lot of things to process, and she was trying to understand everything that was going on in her life, and the point was not just to process, but also to know how to deal with it.

She pushed her thoughts away and got dressed. Today she was going to meet Ari to talk about her training in Amondridia and the things she would have to do.

Although she was enjoying the easy life she had, she couldn't just live there for free without contributing.

The corridors of the palace were more busy than usual. There were creatures clearing some areas and flying objects controlled by, Rosé assumed, some wizard or mage. Some people waved at her and wished her a good morning, something Rosé had already gotten used to.

She just reciprocated with a smile and sometimes raised her hand to say hi.

She met Misty halfway. Rosé thanked her for the dress and Misty asked Rosé to try it on before the party to see if she had gotten the size right, in case she needed to make some adjustments.

Looking out the window, Rosé was distracted by the scenery and did not realise where she was going and ended up bumping into someone. "I'm sorry." Rosé came across a girl with short bronze hair. Extremely thin. Her features and bones were strikingly visible, and her gaze was deep.

Something trapped Rosé in her eyes. They were honey-coloured, just like hers, and round like an almond, larger than normal. She looked like a human doll. Pale by nature, but something in her gaze was alarming.

Rosé's head drooped and a male voice took over her mind until everything turned dark.

<3

(Lucy's memories/mind)

Rosé was on the floor when she woke up again. The man was yelling at someone. She got up and came across a deplorable scene.

"You can't tell anyone, you understand?" said the male voice. He was an old man, probably in his fifties. "If you tell someone, there will be great consequences." His voice was firm and authoritative. Intimidating would be a better description.

The bedroom door slammed.

The woman was in the corner of the room. Her knees close to her chest. Tears running down her delicate cheeks.

Rosé tried to get close. She wanted to cover the woman's fragile body and bring her closer, console her, but before she could do anything, the memory changed.

She got dizzy and a child's voice appeared.

"Mommy? Daddy?" It was a young boy's voice. There was something sinister in his tone. Fear. Desperation. His steps were cautious, yet the wood creaked beneath his feet. Every step he took made his heart race more. Rosé could feel despair taking over the child's body.

Screams.

As he approached the door, red liquid began dripping underneath.

Dizziness and darkness took her body again.

"Hey, it is alright sweety. I am going to take care of you." A lie.

Skin-to-skin noise.

Everything was dark.

"You're not going to touch her," said a female voice. There was a mistake in that voice. A glitch. A hiccup. Despair. A smile. "She was not meant to be touched." One shot.

A scream.

The memories were mixing and only voices could be heard. She was confused and scared.

"Mother, stop. It's all my fault," a female voice shouted. She was a dark-eyed, blonde girl. Her skin was white as snow. The woman turned to face her. They had gone back in time. They still wore corset and long dresses.

A slap.

A kick.

No air.

A dark hole.

She was in a cell, covered in bruises.

"You are mine and no one else's. If I can't have you, no one will." Was that a new memory? Another nightmare?

Skin with skin. "I love you and I'm doing it for your safety." A scream.

Rosé's scream. The memories were mixing faster than Rosé could keep up with.

She couldn't breathe. It was like someone had taken the air away from her. Like her lungs couldn't work anymore. She could feel icy marble on her hands and knees. She didn't know how she got to that position. Her eyes were fixed to the ground. She was crying and her chest hurt like never before.

There were hands on her back, stroking them. "It's alright." There was someone crouching next to her. "Take a deep breath." Rosé tried to sit up, but it was no use, the pain and the crying prevented her from moving.

Her lips were salty from her tears. Her hands were cold. Her chest and spine were in pain. Everything seemed to hurt, just as everything seemed to spin. She was feeling weak and helpless, like the woman in the corner of the room. The pain of someone's toxicity in her chest. The agony of the scream and her heart stopping for a second when she heard the shot.

Fear.

She was scared.

But she had no reason to be afraid.

The images continued to pass through her head. Thinking about the girl and how she felt. So young and already destroyed by the world. The boy's fear as he walks to his parents and the red liquid in front of him. *No, no, no, no, no, no, no, no,* Rosé repeated. She had to save them. She had to do something. They need her. She must save them. The Pure

Soul.

"Rosé, look at me." No, she couldn't look. She didn't have time for this. She had to save them. She had to save them. She had to take them in her arms, and she had see that they were fine and that she would take care of them. She desperately wanted to move, but nothing in her was capable. How would she get to them?

Anger burned in her chest. Pain. Anguish. Sadness. Fear. Everything bad was in her chest at that moment. Burning her heart little by little, hoping that it would turn everything to ashes until there was nothing left.

"Rosé for fuck's sake. Look at me." She raised her gaze. Her eyes burning and yet wet from tears. Grey. That's what she saw. Her body relaxed. Two grey eyes. "Come with me."

"I c-can't mo-ve."

"Can I touch you? Can I lift you up?" Rosé just nodded and suddenly everything went dark.

It was only after a few seconds that she realized she had invaded someone's mind.

Chapter 25

Lucy was almost six feet away from Rosé, in the same position. They had been broken up by someone or something. She could taste poison on her tongue. No. It wasn't poison. It was something acidic, but it wasn't poison. Ari was on her side, helping her up.

(You might be wondering: Who's Lucy? Well… funny story, Lucy had a purpose in this book. I planned her short appearance, but people just got confused and took it to another level. So here I'm, explaining. Who and what Lucy is, comes further in the book, okay? And in the previous chapter, Rosé invaded Lucy's mind and saw those things and now, it's Lucy's point of view of this event after they break away)

At this point, an audience had already formed. Whispers and gossip had already taken over. They looked and judged, but that wasn't the problem. Lucy did not know what had happened, but what she had seen was not pleasant.

These were memories. Memories she had to keep. The darkest ones from people who had requested she remove them, so they could live.

That is what happens when you are cursed.

That is what happens when you are born a Sentiment of Fear.

When, what makes you not Ordinary, is a gift that allows you to control a feeling that might destroy you.

She needed to get close to Rosé, and comfort her, but she was stopped, and Rosé was taken far away from her.

The acidic taste came back to her mouth.

<3

"And you had the audacity to bring this girl into the palace!" Li Wang almost screamed.

"If you're not satisfied, you can leave, no one's asking you to stay," Kay said, leaning against the wall. "Isn't that what you've always wanted? What's keeping you here? You're not going to touch her."

"Are you going to protect that freak? That damn kid?"

"I will protect her to the end. Body and soul."

"Then you will die very soon, dear. Have a good time," she said, leaving the room. She never came back.

Ariady looked at Kay who kept his gaze on the door. "That's a very strong promise," she remarked, getting into one of the chairs. "I'm surprised you took this job, Kay." She joined her hands and left them resting on her lap.

"We all made that promise."

"Indeed, we did. However, I couldn't help but notice how your smell changes when she's around you and … it's not love. It's something different. Something I can't understand. Do you have anything to tell me?" She watched Kay intently.

"There's nothing to be said."

She sighed and leaned against the back of the chair. "I was not born yesterday, dear. I've seen this world fall apart and come together. I've seen years, decades, centuries go by. I've seen a good part of our humanity evolve and you really think I don't know that you're hiding something from me. If you haven't forgotten, I've been part of groups of people who have ruled our world and I know very well that there's something much deeper in it. It may not seem like it, but you, Kay, are very easy to read and I hope from the bottom of my heart you tell me before I find out for myself."

"Will you add 'after everything I've done for you' too?"

"I don't do things expecting something."

"Of course, not." He looked at her. Eye to eye. "You also seem to have some kind of connection with her. Something very personal. Would you like to share?"

Ari smiled and got up, smoothing down her clothes as she did. "Amondridia has been my home for a long time. Made and developed by the only person who really had a brain in this place. She protected this place even though she was pregnant. She put her life on the line for everyone here. Keeping Rosé alive is the least I could do for her. This isn't about the Lysion's tale, this is personal, and I'm going to protect her with body and soul. I've lived too long in this infamous world." She took one last look at him and left the room, leaving him alone with his own thoughts.

Chapter 26

'You shouldn't be here alone,' Rosé wrote in Nikko's notebook when he joined her at the bench. She had not been able to sleep and the same seemed to be true for him. She had been warned about not walking alone through the palace at night, but Nikko was with her, so she was not alone.

'Is this how our conversations are always going to start?' he asked. She denied.

Rosé stopped to think. 'What are you capable of doing? Your magic? You never told me.' Nikko read what she had written and, in the blink of an eye, he disappeared. Rosé stretched out her hand where he was, carefully, but found nothing. Everything in him was gone, even the notebook in his hands.

She withdrew her hands and kept looking at what appeared to be nothing. Just the bench and the grass, like there was no one there.

Nikko appeared again and wrote in the notebook. Rosé was getting apprehensive. 'Sorcerer. When I was younger, I could hear a little. The voices came out like a whisper, but I could hear them. I had the gift of reading minds. Listen to what people thought and imagined, like my Da. I can get invisible, but I can't control it yet''

'Can you still see them? Feel them?'

'Sometimes. Only images without sound.' He took the notebook again and wrote more things. 'People's minds are dangerous territory. I don't want to get inside them, but I can still feel their emotions.' They looked at each other for a while. The sun and the moon in his eyes.

'Your eyes. They are beautiful.'

'Even the white one?' Nikko smiled. A sincere one.

'Even the white one,' she wrote back.

His smile widened and he stole the notebook from Rosé's hands.

'It's good to know that you're not repulsed and that you think it's pretty. I hated it for a long time.'

'You shouldn't hate it. It reminds me of the night. The moon.' He took his fingertips to his chin and, in a subtle motion, extended his hand, muttering *thank you.*

'What's your name? In sign language,' she wrote. Nikko read and turned to her, crossing his legs, and faced her. With one hand he made a C, like a shell, and with the other he lowered all his fingers, leaving only the index finger, positioning it in the middle of the C. Rosé repeated the gesture and he waved.

"Ni-ko," he tried to say his own name. If someone asked her to describe his voice, she'd never be able to. She looked at him. She wanted him to repeat it, but she wouldn't ask him, instead she smiled.

He approached her and put his warm, small hands on her cheeks. Rosé closed her eyes. She could feel his little hands go through the entire length of her face. Her eyes, forehead, eyebrows, chin. Until he lifted them away.

She took the notebook. 'What were you doing?'

'Memorizing and admiring your face with my hands, in case one day I lose sight in my other eye. I was memorizing with the tact.' Rosé read and felt a warmth take hold of her chest. No one had ever done that before. He wrote something else, 'I was also seeing what was inside your mind. I'm sorry.'

She couldn't get mad at him, even though she knew he'd invaded her privacy. Instead, she wrote. 'What did you see?'

'For a moment I saw happiness, I felt it on you. But for a moment I also felt darkness and pain.'

Rosé took the notebook back in a quick motion. She was frustrated. 'You should not be here, alone, with me,' Rosé wrote and handed the notebook to him.

'Why?'

'I am dangerous,' she wrote and rose. She couldn't control her feelings, her power, her magic. Whatever it was. She couldn't do it. What if she did something to him? If she hurt him?

'I'm not afraid of you.' He handed the book back to her, patting the space where Rosé sat a moment previous. Rosé returned to her seat, passing the book back to Nikko. 'You must be proud of yourself'

'I don't know if proud would be the right word. Besides, what were you doing walking alone? Should you not be accompanied at all times?'

'Why? Because this world is too dangerous?'

'~~Yes, especially for someone~~' She stopped writing and scribbled out what she had written, but it was too late. Nikko had read and ripped out his notebook from her hands with such ferocity.

'Like me? Deaf? Helpless?' Rosé didn't answer. She couldn't get the notebook back to answer. She felt terrible. 'I thought you hated the feeling of pity,' he wrote, delivering it to her.

'I do hate it,' she delivered, waiting for him to read. She retrieved the book, 'and I'm sorry for that.'

It took him a while to finish writing.

'The world is more dangerous for you than for me at the moment and I think it's time for you to stop feeling sorry for yourself, don't you think? I felt it inside you. You hate that people feel sorry for you, but what you feel most is pity for yourself. Whining is not going to make me hear anything or make my eye see.' Tears slipped from his face. Rosé took her icy hands up to Nikko's cheeks. She could feel him shiver when her hand found his face. His face was a light shade of red and Rosé could not tell if it was anger or the cold wind.

Rosé dried his tears. She pointed at him and made a sign of crying. Her finger dropped from her eye to her cheek. She pointed to herself and repeated the act. 'If you cry, I'll cry too.' They hadn't talked properly, but that conversation connected them. Rosé felt something in her chest for Nikko that she couldn't explain. He looked like her, but different at the same time.

'I'm sorry, but sometimes it hurts. It hursts so much that I can't stop them,' he wrote. Nikko took his own hands to his face and dried up the tears that came later.

'~~I'm so sorry...~~ it's complicated.'

'It doesn't have to be like that.' When looking at Nikko's hands that fell on his lap, holding the notebook, Rosé saw a scar on his left wrist. Silent tears began to flow down her face. 'Why are you crying?' he wrote.

'I said that when someone cries, I also cry.' She let a sad smile escape.

That image never left her head.

He was very young, and the world had already destroyed him in countless ways. When looking at him, her eyes saw a teenager, almost a young adult, black curly hair and multi-coloured eyes, but her heart saw a little, innocent child.

(A small break for you. Stretch yourself. Drink water.)

Nikko had accompanied Rosé to the canteen to pick up something to eat. It was silent, there was no one around. Nikko was very intelligent which made Rosé feel intimidated and stupid. She would have to study more to do not feel that way. 'It's been a pleasure talking to you, Rosé. Thank you for your time and conversation,' Nikko wrote and said goodbye. Rosé watched him walk away, happy and content for the first time in a while.

Until the alarm went off.

Her heart stopped.

Shit.

Her first instinct was Nikko.

"NIKKO?" cried Rosé. For a moment she forgot that he could not hear her, but surprisingly he stopped at the other door of the canteen and looked toward Rosé. Many thoughts crossed her mind. Why was that alarm for? What would happen to Nikko? He could get hurt or stumble somewhere. *The world is more dangerous for you than it is for me right now.* He was right. Nikko knew how to take care of himself. He was a not a child and, with their world-aging, he was probably older than her. She ran to where he was and pulled him back into the canteen. He seemed confused at first. She didn't have time for his notebook. She took him by the hand and with the other she made a blinking signal, hoping that he would understand the message and luckily, he understood, or he had seen something in her head.

They were heading behind the counter when a voice called her.

"In less than two minutes. I think that's a record." He walked elegantly, proudly, as if he had already won the game. "I thought I'd have to face your guardian angel first, or maybe a dead person, but no. It was so simple."

Rosé didn't react. She didn't know how she was going to communicate with Nikko. If she stopped to write, she'd waste a lot of time. At that moment she wanted to know how to speak sign language. She pushed Nikko behind her. He wasn't the one they wanted, but he held her arm, strongly. Strong enough that it almost made her groan in pain.

She tried to shake him off her arm, but it didn't work out.

He was stuck to it.

"Your son? Another Lysion?" No answer. "Bingo then." He was approaching cautiously.

"If you hurt him, I swear the consequences won't be very pleasant," she said. Her head was held high and her voice was firm. "And no, he's not a Lysion."

"Too bad," he said, making a fake crying face. "Too bad I don't believe you. Until a year ago I believed that your bitchy mother had been the last and that Oldo had stolen her magic." Rosé looked at him, confused. "Oldo. The man who almost got his hands on you. Twice. He carries your mother's blood." He stopped and put his hands on his waist. "You did not know? He murdered her. I'm worried about how much you know of this world."

"I know more than you know," she lied, but the man just laughed. Rosé knew he was right, but, hearing it from another person, it made real.

Coming from a threat, it made it hard to accept.

"Did you know your mother was a whore? She wasn't sweet and cute at all. She kept lying to people and was too good at hiding her true self."

Electricity took over her body and before she knew what was happening, her hand was raised, and the man was in the air. Pure anger flowed and bubbled all over her body. That son of a bitch had murdered her mother. She brought him closer. A stupid move in case something went wrong, but she didn't care.

The man managed to get rid of her and fell to the ground. He muttered something and a red energy ball found Rosé's chest, lifting her from the ground, squeezing her chest. Squeezing what was inside her. She shouldn't have left her room.

When her vision became turbid, she felt the impact of the ground on her bones. "So young and so inexperienced," he remarked, approaching her. He held her hands with a rope that came out of his own hands. "I could kill you now, but … there are a lot of people who could stop me." He helped her up and conjured a portal. A light circle.

"And I really want to hear you scream."

Rosé looked behind her for Nikko, but he was no longer there.

The man held her by the arm and was pushing her.

She turned to him and in the snap of her fingers, she kicked him in the groin before bringing his head crashing into her knee.

She got rid of the ropes.

"Don't you dare talk about my mother like that, and you better give me a good reason to not kill you."

He was the one fighting for air. He tried to talk more. Rosé let go of what held his neck but kept him still. The connection remained intact between them. Nikko wasn't anywhere. He was probably invisible. Rosé went to the man. An electric circuit appeared in his hands, holding them together. He screamed for every shock he received. "I told you to tell me more."

Rosé didn't recognise herself.

He was still having trouble breathing. "He … Oldo arrived at the mansion … arrived in Wysez one day. He was proud of himself, saying he had killed the last existing Lysion. The last woman who held the power. Cursed by the gods—" Rosé was going to ask more, but a bullet shot through the man's neck.

Rosé got scared and he fell to the ground She wasn't responsible for that.

Rosé looked to the entrance and there was Gustav. His eyes were bulging, and the gun was still in his hands. Half of his face was covered with a cloth. Ari appeared after him, panting. Then Ruby and Kay.

Rosé took a deep breath and looked at the man in front of her and then at her hands and placed them on her face. "Am I still alive?" she asked. Gustav nodded then lowered his gun. They were all looking at her. "Shit. I thought I was going to die." The tension had passed.

"That's not funny. Did you have a great conversation with him?" asked Kay, coming towards her. "Instead of doing something or hiding, you were talking to him? Having a chat?"

She almost sighed in frustration listening to his voice. "I was trying to get information out of him, because no one in this place tells me anything."

"And you almost died." He was now in front of her.

"I don't know if you noticed, but it wasn't me who was about to die and be careful of your words because if you keep treating me like that, it's not going to be the bullet that's going to make the blast noise, it's your brain. If you still have one," she informed with her chin high, gathering all her willpower to not attack him or make him kneel in front of her.

Gustav laughed behind them.

Everyone else was silent.

For someone who had been close to death, she felt fine.

Until she remembered why she was there.

Rosé looked back and found Nikko, where Rosé had left him. She went to him and touched his arms. She analysed him for any signs of injury. He closed his eyes and placed his hands on Rosé's face. A vision arose in her mind. Nikko had saved her from having her organs crushed.

He opened his eyes and hugged her.

She took the notebook. '*The next fucking time, you run,*' she wrote, with a middle finger drawn. '*The next time you make me worry about you, I am going to throw you out of this window.*'

He nodded, laughing, and Rosé hugged him once more.

She passed the group with Nikko still stuck to her and left the canteen. Limping and with pain in her chest. She wasn't sure what had happened, but she would only deal with it when Nikko was safe, and she was in her bed.

A woman appeared in the hallway and Nikko ran to her. They began to speak sign language, excluding Rosé from any interaction. Nikko looked at her once more and waved a bye and she reciprocated. The woman thanked her.

Rosé watched them disappear in the hallway.

She looked back and saw Kay leaning against the wall with his arms folded. "We need to talk." Rosé began to walk away, pretending he wasn't there. "Don't ignore me. I'm not joking." He stopped in front of her, blocking her way. She tried to swerve, but it was impossible to get past him. "You almost died."

"Why do you care? I'm just an Ordinary to you." Rosé tried to pass by once more and was stopped. "What's your fucking problem?" she said, staring at him. Her face burned with rage.

"You are my problem. You're the reason for all my problems twenty fucking hours a day. Why can't you stay one night in your room?" he almost shouted.

"Because I can't sleep. Because I have nightmares every night. Because even during my moment of rest I do not rest. My mind is a machine of tragedies. It's an endless black hole. I don't know what happened there," she exclaimed, pointing to the canteen, "and it's not something I'm in the mood to talk about right now, give me a break."

"We've already given you a lot of time and we have what we need to start training you." She closed her eyes and took a deep breath. She didn't want to fight. She didn't want to start an argument with him. Especially with him.

"Can we talk about this later? I just talked to one of the purest souls I've ever seen in my life. I saw myself use my magic for the first time and saw a man die in front of me in a matter of seconds. So … I'm really not at my best to talk to you right now … please. I need to sleep." Tears of anger fell on her cheeks.

Kay cleaned them before she could do anything. "Stop crying, that's disgusting," he said.

"Is that how you calm someone down?"

"Want a hug? A kiss?" Rosé pushed him, even though she wanted to say yes to the hug and, for a second, to the kiss. "That's what I thought." He smirked. "Do you need me to take you to your room? No talking. Only company." She nodded.

Chapter 27

Rosé was back in the library. She had already lost count of how many books she had read since she got there. They were her only true friends, even though they never met her. She fell in love with more characters and real people and experienced more real things through pages than any one person did in real life.

Sometimes she was so intrigued, that she used to spend the whole night reading. Lost in pages and ink.

The library was divided into sections of huge semicircles, and they were themed according to the genre of the books. Other sections were just countless stacks of books with titles and numerous shelves whose books did not have a specific genre.

Rosé spent a good part of her time reading fantasies (which were no longer fantasies but books written by magical creatures) or romances, but sometimes took risks with others. She, sometimes, used to read a little bit about the history of the magical world so she wouldn't get lost in conversations over meals.

After the first attack she had returned to sit with the Elementris, but from time to time she did not understand what they were talking about.

Rosé always sat in an armchair near a large window in one of the corners of the library. It was cosy and there was a coffee table. The light that penetrated through the window was perfect for reading. Mr Bebbols would appear and sleep on her lap and other times he would not appear at all. They didn't talk much. Maybe it was the fact that he was too arrogant and grumpy, or Rosé wanted to read her book in peace.

Today, he had spent time in her lap, then at the table. He wandered around with a toy in his mouth and then disappeared.

Rosé was reading a novel about a warrior and a princess who fell in love after much fighting and was now at a very interesting scene. Her eyes were focused and narrowed, having high self-control not to scream and react, but sometimes the outbreak was inevitable. Nothing could get in the way of that interesting moment.

(Interesting, cough cough.)

A noise interrupted her. Rosé looked sideways and saw no one. So, she went back to her book. She almost let out a scream but took her hand to her mouth, muffling the sound. The noise continued to make it difficult to concentrate. The noise persisted and she was sure it wasn't Mr Bebbols.

"I'm trying to read," she cried, angrily. She was desperate to finish that scene.

"I thought you were trying to get away from your reality," someone said behind a bookshelf. It was a very familiar and formidable voice. "A very interesting book and I think you agree with that since you've been having little heart attacks since you started reading it," Kay commented, emerging with a stack of books floating next to him.

She rolled her eyes. *Him again, to my patience's sake.* She had been avoiding him all week so she wouldn't talk about what had happened.

"How do you know?" she asked, dropping a fake smile. "And how long have you been watching me?" His response would define the amount of shame she had spent in the last few hours that she was there.

"I've read it," he commented, returning one of the books to the bookshelf and then turning to her. "Some time ago. It was hard to finish my book with you shouting and talking with a book." Rosé blushed. Okay, she could live with that. "Actually, it was a great experience."

Her face now burned with shame. She took a deep breath. "Do you read?" she asked quickly, trying to change the subject, one that didn't involve her and her outbreaks.

"Of course," he said, leaning against the bookshelf. "I've come to return some." He snapped his finger, and the books began to direct themselves back to their bookshelves.

"Did you have to make so much noise?"

"Have you ever seen yourself reading? One day I'm going to record it and show you."

"I don't believe you read," Rosé commented, returning to her book, but she didn't read a word because she knew that, if she did, she would turn red. This wasn't a scene to read with an audience.

For someone with a terrible past, 'reader' didn't seem much his style. The image of him sitting in an armchair or bed reading a book popped into her head. A shiver strolled through her body. She blushed. She desperately wanted to see that scene. Maybe he would be without a shirt, exposing his muscles. Maybe he wore glasses. Something happened down there. *Fuck. Rosé, focus.*

"Well, I don't need to prove anything, but ... what makes you believe I don't read?" he asked, leaning against a bookshelf. She could feel his gaze on her when she was trying to read.

"You don't seem like the kind of person who reads, and a lot of boys don't like to read, and ..." she said, raising her finger, "you look more like the rough soldier type and not the intellectual man who read books."

Kay laughed. "Not all readers are smart."

"In our society, they are. Not all are courageous enough to do so. Books are a sign of intelligence for me and—"

"People who don't read books are idiots with a social life?" She looked up in annoyance as he finished her sentence. "I grew up reading books. My mother's influence. She said that what's not real can save someone's life." She now wanted to see him reading and she really wanted to meet his mother. Would she be alive? In Amondridia? She thought about asking, but she would seem very interested and that wasn't the point. "What chapter are you on?" Kay was still by the shelf, watching her.

Rosé looked at the chapter. "35."

Kay ran his tongue along his lips, his piercing was no longer there. His smile took over his face. "That scene is, well ... if I may say, loving. I hope you're enjoying their show of love, even if it's diplomatic," he said. Rosé's body heated up. "Further on has an even more interesting and hot scene."

"Don't give me a spoiler, idiot," she said, hiding her face behind the book and going back to reading.

"He dies at the end," he remarked before leaving. Rosé shouted out in anger and cursed him with countless things, but he was right, further on there was a scene more interesting than the one she was reading. (Clears throat.)

<3

"Rosé, is everything alright here?" Ariady arrived in the canteen and stopped by her side.

"Yes, why?" she asked, confused. Ari had gotten in the way of a great story that Aiden was telling about an epic betrayal that happened between a couple of famous singers.

"I heard you shouting in the library this morning, I thought something had happened."

"The walking-comic-book-shit came to piss me off," she remarked, taking a bite of her food. It was when she looked at Ari once more that she realized her mistake.

"Who?" Aiden tried to hold back the laugh but couldn't. Rosé kicked his leg under the table.

"Hmm?"

"You called someone a walking comic," she stopped for a second, "book shit. Who is he?"

"Or, um I called …? I must have confused the names." She was trying to hide her face. "I was talking to Aiden about this character from the Outer World, you know? Before you got here. And I mixed up the names, but it was nobody … I'm fine. Freaking out about books. That must have been what you heard."

"I'm going to pretend that nothing happened, and I really don't want to know who you called a walking comic, but I think I already have my guesses, but avoid yelling there. There are things in that library that don't like loud sounds."

Ari left and sat at the usual table, leaving her with a feeling of embarrassment.

"Great actress. I'm jealous," commented Aiden, laughing. She kicked him one more time.

"I was going to tell you to shut up, but I need you to finish the gossip."

"Not before you tell me what happened in the library."

Chapter 28

Rosé had just explained to Aiden what had happened at the library and in the meantime, the rest of the group joined them at the table. A man older than them walked over and asked to talk to Misty; Theo explained that he was her older brother.

She couldn't help but notice how the whole palace was quieter. She had woken up earlier and, on her way to the library, everything had been too calm and it was the same when she came to the canteen.

The tables were full, but it was silent.

Rosé could see a girl reading a magazine with the title *Incantus* on the cover. Others were on their phones, but no one was necessarily talking.

Usually, everyone would be talking and debating about something Rosé wouldn't know. Arguing and fighting with each other, defending their ideas, but, looking at them, everyone was in a strange silence. Rosé started messing with her ring.

She was getting impatient with the lack of conversation. Misty returned and sat in silence, which made things even worse. She was the one who always brought a subject to the table and answered most of Rosé's questions about their world. It was hard for a place to be silent when she was around.

Rosé continued eating, thinking of something to say. She looked at her phone and she had the same notification she had received when she woke up.

"What is Astrea's Night?" asked Rosé, pulling away from her juice box, whose straw she had chewed to almost a pulp. That was definitely a bad habit she had to stop. It was disgusting to see.

She tried to fix it, but it didn't work out too well. It got even worse.

She had seen posters scattered throughout the palace and had received a message on her mobile phone that this event would take place later that day.

"It's the noble way to say goodbye to someone. Like a farewell ceremony. That tradition has a lot of names actually. Constellation Night. Zorya Night. Pyxis Night. It depends on where you come from and who introduced you," Misty replies. She'd been playing with the food ever since she got here.

"But who's leaving, who are we going to say goodbye to?" asked Rosé innocently.

She went to get her juice box, interested in what Misty was saying, but when she went to pick it up, it wasn't there anymore. Rosé looked to one side and the other and even on the floor, but nothing. She swore she had just set it down. "Has anyone seen my juice?" Everyone looked at the table, but nothing. Rosé ignored it. She was sad and thought about going to get another box of juice but gave up out of laziness.

The conversation continued.

"Haven't you heard the news?" Theo was looking at her. Everyone was. Rosé lowered her half-embarrassed head but soon lifted her eyes to meet his. Should she know? She didn't remember anything happening. "No one's leaving. Rosé, the Night of Astrea is … for someone who died." Rosé's eyes widened, and her fork stood still in midair. Died?

"What? Who died?" she said, still in shock. Her gaze went from Theo to Aiden and came back. She was waiting for an answer, but it didn't come. Her heart sped up. If someone were closer, they'd probably hear it almost coming out of her chest.

"Lucy." Rosé didn't recognize that name. She had no idea who she was. Would it be wrong to ask them who she was? But Aiden saw the confusion and doubt in her face and explained. "Lucy was the girl who bumped into you in the hall. Red and short hair, you know?" Rosé's body became paralyzed. Countless questions rose in her mind. How? When? Where?

"How? Why am I the last to know?" was the first thing that came out of her mouth. Her eyes were fixed on Aiden's.

"She … She killed her-" He didn't finish the sentence. Everyone was silent. Rosé looked around and realised that everyone had their heads down. Theo was relaxed in his chair, his arms were crossed, and he was looking down. Misty was stirring up her food. Nixie gathered up her things and left. Rosé didn't know what to say. "They found her body last night."

The images had returned to her head, things she had seen somehow.

The kids, but none of them looked like Lucy. Besides she was a Sentiment and they're not easy to kill, right? Ari had informed her what a Sentiment was after the accident. Sentiments are connected to a feeling, and they have the power to control them, and they feed from them.

Lucy's was fear.

Rosé remembered her face and how incredibly beautiful she was. Her hair was bright red. Her face was covered with reddish freckles and her eyes were like honey. She didn't know her, but that news had been like a stab in her heart.

"I don't know what to say," remarked Rosé, lowering her head. She dropped her fork and abandoned her food tray. She had lost her hunger. Why was she feeling a pang of guilt? One day the girl is walking down the halls. The next, she bumps into Rosé and they invade each other's mind, and then … after …

"No one expected this," commented Theo, withdrawing from the table.

"Were you close to her?" Rosé asked, trying to be as sensitive as possible. Maybe she should just shut up.

"Kind of. She was a lovely person, she cared a lot. She was one of my first friends here." Misty had a sad smile on her face as she responded to Rosé's question. Paying more attention, Rosé realised her eyes were puffy. "Welcoming and … For a while, she was responsible for teaching children to control their aura and skill, including me. Well," she said, getting up. There were tears on her face. "It happened. I wish I'd done something. Helped, realised." Her voice was weak. In a second, she also disappeared.

Aiden looked at Rosé and then where Misty was going. "Go after her," commented Rosé.

"Are you going to be okay?" he asked.

"I'm not the one crying." He nodded and left. Rosé stood there looking at the empty table. She thought of some possibilities that might have led her to that decision, but Rosé did not know her, or her story.

She didn't know how long she sat there. Looking at nothing. She wanted to get out. Every day she stayed here, she felt more guilty about the bad things that happened in this place.

Rosé heard the sound of someone clearing their throat and, looking at the sound source, she came across the Elite's desk. Ruby was drinking a red liquid from a glass, which Rosé deduced was blood. Her hair wasn't black anymore. On the day of the invasion, her hair was greyish and long. Today it was a magenta pink and shorter than normal. Gustav had his back on her, but what caught her eye was Kay. Their eyes met for the thousandth time. She smiled and showed her middle finger to him. While looking at him, she noticed it – her juice, in his hand. Kay took the juice to his mouth and drank, without taking his eyes off Rosé, and let a little smile escape.

She lowered her finger and stared at him.

"He didn't—" began Rosé. She looked at the straw more closely and it was half bitten. He couldn't have the same disgusting habit as her. Anger began to grow in her chest. *Who does that son of a bitch think he is to steal my food?* She thought.

Rosé wouldn't fight him. Not when something so tragic had happened.

She didn't get up. She closed her fists on the table, feeling her nails almost cut her skin. She pressed her lips together in an attempt to stay calm. *It's just juice. Just a fucking juice. Calm down.*

He got up along with the rest and passed the table where Rosé was, leaving the juice box in front of her, with a provocative smile in the corner of his mouth, making one of his dimples appear, and he walked away. The piercing was on the side of his lips today. Without thinking twice, she got up and headed toward him, with the little box in her hands.

She poked him in the back. Kay turned slowly until he was facing her. Eye to eye, she squeezed the little box on his face.

Kay closed his eyes instinctively and then dried his face with his hands. "You didn't?"

"Oh dear, of course I did."

"You got me wet," he said calmly.

"Yes, I got you wet," she said, smiling. "Nobody told you to mess with my food," she said, wiping her hands on his t-shirt, realising that the liquid had flowed over her hands, and, in the process, her hands touched his abdomen and she blushed, while Kay watched her.

"Is it over?" He was looking at her in the eye now. "Do you know you're going to have to clean it?" he asked. The juice was still dripping down his face. Rosé wanted to laugh but kept her posture straight and poker face.

"Why don't you clean it up?" she asked, placing her index finger on his chest, pushing him further away, but it was in vain because he was getting closer and closer.

"I don't do that kind of work." he fought back "Besides, I'm curious about how you'd do it," he said, right into her ear. "You'd have to clean me up too." Was he really insinuating totally inappropriate things at this time?

Rosé push him hard. "Don't come near me," and then she let out a sarcastic laugh. "Besides, I've got a better idea. You don't do shit, your magic does. Why don't you clean it?"

"I didn't do it."

"I didn't steal it," she said. She lifted her head up to meet his. "By the way, next time don't steal what's not yours."

"And why would I listen to you?"

Gustav was just standing by, watching them and laughing as usual. Rosé thought about going over there and punching him in the face but gave a 'be quiet' gesture and he raised his hands in a sign of surrender, which only made things worse.

"Because you have ears and I believe you're already too old and mature for it."

"And what will happen if I don't clean up? You're going to humiliate me in front of our incredible audience? You know I can kick your ass," he leaned closer and whispered. "Or better, slap it … so good that it is going to leave a beautiful mark. I'm really good when the subject is punishment"

Rosé flinched. "How sweet of you, but I would suggest using your hands, or better your snap, to clean it up. Besides, sweetheart, touch what you are not allowed to, and you die." Rosé took another step towards him and picked up his t-shirt again, lifting it up and rubbing it in his face. Rosé did not look at his defined abdomen, her concentration was on rubbing his face. "But it is good to know you are interested," she whispered.

Despite her best efforts, she couldn't resist looking at his exposed chest. She liked what she saw.

Rosé focus.

"I don't need to humiliate you." Rosé, with a smile on her face, dropped his shirt, letting her nails scratch his abs. "You already do it alone," she said and she began walking out of the cafeteria. Rosé ran to her room once she was clear of the canteen, laughing loudly down the halls, but scared to death at the same time.

That wasn't appropriate considering the circumstances.

(I was quite concerned about these two scenes. I don't know if it is appropriate to mingle them. They are two separated ones. Sorry if offended.)

<3

Rosé returned to her room. What had that been? Pure adrenaline still ran through her veins and a silly smile took hold of her face. She was happy. Had she just faced an Elite? Yes. And she was happy about that? Obviously.

She was leaning against the door, her gaze locked onto itself in the mirror. Her hair was a little messy, but she was happy. Something a little rare, taking into account what had happened.

She turned on the lights and opened the curtains, letting the light into her room.

Going to the bed she realized there was a box sitting on it. It was black with some grey details. There was a letter next to it.

She took it and, with impeccable calligraphy, was written:

Dear Smurf,

I decided to send you a letter because it will take a while for you to send a message of hate in response, or rub your hand in my face, and because according to you, I'm old. So, I decided to do it the old-fashioned way.

I accept your apologies for:

1. *Splashing your fucking juice in my face in front of everyone.*
2. *Drying your beautiful hand on my shirt.*
3. *Almost breaking my nose by rubbing the t-shirt (which you used to dry your beautiful hand) on my face, in front of everyone, and then walking away as if nothing had happened.*

To excuse myself for my childish behaviour of stealing your food, I hope you accept my little gift. Open the box before continuing this letter.

Rosé did as he asked. She unrolled the bow and opened the box. There was a juice box, the same one he had stolen from her. There was a little note on it. '*Drink now that it's still cold, I know you like drinks like that.*'

Rosé started laughing and took out the juice box. She couldn't believe what she was seeing. Would Kay really send her a present?

Maybe he wasn't that bad, and she had underestimated him.

Taking the first sip, Rosé spat it out immediately. Her mouth began to burn, and she had to run to get her water from the desk. Countless swear words were running from her mouth.

Furious, she took the letter.

However, you have declared war on my person. So, be prepared to suffer the consequences of your misbehaviour.

A huge, burned kiss on your cheek, my Smurf.

Let our war begin xx

Rosé thought of countless ways to kill him.

She took the phone and opened the chat, without thinking, sending an exaggerated number of emojis showing the middle finger, knives, and one with the face dead. She got up from the bed and threw the juice box in the trash. She went back to bed and crumpled up the letter, throwing it somewhere in the room.

The phone screen lit up and Kay responded with laughter, which made Rosé furious. She thought about throwing her phone on the wall or maybe on the other side of the room, but she needed it and it wasn't its fault that some idiot had provoked her. Why the fuck was he laughing? That wasn't funny at all.

Her heart stopped when his name appeared big on the screen. Rosé answered the call, but she didn't say anything.

"Hi princess, did you like my present?" He was laughing on the other end of the call.

"No, and don't call me a princess," she remarked.

"Why is that? Do you want me to keep calling you 'Smurf'?"

"No and I am not yours, I'd rather you call me Rosé."

"Rose?"

"Only if it's your ass."

"Do you want to see it?" That was a question that didn't deserve her answer. He laughed one more time. His dimples were probably showing up.

"That's never going to happen."

"I can call you 'my love' if you want."

"I'm not your love."

"Oh my feelings." He was sly, and she could hear the impact of his hand on his chest.

"I'm glad I hurt your feelings."

"You're going to have to do better, baby."

"Don't call me that," she said, blushing. She was thankful he was not there.

"I can't help it; you do things with my heart." Rosé didn't answer. What was that in her stomach? No, no, no, no, no, no. Kill, kill, kill. She thought about the butterflies. She didn't have butterflies in her stomach for Kay. Impossible.

"You're unbelievable," she said at last. The smile was inevitable. She tried to stay emotionless, but she couldn't. The smile on her face answered for itself.

"Are you smiling, princess?" he asked. No. Yes. She pictured him lying in bed. One of his arms behind his head. Legs crossed. Wait, why was she wondering how he was at that moment?

"I'm smiling at you trying to flirt with me," she said and hung up.

She couldn't deny that she liked his attention.

She slapped her own face lightly.

Rosélina, you stop with this shit. Your heart is blacker than a black hole and you don't fall in love with dumb, proud men like Kay.

Chapter 29

After dinner, everyone gathered in the gardens. There was a small altar in the middle of the circle of people and there she was.

Lucy was serene. Her flame-coloured hair stood out. She wore a white dress which Rosé deduced had been made by Misty since it was slightly wide on her small body. She imagined her making the dress for her friend as a form of thanksgiving and farewell. Her hands were perfectly positioned on her belly. She seemed to be asleep.

Rosé really wanted her to be just asleep.

Nobody wore black. According to their thinking, black meant darkness and pain. Negative energy to pass on to someone who deserved to sleep and rest in peace. Aiden was on her right side, holding her hand, and Misty on the other side. She had never seen Misty so mentally destroyed as she did this night. "She was so beautiful," whispered Misty. Rosé just agreed. Her eyes were still on Lucy. "Death is the only certainty we have, but it still takes us by surprise."

Death is the only certainty we have. We know that eventually, we're all going to die. We talk about death. We joke about it. We argue about it, but it comes so quickly and so unexpectedly that it often seems like a lie. A horrible, cruel lie. Something expected, but not desired. Something, even though you know how real it is, still takes us by surprise.

Death is the cruellest certainty in life and shows how human and fragile we are. The pain of those who stay cannot be measured so we go into a state of mourning, trying to convince our brain that everything is fine and that there are still memories. They don't kill the pain, but it keeps people alive in our minds, comforting a pain that we will one day know how to deal with.

Ari took a step forward and positioned herself in the corner of the altar. She passed her hands over Lucy's body, without touching her.

Within seconds her body turned into bright little balls that began to float in the air, and gradually rise into the starry sky. "People believe that burying someone holds them in the earth, but when delivered to the sky, it means that we are letting them go wherever they want, especially to the Upper World. It's like letting her go, leaving only the memories on earth. Also, when you want to feel close to that person, you don't need to go to the cemetery, you can simply look at the sky from wherever you are. This is where the expression comes from that one has become a star in the sky. This way of saying goodbye to people is from centuries ago," Misty explained, and she lay her head on Rosé's shoulder. "Sometimes we have to let people go."

Tears flowed down Rosé's face. She held Aiden's hand tighter, trying to hold on and control her feelings but she couldn't. He repaid the squeeze.

That was Astrea's Night.

The night they gave their late loved ones to the stars.

Chapter 30

"Who am I going to train with?" Rosé asked, curious.

"Kay." His name was like a punch in the stomach.

"No, no, no …"

"Can I finish?" Ari asked, she stopped what she was doing and looked at Rosé. Aiden had spoken about how Kay was the one who ran the training, but she didn't think he'd be responsible for her. It would be nice for her to be trained by someone experienced, but not Kay. Rosé nodded for Ari to continue. "Thank you. Kay …" Rosé rolled her eyes so hard it hurt, "will train you at the beginning with the basics. He has more patience than the others." Rosé looked at her, doubting what she had said. "Believe me, dear, I know what I'm talking about. He's going to prepare you so Gustav can train you martially. Fights. Defense. Ruby will take care of the weapons and Kay of magic further on." Rosé opened her mouth to protest. "No." Ari raised one finger. "Don't even start."

"What happens if … I end up killing them? It's a possibility."

Ariady let out a loud, hysterical laugh. It took her some time to recover from the shortness of breath it had brought on. "First, two of them, technically," she said, making a gesture with her hand, "… they're already dead. And second, you can try, but I'm sorry to inform you that you're going to fail. They've been through a lot and an inexperienced Lysion won't be able to kill them. Maybe later." She tried to ignore the fact that Ari had just insulted her.

"The instrument classes are going to be with Kay. The first ones at least. Some of it's going to be with Aiden and Misty and sometimes with Theo. He's got a busy life with that boy. They're calm and I think they'd be great for you because, as I heard, you got along very well."

"What about magic with Kay?"

"Forward."

When do I start?"

"Now," said a male voice behind her and it was by the smell of that *thing* she identified him. "Let's go." She turned very slowly, with the biggest grimace she couldn't even disguise. Kay was leaning against the door with his arms crossed. Rosé got up, taking one last look at Ari. "You will pay for this," she muttered. Ari just gave her a bemused smile and went back to doing her things.

"Have a great class, dear." Rosé wanted to show her the middle finger but had a lot of respect for Ari and would not do that.

Rosé passed Kay, bumping into him. "Good morning, Smurf. Happy face," he said, grabbing her hand and leaving a kiss. She still had a sour expression on her face.

"Didn't you have another name? Smurf's old."

"First, you're going the wrong way. Second, don't you like Smurf?"

"First, I'm going to my room to change. Second, how about Rosé?" she asked.

"First, you already have an outfit in the locker room waiting for you. Second … I like to be unique in the lives of others. I told you that." Rosé stopped and looked at him. *He wanted to be the only one?* Rosé laughed internally. *Poor thing.*

"Go ahead then," she commented, stretching her hand, giving him permission to pass. "Guide me to the right path."

"Shall we go?" Rosé just nodded and started following him. Kay was wearing a tighter blouse which left his defined muscles in plain sight. Rosé's eyes followed him until they hit his ass, which consequently he was very proud of, convinced that it was bigger than a normal male or even female ass. She didn't know how long she had been staring at his ass, but enough for Gustav to notice while passing.

"Liking the view, Rosélina?" Her face turned red and she realized they were already in the training camp. How long *had* she been staring at his ass?

"What are you talking about?" she asked, trying to keep herself as neutral as possible.

"I saw that you were admiring Kay's great ass. I thought you were innocent, but apparently, I was very wrong," he said, looking at Kay and then going back to her. "Your ass is a success among girls," he said, beating Kay's shoulder.

"Fuck you," Kay cursed.

"Do you come here often?" asked Gustav, making an annoying feminine voice and leaning on one leg, putting one hand around his waist. Rosé couldn't decide if that was hilarious or the strangest thing she'd ever seen.

"For love's sake," he disputed. "I have work to do. Is room eight empty?"

"Deserted."

Rosé took one last look at Gustav, he winked at her and then signaled an ass being squished, and then made an okay signal with his fingers. She wondered if he had already squished it, and she caught herself wanting to do that. Was it soft or hard due to training?

That was something else she'd have to find out.

Rosé refocused on her surroundings, taking in the training centre. She had never been there before. She just listened to the stories.

"So, you're interested in my"

"Shut up"

Upon entering, she came across grey stones on the walls and a specific floor for fighting. She could see Nikko training in a room with his twin brother, Lux. Kay took her to the locker room and handed her a black outfit. "Put that on and take off your shoes. The curtain is on the right-hand side."

Rosé picked up the clothes, keeping eye contact with Kay who did not take the trouble to deviate. Their hands touched when Rosé took the clothes. Something inside her happened and maybe she wasn't the only one. Kay let go before she could, she took her clothes and sat on the benches.

It bothered her a little to have a man on the other side waiting for her.

Rosé changed clothes, trying to make as little noise as possible, but the clothes were a little tight and charged her for her efforts. The pants escaped her hand, hitting her thigh hard, making her moan in pain.

"Alright, there?"

"Yes. This outfit is very tight."

"But it's elastic enough not to hurt you." But it did just that.

Rosé left the locker room holding her clothes in her hand. Her training suit was similar to Gustav and Kay's. Kay looked at her from top to bottom and headed towards her. "It took you ten minutes to change. Next time be faster," he said, taking the clothes that were in Rosé's hands, which made her protest. "This goes to your room."

"How?"

"What is that?" he asked, pointing to something. Rosé turned to look, but it was too late to realise her mistake. When she turned her gaze back to his hands, they were empty. "Okay, they're in your room. Let's go."

In the room, there were some instruments around, but Kay went towards the bats. "Do you know how to use them?" he said, delivering one to her. Rosé thought to say yes, her father had already shown some her techniques when she was little, if she needed to defend herself. Rosé was only now understanding what it was she was to defend herself from.

"No," she lied.

"What's your dominant hand?"

"Right."

"Great. It goes below and the left hand is on top," he said, showing her. Rosé obviously already knew that and did it without needing him to finish the sentence. "You have a small hand." Rosé looked at his and blinked. She couldn't believe what he had just said. *Bastard.* "Now defend."

"What ...?" Rosé couldn't finish the sentence as Kay was already attacking. Rosé quickly defended and they began to fight. Kay was certainly much more skilled than her, yet Rosé managed to defend and attack for a while until her bat flew up and fell a few feet from them.

"Rule number one: don't let go of the bat. Try to hold it as tightly as you can," he said, opening his hand, which the bat willingly flew to, and delivered it to Rosé again. Sometimes she'd forget she was in a magic-controlled place. "Rule number two: don't lie to me," and then he struck again. This time Rosé lasted much less time than the first. Sweat was already dripping down her face.

"Tired? We didn't even start," he said, a curve in his lips.

And they started fighting one more time.

Kay was much faster than her, besides being much older, and he had certainly done it countless times before. Rosé's ability to keep up with the fight was diminishing with each passing minute. Her body was exhausted. She couldn't take it anymore. She surrendered.

"Already? It took a while. I've trained people who couldn't take five fights." He extended a bottle of water to her. Rosé drank it all at once. Her lungs were fighting for air.

"Have you trained many women?" she asked, going to throw away the empty bottle, but before she got there, she felt a weight in her hand and when she looked at the bottle it was full again. She left it on a table and returned to the middle of the room.

"Are you jealous, Smurf?" he asked, with the tone of satisfaction that infuriated her.

"Not at all. But the female and male bodies have a difference, so ..." Kay turned Rosé around, returning his bat to its place. "Are we done?"

"No. I'm going to fix some things you're doing wrong. In this case, there are several and I want you to practice it in your free time." It sounded more like a demand than some advice. "The first is the legs, you're not flexing them all the time. They're your balance point. A hard hit will make you fall quickly." He demonstrated the right way and how she should move. She imitated him and sometimes he had to touch her leg to adjust it. The heat overcame her body. "You're also making the same defence move, there are others," he said, demonstrating some positions. "The same for attacks. And lastly, connect with the bat."

"How? Making a mental connection with it?" she said, mockingly.

"Yes. Stand in defence," he ordered. Rosé obeyed. Kay moved to the back of her and positioned himself. "Lock your body, you need to defend yourself." His mouth was near her ear. "Close your eyes," he stepped back. A sense of disappointment burned in her chest. Rosé obeyed. "Now connect with it, as if you were one. They are not ordinary bats." Rosé concentrated as much as she could until something ran through her body and Rosé felt ready to fight. Opening her eyes, she could feel them slightly burning.

"Now fight." And that's what Rosé did. She felt more willing to do it. She didn't know what she was doing. Her body seemed to be on automatic and, before Rosé realised, Kay was on the ground and his bat far away, but before she could celebrate, Kay was already standing again, bat in hand, attacking and attacking again.

Then, she was against the wall, her hands stuck to the side of her body. "Another rule, dear: never celebrate too soon and never give up too soon," he remarked, holding her more against the wall. He had a smug look on his face. She wanted to break that cute face. She was tired of him. Rosé continued to stare into his greyish eyes, then she let a slight smile slip onto her face.

Rosé realized that Kay's eyes went from her eyes to her mouth.

"Why are you smiling? Are you enjoying the view?"

"It's not really the view," she said, keeping her smile on her face.

Oh no? Then what?"

"This," she said, lifting one of her knees toward the middle of his legs. His smile disappeared in the blink of an eye.

Kay didn't fall to the ground as expected, writhing. He trapped her further against the wall and rested his head on Rosé's shoulder. "I'll pretend you didn't do that," he grunted. There was a pain in his voice. "You're lucky I'm in a good mood and, believe me, one day you'll regret what you've done."

Rosé let a loud and scandalous laugh come out. “I don’t think so,” she said, dropping the bat, Kay did the same, releasing her. “I’m done. I think our class is over,” she said, getting rid of him and going to the door. Her body was aching. “And that was for the juice. We’re at war, aren’t we?”

“Almost. The class doesn’t end until I say it’s done,” he commented, pulling her arm. Rosé complained. “Is there any way you can stop complaining for a moment?”

“Is there any way you can stop being an idiot?” she countered. She was in his arms, and she didn’t know how that happened.

“Is there any way you can stop getting so beautiful when stressed?”

Rosé opened her mouth to answer but closed it. She didn’t know how to answer that, she just let go of him.

“So that’s how to shut your mouth,” he said, crossing his arms. A huge smile flooded his face again. Fuck. “Interesting.”

“There are many ways to shut my mouth.” Rosé straightened up, waiting for his next answer. She was curious about how far this was going. A curiosity she was no longer able to control.

“I think I’m going to stick with that form at the moment. Maybe one day I’ll decide to use another one. Something more interesting.” Rosé didn’t answer. Kay was the one who moved first to release and put the bats in place. "Or maybe the other way round. Scream" Rosé just admired him. *Asshole, asshole. Son of a bitch.* “The next practice is tomorrow at the same time.”

“Okay.”

“And drink this,” he said, delivering what looked like a tea bag. “Just put it in water and drink. It’ll help with the pain. You don’t have any muscles trained and you need them. At eight p.m., I will be in your room to pick you up. Now you are dismissed.”

“Are you asking me out? What makes you think I’m going out with you?” Rosé inquired, taking the water bottle and putting the powder in it. *I hope it’s not some kind of poison.*

Kay approached her once more. His face was a few inches from hers again. Cheeky. “Can’t I? And it’s not necessarily a date, Smurf. I’m going to take you to a place with a lot of other people in it.” He walked away from her and smiled. “Like hell, I’m going to ask you out on a date.”

“I can’t wander around at night.”

“Right, I forgot that the baby needs time to sleep,” he commented, making fun of her. “As if you spent all the nights in your room.”

"I'm not a baby," she answered. "You pay too much attention to me"

He got closer again. His mouth was next to Rosé's ear. "Eight o'clock and don't worry, I'm not going to let anyone touch you, beautiful thing"

Rosé left the room, leaving him behind. A feeling of anguish was in the heart. She wanted more and at the same time, she wanted to punch that stupid, perfect face. *Don't worry, I'm not going to let anyone touch you, beautiful thing.* She should have taken a stronger knee to him.

She was angry.

She passed Nikko once again, who was training alone but blindfolded.

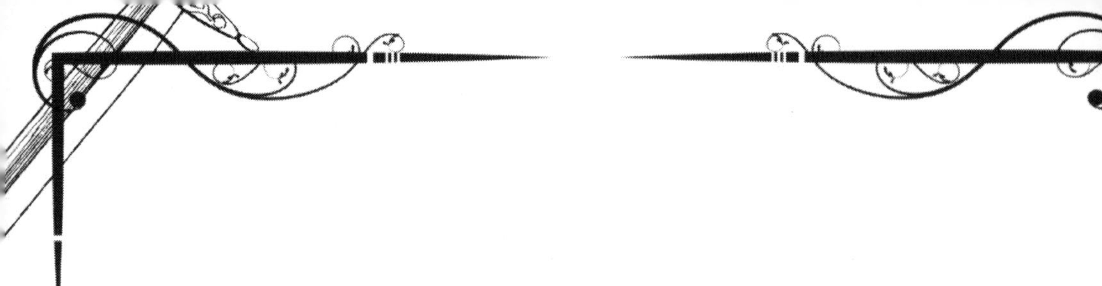

Chapter 31

The wall clock was showing five in the afternoon. Rosé had already gone to lunch with Aiden and her friends. Most of the time was spent trying to cheer Misty up. She was still affected by Lucy's death. It looked like she couldn't sleep.

The rest of the day she spent in the library because she needed to finish a cliché idiotic novel that she had begun a few days ago. Besides going to visit her father in his office.

They were still trying to get along. Both sides were trying to make it work again.

6 p.m.

Rosé took her things and went to take a bath, which took longer than she expected. She washed her body, her hair, and shaved.

6:40 p.m.

"Okay, what am I going to wear if I don't know where I'm going?" Rosé left some clothes prepared and decided she was going to wait for him to arrive so she could ask.

7:30 p.m.

Rosé was still trying to apply eyeliner and finish her makeup. She had already lost count of how many times she had to start over. She wanted to call him and cancel, but she changed her mind.

8 p.m.

A knock on the door made Rosé jump and mess up her eyeliner once more. "Son of a bitch," she cried without even thinking that he could have heard her. "Enter." Kay was dressed in black jeans, matching the black top that made his muscles all too evident.

"I expected to be better welcomed and, by the way, the princess is not yet ready." The two exchanged glances in the mirror. "Why am I not surprised?"

"I'm almost there. I just need to finish the fucking line that you made me miss when you knocked on the fucking door," she complained.

"Relax, sweetie! Are you going to go dressed like that?" Rosé was still in short pyjamas. Too short for him to see her in, but at this point, she didn't mind.

"Of course not. I didn't know where we were going so I don't know what clothes to wear. There are some on the bed, you could pick some for me since you know the place, or you could tell me." Kay moved towards the bed.

"It's a surprise." For some reason, Rosé felt a grip on her heart at letting Kay touch her clothes.

"Does that fit you?" he asked, lifting a black dress.

"Yes, why?" She had managed to apply cat eyeliner and now proceeded to the mascara, to finish.

"Nothing, it must be very tight on your curvy body." He put the dress back on the bed, along with the others.

"Are you calling me fat?" she asked, looking at him.

"Any problem with having more fat? Because for me it's even better." He took another outfit and began to analyse it. He seemed quite concentrated on his job.

Rosé was not synonymous with skinny, but she also did not have many curves. She was in the middle, depending on the part of the body you were referring to. She had never loved her body, but she also did not live in hatred with it.

Well … ups and downs.

"Have you decided on the clothes? Because I'm ready."

"Yes," he said, delivering a black skirt and a cropped black top. Rosé took it and went to the bathroom to change. She tried to be as quick as possible.

"You have many black clothes," he remarked on the other side of the door.

She stopped what she was doing. The skirt was midway on her thighs. Fear invaded her body. "Are you messing with my wardrobe?" Now she was getting dressed more quickly. How could she trust her room with an idiot like him?

"Maybe."

"Get out of there."

"Hmm if you don't hurry, I'll leave."

Rosé didn't take long to change. Regardless of where they were going, she put on a pair of trainers and went.

She was firmly a member of the 'trainers above heels' team.

<3

The corridors were empty, just like any other night. The sound of their shoes echoed in the hallway.

"Are you sure this isn't going to get us into trouble?"

"Of course, not and you are with me," he said, putting his arm over her shoulder, pulling her close to him.

"You're not that much."

Kay let out a laugh that echoed in the hallway and by instinct, Rosé slapped his abdomen "Are you crazy?" Kay kept laughing and pulled her even closer to him. His other hand was on her back.

"Are you scared?"

"I don't know if you know, love, but I'm not a legend that's part of the Elite, or whatever you are. I have rules to follow because, I don't know if you forgot, but there are people after me, wanting me dead, and at any moment they can invade this place." Kay looked at her. She hated it. It was a look that made her shut up and not contradict him, as well as making her stomach become a dance school for butterflies.

His pupils were dilated, and the side smile made her … *Rosélina.*

"I know very well my responsibilities and yours in this palace," he started "As I told you, I'm not going to let anyone touch you. Before they get to you, they're going to have to go through me. And you didn't seem to care about that every night you were wandering around. We've reinforced security measures; you don't have to be afraid and … what did you call me?" There was a strange sensation in her body that shouldn't be there.

"I don't know what you're talking about." Of course, she knew what he was referring to. "Now why don't you step aside?"

"You know very well what I'm talking about. What was it, hm … Love?"

"Irony, have you heard of it?"

"Does that bother you? Me holding you?"

"No, but you shouldn't do that." Honestly? Since when? She couldn't deny it, but the way he held her was different. The right strength and the grip.

"I can hear your heart from here," he whispered against her neck. She couldn't take it and closed her eyes, enjoying the warmth of his breath on the sensitive point of her skin. "It's out of control." His lips swelled around her neck. Her hands went instinctively to the back of his neck. "Have you been told that your neck looks delicious?" She shook her head slightly. "Your neck looks delicious, love." Her legs were wobbly, if he wasn't holding her tightly, she would have fallen. *Rosé focus, but … but …* "Can I?" She didn't know what she said or the expression on her face, but she could soon feel his warm, soft lips on her neck.

The piercing rubbing on her neck.

She wanted more. More from him. More of his touch. *Fuck. Fuck. Fuck.*

A moan came out of her mouth, making her come back to reality.

"Shall we?" she asked with irregular breathing, getting rid of him. "And don't ever do that again."

"Of course, princess." He was smiling. "And I'll stop when you really want me to stop."

Never then. Fuck, little son of a bitch. Why do feelings develop for those who hate us? I do, I want more. Fuck!

They arrived at an old wooden door, which anyone else would not have even noticed. Kay opened the door and, looking inside, Rosé saw a ladder leading to the dungeons.

"Are you trying to kidnap me or what?"

"You like to ask questions. Just enter."

Rosé obeyed and began to descend the stairs. The cold air made her skin tingle. "It's going to get warmer when we get there." They went down a few more flights of stairs and when they finished their descent, she could hear music, it was getting louder. They came to another door. Kay passed in front and opened the door, from there hot air found her skin. The place was illuminated by spotlights of vibrant colours as if it were a ballad. Music was playing at a high volume.

"Rosélina, you came," said Gustav, hugging her. "I thought you'd be too tired after your training. Kay can be really rough sometimes" Gustav smiled looking from Kay back to her.

"Good to see you," said Ruby, who was right behind him. "Come, I want to introduce you to someone." Ruby had never presented Rosé to anyone, and their conversations were always short. Almost nonexistent.

Rosé looked at Kay and cast a glance, asking if she should trust her and he understood the message, whispering in her ear, "She must be drunk."

Ruby's hair was tied in two long braids and was apparently white again.

They moved down to the main hall. There was a wall full of graffiti and a blue-haired girl with a can of spray paint was finishing a lion drawing.

"Skylar, this is Rosélina. Rosélina this is Skylar." The young woman who was previously graffitiing stopped what she was doing and turned around. Rosé couldn't see much of her face because she was wearing a mask. Rosé waited for someone with a Ruby-like personality but was surprised when she took off her mask and jumped toward Rosé, hugging her hard, almost causing them both to fall. Why does everyone here hug so strongly? They want to kill people. Once she let go, Rosé could see her face better. She was a young Asian girl.

Her hair was bluish black, but with red tips. She had orange and gold eyes. Somehow Asian features. Maybe it was her eyes or… she was not really sure.

"It's so nice to finally get to know you," she said excitedly, holding Rosé's hands. "I'm Skylar, but hardly anyone calls me that. You can call me Sky. Feel free to call me whatever you want. Oh, and I'm the Princess of the Down World. Now, seriously, you two need a little colour. There're brushes and neon paint over there, make yourselves at home."

Rosé felt a hand on her back and, as she turned around, she saw Kay behind her. "Let's go." But before going, Rosé turned to Sky. "I've never seen you on the surface."

"I'm not a big fan of that place, I like to stay here." It made sense if she was who she said she was. "Besides, the bullet shots make more noise down here." Rosé stared, wide-eyed, trying to process what she had just said, but Kay pushed her away before she could say anything else.

They headed to a table full of paint pots and brushes of all sizes. "What do you want me to draw on you?"

"I don't trust you to draw something on me."

"Well, have I ever let you down?"

"Many times." She thought a little. "Surprise me."

The cold paint came into contact with the warm skin of her arm. The brushstrokes were light and careful. Looking at him, he was focused, drawing carefully on her. His lips were perfectly full and red.

His piercing on the side of his lower lip moved along with him.

She wanted to grab it on her lips and taste his mouth.

It took him a while to finish.

"Ready," he said, putting the brush in the water. Looking in the mirror, she saw there were several stars drawn around her neck, down her shoulder, and across her collarbone. He had also painted a pair of wings. There was a rose with several circular designs around it.

"Explain?" she said, turning to him.

"It's the first thing that comes into my head when I think of you. I'm your guardian angel and the rose, I think you already know."

"Guardian angel?" Kay didn't answer.

"My turn." Rosé was not quite an artist, but something that she was always good at drawing was roses, because of her name, but she found it unfair and unfunny to do since he had drawn them on her.

Kay's arms were larger than Rosé's and defined. In the light, it was full of tattoos and runes, but in the dark, it was difficult to see them. His skin was warm when Rosé started to draw some symbols and lines, like flames on his arm, and then, without much thought, she began to put the paint on her hand, without drawing attention, leaving a mark on the top of his chest that was bare. She gave a shy smile.

"What the hell did you do? Tell me you didn't draw a dick," he asked, getting up to go look in the mirror, but Rosé held him still and he didn't fight it.

"No, I haven't, and I'm not done yet." Rosé took the white paint and positioned herself in front of him, pretending to make dots above his eyebrow and then two lines on each cheek. But it was just an excuse to put no on the other side of his neck and on his arm. Leaving her mark on it.

Their faces were close, but Rosé had not noticed.

"Do you want to get closer?" His voice was like a whisper. Rosé woke up from her concentration and looked at him. She held his gaze for a while and leaned away. "Your lips are tempting, you know that?"

Rosé started to draw again. "If I didn't know you, I'd say you're trying to flirt with me because you are interested, but people like you throw women away after you have finished enjoying them." She didn't give him time to answer. "I'm done." Kay went to the mirror.

"Not bad, Smurf. I like the symbols, but I don't understand the hands on my neck and on my chest."

"Marking my territory," she said. putting some more paint on her hand and positioning it on top of his t-shit. She put her hand on his face. Kay watched her every move. She wiped clean her hands and approached him again "I also know how to play, Kay," Rosé whispered in his ear leaving a quick kiss close to his lips and moving away, he tried to catch her, but she was already too far away.

She looked at him and smiled, before leaving to mingle with the crowd.

<3

There weren't many people at the party, so she soon spotted the Elementris in the corner. Everyone but Nixie.

"Rosé," they said in unison.

"I love the angel on your arm," Misty said. All of them were covered with drawings and symbols on their faces and bodies. She looked deep into Misty's eyes, trying to find evidence that she was struggling. She soon realised that Misty was doing fine and was glad of the distraction.

A chaotic rap started playing. Misty grabbed Theo and Rosé by the arms and pulled them onto the dancefloor. Aiden followed them and began to dance. Rosé was not a good dancer, so she just imitated the others. Rosé realised almost everyone was on the dancefloor.

She danced until she couldn't anymore.

Rosé realized that Aiden and Misty had glasses in their hand and asked where they had gotten them, she was directed to the other side of the room.

When she got there, she was met with a large array of drinks and a bartender cleaning up some utensils.

"Hey."

"How can I help?"

"One—"

"Bloody Soul," commented Kay after her. "She's never had that drink and I think this is a great opportunity." The bartender obeyed. He seemed nervous. His hands shaking holding the glass. Rosé could see his hands shaking and his gaze lowered when Kay appeared.

"I honestly think you have something with me because you won't stop following me," she remarked, waiting for her drink.

"Don't think you are too special, love. I'm responsible for you, you forget? And … you can't just say things and leave as nothing happened."

The man handed over her drink and she took a sip. She could feel the sweet taste of the strawberry with something acidic and a burning sensation of alcohol in her throat. She smiled at him. "Just watch," she said, going back to the crowd with her drink.

But he didn't know how to just observe.

He pulled her by the waist, making her go back to where she was, spilling some of her drink on her clothes. "Son of a bitch."

"Well done. That is for the juice box." Rosé left her to drink on the table and wiped her hand and arm on Kay's t-shirt once again while smiling at him. "If someone kills me, your DNA would be on almost all my clothes."

"Of course, it will because I'm going to be the one to kill you," she said.

"I have no doubts abo—" he commented.

"What's taking you so long? You're missing the whole shit," interrupted Theo, appearing from nowhere and leaving his glass on the table.

"She's just going to finish her drink. She's already got wet, it'd be awful if she got even more so," Kay said to him, as if she wasn't there. Another phrase that could easily be twisted.

Theo left abruptly.

"I can speak for myself, you know?" Rosé turned the glass over and left it empty on the table.

Kay put his hand on Rosé's cheek and then on her arm. "Of course, you can."

She went back to the dancefloor, to her friends. The alcohol was already working on her blood. She was looser and danced until she felt her body sweat. "What happened to your face?" asked Misty. "Whose hand, is it?"

Rosé put her finger on her face and saw that there was red paint on her. She looked at her arm where he had also put his hand. "Someone who will die soon," she commented.

"I think we both know how to play," said a voice behind her. She didn't dare turn. She knew exactly who it was. She kept dancing until the tiredness hit.

It'd been a long time since she felt that way. Adrenaline. Feeling happy and forgetting that someone was after her. Chasing her.

She felt like a normal person.

She had a few more drinks. She danced with everyone around her and on the way met Skylar who seemed to have drunk more than she did. There were some girls dancing on a table, breaking what was on them. She smiled. Theo and Aiden were great dancers and moved like she had never seen a man do before.

Her legs were already aching.

But she didn't care.

Her vision saw nothing but figures and flashes. She stopped and looked around. Adrenaline, alcohol, and heat took over her body. It had been a long time since she had been parting, and, most of all, allowing herself to drink and actually enjoy it with people she likes.

She used to hate parties. She was always afraid of what could happen. The sexual assaults, drink spikes, etc.

She walked away and sat down at a table, looking around. She tried to dry the sweat off her face, but it was useless. Her body was wet, and she was stinking of alcohol. She tried to get her heart back to normal. Normalize the breathing, but the air was too heavy.

She got out her phone and started going through some social media. She wanted to rest before going back, but it didn't help. Everything seemed too crowded. Too many people and she didn't feel like staying anymore.

Aiden came to sit beside her for a second. He asked if everything was okay and offered to stay with her. He was sweating like her, drunk and a little dizzy. He could barely form a proper response.

She asked him to go have fun.

In another corner Gustav and Sky were graffitiing and Ruby was drinking something and dancing. She was quite sure she saw some people with pointed ears. Maybe some Olvs came here for partying. "Social battery running out?" Kay was by her side.

"For fuck's safe, don't you get tired of chasing me?"

"I'm just chasing you here. We are in Amondridia and not in a perfect country for a woman to go out and have fun without worrying. I brought you here and you're my responsibility. When you come here alone, you will be on your own."

"Why don't you look tired?"

"It takes me a while to get tired, beautiful thing." Rosé kept that information. She knew why but didn't want to admit it.

"You don't even look like you drank."

"I'm on duty." Rosé looked confused. "You're my job, idiot. Let's go. Your battery seems to be almost depleted."

"I hate you," she said, getting up. He held her in place. The world was still moving too fast for her to keep up.

Kay took her in his arms "Tell me something I don't know."

"I've thought about killing you in a lot of ways." she let her body relax on his touch.

"I know that too."

"Your lip piercing is tempting. It makes me want to kiss you." She covered her mouth, frightened by what she had said.

"That was interesting." She didn't have to look at him to know about the smile and his dimples. "If you were not drunk, we could have taken care of it."

"You are so fucking annoying."

"And so fucking delicious."

"I am that," she said, laughing.

"I don't disagree."

Chapter 32

Rosé continued her training with Kay for almost a week. She had learned different defence poses and how to dodge certain enchantments and spells which had been helpful and easy until he began using magic against her and her anger at him only increased more and more.

Ari had made herself available to teach some potions, especially healing potions and some combinations of poisoning, in case she ever needed it, but she did not have as much patience as Rosé had imagined. When she first met Ari, she was calm and her voice was quiet, but that had changed a little.

As she was interested in the subject, she picked it up fast, but she still needed practice.

Rosé finished lunch with the Elementris as usual. She looked at the table where Kay and the others sat, but it was empty, just like breakfast. Rosé began to notice that it was often completely empty, or that one or the other was not present at times.

She went to her room and changed clothes and headed to the training camp where Ruby was already waiting. She was hoping she wouldn't show up so she would be able to take time off or practice what Kay had taught her.

The training was different from the training with Kay. Ruby was more serious and charged more than he did. For a few minute,s she wished it was Kay who was there because Ruby was horrible at teaching, which made Rosé angry and Ruby even more so.

A total catastrophe, but she continued without complaining.

The first thing she gave Rosé when she arrived was a piece of metal that looked like the support of the sword. When she touched it, it turned into a shiny black dagger.

The dagger was much heavier than Rosé imagined, and she was wondering how Ruby could fight with heels on. She was getting distracted by the sound the shoes made with every move.

"How do you know all this?" asked Rosé. Ruby had given numerous tips and tricks to hold the dagger and confirmed that over time her body would get used to the weight to the point of being able to throw it and hit the target easily.

"Because that's how I've survived all my life," she said in the midst of training. Her face was blank. No emotion. She had nothing sympathetic in her voice. She stood tall and firm. Authoritarian. She showed no facial expression at any time.

Daggers were replaced by swords, increasing their size gradually, and then came some 'simpler' guns, according to her.

Rosé's arms were asking for help.

"Don't you have powers or anything?"

In countless books, vampires were portrayed as fast, white, blood-drinkers, and sensitive to sunlight, but Gustav ate and was always exposed to the sun.

"No. I'm a vampire and not a wizard or Elementri or any of these bunches of idiots with something coming out of their hand," she remarked, pressing her lips together, forming a straight line. "Watch your elbow," she said, straightening it out.

"I thought you could run fast and had to hide from the sun."

"Half of what you hear in the Outer World is true and the other idiocy. We are more agile than normal human beings. Our body weighs less which makes us more flexible, and quick to do things, but nothing too abnormal like some books and tales say and I don't know if you've heard but the sun you feel on your skin is pure magic. It's not real."

"Have you ever drunk human blood? Or do you smell it?" Rosé had never dared to ask Ruby that before, even though she had known her for a long time now.

"I thought we were training and not on a Q&A talk show."

Rosé had never realised that she did not have a British accent, she was different and went almost unnoticed. Aiden had commented that her family heritage was detailed in books, maybe one day she'd find out where Ruby was from. "Sorry. I never had the guts to ask you that."

Ruby let out a long and scary laugh. "Courage? Am I that scary? And second," an icy blade found Rosé's neck. "Rule number one of coexistence with me. Never. Ever. Apologise. The world doesn't apologise to you, so don't apologise to the world. Never put your head down unless it's to protect your neck and don't let melodrama in the room. I don't like feelings; they make you look human and I'm not able to feel them anymore."

She took the blade from Rosé's neck and analysed it. "When you've killed countless people and gone through death, dear, feelings are your least concern." She bequeathed the blade to the side of her body and looked thoughtfully at Rosé. "I do not even remember the last time I felt something for someone." She moved her body as if she had felt a chill. "Disgusting. Only one of us was able to fall in love again and today we are suffering the consequences of it." She smiled lightly and then returned to her usual face. "I thought we were training."

"You're intimidating."

"It's good to know that people are afraid of me. I like that, and I've had human blood when things were different. Humans ate real food, not that crap. So, as you can smell food from afar, I can smell blood."

"Does my blood smell good?"

"Not at all."

Ruby attacked her again. The sound of the blade echoed through the room. Ruby didn't seem to drop a bead of sweat or blood while Rosé was sweating like never before and with small cuts on her arm and hands.

Their training continued for a long time. Rosé had already learned to dodge, like falling in style without getting hurt, how to defend herself and how to use certain parts of the body to her advantage. Although Ruby was very demanding, she had learned more in her class than from Kay. Maybe it was because they talked less, and Ruby was more practical. Kay's template was practice, talk, be a jerk, practice.

"In the next training session, we go to another part of the training centre. I'll wait for you at the door."

"What are we going to do?"

"Weapons, not the one Kay gave you. Other. Guns. Bigger and deadlier." A shiver ran through Rosé's body. She told Ruby she hadn't touched that kind of weapon before and didn't intend to. That would be a humiliation. Ruby would have shot a lot of guns in her life by now, and she should be a master at it. Rosé didn't know how old she was, but she knew she was much older than maybe Rosé could imagine.

It was strange to imagine that everyone there was extremely old, at least a part of them. Ruby and Gustav, Kay. Even her father.

She was just a young, helpless soul in the midst of professional killers.

Rosé needed a bath to soothe the horrors from training and was stinking. Her body was destroyed, and she was thinking of eating in her room today.

Chapter 33

Rosé returned to the tower to observe the stars. It reassured her. It made her forget all the craziness in her life. She often ended up sleeping right there and waking up with horrible back pain, but over time she got used to it.

She didn't go to many places in Amondridia. She didn't know the place very well; she hadn't been there long and Rosé didn't know many people to show her the sights.

Besides the tower and the dungeons, she would go find Ari in a greenhouse where they talked about the medicinal properties of plants and how important they were to the world, and she almost freaked out when she found a plant with more than medicinal advantages in the middle of them. They also talked about the magical world, gossiped about people, and Rosé talked about her life in southern Brazil and London.

Ari seemed to be interested.

Ari didn't like to talk about her personal life very much, so they talked about others and Rosé didn't even try to bring it up, although she was very curious. She wanted to know about her family, something Ari had never mentioned before. She wanted to know about boys or insecurities.

Sometimes she was found in the enormous library. Rosé had even lost count of how many times she got lost inside. There were rooms inside a single room if you know what I mean. There were a lot of books in there. There were only a few books she had been able to read from start to finish. Rosé liked to go there because it was quiet.

There were no people wandering around. It was the perfect place to think. Quiet and inspirational. That's why Ari used to spend so much time there as well. She had no one to disturb her.

Ariady didn't feel uncomfortable when she met Rosé there. She always kept quiet, reading something like Ari. There were a lot of cats there. They were one of the only things that seemed normal in that place. Mr Bebbols was the only one who could talk. The rest were cats. Just cats.

The Cielo Tower was probably the last tower in the palace and where she would spend some of her nights. Sometimes she would go back there when she wanted to be alone and watch the kingdom from above, even though there was only the sea and the forest of the Olvs.

There was another tower similar to that one, almost the same height, not far away. Rosé couldn't deny her curiosity, but it wasn't easy. She was certainly a little lazy.

That day, Rosé had decided not to go anywhere different but go find Ari in her greenhouse. She liked to sit on the table and watch her work.

Upon arriving, Ariady was wearing a long white lab coat and goggles. Her usual pink hair was stuck in a high ponytail, half loose and slightly curled. It was impossible not to recognize Ari, her hair was unique. Maybe it was because no one dared to do the same because they knew no one would look prettier than her in that baby pink shade. It was like her trademark.

She seemed very concentrated, dripping something into one of her plants. The greenhouse wasn't like last time. There were plants missing. New ingredients on the shelves. The last time she came, it was raining and today the sky was clear, no false clouds in the sky.

Upon noticing Rosé's presence, Ari raised her head and greeted her.

"Hello," she said, turning her attention back to the plant in front of her and three books floating in the air.

"Hi," Rosé said, sitting on the table, in the same place as always. Ari never put chairs there, not even an armchair, so she got used to sitting there. Sometimes Ari would complain, but Rosé wouldn't care if any acid burned her ass.

As she watched more closely, Rosé realized that the plant in front of Ari was carnivorous, not only that one, but so were the others who were on the opposite side of where she was sitting. Ari carefully dripped something in its 'mouth' and in a quick act the plant closed.

"What's that?"

"Dead mosquitoes mixed with water and sugar," she responded naturally while Rosé made a face of disgust. "I'm just feeding them." The page of one of the books turned and Ari started reading it.

"What about the other tests?"

"Decide to take a break," Ari informed, dripping the disgusting liquid in the last carnivorous plant.

"Why?"

She stopped what she was doing and turned to Rose who stared back. "You ask a lot of questions, you look like a little kid, and I think it was kind of clear why," she said, holding a dropper in one hand and the franc in the other, looking slightly irritated. "I'm sorry."

Silence.

"I'm the one who has to apologise. At times I …" She stopped for a little while. "Sometimes I forget you don't know much about this world and … it's just weird, you know? You've grown away from everything and everyone. I saw you as a baby and then you show up as an adult in such a short time. That's … scary, and the plants were going very wrong. I killed a lot of others after you left." Ari let out a slight laugh. "I want to analyse the results I've achieved so far and then come back."

Ari disappeared into another room. "I have something for you," she called. She came back with a small box in her hand. "I have kept this, and many other things, hidden from the eyes of others. At your mother's request, of course. I think it's time for you to receive it."

Rosé took it and eagerly opened it. There was a black dagger, with decorative red roses, not to mention the spiked ones all over the hilt. "It was your mother's dagger. She carried it all over the place." Ari picked up weapon support and handed it to Rosé who positioned it on the thigh.

Rosé admired it before putting the dagger in place.

"There's a tale about it. Once again in a distant kingdom … lies and more lies and blah blah. Fuck it. In northern Europe, a witch, one of the most beautiful in the village, fell in love with an ordinary man. To her surprise her love was reciprocated. After months together of much love and affection, the man began to feel threatened by the power that the witch had. He was cowardly and an ordinary stupid fucker—" "I don't think that's in history," Rosé mocked.

"It's not, but I thought it was important to point this out."

"They married and had a very happy life. A perfect marriage, despite his fear." Her tone was annoyed, like she has told that tale so many times in her life "But on an unexpected day, a new family arrived in the village and among them was another woman, more beautiful than the witch. Her husband no longer paid attention to his wife, and she suspected that he was having an affair with this other woman. One day she became so paranoid and suspicious, that she started following him and found that her husband used to give that women red and black roses.

"Angrily, the woman decided to poison all the existing roses. A poison that with a simple touch could kill someone in the worst possible way and when her husband touched another rose, he dropped dead, a black liquid coming out of all possible holes. When his mistress went to help him, she touched the rose and there she passed away by his side.

"From that moment on all red and black roses began to be seen as cursed roses. The end."

Rosé couldn't hide her disappointment. "No happy ever after?"

Ari laughed loudly, leaving Rosé uncomfortable. "Happily ever after? Do you still believe that? Oh dear, in real life there is no 'happily ever after.' Stop believing that. Forever does not exist, and let's be honest, no one is happy for the rest of their life. There is no prince and there is no true kiss, and … there's someone out there waiting for you." "Stop ruining my childhood," Rosé said, getting off of the table.

"No. And leave the stuff I gave you here. I will take it to your room."

As she left the greenhouse, Rosé's body tensed. All the hair on her body stood up. The sky looked beautiful. There was sun and few clouds, but it lied. It was cold.

A heavy coat appeared over her. Ari must have realized.

Rosé didn't know exactly where to go. There was nothing to see beside the huge Rocky Mountains that led to the end of the island, whose peak could not be seen as it was covered by black clouds.

Still watching the landscape that was in front of her, Rosé heard a strange loud noise. She couldn't tell what it was. It seemed like a cry of a desperate animal.

Rosé approached. The sound had repeated itself more than once. She flinched, not knowing what she could find ahead.

As she approached, a large, emerald-green creature appeared. She couldn't believe what she was seeing. The animal was huge. Rosé didn't know how she hadn't seen it before. Its wings were enormous. Grey horns came out of its head and something similar to fangs protruded from under its mouth.

A dragon.

Its body was not leather like Rosé had always imagined dragons. It looked like tree roots were wrapped around his whole body.

Looking around, there was a man near the dragon. That's what Ariady was referring to? The dragon?

As she came up to face the creature, the man noticed her and came to meet her.

"You must be Rosé," the man shouted, as he was too far away to be heard in at a normal volume. He was tall and young. He had dark skin and short, curly hair. His eyes were a strange tone of emerald and hazel.

"Yes."

"Josh. Josh Dodin. Sorcerer," he introduced himself, raising his hand to greet her with a sympathetic smile. Rosé held it. "Pleasure." "How did you know?" she asked.

"What?"

"My name. How did you know my name?"

"You must be kidding." He smiled, exposing his perfectly white and aligned teeth. "I don't think you fully understand what you are and that for many your existence is a myth. A story found in books and … Ari told me earlier. She also said she'd send you to see me, saying that, probably, you'd like to see this amazing creature." Rosé could see a different shine in his eyes upon mentioning the creature.

"I thought they only existed in fairy tales." Rosé was fascinated by that. She remembered reading about them in children's books and seeing them in fantasy films, but never imagined that they really existed.

He laughed loudly, "Glad not," as they approached the creature. The dragon sighed, echoing through the Lys. Rosé could feel its warm air on her skin.

She was shaking, not because of the dragon, but rather the cold.

They were getting closer and closer. "Isn't it aggressive?"

"Not if you don't provoke it. Besides, he just ate," Josh says, pointing to a huge stone, marked by blood. Rosé kept her gaze there for a second. "Don't worry, it wasn't a person," he said, still smiling, putting his hands in his pants pocket. There definitely was a different light in his eyes when he looked at the creature. A sparkle. His smile was like a child receiving a gift.

"He? A male?" asked Rosé. The dragon was lying down. Resting on the grass. His head down and wings retracted. It was looking at them both. "Glovn."

Glovn.

"I like it. I thought they were aggressive," said Rosé, hugging her own body. Even being close to a hot source of fire, the wind was not merciful.

Josh approached Glovn and stroked the corner of his body. "Some are. Too aggressive actually. It's in the nature of some animals to be aggressive. They need to defend themselves, but if treated the right way, they're no threat. Your mother demanded that all who arrived in Lys would be raised and treated in the right way. Fed and exposed outdoors, not trapped and kept in captivity. She didn't want to worry about them. That's why they're left on the mountain."

"They?" Rosé tried her best to hide her surprise. She was afraid of reacting too much at it. At everything. Everyone was so used to this, and she was the grown-up discovering the world.

"Apart from him, we have five more. They are three females and three males."

"Wow."

Josh laughed at her reaction.

"Where are the others?"

Josh pointed to the top of the mountain from which a waterfall cascaded.

"He's my favourite. He's the quietest," he informed. "The others are very agitated, difficult to deal with. Besides, he is the only one who doesn't complain about the weather here, even with our effort to make the most of it to make the weather good and pleasant for them. They're hard to impress."

There was a short silence, until Josh whistled. In a matter of seconds, the colossal dragon arose, obeying Josh's commands, exposing its huge wings. Josh had to dodge so he wouldn't get hit. "Wow buddy. A dragon's wing like that knocks you unconscious or even worse."

Josh was now at the creature's feet. He whistled again and the creature lowered his head so Josh could touch him.

"You can come. He doesn't bite. Just breathes fire and burns you," he joked.

"That's not funny."

"Of course it is, just stay away from his mouth, of course. And from the nose," he warned and made a noise with his mouth. "People who do not like dragons are strange."

In slow movements, Rosé approached. Memorizing every detail she could. Maybe that was her last living sight. Her heart was racing. The dragon was now watching her. She had never seen such a beautiful creature before in her life.

It was like one of the wonders of the world.

The dragon made a sudden move that scared both Josh and Rosé. She froze, not know what to do. Her breathing was heavy. Her hands were sweaty. Her eyes were fixed on the whitish eyes of the dragon that returned her look. A hole opened in her chest.

"Don't move," he advised. *Why the fuck would I move?*

The creature slowly moved his face closer to Rosé. She could feel the warmth coming from the dragon's nostrils again. *Fuck*, she was right in the spot she shouldn't be. Soon after, he lowered his head until it was on the ground again. Rosé shot a slight look at Josh, waiting for his command. She had noticed that he had also stopped breathing when, after a few seconds, his chest returned to moving up and down.

Rosé also breathed again, not knowing she had stopped doing it.

Slowly raised her hand and stroked Glovn. He was hot and rough.

She spent some more time talking to Josh about dragons. Josh explained how he became interested in dragons, about some curiosities about them and that he had just graduated in Dragology at C.A.E. He also said he would travel to China in a few days to take a look at some specific dragons there at a place called Cante.

"Do you speak Mandarin?"

"Not much, but they speak a little English. It's going to be a mix of the two."

"Good luck."

"Thank you. Besides, I'm going for the dragons. They don't speak any language."

They both laughed. Fair.

The dragon rested on the ground. Josh was leaning against his long neck. "How do you get there?" she asked, pointing up to the mountains. She felt stupid sometimes asking those questions. She was still young in this magic thing and, when she spoke loudly, she was ashamed. She could feel her cheeks flush with colour.

"Flying," he said half pensively. "I always call them through these whistles," he added, taking out of his pocket six whistles attached to a rope, as if they were keys, each a different colour. "Sometimes I use portals."

Glovn grunted and opened his eyes.

"Do you want to try?" Josh asked.

"What?"

"Flying," Rosé's eyes widened with the idea. She wanted to, but she also wants to stay alive a little longer. "You won't fall. I promise." She hesitated for a moment.

"Okay."

Glovn was still lying down. Josh held Rosé's hand and helped her climb the dragon and then Josh positioned himself in front of her. "Hold on tight," advised Josh. Rosé held his waist so hard that she could have broken his bone.

She didn't know if she really wanted to do this, but it was too late to reconsider. Josh had hissed and Glovn was already getting up and moving his huge emerald wings.

Within seconds, they were both flying.

It was even colder up there. The wind hit her in the face which kept her from enjoying the view a little. Lys seemed smaller from up there and the sea immense. It was funny to see Amondridia from above, the palace was not very attractive seen from above. Everything was beautiful, but in its own separate way. She was desparate to open her arms, but the fear was bigger than her.

She felt alive in the sky. Observing the world from another perspective.

Glovn took a few turns around the island before returning to the ground.

Her arms ached from holding Josh so tight.

<3

Ruby and guns should never stay in the same room. It took Rosé a few hours to recover from her last lesson.

Chapter 34

"You're not concentrating," Kay announced, irritation surging up inside him. His muscles were tense and veins bulged out his arms. Rosé couldn't take it anymore. She had started magic training with Kay and had not been able to do much other than making them both angry. "I've already told you to focus on your body. Your magic relates to your inner energy."

She took the dagger from her thigh and pointed it at him. "If you call me 'thing' one more time, I swear I'll cut your dick off."

Kay had come back from his mission, wherever that was. She had already asked them if one day she would be able to do something like this, but he said that was all in the future.

She was trapped in a palace and wasn't even the princess of its history.

Kay's magic training was different, yet annoying. She preferred it when it was fighting, because at least she had control over it, and it was a bodily and a human issue, not like her magic.

At times, she really thought about picking him up by the hair and rubbing him with asphalt.

Her life had been based on training and training. She had it in the morning with Gustav and the afternoon with Kay.

Sometimes morning training was alternated with Aiden, Misty, or Theo. They helped her master some of their matter since according to the tale she would have access to all the powers they had. She had managed to do some things, including making a flame appear in her hand, as well as almost rubbing it off Aiden's face, who wasn't too happy.

Air, she had greater domination over, since virtually every time she had access to her magic she was connected to the air. Misty had been patient about teaching her and gave all the details possible to help her with this.

Theo was the same. She loved the energy he was going through which made her feel more comfortable. He had taught her to make branches grow and to trap people in them. He taught her to use her arms and legs more specifically and she had done it with Ari once to test it and had succeeded.

"It's hard to do that when you're distracting me." They were already arguing from the moment she stepped into the room, in which, according to him, she was two minutes late and was not wearing the boots she was supposed to. They were protective and mandatory in all trainings. Did I mention she wanted to grab him by the hair and rub him with asphalt?

Kay stopped for a second, admiring her. "I'm a distraction to you?" There was malice and pride in his tone. Rosé wanted to puke on his face, but rolled her eyes and took a deep breath, ignoring that will. She wouldn't do that until she knew how to control her powers in case she had an outbreak.

Or not.

"Yes, you are. That sculpted body of yours and your enormous pride and ego." Regret struck immediately, but she was too angry for it. "And the fact that you're admired for your talent and you're part of the Elite without talking about the fact that there are countless people hoping I can do some shit. So yes, you're somehow a distraction and it makes me nervous."

Kay looked in the mirror and started contracting his muscles and making positions. "Sculpted body? I like it." She smiled and made an obscene gesture and he reciprocated, Rosé raised one more hand and the gesture was reciprocated one more time. "Have you finished showing off your beautiful middle fingers?" he asked. She nodded. Kay muttered again and a hand showing the middle finger appeared in the form of smoke.

Idiot. She needed to learn this shit. Rosé got up off the ground and took one of the bats that were there and hit out, but, as expected, nothing happened, because THE FUCKING BAT WENT THROUGH THE FUCKING CLOUD.

Kay started laughing at her. She took the bat and headed for his groin. He was too distracted for this, and Rosé saw an opportunity. She was tired of his ego and how he bragged. She needed to get what she couldn't get in the library. She wouldn't let the feeling of inferiority take over.

If you can't affect someone in one way, you find another way.

The bat was just short of hitting his precious jewels when one hand caught it before it found its target. Their eyes met. Bloody grey eyes. A dimple formed in the corner of his mouth. She hated them. (A big lie.)

"What do you have against it?" he asked, pulling the bat from her hands, but Rosé was holding it so tightly that she ended up being pulled along. "Any particular interest?"

Rosé could feel her face burn. She straightened up and fixed her blouse and then looked at it.

"Every night," she started, approaching him and playing with the collar of his shirt. Kay followed her movements, "When I'm alone in my room with lights out, I imagine putting my hand on them," she wet her lips and held his gaze, trying to make a sexy and sweet voice at the same time, she approached his ears lightly, getting on her tiptoes to get closer to him, "and nailing them to the wall. Tac. Tac. Tac," she whispered with an imaginary hammer in her hand and then she walked away, going to get her purse. "You, twisting on the floor, is my pleasure. And since you're not helping me at all, I'm leaving." Rosé passed through the door and hit it hard, making the glass shudder, but it was in vain because she was soon in the air and being brought back into the room, stopping in front of Kay.

"That was very rude. Poor door and my balls," he said. His head tilted to the side. "Now, let's get to the point." His jaw contracted. *If I slit her finger over there, would it cut her fingers?* Rosé pushed the stupid thoughts away from her head and watched him.

"Your magic is linked to your intense emotions and self-protection," he commented, walking from side to side with his hands behind his back. "So …" he stopped. "Let's make you feel intense emotions, Smurf."

"Don't call me that."

"Why is that? It's just reality. Also, I did not complain when you called me a walking comic, *Smurf*." Rosé bit the inside of her cheek until she tasted metal. "I could paint you blue and leave you only in a white dress, with a beautiful hat on your head," he commented in an irritating and thin tone, as if talking to a baby, looking across the length of Rosé's body. "What do you think?"

"You wouldn't do that," she said. Her whole body tensed.

"Stop me." Kay raised his hands to issue an enchantment, but Rosé kicked out in frustration. Kay swerved and prepared to cast another spell. She ran up to him, but he was faster, this time he not only swerved her, but he also pushed her against the wall and held her wrists with one hand just above her head. His eyes were locked on hers. One second, two, three … "Too sexual," he said, dropping it and taking a step back, breathing hard.

She rolled her eyes at him, and he grabbed her again. "Don't you ever do that again"

"Or what?" she provoked, her hand moving down his abs. "Are you going to punish me?"

A shiver passed through her legs and arms. She looked down and realised she was wearing a white dress. "You're wasting time," he said, threatening to raise his hand. Rosé lunged at him and began to fight once more. She swore she had kicked and punched him in the arm and leg, trying to take him down, but, in one of those attempts, he fell and took her with him.

Their faces were close once more. "I think you like my face," she commented.

Rosé could feel his hands on her waist. "Watch your hat, it's going to fall." Rosé put her hand on her head and there was the damn white hat there. "You're getting too close to me, I'm starting to think that *you're* interested, Smurf," he said, laughing. "Get up first," he commented, closing his eyes. "I'm not going to be perverted and look. Also, you have to use your magic and not physically attack me," he commented, rising when Rosé was already in position. "Only the blue is missing."

Blue is his huge and round ass, she thought. Rosé gathered her strength and when Kay got up to do something, Rosé pushed her open hand forward, palm pointed at Kay. She closed it. Kay's hands and feet came together in a sudden movement and he fell back. Rosé went to him, putting one of her feet on his chest, victorious. "I need to remind you that you're wearing a dress, sweetheart," he warned.

"Interested?" she asked, ripping off her hat and throwing it in his face.

He smiled. "Do you really want to know?" That question made her guard fall because soon he was free and over her one more time. She didn't know how it happened because she didn't feel the impact on the ground. His hand went from her waist and down to her hips, it stopped there hesitating. She could feel him pulling the dress down. "I told you I'm not a pervert," he repeated, taking his hands off her body. "I don't have a habit of playing where I can't, but I can't let you expose yourself too much either." He smirked. "I can't deny that I find it amazing how your body connects perfectly with mine and I'm intrigued by it."

He stood up, helping her, but when she stood up, Kay fell to his knees in front of her. Hands behind his back. Rosé didn't have to touch his chin for him to get up. He hadn't been the only one to realise that connection, but she was angry that he didn't have to use his magic to disarm her. Just words and his body on hers.

He made her vulnerable and she hated this. Just like the smile that formed on his lips as he stared at her.

"I love the objects behind you, waiting to attack me," he remarked, looking behind her. She didn't have to turn around, she could feel a line connecting with each of them.

"Aren't you going to stop me?" Kay laughed. She looked at his lips and his throat but turned her thoughts away. She took a deep breath. One time and then again.

"You would never do that." He was sure she wouldn't. But she pushed him into the mirror that broke with the impact of his body against it.

She hated this vulnerability and that's why she hated him.

Rosé went towards her purse. She needed to get out of there. "Congratulations Rosélina." Gustav was entering the room. "Hey, what's this blue thing on your cheek?" he asked, pointing. Rosé ran to the closest mirror that was still intact but saw nothing.

Gustav and Kay were behind her, laughing. She went up to him and kicked his cock, causing him to fall to the ground, and she laughed. "Who's laughing now?" She cast an angry look at Kay and left. She could hear them say something.

"She has a serious interest in dicks."

<3

"Won't you tell me?" Gustav asked as Kay fixed the mirror.

"What exactly?"

"Today's training was intense, Kay. Very intense. What's going on between you and *Rosélina*?" Kay didn't answer. He went to another room and came back with an aid kit. The mirrors had done a little damage to his back and arms. "Don't tell me the prince of walking comics is in love with the cursed princess?"

Kay raised his head to finally look at him. His eyes narrowed. "Don't call her that again and I'm the king of walking comic books. I have more tattoos than you, the title of prince is yours." Gustav began to laugh and lay on the floor.

"Shit, this is more serious than I expected." He sat down. "Fuck, that's crazy, you know that, right?"

"I'm not in love with her," Kay commented, putting on the last bandage. "Loving her would be like loving your own destruction. She may not have mastered her magic, but … that girl can destroy the whole world if she wants to," Kay remarked, getting up and raising his arm to help Gustav. "I'm just teasing her. Trying to figure out how far she could go. Trying to understand her vulnerability. But you need to agree that she looks fucking good when she's angry."

"Keep lying to yourself." Gustav went to the door. "She is your type. More than the other ones."

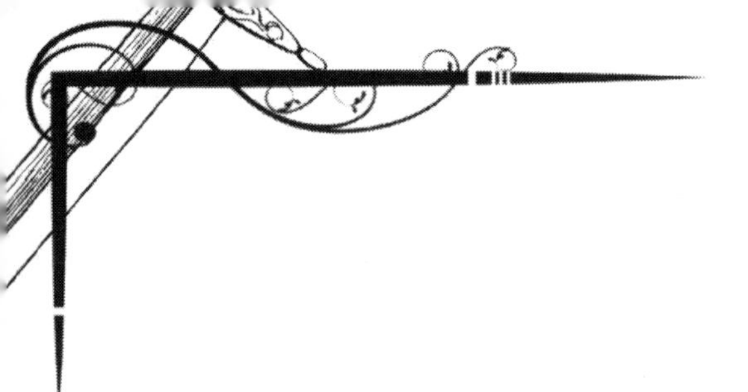

Chapter 35

Rosé was already in the training room when Ruby arrived. Rosé could hear her from miles away. Her heels making a distinct noise as she approached the room. This was one of the things she most admired about Ruby, the fact that she didn't need to say anything, but everyone felt her presence in the room.

She was like fire in a cold room.

Everyone knew her, but few knew about her.

She arrived in the same way, upright spine, hands together above the navel. The closed and mysterious face. Hair stuck in a high ponytail. Today, it was white. "You're not wearing the right clothes, go change," she said, sitting on one of the chairs and crossing her legs, looking at her.

Rosé looked at her black training outfit and then turned her gaze to Ruby, who kept staring. She raised an eyebrow. "The clothes are in the locker room," she spoke in a cold voice, making Rosé's body shudder, as if she had been struck by an icy winter air.

In the locker room there was only a long black dress hanging and a pair of heels.

"Ruby?" she shouted. This must be a misunderstanding or something.

"It's that outfit." She didn't shout but spoke in an audible and clear tone. "And fast." Rosé wore the black dress, which to her surprise was her size. She wondered if Misty had made it. She didn't know if she was going to train or maybe go to a dance.

On returning to the room fully clothed, Ruby got up, showing no reaction other than a 'Hmm' and then headed towards the mirror to straighten her hair. "You took too long," she remarked, turning again.

Although Ruby always had a closed face and intimidating expression, she knew that today wasn't her best day. Rosé knew not to question her methods or engage in too much conversation. Ruby's tone today was more authoritarian and harsher.

"It wasn't easy to put on," she said, without complaining too much that it was slightly tight at the waist or that the heels were horribly uncomfortable. It wasn't even half what Ruby normally wore and it worried her.

"I know," she said, her mouth barely moving, still a few feet from Rosé. "Today it is what you will fight me in. People attack their enemies at vulnerable moments. A naïve man or a badly disciplined woman wouldn't think a woman like …"she looked Rosé from top to bottom, "you, would know how to fight in heels or a dress at a party like the one we'll have in a few days. Too much fabric, a lot of pain, a lot of distraction, for a woman to fight someone in pants, t-shirt, and boots, more than comfortable. People hope that a woman doesn't know how to fight, especially in this situation, they barely know who they're dealing with."

She stopped to retrieve a breath.

"If I hit you" she said, going towards Rosé and pushing her arm, causing her to fall. "This is not to happen," she said, reaching out and helping Rosé get up. "If I kick," she said, doing the same. Rosé fell to the ground once more. "That's not supposed to happen. If I hit you with a bat—"

Wait, where that bat came from? Rosé stopped it before it hit her, almost losing her balance. "I fall, my ass on the floor, it is not to happen," she interrupted Ruby. "I get it."

"Great." She spun the bat in her hands and smiled lightly. She went towards Rosé, watching her, and stood with firmly with the bat in her hands, as if Rosé were a pinhata. Rosé tried to defend herself and maintain her balance, but she soon fell to the ground. Ruby helped her up and so they continued until her body couldn't take it anymore.

"Impossible."

"Nothing is impossible for a woman."

"It would be better if you didn't use a fucking bat."

"Gives a taste of real life, just accept it." Ruby leaned over her body and whispered, "Stop me."

Ruby attacked her again with the baseball bat. Rosé swerved and defended, but Ruby was too fast. She wasn't as fast as she expected from a vampire, yet she was much more agile than a normal person. There was a slight noise in the air of the bat going from side to side.

The noise of the heels on the floor.

Rosé had her hands on the side of the dress, pulling it up. She lifted it up when she needed her feet and lowered them when she needed her hands and arms, but in one of the moments her brain couldn't handle it and she ended up getting smacked in the arms, unbalancing her and causing her to step on her dress. She fell to the ground.

The sound of tearing fabric echoed in the air.

"Rwvka." Ruby helped her up. "You tore my dress."

"It's not yours. If it were yours, you wouldn't be lending it to me and you especially wouldn't let me use it in training," she said, taking a break and drinking some water. "You wouldn't let me even get close."

Ruby nodded. "Truth."

She couldn't explain how uncomfortable that dress was. She imagined showing her boobs to Ruby countless times simply because her breasts wouldn't stay where they were supposed to. The dress brushed and squeezed her belly. Not to mention the straps that kept falling and the pectoral was almost loose.

She was wrong. The dress wasn't her size.

"I'd say you were doing very well, but … there's a little something you've been pretty dumb about," she commented, joining her thumb with her forefinger. "Rule number one in a fight with a dress: analyse if it is over your knees, because if it is, you can't fight like that. Tear the dress and use its fabric as a weapon," she instructed. "It is great for hanging someone. Cause a distraction, in the middle of the twenty-first century, there are still men who think too much with the 'down' head. Exposed legs allow you to get a few extra seconds." She rolled her eyes. "Unfortunately."

Rose's feet were swollen and almost purple. She wondered how she hadn't broken her foot at this point. Her hair was messy and fastened in a bun. She got up once more, despite the pain she felt. She knew she would fall onto the ground again soon. Her legs were wobbly and her arms sore.

Ruby she was still intact. She wasn't playing the part of the piñata, but the aggressive girl thirsting for candy, besides, she wasn't blindfolded. "You put up with more than I expected," she remarked, walking away. Kay had said the same thing. How could she be perfectly intact? She was in high, high fucking heels all the time. Bigger than Rosé's. "You need to work on your balance. The problem is not so much the dress, but rather the heels, it hinders you in a fight or conflict.

That's your downside," she remarked, raising one of her hands. "But heels are a weapon. I've seen women kill, shove heels down men's throats." Rosé swallowed the bile that rose in her throat. "Sticking, slitting, crashing down. Learn how to use it as a weapon and keep your balance. You can leave them behind or carry them in your hands."

"How can I do that?"

"Old style. Lines and books." She went up to one of the cabinets and picked up a white spray and drew a straight line on the floor. "Go there, acrobat." Rosé cast her a look of anger. How did she expect that after being a punching bag she would manage to walk in a straight line?

Every time she used to step out of the line, Ruby would make her start again, while she hit Rosé with the bat.

When she tried to defend herself from Ruby's attacks, she was not fast enough, being defeated by her. "When I say something it's for you to do without question," Ruby commented, leaving the room. The heels made their trademark noise as she left. "We're done for today." Rosé sat there on the floor. Her body was sore and tired.

She tried to get up, but she was too weak for that. She took off her shoes and threw them away. Her legs were sore from so many kicks she had taken, as were her ribs. She couldn't sit upright. Her spine wouldn't let her. She looked around and had no one. She was alone, looking at the clock it was past midday, everyone was having lunch.

Rosé never felt so humiliated as she did now. Weak, on the ground. Alone.

She crawled from where she was to the locker room to pick up her phone and call someone. The dress hindered her crawl. That was humiliating and she couldn't do anything about it. She just had to survive. Make more effort.

She came to the locker room and picked up her phone, opening the contacts.

Aiden answered on the first touch. "Hey, where are you?" Rosé began to cry and sob. Upon hearing his voice, her world seemed to fall apart. She could hear him getting up quickly from a chair, the sound of it creaking on the floor.

"Locker room, room seven," she commented without strength and dropped her phone.

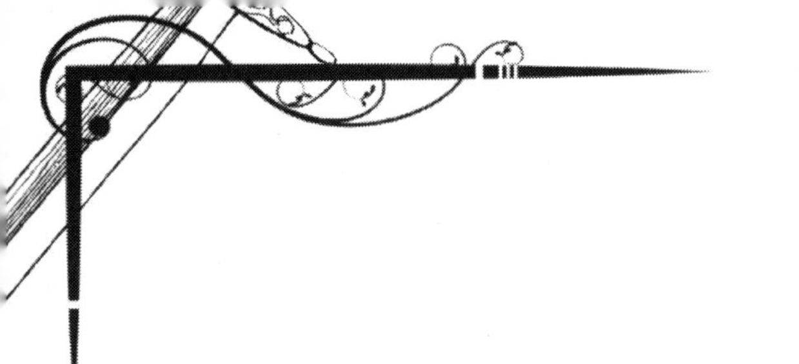

Chapter 36

She was balancing the books on her head.

Trying to develop the balance that everyone valued in this place. The library was quiet like always.

She hadn't seen Ruby after practice yesterday and she hadn't shown up for practice in the morning, so Rosé thought it was fair to practice alone, but not in the training camp. She went up to the library as she would find the books she needed, and silence, out of the eyes of others.

Aiden had appeared shortly after she had called, along with Misty and Theo. They gave her something to drink that looked like what Kay always gave her. It tasted horrible, but it helped with the pain. Theo carried her to her room as Misty and Aiden had things to do.

She felt bad about being so vulnerable in other people's arms.

Aiden later showed up in her room to ask if she was okay and spent a long time complaining about how intense training could be. He had become furious with Ruby and intended to talk to Ariady, even though she asked him not to do so. Ruby was right about people taking you by surprise and it wouldn't be bad to know how to fight in high heels and a dress. She did it without a problem and Rosé wanted to learn.

She had not forgiven Ruby but tried to understand her, even by hating her.

Rosé was quieter today, more on her own. Lost in thoughts. Her body had woken up sore and she thanked Ruby for not showing up. She didn't know if she'd be able to look at her face or move her body in any way.

Today, she didn't want to talk to anyone. She didn't feel like opening her mouth to say anything or explain anything. She wanted to be on her own. Besides, she was never alone. She had herself.

(Un)fortunately. She always has herself.

Inside her mind, many things were happening. Would it be wrong to appreciate the pain?

That day she wasn't feeling anything. No emotion inside her chest. She was feeling empty. It wasn't the same hole that formed when her heart beats fast. It was simply a feeling of emptiness. As if her body had gotten rid of everything and any kind of function.

She felt light, but not in a positive way.

The pain in her body had no effect on the rest of her. She was actually enjoying it. Every bruise, every pain, every stain on her body. Every move caused her to contract from the inside. She wasn't too disappointed in them.

Maybe she deserved it. Every colour covered her body. Every single one of them. It reminded her of every shot Ruby had given her and reminded her that she was preparing for a fight. For something bigger than she could have imagined. What she felt outward, was nothing compared to her inner self.

It wasn't much stronger than what was going on inside her body. In her mind.

Rosé already had more than three books in her head, which was a miracle. She followed the lines of the library floor made of clear wood, trying to maintain her balance. And every time she fell out of line, she'd start over.

She wanted to work it out first barefoot and then add the heels.

The library had become her place of refuge during the hours without training. When she was at the library, she felt at peace, surrounded by stories and fictional people.

She was alone, but she didn't feel alone, and that was enough for her.

Her room could be too quiet. Too dangerous sometimes to stay silent.

Hardly anyone went to the library. Sometimes she saw Ariady there, reading in silence, but it didn't last long because soon she was gone and Rosé couldn't hear either her breathing or footsteps through the library, thinking it was too easy to get lost. She'd get out of one section and magically show up in another. Some books sighed or murmured something; others whispered. They stopped when they were asked or left alone after a while.

Other days, she would find Skylar testing her balance on the stair's handrails, reading a book.

It was a warm morning. She wanted to put on a dress, but it would show all the bruises from the previous day, and she didn't want to draw attention. She wore a long skirt with a tear on the side, which was good because it did not roll on the sensitive parts of her leg and was fresh, not to mention that it looked like a dress.

She wouldn't give up so fast.

She wanted to prove to people that she was capable and wouldn't accept being the only poor girl who has a lot of power and doesn't know how to use them. That was ridiculous and was the reason she didn't care about the bruises on her legs and ribs. That was part of the trajectory. She just needed to try a little harder.

Nobody said it would be easy.

It was waking up every day and trying again. Every day was a new day that she needed to get out of bed and fight. She'd done it before, and she wouldn't stop now. It was only a matter of time. And she was going to get what she was looking for.

She always did.

She was changing book sizes and quantities, and wanted to test all possibilities. Sometimes it worked and sometimes it didn't. She went up and down steps. Her feet were barefoot on the icy wood.

She could hear nothing but birds out there and the whispers of the books.

One step at a time.

One step at a time.

Then, she put on her almost white pair of high heels and eventually began to make some fighting moves in spacious places. Some positions and actions succeeded, and others went wrong, and in one of them books fell on her feet, making swearing and leaning against a desk a temporary necessity for her.

A pair of black boots appeared in front of her.

"Swearing doesn't look pretty in a woman's mouth," Kay commented. Rosé stared at him and cursed a little more. His lips bent in a slight smile. "I take it back. It's beautiful coming out of your lips," he said, helping her, lifting her up until she sat at the table. "What were you doing? Playing princess?" he asked, kneeling and taking off Rosé's white shoes.

She took a long time to respond, wondering if she should move his hands from her feet just and leave the library, but her body did not seem to be in agreement with her brain. She didn't feel like talking to anyone.

She was still sensitive. She was recomposing her energies and, if she answered, he would ask what was going on. And if he did, they'd start a conversation.

She didn't answer at first. He was silent for a few seconds, so he could get the message. She kept her face neutral, avoiding showing her discomfort. Kay looked at her. His grey eyes were shining. "Practicing," she finally replied.

Simple and straightforward, she looked away. Kay had already taken both of her shoes off and was analysing her fingers.

Why was she still there?

Rosé looked at her thumb and it was red. "Nothing serious," he remarked, putting the shoe back on her foot and getting up, supporting Rosé as she stood, but keeping his distance. "Ready Cinderella. I do not recommend you use these shoes though." Rosé observed him without saying anything, trying to read his face. Why does he care? (We all know the answer.)

He didn't say anything either.

"Why do you appear at the most random moments?" she asked.

"I'm always watching you. I thought I'd made that clear." A smile popped up on his lips. "I am your guardian, princess, or who knows, the dragon in the tower."

"You look more like the prince."

He smiled sarcastically and looked away from the table. "I don't want to be the hero of history. I'm not the type to save the princess, I'm the one who steals her. The heroes of the stories disgust me," he commented, leaning against a bookshelf and crossing his arms. "I like to be the villain."

"You like the attention," she commented, crossing her arms as well. And there they were, talking.

"No, sweetie. You're confusing it again. It's the heroes who enjoy attention. I like to be feared." Rosé looked down and smiled, not knowing why.

"Maybe you're not the bad guy."

"And what makes you think I'm not the bad guy?" Rosé looked at him and exchanged a long glance. He seemed anxious for the answer. He didn't break eye contact for a moment. Maybe he even stopped breathing for a few seconds.

"You are my guardian, who does not make you my villain." He showed no reaction. He was too focused on the words that came out of her mouth. "You're just a stupid fucking asshole sometimes, but not the bad guy, so … it depends on the side of the story. For the people who want me dead, we're the bad guys."

"Deep."

"Don't think that thought is mine. I read it somewhere, in so many words. That's how I survive, even though I don't want to be living. Words, phrases. 'I'm going to survive, because somehow I always do', 'Control your emotions', 'I still have a lot to explore', 'Go and if you're scared, go anyway', 'I know who I am, and that's enough." She laughed. "Bullshit."

"Deep and sad."

Rosé smiled once more. "I met hell when I was still very young."

Kay made a noise with his mouth and leaned away from the bookshelf, he approached Rosé. "Ironic you say this to someone much older and who has known hell personally. The king of the Down World is very good person, you know?"

"Are you—?"

"No. I was just kidding. Stay away from him."

She looked at him again. A lot of things were going on in her head at the same time. Thoughts she had no control over.

"Skylar."

He lowered his head and sighed. His arms were still crossed in front of his body, flexing the muscles of his pectoral and arms. Rosé could not deny that the vision was pleasant. His gaze rose to her face again, the silence still prevailing. She wasn't the only one with a head full of things.

"Skylar is different. You don't go around telling people that you're the daughter of the man who controls demons, but she's different, just like she might be faking it all. Anyway, this is not a discussion I'm going to have with you." Silence.

Kay walked away and headed for the stairs.

"You weren't there yesterday after my training with Ruby," she remarked, playing with her hands on her lap. Thinking about the situation she was in when the practice was over. The feeling of humiliation burned in her chest again. She remembered the feeling she felt in her mind and body.

Kay stopped where he was and turned to her.

"When you're with Ruby, you're her responsibility, the same for Ariady, Gustav …" Responsibility. That's what she was. How people saw her. Not like a grown woman who can take care of herself. Not a friend, a person, someone they appreciate.

Responsibility.

A baby they needed to take care of.

"I thought you were my guardian," she observed, teasing him, because an almost invisible smile formed on his face.

Kay approached her once more, placing his hands on either side of her body as he had done before. He didn't say anything, and she didn't say anything. They stared at each other for a while until Kay placed his mouth near her neck. His breath tickling her. A heat wave travelled all over her body. The shiver went through her spine.

There was warmth and softness on her sensitive skin.

He left a quick kiss.

"Do you want me to be your guardian all the time?" Her body no longer corresponded to her commands, and she discovered this when unintentionally her head moved to the opposite side, giving free access to her neck.

She felt the smile on his lips against her neck. The tip of his nose stroking and making circles on it. She could feel the weight of her clothes on her body. Her hands were on the edge of the desk, squeezing it. Keeping the rest of her sanity intact.

"Won't you answer me?" he asked, still against his neck. She tried to form the words in her mind before speaking again.

"No. I don't want hi…" Kay stopped where he was. "I don't know if I could do it with you." She cleared her throat. "I couldn't deal with you all the time." He smiled and walked away. "You have to stop doing this," she informed, recovering from what had happened. Her breathing was still heavy. Her heart beating out of her chest.

"We're still at war, remember?"

"Are you going to use it against me now? Every time?"

"I told you, it's effective."

"Maybe I'll learn to defend myself from it."

"You won't," he said, leaning from where he was and whispering, "You love it. Your body reacting to me is entertaining."

"I am a fool now?"

"Never."

He was no longer as close as before, but close enough for her to try to hit the middle of his body, but Kay held on before she could hit him, squeezing her legs, causing her to moan over the previous day's injuries. "Nice try."

Kay let her go and walked away from her, leaving her free to leave. She raised her leg once more to look at her shoes, to see if Kay had done anything to them.

Precautions, she thought. She'd gone too far, and she wouldn't doubt it if he did something to her. Checking that everything was fine made her realise that the open part of the skirt was showing her bruises. Rosé lowered her skirt and looked at Kay, who was looking at her legs, she tried to get up quickly and disguise it. She was not in the mood to answer any questions, besides, he should be happy to see it.

It showed that she was training and that she was suffering.

Bruises were common, right?

She got up and started walking, but soon she collided with the hardwood again. He knelt once more, making Rosé's foot lean on his knee and he lifted her skirt to her knees. He looked at the bruises ranging from purple to yellow and some minor ones in a light shade of green.

He ran his hands over them. A mixture of pleasure and pain strolled through her body. His hand was warm, and his touch was soft, but certain parts were too sensitive to be touched and she couldn't help pulling her leg every time his fingers caressed a sensitive bruise. "I'm sorry," that's what he said every time. He lifted her other leg and checked the other bruises. "Somewhere else?" Rosé lifted her blouse close to her breasts. Kay ran his fingers over her skin. "Who the fuck did this to you?" Rosé opened her mouth to respond but was interrupted. "No. I really don't want to know who did this to you, because I'm not in the mood to torture and commit murder. It would take up a lot of my time, but if it happens again, I want you to come to me." His voice was firm and protective, removing her shoes. "Don't use them. You need rest."

He was angry. The sparkles in his eyes were gone, there was no smile or anything like that on his face. His jaw was locked.

Rosé just agreed and he helped her down.

"They're not very serious, but if you want to talk to Nina, I'd be more than okay with it. She's the nurse here and she could take a closer look. Her number is on your contacts. Is there anything else you need?" Rosé declined. She didn't feel like talking anymore. Not after what he saw. "If you need anything." Rosé only agreed. He took the books off the floor and in a blink of an eye they were no longer there.

Rosé began to go toward the door, her shoes in her hands, but stopped midway and turned to him.

"Thank you," she whispered and gave a faint smile. She turned and started walking but stopped once more when he cleared his throat excessively. She looked at him again and he smiled, approaching her. The smell of masculine perfume and books overwhelmed her. At that point she had to look up to meet his gaze.

He took her hand and kissed the surface without breaking the eye contact. "Did you really think I was going to let you leave without me properly saying goodbye, Smurf?"

"Do you do that to all the women?" Yes, she wanted to be special. He didn't call her by her name to be special. She wanted something special from him, too.

A broad smile appeared on his face. "Jealous?"

"Not at all." Just too much.

"Some," he commented, "special."

Her heart warmed. "I'm sorry for them," Rosé said, holding his gaze.

"Why?"

"Because now you only do it with me," she informed him, trying to hide the smile. "You are just my guardian. I deserve something special from you."

He kissed her hand again. "You deserve a lot from me, baby" Rosé got loose from his hands and started going down the stairs. She looked back enough to see him looking for a new book to read on Section B.

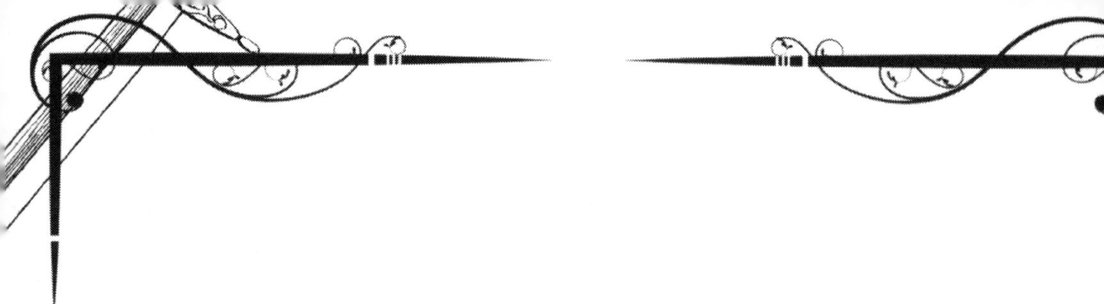

Chapter 37

"You should have seen the face of some girls when you arrived with him. I'd die painfully to see that scene again. The jealousy was so fucking evident in their faces, you know?" Skylar laughed, taking Rosé with her to her mental session. According to her, it would be good for Rosé to know how to control her own mind.

"Does he have some kind of relationship with any of them?"

"No," she said, slightly turning her head to the side and frowning. "Maybe casual sex."

"So then why would they be jealous?"

"Come on, look at him. He and Gustav are THE sexy boys in this place. Many would kill for their attention. Several girls have tried to be my friends to be close to them. You, my dear, have both and the Elementris."

"And what have you done?"

"Some I threatened and some I killed." Rosé choked on her own saliva, while Skylar laughed. "Alright, there? Rosélina, we are killers. Deal with it. Well … I am technically a demon."

(Water reminder.)

Rosé knocked on the door and unsurprisingly, it opened by itself. That was another feature of the library. Rosé recalled Ariady commenting on the palace having several unique oddities.

"Enter," said a familiar voice. "It's so good to see you again." As she looked at the man in front of her, Rosé recognized him immediately.

"Mr Watson?" she asked, going towards him to greet him.

"I work with minds, I thought I'd told you this before in our sessions."

"Are you a mage?"

"A wizard, and I have the power to read and get into peoples' minds. That's why I did psychology in the Outer World, to understand how the ordinary brain works. Stupid creatures that don't write a more simplified book," he complained. "Sit down, dear. Let's talk." Rosé obeyed and sat in the armchair in front of him.

"I thought I'd never see you again."

"You thought wrong," he said, sitting down with difficulty. "I'm getting old, Miss Johnson, or better, Miss Lysion. Ouch … soon I'll leave and I hope you don't replace me so easily. Long lifespan is not in my blood."

"Impossible."

"Good to know." He crossed his arms and watched her. "I don't have a clipboard this time. I know you hated it. You kept looking at it so much with disgust that even I started to feel angry with that thing."

"Mr Watson?"

"Yes?"

"You said you can read minds or penetrate them."

"Correct. And you might be wondering if I've ever done that in our sections." Rosé just nodded. "No. At least not entirely. Rosé, when I first met you, you were a girl who had just started in her adult life and had trauma in the past. I think talking to an old man about your feelings might not have been the thing you most wish you had done at that moment, so I needed your trust. It put lull so that you could be honest with me, but nothing more than that." Rosé remained silent.

"You said my brain was interesting."

"Indeed, according to what you told me, yes. But that's not what we're going to talk about today, it's about your mind. The other part of it. If all of us are right, inside you harbour so much power and … like anything powerful and valuable, we need to keep it safe. According to past studies by creatures, our brain is the centre of our magic. Ari told me about some incidents that happened recently, and I must admit, I'm impressed with them. Now if you'll allow me, I need to get inside your mind."

"Do I have a choice?"

"No. In this case, I am sorry to inform you that you do not have many options unless you know how to block me."

Mr Watson closed his eyes and, when he opened them again, they were completely white. Rosé felt tiredness in her mind. Her eyelids began to get heavy, and the world began to spin, but in seconds it all passed, as if nothing had happened.

Looking at Mr Watson, it was clear he was intact. In the same position as before.

"Interesting," he commented.

"What's interesting?"

"Your mind is more interesting than I thought. Honestly, I hope I don't have to go back in there again. Not until you have control of it."

"Is it that ugly?"

"Ugly is an understatement, dear. That's a death zone. Deplorable and scary, I'm surprised you're still alive. Your past still hunts and hurts you in a horrible way. You need to fix it," he said, pulling out a sheet from somewhere and delivering it to her, along with a pen. "I want you to write on this sheet everything that hurts you. Moments, people, phrases that have already been told to you. Everything."

<3

"A lot of things that hurt you, I can see." Mr Watson had not returned from his walk when Rosé called him, but his voice was loud and clear. "Now I want you to read each of them to yourself and ask why they are hurting you, explain to yourself as if it were an unknown person. You can do that in your mind," and Rosé obeyed. But tears ran down her face and a few times she had to stop to control her breathing.

"I think you've heard that phrase before, but our mind is the most dangerous thing in the world and something that destroys thousands of people every year, month, day, second. Our mind is the darkest and most terrible place there is and if you can't control it, you die. Our brain processes countless information per second and still has time to destroy us.

"Pain feeds on past memories and feelings. Do you realize that when you're sad, horrible memories come to your mind? It feels your pain. When I asked you to write down everything that hurts you and talk to yourself about it, it helps you process the information again, only this time rationally, and when you explain you get familiar." He fed her with information. His hands, behind his back.

"The point is, you can't let those emotions control you, and I need you to work on it in the next few weeks. Befriend your past. Make peace. Until it doesn't hurt anymore. What hurts today, must stop hurting in the next few weeks."

"I am sorry, for not having a strong mind and for being stupid."

"That is not what I said."

"Do you care about me?"

"Why the question?"

"Sometimes when I look at you, you don't seem to mind. It seems to be monotonous, and you were only doing this out of obligation."

"You are my only patient."

"Still."

He sat in a more comfortable armchair when he returned. "No. I don't care about you." He fixed his glasses and put his hands together in front of him. "Funny you ask me that, because, again, anyone else in the Elite would know that, and the fact that you question me worries me." Rosé rolled her eyes. "I don't care about you. Nobody cares about you. No one cares about your well-being, your dreams, about your imperfections. People just don't care about you. Put that in your head. It's not a personal thing. People don't care about others. They pretend to care. There is pure mathematics, pure science. This … is the pure reality of life.

"We are driven by selfishness. I'm here because I need you to know how to defend yourself mentally, because if anything happens to you, the world is fucked up and I live in this world. It affects me so I need to make sure your lack of experience doesn't affect me. When we help someone, we don't do it because we care, but because we need to keep our conscience clean and show and convince our brain that we care, but we don't care because the human being is selfish. So Rosélina, I don't care about you, but I have consideration for you. Don't confuse the two."

"You session is scarier each day."

"Realistic I would say. We don't have much time, Miss Lysion," he informed, looking at a clock on the wall. "From now on, we don't. People are becoming aware of your existence. We, you, all of us. We don't have much time to play considerable people. Dark times are coming, be aware of this."

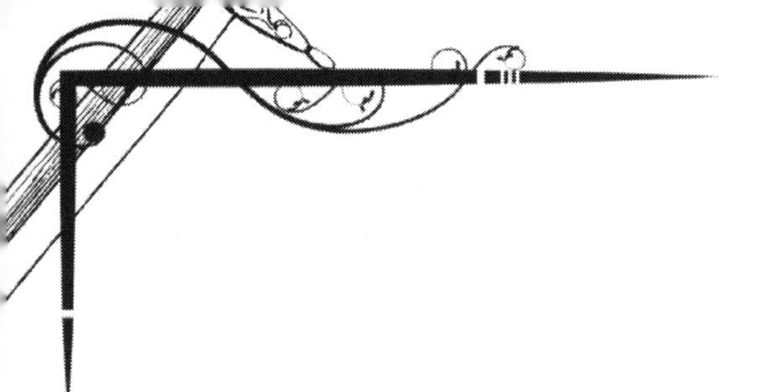

Chapter 38

"I'm not going."

"May I know why?"

"I am not going. At least not in this dress." She didn't want to insult Misty, that was the last thing she wanted, but … it just didn't do it for her. It wasn't really a dress, but two pieces. A turquoise lace top and a skirt that fell just above her knees of the same colour. It was beautiful.

"I don't understand you." Ari was looking at her, trying to comprehend.

"I look fat …" she stopped and rephrased "It doesn't suit me. And, my arms, they're fat. I … I'm not going. I think I'd rather stay. Besides, look at my face, it's full of pimples and scars. No makeup will cover it." She was looking in the mirror now.

She tried pulling her skirt up so that she could hide her belly, but when she lifted it, her legs became very exposed, almost showing her ass. She pulled it lower again. She turned to one side and then to the other. Watching the fat in her belly and then on her arm.

She contracted her belly.

She straightened her spine.

Relaxed.

The thunder tattoo definitely did not go well with the delicacy of the dress.

She had lost a little weight because of the training, but it was still not enough.

The top was not in place, and it exposed her back acne.

She looked once more.

Turned.

Rolled.

She stopped and watched.

"No. I think I'll stay." She looked at Ari who was wearing a red dress. She looked great in it. "I want to have your body. Oh, look at you. You're flawless. Everyone here is, I'm the fucking ugly duckling. No one's going to miss me.

You're going to live your diplomatic life and the others are going to start talking about things," she said, sitting in bed next to Ari, throwing herself backwards.

"You are ridiculous, Rosélina." Ari watched her for a while without saying anything and then stood up. "Come here," she said, calling Rosé to her side in front of the mirror. Rosé obeyed her. "Look at my reflection." In the blink of an eye a fat woman appeared in Ari's place. "That was me. Years ago, they called me Pinky Ball." They exchanged gazes in the mirror. "I used to look in the mirror and cry. I'd scratch my fat belly until it bled." A shy smile lingered on her lips. "I was a child. By that age the world had already taught me to hate myself." The reflection disappeared, and Ari sat back in bed.

"One day my mother came into the room and saw all my body scratches and said I couldn't go on like that, crying and scratching it. As much as I wanted that, my body wouldn't change. 'The time you spend crying and weeping, you could be doing something to change it if it bothers you so much. Or you can accept yourself the way you are and fuck people and society. The decision is yours, but no matter what you choose, you will have to learn to love it. This is your temple. Your house. Don't let them rule what's only yours by right. Including your paranoia'."

They exchanged a long glance. "I'm not going," Rosé said, looking at her reflection in the mirror. "I am sorry."

Ari looked at her one more time. She closed her eyes and when Rosé observed her reflection in the mirror one more time, Ari's entire body was covered with scars. It looked like a mutilated body that had healed over time.

"What you see from people is superficial." Her voice this time was rougher and cold. "People hide their imperfections, and you don't even know it." Her skin had returned to 'normal'. Clean and smooth. "Remember these words: no one sees you the same way you see yourself." She arranged her dress. "I think you look amazing. You are beautiful. We all have many scars, but we only show what pleases us."

Rosé looked at her and then looked away at the window, where the sound of the party sound was coming from.

"If you know of your imperfections, you won't mind telling yourself

you're an idiot, for stopping yourself from living an amazing life, having incredible experiences, because of appearance." Her voice was firm but calm. "I will wait for you at the party, but I won't mind if you decide to stay in this room, with your own mind, listening to people have fun while you cry."

"Is that psychological manipulation?"

"Or is it just the truth you try to ignore? Honey, life doesn't get any better."

Those were her last words before she left Rosé's room.

<3

"I'm sorry, but what the fuck happened to your face?" Misty had knocked on her bedroom door. She was wearing a short white velvet skirt, a cream blouse, and numerous pieces of well-chosen jewellery.

She looked beautiful and didn't seem to care about her exposed fat and large legs.

Before she looked at the disaster on Rosé's face, she marvelled when she saw Rosé wearing the two-piece outfit and said she looked amazing in it. "I thought I was wrong about the measurements, but I wasn't." Rosé asked if Ariady had sent her, she wouldn't be surprised if she had. Misty said she wanted a girls-only moment and that they never had the opportunity to talk together because Aiden or Theo was always together.

Rosé vented a little with her, taking care of the words she used and what she said.

Instead of arguing or her giving some lesson in living, Misty took Rosé by the hands and made her sit in front of the dressing table. They talked while Misty fixed the disaster her tears had made.

"Honestly, I love stretch marks. The clear ones in particular," Misty commented smiling, putting some blush on Rosé. "Like, they make me feel human and not those Photoshopped women from magazines. I have them in so many places that every time I look in the mirror, I find another." Misty lifted her skirt and showed off her stretch marks on her ass and thighs. Rosé was startled by the intimacy but was happy that Misty shared it. "I may be fat, but honey," she stopped and posed with the brush in her hand, "I'm still beautiful. Of course, I have my ups and downs, but that's life, right?"

Misty finished Rosé's makeup. She looked in the mirror. She blinked once, then again. Misty had performed a miracle and Rosé didn't know how. "That's not me."

Misty laughed. An infectious laugh. "Of course, it's you. A little different, but still you." She took her phone out of her pocket. Yes, her velvet skirt had pockets. And she started taking pictures of Rosé and her together. She pulled Rosé's arm to the door, but Rosé shook her loose stopped. Misty also stopped, looking confused.

"I'm not in the mood for this. For a party," she reported, holding one of her arms, stroking her skin.

"You have got to be kidding me That's a waste of beauty and—"

"I just don't … I really don't like partying."

"An hour, that's all. Just an hour and then you can come back. The party is not far away, it's stumbling out of the palace," she joked. "Besides you've never been to a party here. Trust me on this one. You'll love it and, if you don't like it, you come back." Rosé looked at her and blinked. She looked so excited for this party. "An hour? Forty minutes?" She went to Rosé and held her hand. "As much as you want, just come. For me," Misty commented, making a sad face.

"That's emotional manipulation."

"Always works."

"I hate you."

"Don't hate me," she said, pulling Rosé out of her room. "You don't hate me, right?"

"Of course not."

<3

Music and conversations could be heard from afar. When they left the palace through the side door, Rosé could smell the food and hear laughter and glasses clashing with each other. The training camp had become a huge hall and outside a tent had been set up with more space for people to sit and chat.

Misty held Rosé's hand and guided her through the crowd. The training room was unrecognizable. There were no walls, tatami mats, or instruments. The hall was taller and covered in amazing lights. According to Misty, people from other Lyses were there, but they were not any threat. She also asked Rosé to introduce herself as a mage, and nothing more.

The Heir of Lysions returning was still a rumour.

They passed through countless people before joining the Elementris. There was a huge piano on one of the stages and Mr Watson was playing and singing a song that Rosé had never heard before. He hit his foot on the floor and sang, followed by a choir of people, while some danced.

Rosé saw Ruby in the corner watching people. She was wearing a black outfit, to the surprise of no one. Her dark red hair was tied in a ponytail. A huge gun was strapped across her body, and Rosé noticed a large scar running through her right eye.

Gustav was by her side. He wore navy-blue trousers, a white t-shirt, and a social vest on top. Unlike Ruby, he didn't carry a gun. At least, it wasn't exposed.

Most women wore long dresses and high heels, and men wore suits. It was a gala and, as always, Ruby was the only different one. Nixie wasn't there, as usual.

She thought about asking, but she didn't bother.

They spent a good part of the party eating, as they had got a table near the food that Aiden argued had been won through the 'silly lost.' She lost count of how many glasses of wine she had consumed, but she was not yet drunk because she drank cold water to stagger the effects of alcohol.

She tried the m. cookies everyone talked about, and the name matched the taste. The dragon egg cakes were a treat as well.

She ate until she couldn't take it anymore. Looking at their table, they saw all the empty plate and realised there wasn't much food left. They had only stopped because Ari had come to yell at them over it.

"I'm sorry guys, but I'm going to have to open my trouser buttons," Aiden announced and did just that. Theo agreed and the girls complained, but they thought it was fair at the same time.

Another hour passed.

Mr Watson had returned to the piano. She had seen countless people dancing and others stealing a bottle of wine and another strange drink.

She saw Lux, Nikko's twin brother, stealing some food with JJ, a little, blond girl. They put the food inside their pockets. She had met them a while back when Theo explained about his family and that they were actually Nixie and Theo's siblings. Nina's children and Mr Watson's grandchildren. And beside them, there was another girl, called Ascelin.

Several women had taken off their shoes and now danced barefoot.

Some men had already taken off their blazers and ties, lifting the sleeve of their shirts to the elbow.

Looking at the Elementris, Misty was on her phone. Theo was almost asleep, leaning on the chair, and Aiden seemed to have entered a state of vegetation by eating too much food, looking out to nowhere.

"I think I'll be going," she remarked. Aiden returned his attention and Theo opened his eyes.

"We need to dance, yet" remarked Misty.

Rosé had realized that most of the songs had accompanying choreography and she definitely didn't know it. When she commented on this, they said they would teach her. Aiden got up (and before you ask yourself, yes, he fixed his pants. How do I know? I'm the writer so, yes, he fixed it).

They began teaching her the steps and she paired up with Theo while Aiden and Misty were coupled up. The choreography made her feel like she was in an old princess movie. Theo informed her that that was the dance of Evlayin, an ancient kingdom in the Outer World which had been adopted culturally in Amondridia and was modified a bit.

The song soon switched to a rock ballad from Full Nappies, and they danced until they couldn't take it anymore, rocking their hair back and forth. Misty and Aiden returned to the table, but when Theo and Rosé sat down as well, someone called them.

"Rosélina!" It was Josh. The dragon tamer. He embraced Rosé. "It is good to see you again."

"It's good to se—" She stopped abruptly in surprise when, instead of hugging Theo or giving him a handshake, he kissed him.

Like, they really kissed on the lips.

Rosé's chin must have dropped in response to her shock. They looked at her and asked if everything was okay and if there was something wrong. She didn't know how to react, and it wasn't in a negative way.

She looked at them and smiled.

"Sorry, I just wasn't expecting this." She opened her mouth to say something else but closed it again. "Good … I mean, wow …" She tried to formulate something. She was shocked at herself for not noticing and looking more closely. They were meant for each other. "I think I'll leave you alone and wow, you guys look great together." Both blushed.

I WANT TO KEEP THEM IN A LITTLE POT.

"I'll join you."

"Well, actually, actually … I was already withdrawing. My social battery is dead and please …" she said, holding Josh's arm. "I'm not leaving because of you. Let that be clear," she commented, hugging him and then embracing Theo. "Thanks for the dance, I'll be going."

"Are you sure?" Josh asked.

"Yes, I'm sorry. I have a socialization limit, really. And … how didn't I notice this?" They both laughed. "I mean … aw."

She finished saying goodbye to the rest and left. She was so happy for them. In her head she never imagined this happening, Theo had never mentioned anything … but you do not go to people saying that you are gay or straight or … you know.

(Stretch your body and, if it is night, finish reading this book … I mean, chapter, and go to sleep.)

Rosé thought seriously of returning to her room, but knew that if she returned, she would stay awake for a few hours, so she decided to walk through the gardens a little further ahead of the hall.

The conversations were lost in the air. Rosé could hear the sound of music and laughter. The place rejoiced. It was late. Looking at her phone, she realised it was almost 2.00 in the morning. It wasn't cold, but it wasn't hot either. The breeze was soft on her body.

The stars were shinning in the sky.

There were several arches adorned with flowers all the way to the hall door. The breeze softened lightly on her face and the sweet smell of the plants, and the night entered her nose. For a moment, Rosé thought she smelled an old book. Maybe she was spending too much time in the library.

A strange sensation began to bother Rosé, as if someone was watching her. Looking around, she didn't see anyone. The conversations were far away, and she was alone. Maybe she shouldn't be wandering around out here because her life was in danger, but she needed to breathe. She needed to be alone, and she couldn't do it anywhere else.

Rosé needed to be outdoors.

The feeling of being watched intensified and, despite trying to ignore the feeling, she just couldn't. She started frantically looking around her, but there was nothing. She was all alone. She looked back once more, but again, nothing, until she turned around and she collided with something hard.

"Looking for someone?" Kay asked. He was wearing black pants as usual and a navy polo shirt, almost black with the lack of light. He had a watch on his wrist and his usual lip piercing. The smell of manly perfume and books drifted off him.

She smelled him as discreetly as possible and passed him by. Her chest tightened.

"No," she lied. Rosé started walking and Kay followed her.

"Your senses are sharpened," he commented. "Congratulations. I know you were trying to find me. You were feeling something."

"Thank you and I wasn't looking for you, but I was feeling someone close." She didn't look at him. She kept her focus ahead of her, watching the flowers, but it was hard to concentrate. His presence had a strong effect on her. "Besides, haven't you forgotten something?" she said, reaching her hand out to his.

Kay let out a laugh and held her hand, depositing a soft kiss. "You amuse me, and you look beautiful." Rosé blushed, but Kay did not seem to realise. She hadn't gotten used to receiving compliments yet, especially from men like Kay. "You shouldn't be walking around alone." The idiot came back.

"You're here," she argued, looking at him this time. They exchanged glances and then turned away.

"Before," he observed "I wasn't here before." He pulled at her, hand forcing her to stop. "I'm serious, Rosé. You have to be more careful. Where we are now, where I found you, is well hidden. Anyone can show up and …" It took him a while to continue. "If anything happens to you, I don't know what's going to become of me."

He was serious. Rosé could not resist and laughed at him and continued to walk. She knew he was only saying this because he was her guardian and he would have to go after her.

"I know there's always someone taking care of me," she remarked, still smiling. "I have babysitters and a guardian. I'm not afraid." When she didn't hear anyone coming up behind her, she looked back, and she was alone again. She looked for him, but she couldn't find him.

She kept walking. She wouldn't wait for him. At some point he'd show up.

She kept walking, breathing the fresh air and watching the flowers.

She felt a shiver in her spine. She needed that moment alone, trapped in her thoughts.

But as with all things good in life, it doesn't last long.

She heard the sound of footsteps near her. There was no one around. Would Kay be testing her? If she's right, she knows very well what she's going to do (can you guess what?).

Something was approaching. She could feel it. It was a strange feeling. Like a sixth sense. An intuition. She looked on one side and then the other, but nothing. Then something seemed to materialize on her side. She turned back and raised her knee, making full contact with where she expected.

He fell to his knees.

"I told you I was going to be okay," she commented, lowering herself without hiding the smile. "I know how to defend myself."

"I really think you have a serious problem with my dick," he commented. The words coming out with difficulty. She could see a tear coming out of his eyes.

"Did I ever tell you I want it nailed to the wall?" and it was with this reminder that they started a fight. Kay was agile but didn't take Rosé by surprise.

Training with Ruby had been effective. She was in complete control of her body, even with heels on and a skirt, although she was too short for it. So, she had to keep lowering or capping, but Kay didn't seem to care about it, or he disguised it very well.

He didn't use magic, nor did she. She didn't want to do any damage here.

They went for punches and kicks. Deflections and grabs.

However, she was still no better than him. As last, he passed behind her, trapping both hands behind her body. "I almost believed you were going to beat me," he whispered in her ear, making her whole body shiver. Both were breathing with difficulty.

"You have a serious problem with me. You should stop following me."

"I do have a huge problem with you, Smurf. Many actually."

Rosé tried to lift her foot from behind, but he was quicker. He managed to trap her against a pillar. His thigh was between her legs, pressing her so she wouldn't make any other movement, holding her hands above her head. She let a sigh escape. The friction… she wanted to move.

Rosé took a few seconds to comprehend what had happened and understand why his mood had changed from convinced to stressed.

"Stop trying to kick my dick." He was dangerously close, his eyes darker than ever. He was shaking, holding her firmly and breathing hard. "My patience with you is ending."

"Stop whispering in my ear or approaching my neck or even getting close." He let her loose, taking a few steps back. Just like her, he was panting. Kay ran his hands through his hair, trying to fix it again.

"There's a big difference in what we do here." Rosé crossed her arms, listening to what he had to say. "You bring me pain, I, on the other hand, bring pleasure to both of us," he argued. "I am still suffering the consequences of the first one and you have not even apologised."

"I'm sorry."

"I'll decide if that's sincere or not."

A loud noise emanated from the party. They both looked to where it came from, but they couldn't see anything. There view was blocked by plants. They stared at each other again. Nobody said anything for a long time.

"What's your favourite smell?" Kay asked.

Rosé observed him for a long minute. "That's the worst question I've ever heard."

"Answer."

"What the hell?"

"Just answer."

She looked at him and blinked. "I think the smell of the night. From the sere. The smell now. I don't know," she commented, looking around. "It makes me forget the times of the world, because walking at night in a safe place sometimes doesn't even seem real. And book smell. I'm addicted."

"What are you smelling now?" Kay was terrible at chatting. If he had asked, 'Do you like bread?', it would have been more interesting than that.

"The smell of the night, of course, because it is dark." She stopped to take a deep breath, be sure of what she was feeling. "Your perfume and the faint smell of books, why?"

A portal appeared. "Let's go on a trip."

Chapter 39

"Where the fuck did you bring me?" Rosé demanded, now in the middle of a street. Her body was chilled by the touch of the wind on her warm skin, which caused Rosé to shrink and embrace her own body.

They weren't in Amondridia.

"Welcome to Rome, *amore mio*. You wanted an adventure so here we are," he announced, making a blouse appear of nothingness and putting it on Rosé's shoulders. The heat made her muscles relax. Rosé stared at him for a few seconds, there was a shy smile in the corner of his lips, making one of his dimples appear. "What? As you love to emphasise, Smurf, I'm old and a great gentleman." Kay began to walk.

"You shouldn't have brought me," she disputed, following him.

"You wanted to go on a mission. Here we are." Kay put his hands in his pockets, facing forward.

"Have you forgotten that I'm in danger?" Rosé pulled him by the arm, stopping him. She expected some reaction from him, but mostly, she expected him to take her home.

Home. She didn't even know what that was anymore. She has never thought of Amondridia as a home, at least not until now. For her, Lys was just a temporary place she was staying in.

"No, and that's why we need to get off the street." Kay took her hand. She could feel her cheeks burn. Why was her body reacting like that?

They wandered down the street. The buildings around them were old and rustic, as Rosé had always imagined. The historical air made her feel like she was in an old movie or in a princess universe she had read in books. "Your hand is cold," he said, holding her harder.

"My hands are always cold." Rosé was surprised when he took her hand up to his lips and began blowing hot air at it, then he left a kiss. Rosé looked at him, she didn't know how to react, but he didn't reciprocate the look.

She never wanted to kill the butterflies inside her stomach so badly.

Kill. Kill. Kill. Don't kill.

Why was she reacting to that? Why didn't she take her hand back or refuse his coat?

"Does Ari know I'm with you?" she asked.

"Of course not. She would never allow this, but I sent someone to warn her." Rosé made a noise with her mouth and rolled her eyes. "Are you worried? I thought you wanted this."

"There's a bunch of people after me, wanting me dead." She looked at the floor. She was wearing the same cream heels that Kay had taken off when he checked her bruises. There were times when it had become so common that it made no difference when spoken out loud, but at other times, those words hurt.

If someone had said that to her some time ago, she would have laughed. She had always been the almost invisible girl who didn't have confrontations or got into a fight with anyone.

A feeling of sadness took over her. She missed her old life and she mostly felt angry about it. Her life was miserable and sad, but it was calm.

Do I really miss it?

"You can stop worrying so much. You're with me and I've told you, I'm not going to let anyone touch you and before you die, they're going to have to kill me and good luck to them, because I've been alive for a long time," he said with a proud and arrogant tone.

"You think too much of yourself," she said, looking to their hands together, freeing herself from him, but she missed his warmth, of his strength against her hands, but he didn't seem to care.

She didn't understand him. One minute he cared and the next he ignored her and the next he seemed to care again. Rosé had thought of him differently. She wouldn't just be a hypocrite and ignore that there was something extra there. At least on her side. But every time she thought about giving it a chance, he showed no interest or gave her a reason not to let herself be fooled.

She could hear her heels hitting the ground. She could feel the warmth of his body by her side and the sound of his breath. She could hear the sound of her own heart beating quickly.

"I know my worth, darling."

"Don't call me darling."

"Smurf." She didn't complain.

Silence.

"I learned a word in Portuguese." Rosé couldn't help but show her surprise at that. She smiled at him, waiting for the horrible accent and mispronunciation.

"Really?" Their eyes met, and he smiled then looked away.

"Vida. I think I'm going to start calling you that." They exchanged another brief look. She had not realized that a few strands of hair had gotten stuck in her lips until he removed them from her, causing her to turn her face in the opposite direction to hide her red face.

She hugged her body again. Her heart was beating a thousand beats per minute. And her stomach was dancing with butterflies.

"Don't you dare. That's what people call their lovers and there's nothing between us," she finally replied. This man would be the end of her. "It means life."

"I wasn't thinking of it that way, Smurf. My whole life depends on you and keeping you alive."

"You say that all the time without even knowing what they're planning. Sometimes I think you're overreacting. Why don't you give me to them?" He was looking at her. Examining her face. "I am a cause of concern. A weight on your back. For all of you. Give me to them, you'd be famous for it. You would participate in their perfect plan, go back to being the great killer and bla bla bla."

"You have a great dying wish." Rosé did not answer. "I don't want to be that man again, even though I still have a great reputation among them, and they hope for me to come back to that side."

She smiled, as a thought entered her mind. Something she chose not to share with him. It wasn't a sincere smile. It was just a smile that said,

'I've reached this point in my life and even failed at that.'

They arrived at one of the buildings. Kay took his phone and checked the address and then opened the door, holding it until Rosé could enter, and together they headed inside.

They had a few flights of stairs to navigate before they got there. Kay offered his arm and she accepted. She wasn't in the mood to fall down the stairs in case she stepped wrong. She had survived until now; it would be unfair to die falling down some stairs.

Upon entering it, she saw it was a studio apartment. It had a small kitchen, TV, a bed, plus a spacious bathroom.

Enough for them.

`Just like she always did, she started looking at everything. She opened closet doors and snooped everywhere possible. It was a modern apartment which Rosé deduced to be very expensive. There were more modern appliances and the furniture seemed to be new.

"What are we doing here?" Kay was lying on the only bed in the place, his hands behind his head, watching her as she explored the whole place. The bed was huge, and Rosé looked around, searching for a couch but saw none. She took another look. "And where are you going to sleep?"

"I'm going to sleep in this bed, close to you," he said with a smile on his face, patting the empty space by his side.

"No. No way," she protested. They wouldn't sleep together. They weren't close to it. *I mean … Rosélina, focus,* she mentally discussed with herself. She sat on the countertop and stared at him, waiting for him to say it was some joke or something, but nothing.

"Well, I'm not going to sleep on the floor and, like I said, I'm a great gentleman and I'm not going to let you sleep on the floor either." He closed his eyes. "My friend thought that only I was coming so … Tomorrow night there's going to be a party and we just need to get into the party and kidnap a man to torture him to get information from him about you and what the Moridom-Blakes want to do."

"What?" she almost cried.

"Don't make me repeat it again, Smurf." Rosé cast another angry look at him, followed by a middle finger that was reciprocated with a smile.

"And how are we going to do that? Probably in your world—"

"Our," he corrected. "Our world, Rosélina." Rosé rolled her eyes.

"Someone will be aware that we've left. The portals are controlled, aren't they?"

"Yes and no. We were trying to extract information from several people in secret and my coming here would start to arouse suspicion, so Gustav had the brilliant idea of having a party. That would attract the attention of those who run the portals, thinking that someone from Italy decided to leave, and I could get into Rome for good, but then I looked at your amazing lively face from that party and decided to bring you along. I'm surprised it didn't explode from eating so much."

Rosé embraced herself again, hiding her belly. "I was having fun, and were you watching me?" He rolled his eyes and opened his mouth to speak, but Rosé cut him off. *"I'm always watching you,"* she tried to imitate his voice, but it went wrong.

"At first, maybe, but then …"

"And you seem proud of what you did." Kay opened his eyes again and just looked at her before closing them again. "I need a bath," she commented, turning her eyes away again and coming down from the countertop.

"There's everything in the bathroom"

When Rosé came out of the bath, she found clean clothes inside a wardrobe, and she brushed her teeth. When she returned to the bedroom, Kay was shirtless, exposing his defined muscles. Rosé looked at them and swerved. Was she bothered by it? No, but she needed to act like it. "Is this serious?"

"Is there any way you can stop complaining for a minute?" he asked, folding the clothes he was wearing before.

"Is there any way you can stop acting like an idiot for a minute? Now, I was thinking of putting one of the covers on the floor for you to sleep on."

"Look here, let's do it like this, I sleep on one side and you on the other and we'll have the neutral zone that no one can get through," he said, placing one of the pillows in the middle of the bed. "We can't get over." There was nothing kind in his tone. "So, the two sleep comfortably in bed and without stress. Stop finding more problems and get solutions."

Rosé thought a little, her arms crossed. "Okay." She wasn't okay yet, but she didn't really have a choice. She didn't have another bed or a place to sleep. Rosé went to lie down, and he did the same. Suddenly, Nikko came into her head.

She had met him during the nights at the castle when she couldn't sleep. They had talked about countless things and one of them was Kay.

'It's kind of obvious what's between you two,' he wrote in the black notebook.

'He's my guardian, of course there's something else between us, but not the way you're thinking.'

'DO NOT PRETEND THAT YOU KNOW EVERYTHING,' he wrote in capitals, not in an arrogant manner, but to get her attention. They both laughed.

'Write me then.'

Meanwhile, she looked at the stars. Admiring them and trying to identify the constellations in the (non-real) sky of Amondridia. When Nikko returned the notebook, there was a small paragraph.

'Well, before you, none of them sat in the canteen to eat, especially Kay. I might never have talked to him properly, but I've known him a lot longer than you, and he's never looked at anyone like he looks at you. There's something about him that says a lot of things, if you know what I mean. I think he wants to fuck you." Rosé eyes widened, she had to remember Nikko was old enough for this vocabulary, but still. 'He's always there. Besides, I can read/sense minds.'

'Language,' she wrote, getting up to go back to her room, but he held her arm and wrote something.

'Do not forget that I am much older than I appear. I am not actually sixteen, as I am in the Outer world.'

'I don't give a fuck, Nikko,' she countered, and he laughed.

<3

She was back amid the concrete walls. The rain wet her hair and her clothes. Her lungs struggled to get air. There were no voices this time and no one she couldn't save.

That time, I was suffering.

I was in pain, but no one could feel it. I was screaming, but no one was listening. I was breaking into a thousand pieces, but no one could see. I was burning, but no one knew. It's always been like this. I was always breaking and there was no one helping me put the pieces together, but they stepped more on the broken glass, breaking it into even smaller pieces. No one was ever brave enough to look into my eyes and see the black hole inside me, swallowing me little by little.

I closed my eyes, letting all the pain show up, until something hot engulfed me.

<3

Rosé woke up with something hard and hot behind her, not to mention the weight on her waist. As she put her out hand, she felt Kay's arm around her. *We're going to have the neutral zone where no one can pass,* recalled Rosé. *Great, the mission failed.* Rosé lay there for a few seconds, wondering what to do.

It was a strange, good feeling.

Rosé tried to get out of bed, but Kay's arm squeezed her even more. His muscles were hard against her. She froze. She could feel her whole body getting tense and contracted.

He was awake.

"I thought we had a neutral zone," she said. Her hand was still on his, with the hope that when her courage really hit, she could get his hand out of there, but she didn't want to. Not really.

"Oops," he commented with a hoarse voice, getting even more closer to her. "We had," he said, close to her ears, "until you woke me up in the middle of the night moaning and writhing." His breath stroked her cheeks. "I thought it was something else and I was ready to … anyway. I realised that it was not what I was thinking."

"Was I screaming?" she asked, turning to him. His hair was all crumpled and his eyes were swollen and yet he looked incredibly handsome. "I'm sorry." Rosé removed a wavy hair from his eyes. What was she doing?

"You don't have to apologise, but don't you remember me waking you up? Our conversation?" Rosé frowned, confused. She didn't remember waking up or talking to Kay after they went to bed. "You were moaning in pain and kept moving, until I woke you up and brought you into my arms and tried to calm you down. Honestly, you seemed a little doped up, but I thought you were just asleep. You started talking about being stuck somewhere and about some voices talking to you."

Rosé didn't respond for the first few seconds, or maybe minutes. The only person who knew about this was Mr Watson and knowing that this was manifesting itself outside of her head, especially in front of Kay, worried her. She didn't want him to know that. It was too personal. "It must have been just a stupid nightmare."

"Don't lie to me," he said, his jaw tightening. "You said you've been dreaming about it for a long time." What else had she said to him? Rosé tried to get up, but Kay was stronger. Only now realizing that her leg as on top of his. "Stay" he asked "This position is good. I'm not going to cross the line."

"You crossed many," she protested.

"What lines exactly?" He closed his eyes. "Kiss you on your neck? Touch your hand? Not let you sleep on the floor? Hold you?" Rosé didn't answer. "Can I tell you a story?"

"Hmm?"

"In our world, when one person falls in love with another, the person starts to smell differently to you over time. Your favourite smell mixed with the smell of the person itself. What you told me last night seemed like a declaration of love." He opened his eyes and stared at her. "I thought you were enjoying our moment. You feel something in your heart, don't you? It is like your heart stops for a second." She didn't respond. "There is a tale that says this happens as the two hearts synchronise. The nexum."

Fuck. "Get your hands off me," she asked as nicely as she could.

"If that's what you want." Kay let her go and turned to thc other side. He ignored her so easily it made her want to hit him.

His perfume and books. Fuck. Fuck. Fuck. He could be wrong, but he just described it.

She stared at him. The muscles of his back with a huge dragon tattooed in red. What's the point of hiding it if he already knows?

"Yes, I have feelings for you. I don't know if it's love, but I have a thing for you, but you know what? Irrespective of the fact, it doesn't matter that I feel something for you. I'd love for you to stay as far away from me as possible. I'm fine on my own."

Kay stayed in bed when Rosé decided to leave. He didn't say anything about her little speech.

Rosé looked at the floor and saw one of the covers and a pillow. "What the fuck is that?" she asked Kay.

"I slept on the floor, till you woke up in the middle of the night almost screaming," he replied, drowsy.

"Why?"

"Because you were visibly uncomfortable," he commented, turning and opening his eyes to stare at her. "I thought you would fall out of bed, being on the edge as you were. I was going to go back to it, but you grabbed me, and I didn't have the guts to try to go out and wake you up. Not to mention the fact that the bed is much more comfortable." Kay muttered something else to the pillow, but Rosé didn't stop to ask what it was.

She went into the bathroom and held on so she wouldn't scream.

Why does my heart need to do this to me? Fuck. Out of the many people in this fucking world, why him?

Chapter 40

When she left the bathroom, Kay had his back on her. She could see in more detail the huge tattoo on his back. Rosé stared at it. Staring and looking for every detail of the tattoo that moved according to his movements. He had defined muscles that were very evident. Expected someone who trains like him.

Rosé began to approach; she was intrigued by the tattoo. She stretched her index finger to touch it, but suddenly Kay was facing her, holding her hand. "What were you intending to do?" Their eyes met. Despite feeling angry at him, she loved looking into his grey eyes. "I hope you can still talk."

Rosé swallowed and looked down, pulling her hand away. Her heart was racing, and she needed it to get back to normal. "Your … your tattoo." Kay looked at his body and then stared again at Rosé.

"I have several." He was serious again. Maybe he didn't like what she said earlier. "But of course, you know that. You have a nickname for me."

His mood switch would kill her one day.

Rosé looked at him again. Was he stupid or brainless? She couldn't decide. Maybe both. "There's only one on your back," she replied. "The dragon."

"What about the dragon?"

"It's beautiful. Turn around." Kay watched her for a few seconds then obeyed. Rosé had never fallen in love with a tattoo before. She couldn't take her eyes off it, she took her index finger and touched the tattoo, his skin was warm. His muscles contracted with her touch, but soon relaxed when Rosé began to follow the lines. "Wisdom, courage, protection, strength, nobility. Symbol of good luck and spirituality." She had read this in a book.

"Correct." He turned to her. His breathing was heavy. As was hers.

Rosé looked at his left arm. A phoenix. It was going from his arm until it got close to his neck. She gently caressed it. Kay's body reacted to her touch. A smile escaped her lips, he seemed to be struggling to stay in control. Below the phoenix, there was a snake that enveloped his arm and ended up in his hand and, slated around it, random symbols Rosé didn't know.

Runes?

Rosé went the other way, but before that their eyes met. Their faces were very close to each other. She smiled. She liked the eye contact they always had. It seemed like communication.

"Rosélina" he whispered her name and she almost melted on his arms when his arm involved her waist.

"Yes?"

On the other side there was a skull and roses. Rosé remembered that's where she painted him, at the neon party. Below, there were symbols in Japanese and a dagger, butterflies, feathers, and symbols of money, in addition to the Elite symbol that Gustav had spoken about. But there was one that had caught Rosé's attention, the phrase 'Kiss Here' on his neck and that's where her gaze ended up. She did just that like he did to her. Her gaze rose to Kay's lips. She followed the small dagger on the side of his face until she found his eyes.

She knew he was watching her every move, every action and touch. "You shouldn't go around touching people. They may think you have second thoughts."

They were gazing intensely at each other. "Maybe I have second thoughts," she whispered, and she walked away. A difficult action she had to take.

She didn't know if what she felt was necessarily love. Nikko might have been right. Maybe it was, she didn't feel any regret when she had expressed her feelings earlier.

Rosé began to laugh alone at her own thoughts. Why would someone like Kay fall in love with her? Not that she wasn't enough, but there are countless women in the world. Several lying at his feet. Kay looked at her, confused, probably finding her crazy for laughing by herself. She looked away from him and sat on the bed, taking her phone out of her pocket and trying to disguise it.

She hated this place, she had nowhere to go.

"What's so funny?" he asked, putting on his shirt and heading toward the kitchen.

"Nothing." She pretended to be doing something on the phone and tried to control the laughter but was failing.

"I'm finding it unfair that you laugh alone, I think you should share it with me," he said, making a face of annoyance. Rosé couldn't help looking at his lips.

"I've said it's nothing. Just something in my head."

"I want to know what goes through your head." They exchanged glances, but Rosé swerved once again when the butterflies in her stomach returned. "A thousand Euros for your thoughts," he said, sitting on the edge of the bed with a glass of soda in his hand.

"That's a lot of money for my thoughts."

"Exactly. It just demonstrates how curious I am." He took a sip without breaking eye contact. That was too sexy. Rosé couldn't help but keep up with his movements. *What the fuck is going on with me?* she mumbled to herself.

"So?" Rosé thought a little. She could lie. He couldn't read her mind so anything she said would be enough. "Don't waste your time trying to create something. I'm paying for your true thoughts."

"Can you read minds now?"

"No, but I know when someone lies, especially you, plus you're taking too long which makes me deduce that you're up to something." He moved closer.

"What do you mean by *especially you?*" Fuck the butterflies.

"You do a thing when you're lying."

Rosé took the glass from his hands, drank a sip, and returned it. "What exactly?"

"Do you think I'm an idiot?" he asked. "If I tell you, you'll stop doing it. Now, your thoughts. I'm paying too much for them." Kay put the glass on the floor. He started making a clock noise with his mouth.

"I can't."

"Why?"

"They're too shameful."

"You were laughing."

She put her lower lip between her teeth. "I was … I was thinking about … if it was possible, for you to be in love with me." A shy smile appeared on her face. "Now that I've said it out loud, it doesn't seem funny anymore. Everything inside my head looks better or worse."

She smiled, trying to disguise her confusion and improve the situation.

"Why did you think that was funny?" Looking at him, Kay no longer had a playful smile on his face, but a rather serious expression. His forehead was frowning, and his lips were pressed together, he seemed almost angry.

"Why do conversations with you have to be so intense?"

"I'm too intense, Smurf."

"You said that love makes people weak. Besides, you don't look like someone who would fall in love with someone like me. Young." She smiled with the last word. She had no idea of the age difference. "Weak and …" She took a deep breath, playing with her fingers on her lap. "You have countless women at your feet, and you don't even care."

"Love makes people weak, but that doesn't mean I'm not able to love. I just told the truth. I've lost a lot of people and believe me, losing someone close is not cool so I avoid it as much as I can. I can't love someone that easily," he commented. "Love is disgusting."

"That's sad." Silence.

"You …" Rosé didn't finish her sentence. Courage was lost on the way. She got up. She needed to get out of there. Why did she want to know that? He was clear. Ari was clear. No one cared about her.

Kay pulled her to sit down again, bumping into her leg.

Rosé looked at him but quickly averted her gaze.

"You feel something—"

"It doesn't matter," she interrupted. Kay doesn't answer and doesn't bother to say anything. He gets up and goes to the door that leads to the balcony, facing the rain that falls. She looks at him. His profile. Rosé began to reflect on the countless things he had already gone through and how many people he had already lost. Family and friends. "What keeps you alive?"

"What do you mean?"

"We all have something that makes us stay alive. A person, a memory, a goal. What makes you want to stay alive?"

"You ask strange questions."

"Me?" she gasped. "Says the one who …" *made me confess my feelings.* "I want an answer." Kay joined his arms behind his back and thought for a few minutes

"There's a lot I want to do in life. Besides, I like fighting for it. Test my limit. Go as far as I can." Rosé nodded her head. "What about you?" he asked, turning to her.

Shit, he wasn't supposed to ask her.

She had that answer a long time ago. "The same thing that makes me want to end my life." She stopped and took a deep breath. "My mind. It's the only place where, for the most part, I have control. It's the only place where at the end of the day I can run away and create things that are never going to happen, but that are real at the same time. Everything can go wrong, but if I want it, in my mind, everything can work out. The illusion keeps me alive because I don't have the courage to live what I imagine." Her voice came out like a whisper, low and calm. "Books keep me alive"

Reflective.

Kay didn't answer. It had become his thing. Instead, he went to her and reached out. Rosé looked confused but took his hand and he led her to where he was before, facing the balcony door. He got down on one knee, put one of his hands on his back, and with the other he held Rosé's hand. For a second her world stopped.

WHAT THE FUCK IS HE DOING? I'M NOT READY FOR THIS.

"Do you agree to dance in the rain with me?" Rosé couldn't take it and started laughing hysterically, almost spitting in Kay's face. She took her hand up to her mouth. Her belly hurt. She tried to control herself, but she couldn't.

"Okay, I thought … I thought you were going to ask me to marry you." She continued laughing. "But yes, Kay, I agree to dance in the rain with you."

He got up. "I am beginning to feel offended already."

"No one told you to get down on your knees and get serious," she protested. She took his hands and followed him.

"You are too small. That was the only way to be the same height as you." Bad feelings seemed successfully removed. No offence was taken from him. "Believe me, if I asked you to marry me, it would be in a much more creative and romantic way than that," he said, looking at her and smiling. He opened the door with one hand as the other was still holding Rosé's. Soon they were in the rain. The icy drippings touched her skin and soaked her clothes.

Kay approached her and there they started dancing. "No music?"

"We don't need music. Not when we're together." Rosé was shocked, she blushed right there in the rain. "You talk too much sometimes; the music would be useless." For a second, she thought it was a compliment.

They stayed there for a moment. Dancing without music. Their bodies, soaked.

"You … Have you ever asked someone to marry you?" Curiosity had struck. Kay had lived for years and that was people's life goal, right? Most of them. Find someone and share life.

"Lost before I could." If Rosé had not been so close to him, she would not have heard what he had said. He had whispered, as if he did not want to be heard. Just like she did earlier. Rosé felt a pain in her chest and got closer. Even if it wasn't her, she hoped one day he'd have the courage to propose. "Thank you for sharing your thoughts for free."

Rosé widened her eyes and walked away from him. "What about my thousand Euros?"

"I was going to go buy your dress," he said, laughing at how quickly she had changed her expression.

"A dress?"

"We have a gala to go today. Did you forget?"

"You're unbelievable," she said, trying to get rid of him, but he was stronger. Holding her in place. He stroked her back, going up and down her spine. This was going too far. But she wanted more. Her body wanted it.

"I know," he whispered close to her ear. "And we haven't finished our dance yet." Rosé didn't complain, she liked it, even when she shouldn't. She liked his attention on her, and she knew, deep down, that this was going to end soon.

When she thought of him with other women, anger flowed in her veins. She shouldn't love him; she had many reasons for that.

"How do you get money?" Rosé knew this question was very personal, but she wanted to know. Aiden had already explained that some people worked in the Outer World, but Kay had never mentioned where he worked. "I know it's very personal, I'm sorry."

"I'm from the Elite, I make money from it."

"Oh, that's it?"

"You have an incredible talent for belittling people's work. I risk my life every day to save people. I've lost count of how many times I've been threatened with death or something similar. Tortured, stabbed, shot and so on."

"I learned from other people how to diminish things. They've always done this to me. And I can't go out and buy a dress, I'm being threatened with death right now too." Rosé could hear her heart rate go up just thinking about it.

"1. If you say that one more time, I swear I'll go crazy. You shouldn't live in fear. I'm training you to make sure it doesn't happen. 2. That's part of my plan. They need to know that you are here and not inside a highly protected Lys and 3. If you die, at least you will die in a nice dress or while trying to buy it."

"And now they need to know that I am very poorly protected?"

"They need to think that, even if you're not." Rosé walked away from him, once again confused. "Did you really think I'm the only one protecting you right now?" Rosé confirmed it. "Well, I could handle you fine, but I can't afford for someone like you to be ripped from me so easily. There are others in this building and a few others on the street. All I have to do is make a sign and they all appear." "So, you care about me," she said, satisfied.

"Of course, I do." he said "My life depends on you."

There was something there. Something else hidden in the phrase.

Chapter 41

"I don't know if I should accept this money," Rosé said. Kay rolled his eyes and snorted. He crossed his arms and began walking. They were very close. Their shoulders bumped from time to time, which made Rosé move away. Through the corner of her eyes, she could see him watching her sometimes when he thought she was not paying attention.

The rain had already ended, and they were on their way to the dress shop Kay knew. The smell of wet grass took over the place.

The smell of rain was something else she loved. It was comforting and made her feel content. The smell brought back a lot of good memories which she didn't even know she had; sometimes she thought about when she would dance in the rain as a child. Or the times she was just reading a book and listening to its sound against the window. She also remembered the moments running home from school, or maybe it reminded her of the moments when she just gave in to the rain.

Letting it take away all the pain.

Not to mention her dreams, but in it, she couldn't smell it.

She looked at Kay once more. At each step he seemed to play in the puddles of water that had formed, stepping harder or just kicking. He was not as tough as he seemed. He wore his usual black training boots and uniform. It highlighted his sculpted body after years of training.

When she asked where he got the clothes, he just said one word, 'contact'. Of course, he should have contacts everywhere.

He let out a loud sigh, resting his hands on his back.

"I brought you with me and you need a dress. I'm responsible for you."

That was still wrong to her. She didn't like to depend on others financially and that was something that had gone through her mind now. Since she had arrived in Amondridia, she had wondered who was paying for her stay there.

"I wish I had my own money," she said.

She couldn't tell how much time she had spent in Amondridia. She never paid attention to the dates since it made no sense to her. She recalled that it had been some months since the new year when she was taken to Amondridia and, according to the almost icy weather, she deduced that they had already passed the middle of the year.

Rosé had never felt fully comfortable walking the streets. She was a short, baby-looking woman walking around helplessly. She was always attentive to her surroundings, watching to make sure no one followed her. She was then startled when she found out that she actually was being followed this whole time and he was on her side.

She'd never noticed him before. She had never seen him around and it worried her as it showed that she was not being careful enough and that, besides him, there was another man also following her and she did not realise. But this man, no one commented on much.

But …

Kay didn't count, did he? They were using magic. They might as well hide more easily.

Even after everything that happened, she was still afraid to walk the streets, but this time it was worse: countless people wanted her, and it wasn't even in a good way. She was famous now. People wanted her dead for their own benefit, but they wanted her dead. Not one. Not a maniac or a mental patient.

Powerful people wanted her and were desperate for it.

Something that was ordinary now made her feel exposed and vulnerable, but Kay's words were still in her head. *You shouldn't live in fear.* Maybe he was right. She shouldn't live in fear.

"One day you're going to have money," that was the first thing he had actually said since they had left the apartment, other than a word or a tiny phrase. "We just need to make sure you're going to be okay alone. We need you well trained for this, and then you won't need me anymore. You're going to start working. Turning into a possible Legendary and an Elite," He was watching her now. He had no humour or pride in his voice, but he also did not necessarily show sadness or seriousness.

Legendary, a group of people with years of experience and were famous for it. There was a book with their names and photos.

"If I stay alive." The words came out without her thinking straight.

Kay stopped and looked at her. A vein popped out of his neck "Really? If you keep saying that … Damn Rosé, for fuck's sake." He went back to walking. "I'm worried about your death wish."

"Oh, you're worried," she remarked, pushing his arm. "Don't worry, I won't tell anyone. I know you have an image to maintain." Rosé kept walking. "Why can't I wear the dress I was wearing when you technically kidnapped me?" she commented, hoping for his reaction to the word 'kidnapped' or to the comment she had made about him caring. But that never came.

He didn't seem to be excited to argue with her today.

"Because we are going to a gala, and you need a fancy dress."

From the bottom of her heart, she wanted her heart to listen to her brain, at least once.

<3

The dress shop was on one of Rome's busy streets. It wasn't any designer brand, but it had several beautiful dresses in the window. Inside, it was an almost vintage and well-organized shop.

It was small and smelled like lavender. Kay went to the front and began talking to the woman in Italian while Rosé looked at some dresses.

Her goal was to spend under a thousand Euros. She didn't want to abuse his willingness to buy something for her, but of all the dresses she saw, the prices were not below eight hundred Euros. Not to say that one of the dresses which had caught her eye on a mannequin was over a thousand Euros.

She turned away, acting as though she hadn't seen it.

"Did you find one that interests you?" asked Kay behind her.

"Not yet," she lied, fiddling with the dresses on the clothes rack. "I didn't know you spoke Italian," she commented without stopping to pass her hand through the numerous dresses, seeing the price. They were beautiful, but out of her reach.

"I can speak many languages, because—"

"You're a grumpy old man." Kay laughed behind her.

Rosé took the cheapest dresses she had found and took them to the dressing room. She hadn't liked them very much, but it was only one night. The first was baby blue without straps, which left the top of her chest too exposed. The skirt was composed of several layers of a thin and transparent fabric, which together prevented people from seeing too much of her legs.

Another lady was helping her with the dresses.

Coming out of the fitting room. Kay was sitting next to the woman, talking and laughing, but they stopped as soon as she came into their view. They both looked at her and then exchanged glances. "Next," he said.

The other one Rosé tried was emerald, green. Her straps hung off her shoulders and it had a plunging neckline. She didn't have much chest to show, so the plunge was almost empty. There was an opening in the leg, but it was too long for her height. When she modelled it, she got the same answer.

The last dress she had brought in was cream with the same opening in the leg as the emerald. It had transparent sleeves that, when Rosé first looked, she thought would look beautiful, but when she put it on, she didn't like them. It was covered in small brownish flowers.

Delicate, but not her type.

"*Non andrai a un matrimonio, vero?*" asked the woman and Kay denied it with his head. No, they weren't going to a wedding.

"Next." Rosé tried numerous dresses of numerous sizes and shapes, but her eyes always returned to the same dress on the mannequin.

She tried on a few more and over time could no longer hide her anger and began to catch a hatred of the word, *Next.* It was impossible that none of them looked good. Maybe it wasn't the dresses, it was her. Maybe it was her body that wasn't helping.

She had already tired of taking off and putting on dresses. That was exhausting. She was sweating like a pig and if she didn't take care of it, she would start to stink.

Rosé was already taking off her thousandth dress when a hand appeared, scaring her. One more dress. It was a Port Royal colour, but more red-ish and very similar to the emerald green she had tried before, the difference was that the bodice was lace. Same as the mannequin. When putting it on, Rosé looked in the mirror for a few seconds, perhaps minutes, admiring herself. She had never felt so attractive and sexy at the same time.

But the price discouraged her. She couldn't buy it.

She left the locker room, confident, even if she wasn't buying. She stepped out on her tiptoes, imagining being in high heels and on a red carpet. No. White carpet, for her dress to stand out from top to bottom. She wanted to enjoy this moment. Even if it lasted only a short while.

Her eyes met with Kay's who had one of his arms resting on the back of the long armchair, the lady who had helped her put some of the dresses on was sitting next to him. He held her gaze for a few seconds and looked her up and down. Rosé even turned a little, with a smile on her face.

"I know you won't take it. It is over the budget, but the emerald green looks similar and is cheaper." He paused, expecting some reaction. "I liked that one too," she lied. None compared to the one on her body.

They looked at each other and started arguing. Kay looked at her and then at the dress. Just like the woman next to him did. Kay took a glass of wine from the table and took a sip, listening to what the woman had to say.

They stopped.

"Bellissima!" said the woman, pounding her palm.

"Let's get it," he remarked, putting the empty glass on the table and getting up.

Rosé's face got serious. "No!" That word hurt so bad.

"Don't you like it?"

"Yes, I love it, but—"

"That's what I imagined. You've been staring at it ever since we got here."

"I haven't," she lied.

Kay approached, keeping eye contact with her. Every step he took threatened her heart to stop beating or come back ten times faster. She didn't know. With his every step, her brain failed. "I thought I had told you about not lying to me and …" He approached her ear. "I wasn't looking at the dresses or price tag, love."

"Where were you looking at then?" she teased.

"Your eyes and your body" he said. "And you look beautiful on i-"

Kay was interrupted when the woman asked him something. He stepped back and answered her, which gave Rosé time to get back to the argument.

"It's expensive," she whispered. "I'm not going to let you spend it all on a dress."

"It's my money and I decide what to do with it," he said, clenching his jaw. The asshole had come back. "And if I want to spend all my fucking money on you, I will. Now I would tell you to go change unless you want to go out with it on the street, but I think you're going to end up ruining the dress or draw too much attention and honestly, we don't have time for my jealousy."

She sauntered towards the changing room and started taking off her dress with the woman's help. She didn't know what to think at first. Whether it was the cost of the dress, Kay, or his words. When she left the fitting room in her training clothes again, her dress was already paid, inside a box and a bag, and in Kay's hands.

The next stop was to buy the shoes, but that didn't take long since there were few shoes that matched the dress.

<3

"Here's the plan," Kay began. There was a projector displaying a map of a large establishment. "We're going to go into the party and enjoy it, like we're normal guests, and during this process we're going to look for Lorenzo, one of the Black Circus members and ex-Wysez citizen. Your goal? Seduce him. Well … he'll probably already be interested from the moment he realises it's you, so—"

"Wait," interrupted Rosé. "Am I the bait?" She was eating pasta while Kay explained.

"Technically." Rosé opened her mouth to say something, but closed it, waiting for Kay to continue. "I don't like that plan either, but you're going to get him to approach you and when you realise, he's coming towards you, you're going to start walking down this hallway here," he said, pointing to one of the corridors in the west of the hall. "From here you're going to turn left and then go to that door." His finger was snaking through the holographic map.

"What about you?" Rosé asked taking another forkful of pasta.

"Then I show up behind the corner and the torture and extraction of information begin."

"I don't like the torture part," she said, taking her plate to the sink and starting to wash up, but it disappears before she could get the soap. She looked at the sink, confused, and then remembers that she was with a magical being.

I need to learn that. It can be very useful. No dish to wash. Cool.

Kay did not answer and when she sat on the bed next to the hologram, she throws out one more question. "No one's going to come into the room. He could be accompanied."

"Few have access to that room, and he likes to walk alone at these parties. He is never going to be accompanied because he always comes back with someone… a woman." Rosé felt like throwing up all the pasta she had just eaten.

Chapter 42

Rosé was almost ready for the gala. She had taken a long bath and put some makeup on with products they had bought in the town centre. Finding Kay's eyes here and then as he tried secretly observe her as she get ready.

She didn't feel comfortable spending money that wasn't hers, especially Kay's. Not only did she feel like she was taking advantage of him, but she didn't like the feeling of dependence.

She took the dress to the bathroom where she had privacy and put it on. She struggled to perform that task and hit her elbow on the wall twice, but the biggest problem was closing the zipper. She tried countless ways, but she couldn't, almost breaking her back doing it.

In the shop, she had help. Now she was alone.

Rosé took a deep breath countless time until she unlocked the bathroom door and left, holding it so it wouldn't slide down her body. His attention on his phone.

He was ready. He wasn't wearing a suit, as she expected, but rather a suit pants and a black polo shirt with the first buttons open. Her body ignited in a way she never felt before and only she knew how much she wanted to touch him. His hard muscle under the shirt and his smell… fuck!

For a moment Rosé was jealous. Man, it was much easier for guys to get ready.

Why wasn't I born with a snake and two balls between my legs?

Rosé cleared her throat, causing him to turn to her. "I need help with the dress." Her voice came out shy. Nervous. Rosé turned her back. She was feeling exposed, but not totally uncomfortable.

Kay went to her and carefully lifted the zipper. A heat wave wandered through her body as his fingers touched her bare skin. "What happened with your back?" Rosé tried to look at it but couldn't. "It looks like you have been hit by lightning."

"I don't know. Maybe it is my magic."

"We will have to check this." She nodded. There was nothing seductive about his act. He lifted the zipper as quickly as possible and walked away. "I should have found someone to help you."

"Not necessary. It's okay, it was just the dress." Rosé sat on the edge of the bed and put on her shoes. She could feel Kay's eyes on her. He seemed to like watching her recently. Or always had.

"No, it's not okay," he said, harshly. "I'm sorry." The mood changes again. She thought, for a moment, that there might be something else there, but she put those thoughts aside. "Do you need help?" Rosé just shook her head. As she stood again, she turned to Kay.

He came over and took her hand, kissing it and encouraging her to turn around so he could have a look. "You look amazing," he said. There was a twinkle in his eyes that Rosé had never seen before.

"I know," she replied, showing confidence. High chin and straight spine. It was the first time she said that and really meant it. Beautiful and elegant. Kay somehow made her feel that way. Worthy of something.

Kay went to the countertop and came back with what looked like a black ribbon.

"What's that?"

"It goes on your thigh." Rosé took it from his hand and sat down again, putting it on, she could feel Kay's gaze with each movement once more, but did not say anything. She let him look. Admire her. If she was going to be his bait, she expected him to look at her, realising what he was missing.

"And what exactly is this for?" Key went to a briefcase on the table in the corner of the room and pulled out a gun. Her stomach turned and she could feel her heart stop for a second, or two.

"That," he said, going to her. "I think Ruby taught you how to use one. It's simple, active, and shoots." He demonstrates how to activate and disarm it. Simple? It wasn't at all simple. "Remember to hold your arms tight and hold it with both hands or you'll miss it. It's just in case of emergency and there's only six bullets so shoot wisely."

"Any more surprises?"

"You wouldn't need all this if you knew how to master your magic."

"I'm trying"

"I know, it was just a reminder. And yes. I have one more." He pointed to the table with his head where the briefcase was. Two Italian masks. They weren't quite like typical Italian carnival masks, but party masks.

"Masquerade ball?" Kay waved and they both put on their masks.

"Amore mio," he said, offering his arm.

<3

The party was full of people. The conversations mingled and, as in Amondridia, music and laughter could be heard. Kay went over the plan, whispering it in her ear as they moved further into the hall. They didn't stop for security. Kay only escorted her inside, holding her hand tight on his.

"The man we need has a glass in his hand to the right of the column with an angel on it. He has a huge watch on his wrist." Rosé discreetly located it. He was distracted, wearing a full suit and gold mask.

After a few minutes, they split up.

Rosé lifted a glass of champagne and took a sip; the alcohol went bitterly down her throat. She made eye contact with Kay who was a few feet away, watching her.

She moved closer to the man. She thought about stumbling into him but decided it would look too cliché. She didn't know how she would make him notice her. Especially with a mask on.

She rolled her eyes at her idea that were interrupted.

"WHAT THE FUCK?" she cried out in indignation when a man touched her body inappropriately, but when she looked to confront him, he was not to be found. She looked around looking for someone suspicious, but when her eyes caught something moving fast, the way was blocked.

She looked for Kay expecting him to do something, but it never happened, because he too had disappeared.

That was not what she was thinking about, but at least it got the target's attention.

The blood boiled inside her. She couldn't believe her body was involved in this. She looked at Lorenzo again, he was looking at her, even though everyone had returned to their normal lives.

Touché. Unfortunately, in the most disgusting way.

She started walking and mixing with people.

Enjoy the party first.

Rosé didn't speak Italian, but many there spoke English. She went to a table where they were playing cards and betting. She sat down and played a game. She knew very well how to play any kind of card game. Her father had taught her how to do this, but she had no money to bet so she bet her earrings, saying they were gold.

It didn't matter if it was a lie or not. She was going to win.

She always did.

She was not surprised when the man sat at the table on the opposite side and played a match. Lorenzo was his name.

She left the table after few games, beating even Lorenzo. The target. Drinks arrived to her, but she only ignored them.

Rosé took a few more turns paying attention to the people around her. Trying to find someone else interested in her.

He might not be alone.

Another glass of champagne.

The events seemed to be passing quickly as adrenaline took her body. She played, she talked with an old man in brown suit. She danced alone and had some fun and obviously couldn't deny some fancy food.

Most of the people who were there were much older and probably very rich. They wore jewels and gold watches with stones so shiny they looked like they could blind her. They wore branded dresses and very well-crafted masks.

Rosé was already starting to get mad at hers. Pining and hurting her face, but she couldn't take it off.

Not yet.

Her gaze was on people. She had lost sight of Kay but did not bother to seek him out or worry. She wasn't scared. She was tired of him. It was at that moment that she stopped and realised. Her heart was not beating heavily in her chest due to anxiety or sadness. She could feel the adrenaline and even in danger. She felt good.

She let a light smile slip away.

She was feeling alive.

Doing something that really mattered.

The man continued to follow her discreetly, but not discreetly enough for her not to notice.

She was on the edge of the dancefloor watching countless couple dancing, some better than others. The music was slow and had no specific choreography.

The man was a few feet from her. Watching her from the side of his eyes, while talking to someone. An older woman. Rosé couldn't see her. She had her back to Rosé, but by her kind of wrinkled hand Rosé could see she definitely wasn't young.

She looked at the crowd again, stopping to look where her target was. She couldn't be obvious. She bit her lower lip and that's where the trouble started. The woman said goodbye with two kisses on the cheek. He stood still for a while and began to approach subtly. Was now the time? She was a long way from the final destination. Where she had to take him to.

She'd have to go a long way.

Despair began to overwhelm her. Maybe she was scared. Where was Kay? Where was that damn creature? If she squeezed the cup harder, it'd break in her hands. She searched for Kay once more, discreetly, but nothing. She was going to start walking when she felt warm, firm hands touching her waist and one of them gliding down her back, holding her in place and bringing her to his hard body.

"Looking for me, baby?" he asked against her neck. Rosé didn't answer. "Not yet, *beautiful thing* ... but how about a dance?" He stood aside, offering his hand. Rosé straightened her posture and accepted Kay's hand. They went to the middle of the dancefloor. Rosé kept one of her hands connected to Kay's and another went to his shoulder.

He looked at her intensely and it embarrassed her. She didn't want to look around because she knew there were more people watching them.

Most of the couples had decided to leave.

"Really? The middle?" she whispered, approaching Kay, but then she pulled away a little. Their proximity was a danger zone. They began a light and subtle dance, just like the other couples around them. Basic and simple.

"He can't hear us from here," he remarked, squeezing Rosé's waist more and pulling her close. "I don't bite, princess. Well, maybe tonight can be an exception," he commented in her ear. "I heard you bite." Rosé was not in the mood to look at his face, but from the corner of her eyes, she could see that a smile had formed on Kay's face.

"To shut people's mouth."

"Maybe you could shut mine."

She ignored him. "Do you think he's going to follow?"

"He seems very interested. Too much I'd say." Kay looked at the side where the target was and then looked at Rosé again. "Look at me, we need to look like a couple."

"We're not."

"That's why I said, 'look like'," he grunted, making her whole body shudder.

Rosé looked at him, regretting it as soon as her eyes found Kay's. She could never decide if his eyes were light blue or light grey, but knew it was a unique colour.

A red tear ran down under his mask. She caught it before it went lower. "What happened?"

He held her gaze and then swerved, looking down. Rosé took her hands off his shoulder and slapped him lightly on his face. "Hey, my eyes are over here." Another smile formed on his face, causing the two dimples to appear. His gaze was down, like he was drunk. That was the last thing she needed at the time.

Kay drunk.

"What do you think? No one walks away freely after touching what they shouldn't," he said, leaving a quick kiss on her cheek. Her hands grabbing his shirt "Unfair, don't you think? And I wasn't looking at your boobs. Well … maybe. You look incredibly beautiful, Smurf," he said, turning her around. Rosé gave him a disbelieving look. "I'm serious. I can't stop looking at you."

"Thank you, you too." This time he was the one who looked away. "I don't know why you're discrediting my word."

"You lie too much."

"Does that bother you?"

"It drives me crazy" Kay pulled her closer. Their faces were close to each other. Their lips close to touching. If she moved, that's what would happen and she wanted it to happen.

"Sorry if you doubt me, Comic Book," she said, leaning backward, her nails sliding down the side of his face.

Rosé thought the world went by in slow motion as he leaned her toward the ground. His hands held her back so that she would not fall to the ground, then he brought her back slowly.

"I'm not doubting them, I'm just surprised they came out of your lips," he whispered. She could feel his hot breath on her skin. Kay left a kiss on her cheek this time. "Don't ever call me that again, or you'll have to suffer the consequences." Rosé didn't have time to ask what the consequences would be. He started to walk away.

"Now," he whispered.

Rosé began to walk towards the other room, according to plan. She didn't risk looking at Kay. She trusted him. She kept walking. She lifted a glass on the way. She wasn't walking fast enough to seem suspicious, but not as slow as someone who was not up to anything.

Inside she was shaking.

What if it went wrong? What if they couldn't get the man?

Her shoes were the sound that prevailed in the corridor, which was almost deserted. She could hear the sound of his footsteps behind her. But they were low. Is the plan really working? Rosé kept walking. Her hair dancing at every movement of her body. Her hand was warming up the glass and the drink inside it.

She took a deep breath once, twice, three times.

She could feel the heavy metal on her thigh.

Upon arriving at the end of the hall, Rosé entered the last room, as Kay had said. It was a huge room full of furniture covered in white sheets, with a wall of windows that provided an incredible view of Rome.

Rosé went towards the windows. The sound of the door popped. "I thought it was a lie, but our dear Sarah really had a daughter." His accent thick and confident. Was it a thing for these people to always be confident? "The Heir of Lysions."

"My mother was smart," Rosé said, turning around. She swigged the drink and then took another sip. She needed alcohol if she was to put up with a man like him. "Just like my father. It took a while for everyone to find out, didn't it?" She removed the mask. The man was no longer wearing his. He looked like he was in his thirties, but she knew that was a lie, he was probably a lot older than that.

"I must admit, it did. Twenty-one? Twenty-two years? But now tell me, Rosélina, is it real? What do people say? I've never met one of your kind in my life," he said, taking off one of the sheets and revealing an armchair, in which he sat. "I've heard a lot of rumours about you. Theories. Gossip."

"Maybe yes, maybe not. People like good gossip. They believe everything they're told." She didn't know where all this confidence was coming from. "But that's not why I'm here."

"Of course, it's not." He adjusted in the armchair. "Why did you bring me here?" He had crossed his arms and legs. He looked at her, waiting for an answer. His was exuding confidence. According to the plan, Kay was supposed to be there, but he wasn't.

Dickhead.

Rosé improvised. She stood with her back straight. Head higher than normal too. If they were going to argue, let it be on the same level.

"I didn't bring you here, you followed me."

"Wasn't that the point?" he asked, leaning his face to the side, frowning.

"Maybe." Where is he?

"You must be very brave to be here alone," he remarked. She wasn't alone. Kay would show up any minute.

"Maybe I am. Are you bothered by that?"

"Not at all. I like a domineering woman. Empowered, but mostly I like an easy target." Rosé turned her face, showing her disgust at the comment. She wanted to throw up right there over him. "This conversation is getting very boring. I have a party to attend. Why don't we get down to business? What do you want from me?"

"I'm here because …" she let out a sigh. Where the fuck was Kay? She didn't know what to say or act or even how to breath properly. "I want information." She was direct. She didn't want to stall. She didn't know how long that trust was going to stay there, but she wasn't intimidating at all. Her voice had failed.

"Hm that won't be possible." He informed "My mouth is a sealed tomb." He passes his fingers over his mouth as if it had a zipper.

"Oh," she said, leaving the glass on the table next to her. "Won't you talk?" she faked a sad face, and he denied it. Her face went from sad to serious. "Okay. I'm not going to beg—"

"Of course not, because you know nothing about our world. A little girl like you is so naïve."

Naïve: innocent. No malice. No attitude. She kept her head up. *Because you don't know anything about our world.* She took a deep breath, hoping that her patience would return to her body again. And then she smiled. No. She laughed. "Naïve?" She was still laughing. She leaned on the table, six feet away from him. "Says the man who followed a Lysion out of the eyes of others. Alone. You are not all that."

"What made you think I came alone?" Her heart missed a beat, but it was in that comment that the mistake happened.

"Oh." She began to laugh even harder, seeing the discomfort on the man's face. "You're saying then, that you were afraid, and you brought your companions with you because you did not have the ability to face a naïve girl? Oh, so sweet and delicate." She leaned over the table and whispered, "Coward."

Ego successfully damaged.

He rose up, coming towards her. Fury burning in his eyes. Men with an affected ego are like spoiled children when they don't get what they want. Rosé was excited for a moment, but she was not feeling threatened.

Time to play.

In a quick movement of her hands, he flew back to his chair and spindle branches began to hold his hands and legs until they reached his neck. He struggled and moaned in pain.

He pressed a button, it was secured in the back of his shirt. Rosé stopped the branches, looking at the door, but no one showed up.

"Waiting for someone?"

They exchanged glances.

"That's what I thought. You're alone, sweetie. What a pity."

"I am saying nothing."

"Okay, we can handle that." She moved her hand once more, until the branches were wrapping around his neck. "I may not have grown up in our world, but that doesn't mean I wasn't prepared or that I don't know how to take care of myself." She drank another sip of her Champaign. "I may as well be loving and understanding. A woman who respects, but you know, I can be disgusting and nasty, too. I might be a bitch if I want to." He spat at her. "Let me tell you something about women. Real women. If they really want something, they're going to do everything they can to get it. If you take one down, two get up. We don't stop. We don't let others win. We take the pain and turn it into fuel and energy."

She stopped for a second.

"Great speech," he said, with trouble breathing.

Rosé closed her fists. "I'm sorry you won't be alive when I'm done with it."

Adrenaline and anger. That's what was taking her body.

Something touched her hand, relaxing her. His touch on her skin "Don't you think that's enough? We need him." Rosé relaxed even more and so did the branches. Within seconds, he was loose again. His hands on his neck, bleeding.

Rosé didn't look at him. She didn't want to see his face. Instead, she looked the opposite way, setting loose her hand.

Late. He was fucking late.

"Now ..." He leaned further forward, leaning his elbows on his legs and joining hands. "If I may," Lorenzo coughed, "I wondered if the legends were true. Don't worry, it will end soon," he said, lunging at Rosé, falling hard on the floor.

"You missed," said Kay. He was leaning against a table. "The conversation was very interesting, in fact, but—"

"Interesting?" Rosé interrupted, hitting his chest, her face bright red. "How long have you been in there? Where the fuck were you? And why is your nose fucking bleeding?" she asked getting a tissue from the table and cleaning.

"Calm down, love, I didn't leave you alone for a minute. I've always been here, but you didn't notice," he said, approaching her and stroking Rosé's chin. "You were too busy almost killing our victim. Well, I was taking care of some people," he moved the guy back to sofa "Now we wait for him to wake up." The chair moved quickly and was soon in front of them, scaring Rosé "You freak out easy."

"I don't have time for this," she said, throwing the drink in Lorenzo's face, making him wake up in fright. His gaze confused looking from Kaydan to Rosé.

He closed and opened his eyes a few times. "Kaydan Dagon, how long has it been?" he said, smiling, showing his yellow teeth. Rosé wanted to punch him in the face.

Hadn't he noticed Kay before?

"Whatever, now … I need you to tell me what the Blake family and their fucking followers are planning."

"I'm one of them."

"I know. Now, tell me. What do you plan to do?" Kay leaned over him. The man said nothing. "Aren't you going to tell us?" He remained silent. Kaydan closed his hand, murmuring something bringing a scream from Lorenzo's throat. Lorenzo's head falling backward as his face turned red.

Silence and no reply from Lorenzo.

Rosé was already getting impatient. She lifted one foot to the middle of the man's legs. Kay's eyes widened. She began to push, squeezing her foot, on Lorendo's jewels. The pain became evident with every push. He went from pink to purple. "Look here, you piece of dry shit. You've seen the branches and look, I have a gun here with me," she said, taking the gun from her thigh. "I have six bullets. They all have poison inside them and as far as I know you are the only target." Rosé came closer to the man, forcing her shoe further into him. "And I'm seriously thinking about shooting where my shoe is, not to mention I have a Kaydan Dagon here next to me." Before Kay could say something, Rosé issued a warning. "Save your ego for later, the only voice I want to hear is this man's."

He stared at her. Rosé removed her foot, letting the man regain his breath. She walked away, putting the gun in place, and returned to get her drink. She drank what had been left in the glass by the window, watching the view of Rome.

Both of them were quiet for a while. Rosé turned to Kay, he looked at her from top to bottom. His eyes revealed his shock, and his mouth was slightly open. "You have serious problems against dicks."

"I don't."

"Yes, you do."

"No, I don't."

"Yes … you do."

She took a deep breath.

"Yes, I do. I love kicking them and watching men writhe in pain. Is there a problem?"

"When the dick is mine yes, but with those of others, do what you want."

"Can I?" she provoked.

Kay's jaw clenched. "You do what you want, Rosélina" her full name. *Oh, jealous baby?*

"Has she kicked yours?" Lorenzo asked, they both turned around.

"She's tried countless times, but only succeeded twice." Rosé showed him her middle finger. She was getting tired of this game, especially when no torture was actually involved, and she was getting annoyed.

Lorenzo began to laugh, still trapped in the chair. "Weak." Rosé went to him and drove her foot into him much stronger, almost making the chair turn back. He swore at her. She didn't kick if dick, she perforated.

"The next one's going to be a bullet. Come on, creature, we don't have all the time in the world, I'm done playing dick-kicking." She got closer to Kay. She was trying her best to be like them. Maybe it was too much. Maybe she was just embarrassing herself, but she was trying.

She was fucking trying.

She was …

He took his time to pass on the information. "They are thinking of attacking Amondridia at night when everyone is asleep."

"This isn't original, Wysez are worse than that," Rosé commented, with her back to them. She didn't want to see the man. She didn't really know if what she said was right, but she deduced it.

"Can I speak?" he asked with a tone of indignation. "This, during Tramocult. They will attack by surprise and in large numbers," the man informed, not her, but Kay. She was just an idiot girl for him, she could see how he treated them differently. Kay was a man of business.

"Now we are getting there," began Kay.

"What is Tramocult? A cult?" Rosé asked, confused, turning to them. No one had ever commented on it to her. There were a lot of things people hadn't told her.

"It is when we spend a week living from ancient customs and we return to ancient times to remember our ancestors. Living the way they lived, including technology, i.e. without the security alarms and all the protection of Amondridia. Honestly. I thought they were smarter." He sat at the table. "It's a tradition we don't follow in our Lys."

"That's not all."

"Go on," Kay and Rosé said in a chorus.

"It's not just going to be Wysez." Kay crossed his arms. He frowned. He was focused. "They are recruiting other people and creatures. The ancient Legendaries, half-dead, dragons, black phoenixes, demons, Guyques. The Quintuples are on their side. Aware of her existence. They … they want her and they're desperate for it. And they're going to do everything they can to get her," he said, pointing his head at Rosé. He wasn't confident anymore. Rosé could see that his hands were shaking. His voice failed. Kay looked at her and then at the man. "They want her alive. He wants her alive."

"Why?"

"I don't know," he said with difficulty. "They stopped telling me a lot of things, but… I heard rumours of duplication. Some sort of Lost Ones scientists and machinery"

"Duplication?" Kay asked. His lip twitched as he looked at her for a few seconds.

She had also changed her mind. She was no longer playful. *And they're going to do everything they can to get her.* She could feel the bile burning at the bottom of her throat. She wasn't confident anymore either.

"Thank you for your help."

Kay took Rosé by the hands, and they turned to leave.

"Wait," he cried.

"Yes?" Kay stopped halfway, without looking back.

"Kill me!" Lorenzo almost screamed, "I beg you, Dagon." She had never heard anyone call him by his last name.

"What?" Rosé looked at Kay and then Lorenzo.

"They will come after me and torture me until I beg to die. I cooperated with you because I'm not very much in favour of what they intend to do and I'm going to tell you that … if they keep the girl, our world is over. Please. I helped you because the moment I saw you, I knew it would be the right thing to do."

"Rosé, pass me what I gave you." Kay still did not look back.

"Are you really going to kill him? Use your magic. It will attract less attention," she said, searching his eyes.

"Magic doesn't kill, Lysion," Lorenzo screamed, laughing. "You are teaching her wrong, Dagon. You are fucking up. Clean magic only hurts, your body does the rest."

Rosé handed the weapon over to Kay. Her hands were trembling. He held them before he took the gun and whispered, "I can't risk you leaving this room alone. I'm sorry," he said, giving her hands a kiss. "Look to the side and cover your ears if you want."

But she didn't. Kay didn't hesitate for a second or think twice. She should get used to it. She looked at Lorenzo's back.

The sound echoed through the room.

His body was limp and lifeless.

Chapter 43

Rosé and Kay left through the emergency exit. Kay's hand intertwined with Rosé's. He was holding her like he didn't want her to get away. Maybe he was saying something. Asking if she was well or something similar, but the only thing she could hear was the man's words echoing in her ears.

They want her and they're desperate for it. And they're going to do everything they can to get her.

She had just seen another man being killed. Just remembering the sound of the gunshot, her body shuddering.

No one has ever wanted her so much in their lives. She laughed and cried internally. The despair in his eyes as he mentioned 'they' seemed to be referring to something bigger.

They wanted her. Although it was no surprise, those words echoed in her ears for a long time. *They want her … they're going to do everything they can to get her.* Wanting her wasn't the main problem. She thought they wanted her dead, but now they want her alive. What had made them change their minds? If dead, she would feel nothing, but alive …

They wanted her magic. The same magic she had carried inside her from the womb. The same magic who broke the mirror. The same magic that made the earth tremble. The same magic who protected her. They wanted something she couldn't control properly.

To hear those words coming from people she didn't know, from strangers, that hurt because it made it real.

Her gaze was confused, lost, empty. A thousand and one thoughts were going on in her head. A thousand and one images. Two thousand and two things in her head and at the same time, nothing. Sometimes she'd look at Kay. He watched her, his eyes tried to look for her, understand her, but they got lost.

Since when was he holding her hand?

Maybe he noticed her absence in the real world. Maybe he didn't care about her.

She couldn't understand how she was walking. Her feet were in pain.

Her legs were heavy. Her back seemed to have been hit by something. The world seemed to be passing in slow motion.

She was tired. Tired of everything. She didn't want to be wanted. She just wanted to wake up in her room at the university. Where she could cry with no one judging. She wished to be alone. She wanted her normal life.

Fuck the magic.

Fuck Amondridia.

Fuck the world.

Fuck the Lysions.

Their eyes met. She could see his mouth moving, but it looked like someone had pressed the mute button.

Rosé closed her eyes hard. She moved her head lightly, opening her eyes she looked at his mouth, trying to understand.

"-Do you want me to take you? Your feet look swollen and—"

"No need. I'm fine." The words came out with more difficulty than she expected. Like they were ripped out of her throat. She didn't mean to look weak. Not in front of Kay. He's probably done a lot of that before. Killed or threatened.

She thought about what she had just done. She felt embarrassed. She didn't know how to extract information. They all already had it and she was just another helpless girl they were protecting.

One more on the huge list.

"You're not well." He stopped. "I've never seen you like this, and I've seen you in countless bad times." Rosé sometimes forgot that Kay had been responsible for protecting her without her knowledge. He'd probably seen a lot of things.

Shame. That's all she felt.

"I'm fine," she almost cried, there was frustration in her tone. She closed her eyes and breathed, walking again. There were tourists on the street, talking and laughing. She looked at a group. Happy. She wanted to be one of them.

Before she could take any more steps, Kay took her lightly by the arm, making her stop again, he took her hand and, once again, he left a kiss there.

Eye to eye.

Shit, his eyes. She liked the kisses. It was somehow archaic, but kind and caring. Hers, just hers.

"I'm sorry about what happened, it wasn't in my plans."

"Of course, it wasn't." The tears fell. "You don't seem to be the kind of person who follows the plans, but I follow, okay?" Her gaze strayed from his. "You were supposed to show up earlier. You didn't tell me you were going to give me a gun to carry when we got here. You lied to me." She got rid of his hands, taking a few steps, and then letting her arms fall by her side. "I … I wanted to be like you. Brave, fearless, and heroic. Fight for what I think is right. Fighting for my life, but the only thing I can do is cry and feel weak. Feel sorry for myself. I … I … What I did … what I tried …"

You should stop feeling sorry for yourself, Nikko had said once.

She could barely breathe. "I'm tired of being useless. To be protected. To feel scared and, damn I hate these shoes," she said, crouching down to take them off, leaving them on the floor. "I don't want this anymore. I don't want to live anymore. Maybe …" she stopped. She was about to say it out loud one more time. She wanted to, but she couldn't. "I hate Amondridia and all the people there because it doesn't matter what I do, I will never, ever be like you." Before she could react, Kay brought her into his arms.

Fuck. His hugs were … she didn't have an adjective to describe them.

She wanted to scream. Drop everything she'd kept inside her for a long time. She wanted the pain to go, but …

But if she screamed, everyone would know how weak she was, and worst of all was that no one would care about it. Because people don't care about other people's weakness, only when it effects them.

They stayed that way for a few seconds.

"You're not weak," he whispered. "You did great there, you—"

"Yes, I am," she whimpered back, the sound muffled. Her face squeezed into his chest.

In one second, she was in his arms. In his warmth. And in the next she was being gently lowered to the ground, like in the dance they were performing some minutes ago. She almost hit the floor; their eyes locked. A few seconds passed before he brought her back.

"If you weren't Rosélina, you would probably be alone and on the floor for being so fucking emotional and …" A tear ran down her cheek, making her body shiver. "But you are and fuck it … you are destroying me," Kay said, leaving her there as he started walking away.

"I am sorry," she whispered to his back. He turned around. "I am sorry for being emotional. I am sorry for being useless. I am sorry for being a Lysion. I am sorry for not being enough. I am sorry, for my dad to make you, my guardian." She let out a weak smile. "Yes, I am wea..." She stopped. "You know what? Fuck you." He fully turned to her. "Fuck you," she repeated. "I went there, I sacrificed myself. I did it. I tried, and it wasn't perfect, but I fucking tried. I tried every fucking day of my life and if you or anyone else are not going to recognise this, then I will. I will for myself."

There was a difference between thinking you are not worth it and accepting what people thought of you. She might think she didn't deserve the air in her lungs, but would never, ever in her life, let someone think they could put her down.

He placed his hands in his pockets. "I told you, you were not weak and that you did great. We all told you. It was you all along who was not seeing this and were lying to yourself," he said, coming to meet her. "What you did now, recognising your worth, was a fucking step forward."

"You said I was emotional, and I was destroying you."

He held her face in his hands. It was hot even in the cold streets. "A great number of the people I know, are emotionless. They lost so much; they can't let out a tear anymore, if not for something they really, really care about. You, being emotional, is so human and so innocent, and then the next moment you are threatening, like ... fuck. You can be both. That is amusing."

"Why am I destroying you?" she whispered. Her small hands rested on his chest.

"Because you're dominating my mind" he raised his voice "You're becoming something I can't live without" The butterflies danced in her stomach. "And I hate you for that. It's pathetic how much I want to touch your skin and hear your voice all the fucking time. How I constantly want you all by myself and I'm selfish, I'm so fucking selfish, I brought you here because I wanted you all for myself" he confessed.

Rosé approached him even more, looking deeper into his eyes. She could already feel his hands on her body "Can I?" Her gaze went down to Kay's lips and then back to his eyes. Kay wrapped his arms around her, pulling her body to his. Their faces, close to each other, inches away. The cold was non-existent as their bodies touched.

"Fucking yes, baby," he said "You'll never need to ask for it. They're all yours." he commented with a smile. Rosé took her hand to his cheeks, feeling warm but flushed skin around the rough beard that was beginning to grow again. She closed her eyes, feeling his face, just as Nikko had done before with her. Feeling every trace and trying to memorise every corner of his face, those she had not yet found. Until their lips met.

(Finally!)

That doesn't mean anything, Rosé. She lied to herself because it did mean something. Many things.

His lips were soft and warm as she had imagined. Possessive over hers. She could taste the metal and alcohol on his lips. Rosé's hand slid to the back of his head while the other was in his hair, stroking that area. A strange feeling ran through her body and stopped in her chest and between her legs. An explosion of emotions and feelings and, for the first time in her life, she had forgotten the world outside.

Kay's hand caressed her back, pulling her even closer. Owning her. Rosé had never felt wanted like she was feeling now. She felt like she had lightning in her body. A moan came from the back of her throat. She buried herself in his warmth, his smell. Books and perfume. His hard body, yet soft and warm against her.

Their tongues met. Their bodies were glued together, but not enough. She wanted more. Kay was tall, and she needed to be on tiptoe to be able to kiss him. She could not describe the way he grabbed her. The possession. The strength and yet lightness on her body. Just the perfect way.

Rosé felt one of Kay's hands stop at her ass and squeeze it, making her break the kiss. "Manners." she said, laughing, but worried at the same time. His eyes were dark and shinning, his lips red from the kiss and lipstick.

Everyone must be looking. Affection in public draws a lot of attention. There weren't many people on the street, but no one seemed to be looking at them, it was like they weren't there. They were minding their own lives.

"Like I give a fuck about it" he said "No one is looking anyway," returning to kiss her. Hungrier. More desperate than before. His hands went to the opening of the dress on her left leg, touching her bare skin. She moaned against his lips as his hand reached her ass under her dress.

The shortness of breath came faster than she expected. She could feel *him* on her. "You look so fucking delicious today," he said, smiling at her. Rosé bit her lower lip, trying to hide the smile. "I wish I could have told you before, but it would have been quite inappropriate."

"I would have cursed you," she informed him.

"I presumed this." Rosé laughed, hitting his chest. "You do not know how much I wanted to do this." She could say the same. "Are you sure you don't want me to take you home in my arms?" Their foreheads were glued. Breaths becoming one.

"I'm fine." Her feet were still barefoot and wet on the cold stone, relieving a little of the pain that the shoes had caused. The rain was falling on them. She held his hand, and they start walking.

Rosé had taken a few steps when Kay took her in his arms. "I can't just ignore your feet, they're swollen and almost purple, and are now getting cold and wet." She watched him for a while. His profile was even sexier. "And guess what?" Rosé stood silently, waiting for the answer. Their eyes met for a second. "I'm old and one thing I've learned in my life is that women can be very good at hiding things." She stroked his reddish cheek. "And I think I have to remind you for the thousandth time, to stop lying to me."

She was broken inside, but she still smiled.

Rosé approached his lips and bit them. Kay groaned in pain. "you said they were mine, and I wanted to bite them. You know I love biting."

<3

Kay's phone beeped once more in his pocket, but he didn't answer. It had beeped countless times since they had arrived at the apartment. They needed the approval to cast a portal. They needed to go unnoticed. When she asked, he just said that they had to wait.

"I thought our torture would be more interesting," Rosé commented from the bed. A blanket wrapped around her wet body.

"You wouldn't let me do anything."

"You were too slow and late." Even after kissing him, they were still poking fun at each other.

"The best part of dizziness is you wait for the person to wake up and realise how fucked up they are. Then they panic. The heart accelerates and they begin to sweat, then you begin the torture." The phone beeped once again. Kay swore then looked at her. "Do you still trust me?" Kay asked with his phone in his hand.

"Perhaps. After today I have my doubts."

"I'm sorry, but I need you to trust me one more time," he said, holding her by the waist and pulling her closer, leaving a kiss in the corner of her mouth. There was something in his eyes. Worry? "Pleas-" He was interrupted with a sound at the door. Kay dropped Rosé, pushing her hard as she hit the wall, something soft damed the impact.

"Look at her, the golden egg," said one of the men. "It looks like her mom; only more beautiful and sexier." He looked her up and down. The bile burned in her throat.

Rosé was confused. Kay had not reacted, he simply crossed his arms. "Thank you, Kay." Thank you? Rosé raised her eyes to Kay. What did he mean? Did Kay know these people?

"No problem. Now I want my payment." That definitely was not the answer Rosé was waiting for. Who were they? Rosé's gaze found Kay's. He soon swerved to get the money, beginning to count it. "Um, I think there's two hundred pounds missing here," he said, reaching out for more money.

"Wait, for what? Did you sell me to them?" Kay didn't answer. He took the money and put it in his pocket.

"Seriously, Rosé." He approached her, meeting her gaze. "You really thought I didn't know all that. Oh, wait, you thought I worked for the Elite?" He started laughing in her face. He held her gaze for a few second. His eyes were trying to pass a massage, and then he walked away. "I just needed an excuse to bring you here and Gustav helped by bringing the perfect plan to the table. We distracted the others with the damn party so I could take you here," he commented, gesturing to the air. "I knew that eventually your social battery would run out and you and I would be alone. I know you're not a big fan of parties and eventually you'd go out." Kay took a candy package and offered it to friends. "Do you want one? The best in Italy." Almost everyone accepted.

I need you to trust me one more time, is that what she needed to trust him with? She couldn't believe she was being used as bait again after what just happened.

"Son of a bitch," she said, fist formed; her jaw tightened. One of the men was handcuffing her, but they weren't normal handcuffs. It's touch on her wrist burned. What they did not know was that the handcuffs couldn't retain her magic. It was just a toy on her wrists. She didn't know if she could trust him anymore. She didn't know if he had a plan or not. Everything seemed very surreal. His expression was neutral.

She felt stupid and annoyed for trusting him.

She rolled her eyes.

"Oh Smurf, there's nothing new to call me?" he commented, raising Rosé's chin with his finger. Their eyes met and his corner smile made his dimple appear. Damn dimple. He left a kiss on the tip of her nose. Light and subtle. "Keep it up!" he whispered.

She spat on his face. "You are fucked up," she hissed at a volume only he could hear. He smiled at her. "You tricked me and sold me to a bunch of freaks!" she said out loud this time. Kay walked away and wiped his face. Tears were threatening to escape, so she let them out. Maybe she was exaggerating but looking weak was an advantage. *I'm going to kill all of you*, she thought.

Anger ran all over her body. Kay could have been fooling them, but he was still using her.

"Look, I don't have all the time of the world," the man, who she discovered was called Montiero, said. "Shall we?" he asked, with his hand just below Rosé's waist. A blond man opened a portal, and they all went in.

Kay was in the corner of the room, observing her, especially where Montiero's hand was. She never saw so much hate in someone's eyes as she did in Kay's.

Rosé felt the same sickness but swallowed the vomit. "Kill them all but let the three of us live," a familiar voice whispered in her ear. Everyone was too distracted to pay attention.

Kay stayed behind as they walked to the entrance of a huge mansion. It was different from any she had ever seen. It was made of a dark material which gave it a rustic appearance. Rosé looked around and realised that it was the only building in a vast field. Lonely.

No stars in the sky. Cold. Rosé wrinkled her nose at the smell of death. She swallowed her vomit for a second time. Her throat burned.

Rosé began to reflect on what she had heard. She wondered if she was freaking out. She couldn't just kill them, but who said she needed to kill? Who knows, maybe a serious injury or something similar? A cut on the thigh, a kick in the jewels (she really wants to kick there), a stab wound? No.

They were almost at the gate; the smell was getting worse. There was something lurking behind the gate. Like shadows. Rosé's heart began to beat faster. Montiero's hand was still holding her. She looked back to where Kay was. He watched her. His veins were visible. He was trying not to lose control.

She looked forward again.

She closed her eyes. Killing someone wasn't what she needed to do right now, but the man next to her might be the exception. The rest wouldn't do anything to anyone, would they? She began to think about it, imagining it as she had been trained countless times.

She focused on her body.

She was still wet from the rain, the dress danced to her movements. The wet and icy ground kissed her feet. She thought of her beautiful reddish shoes. She hadn't gone to the trouble of dressing them up. The gun weighed on her thigh.

Hidden. The icy metal against her warm skin. She focused on the men around her. Her hands were stuck in front of her. She let out a sigh. Her eyes burned lightly.

"But what?" Montiero murmured. When she looked around, everyone was on the floor. Nobody moved. They looked like corpses strewn across the floor. Lifeless.

"I'd drop her if I were you." A warning. Montiero was confused. His jaw contracted.

"What did you do?" He turned to Kay, holding Rosé closer to him. He held her so hard that it made her groan in pain. Her body was too sensitive and exposed to the cold.

"Nothing," Kay commented with that tone of satisfaction that Rosé hated. "That was the work of the person next to you." Kay pointed his head at Rosé. "And I won't say it again. Take your fucking hands off her," he said, closing his hands and, with it, causing pain in Montiero's hand who let her go quickly. Kay eyes were dominated by black. It took some seconds for them to come back to normal.

Montiero raised his hands, but nothing happened. "WHAT THE FUCK? What did you do?" he screamed, a vein popping out in his neck, looking at both hands. Despair was taking over him.

"Did you like the candy?" asked Kay, throwing the bag up n the air. "A little cursed weed and boom, means no magic for you. Funny how things are so simple. Magic too sleepy to bother with."

"What did you do to my people, you son of a bitch?" he said, trying to grab Rosé once again, but failing. His hand froze an inch away from her.

"Are you deaf?" Kay asked, approaching, he closed his hands again. And this time Rosé knew Kay had just broken Montiero's hands. The sound made her body flinch. "You won't put a little finger on her," he said with his hands still in the air. Rosé covered his hands, and, just after that, she could feel him relaxing under her touch.

"How dare you betray me."

"Oh my friend, look at the most precious and perfect thing you were holding in your hands. Did you really think I was just going to give her to you? You know me very well and you know that I'm too selfish to share things, especially her." Rosé tried not to smile, but *was he calling me his property?* She wanted to laugh sarcastically and explain things to him, very much, but held on for another moment.

"You're a lot like your mother," he said, laughing and spitting on Kay's face. It must be something people do quite a lot, she thought. He cleaned himself using Montiero's blouse.

"Stealing personalities now?" Rosé asked, indignant at what he had done. Besides using her as bait twice, passing it on, calling her his property, now he would steal her incredible deeds? Not a chance.

"Sorry love," he apologised and wiped the residue of Montiero's spit in his face. "Happy?" Rosé didn't answer. "Now," he returned to looking Montiero in the eye. "Don't you dare talk about my mother," he growled.

"She was going to be the next one, but your sister came first. Poor—" Montiero didn't finish his sentence, Kay was already throwing him against the enormous gate. "Two bitches waiting to be fucked," he commented from the floor, laughing as if it was a brilliant joke. Kay took his dagger and threw it at Montiero, making an impact with his hand.

He screamed. "Go to hell, Dagon!" Kay lunged in anger and hit him. He ruthlessly continued hitting his face, while Montiero only smiled. His mouth bleeding.

"Kay." Rosé pulled back his hand. He was sweating from the beating he was delivering. "Enough." She knew she should not had stopped him, especially after what she heard. The assumptions she made.

She was crying for them. Kay have never talked about his family and now she knew why … she held his face, trying to find his eyes. Calm him. Saying that she was there for him.

He was tense. "You got free of …" He couldn't even speak properly. Rosé only nodded. She had a long time ago. Even before Kay had spoken. They were too busy insulting each other that they couldn't even pay attention to their surroundings. "I am sorry, I … are you okay?"

She was going to answer, but Montiero's weak laugh penetrated the air. "So weak. She is changing you," he commented. His eyes were swollen from the beating. He was facing the floor. "He is not like that," he tried to inform Rosé. "He is worse, Rosélina. So much worse."

"Shut up," Kay hissed. A mistake. Montiero kept laughing.

"Don't lie to her. They lied too much, don't you think?"

"Pass me the gun." Kay didn't even look at her. Rosé just took it from her leg and gave it to him. She didn't know how to react. How to deal with it. *He is worse, Rosélina. So much worse.* She questioned herself. Where did she fall in all this mess.

A single shot and a scream of despair.

Right in between his legs.

“Do not … ever mention any woman I love even again.” Kay crouched in front of him, using the gun to lift Montiero’s face. “I swear on my life, that if you dare touch Rosélina or my family, you will be tortured as you have never been before. Cross my way again, I fucking dare you” he creamed “You will only stay alive, because Oldo will know what to do with you.” Kay was the one who laughed this time. “I know he is going to take care of you. Lost his money. Lost a Lysion. Trusted the wrong guy. So. Many. Mistakes.” A little note appeared on Montiero’s forehead.

Kay conjured a portal and took Rosé’s hand. She was looking at him. So much was going on inside her mind.

They should have killed him.

Chapter 44

Her nose was overwhelmed by the smell of flowers. They were in the greenhouse. Tears were running down her face. Her whole body shaking. Kay lay her on the floor, he hugged her in his arms as she struggled to breathe properly. She didn't know how she had ended up in his arms.

"I'm sorry. I needed a way to bring us back to England … I couldn't use my magic because …" He too could barely speak. "And the people who were helping me betrayed us. Rosé, I'm sorry. For everything. Fuck … I … he …"

She didn't know how to react to that. Neither knew how to react.

"WHAT THE FUCK HAPPENED HERE? WHERE WERE YOU WITH THE HEAD—?" Ariady came in, screaming. Rosé had never seen her like this before.

"I'm sorry," Kay was still hugging Rosé. His voice was weak. He fell to the ground, taking Rosé with him. The floor was hard against their knees. She didn't understand the sudden change of mood. They were alive and home. She had never seen Kay this way. He wasn't crying, but he seemed to have lost control.

"Kay, what happened to your back? Rosé, let go of him." Rosé obeyed, still confused. She tried to dry her tears. Kay stayed on the ground. He hadn't gotten up. He was still on his knees, weak and out of strength.

She turned around and, looking at his back, she saw two knives had pierced him.

"ARE YOU AWARE OF WHAT YOU'VE DONE?" It was her father this time. "Rosé, go to your room, Ruby will escort you." It wasn't a request, but a command. One she would not follow. Ari was moving through the greenhouse, gathering ingredients. Rosé had not noticed Ruby's presence until her father mentioned her.

So, like Ariady and Tom, Ruby was concerned. She was in front of Rosé, groping her arms, looking for something and checking if she was okay. Her touch was not like anyone else's. It was rough and strong. "Is something hurting? Do you feel anything? Nausea? A headache? Dizziness?" Rosé denied all. She pulled Rosé by the arm. No delicacy.

"No." Rosé got rid of Ruby's hand, who stopped looking at her, fist formed. Ruby seemed to be looking inside Rosé's soul.

"I told you to go to your room." Angry was a cute description for Tom. He was furious.

"Rosé, just obey," Ari commented, gathering some more ingredients. "Tom, I need help here." She was shaking as she gathered everything she needed. Dropping things on the floor. Her chest moving up and down. If Rosé had time to observe her better, she might have seen her cry.

"I'm not going. I want to help." She went towards her father.

"No."

"Rosé, let's go." Ruby grabbed her by the arm once more, she gripped so hard Rosé could feel it in her bones. Penetrating her skin. "This is not the time to play hard, or be a hero," she almost screamed, grabbing Rosé even harder.

"I said NO" A wave went through the greenhouse and Rosé knew very well that it had been her. "Stop treating me like I'm a child. I'm staying and I'm going to help. You're more focused on getting me out of here that you forgot about him on the floor with two fucking knives in his back." Rosé broke free from Ruby's arms and knelt before Kay again.

"Are you alright?" she asked, her hands on his cheek, raising his head to meet his eyes. She could see his eyelids were heavy. *Breathe,* she repeated to herself. *Despair is your enemy at the moment.* "That was a stupid question, I'm sorry."

"I have two knives in my back. I don't think I'm okay," he said, laughing. He tried to kiss her but failed.

"I really want to slap you now for laughing," she replied.

"I'd love that."

"What can I do?" she asked Ari. She exchanged looks with Tom who looked away and then gave the commands. "Cut off his shirt and clean his wounds with water. There's scissors on the shelf, you know where to find the stuff." Rosé obeyed "Kay, can you get up?" He tried and failed. Before cutting the t-shirt, Rosé grabbed a chair and went to him, she helped him get up.

"You should listen to your father and go to your room," he said, moaning in pain.

"Don't you even start."

Kay was heavier than Rosé had imagined but managed to help him sit down. His back was arched, preferring to sit backwards onthe chair. Rosé took the scissors and started cutting his t-shirt. Her hands were shaking, and she could feel warm tears running down her face.

Her hands caressed Kay's hot skin.

By the time she finished cutting, there was already fabric and water on her side that her father had brought.

"I didn't want you to see me like this."

"Shut up."

"I'm serious," he moaned. "Now and before, with—"

"Shut up," she commanded. "Please."

Rosé cleaned each of the wounds with water, carefully. She was terrified each time Kay let out some groan or contracted his muscles. She'd lost count of how many times she apologised. She was asking herself what had happened lately and how, how the fuck all of this happened.

The water in the bucket was red when Rosé finished.

"Get some more clean water and another cloth," Ari warned. "I need to take out the daggers and the wound needs to be cleaned again." Ari headed over to them. "Tom, finish the potion. Ruby, grab an empty bucket for me from the closet near the door." Ari put her hands on the handle of the dagger.

"Have you done this before?" Rosé asked.

"Many times, sweetie," Ari informed. "Kay, I'm going to pull the first one."

"Okay," he said, seeking Rosé's hand, she didn't hesitate to give it to him. Kay groaned loudly when Ari tore out the first dagger, squeezing Rosé's hand. She thought for a second that he had broken her hand, but when she tried to move her fingers, they still answered the command.

Ari's face turned white.

"No, no, no. Fuck."

Gustav had arrived in the room. "It is good to see … oh shit."

"What's up?"

"It's poisoned. It's penetrating your body. Ruby, we need Nina. Now!" Ruby rushed from the room, phone in hand. Ari let out a few more swear words. Gustav approached to examine and gave some commands.

Tom had already finished the healing potion and now examined Kay's back. "Imagine if this was in Rosé? We could have lost them both."

"When I said … it would be just over my corpse, I wasn't kidding," he remarked, gripping the chair harder.

"Will he survive?" Everyone was silent. Rosé could no longer contain her tears. As soon as one dried, another one fell in its place. *Fuck Rosélina, stop fucking crying.*

She was standing before Kay once more. Her knees were sore. Her heart was racing. Her eyes looked for Kay's. He was weak. Sweat was dripping down his face. His hands were warm in contrast to Rosé's.

She took the cloth she had used on the wounds and washed it in the sink and twisted it above Kay's forehead. "Why doesn't anyone ever answer me?" she said in a whisper. Drying drops that ran down his face.

"If we act fast, I will survive, Smurf. We need Nina," he said, taking one of his hands to Rosé's face, drying her tears. Rosé kissed the palm of his hand and held it hard. A few thousand thoughts crossed her mind and none of them were pleasant.

The rest had started an argument, but Rosé had only noticed when she looked away from Kay.

"You need to rip out the other one," Gustav commanded.

"We need Nina. Kay's is weak, if something happen—"

"The poison will spread faster if we don't take it out."

"Are you sure?"

"Yes."

"Kay?"

"Take it out of me," Kay moaned. Rosé's heart stopped for a second and soon Ari had torn it from his body. Kay moaned in pain, tightly holding on to Rosé's hands. "Rosé," he started. "I don't know if I can take it. I need you to do something for me."

"What?"

"Close your eyes and imagine you're draining my pain."

"Bro, this isn't going to work," Gustav said, approaching. "This is too dangerous for both of you."

"Shut the fuck up," he muttered to Gustav. "Love, please." Rosé held Kay's hands tightly and closed her eyes. *Focus, you can do it.* It took a while. She had to hear many voices complaining. "You can do it. I trust you." Eventually, she could feel his blood running down her own body. Every vein, every cell in his body, connected to her. Something black had taken over her vision. Her heart rate started to get quieter. There was only silence. She wanted to scream with the burning in her chest and back but held on.

She heard a liquid noise. Like his blood was flowing in her own veins.

Silence.

Rosé was startled by the door opening with a bang, making her open her eyes quickly.

As she looked around, all eyes were on her. Was it working? Or was she playing a stupid role one more time? Rosé looked at Kay; he was alive. He watched her for a moment. He blinked. "You did it," he murmured. His voice was still a little hoarse. Kay got up, still trembling, and stood in front of Rosé.

Everyone was still looking at them both in silence. "I need to rest, and I need you to do the same. You were amazing." He kissed her hands. "Rest. I mean it. Good night," he said, leaving a kiss on the corner of her mouth. "Gustav, I need help." Gus went to Kay and passed one of his arms behind his back and they left.

Seconds.

That's how long it took him to disappear again. Like a click of fingers. So, fast she couldn't even process. She, did it? She did what exactly? He was dying and then …

Silence dominated the room again. Rosé didn't look at anyone around her, gathering the strength to get out of this place.

What had happened?

The corridors were empty and quiet. Her body was on automatic. One step after the other. When she arrived at her room, Rosé closed the door and sat there. No reaction.

<3

"Why do people hide things from me?" she asked. "Don't answer, I don't know if I want to know," she commented, sitting on the floor, leaning against the wall.

Mr Bebbols approached her and rubbed his head on her leg, then climbed on them. He was heavy. "There are things in this world that are not worth knowing. Things that aren't worth saying or being heard." Rosé began to caress him, listening to him purr. "You know what?" he said, standing up. "You're Rosé Lysion, if they don't give you information, you get information, and if they try to stop you, you rip their heads off." She looked at him, bemused. "But I didn't tell you that," he said, disappearing into the shadows.

Rosé smiled.

<3

Rosé looked round to find out where she was and realised, she was two corridors from Aiden's room. *Is he asleep*? she asked herself. Rosé approached and knocked on the door. No one answered. Rosé didn't want to knock again. She didn't want to wake him. She turned to go away and go back to her room, until a noise made her turn to look back.

Aiden was shirtless, just in striped shorts. His hair was messy, and his face crumpled. He was asleep and Rosé had woken him up. "Hey, is everything alright?" he asked, yawning. Rosé stared at him for a few seconds without reaction. She had acted without thinking. What would she say to Aiden? That everything was, okay? That she didn't want to disturb him, and she acted without thinking? She opened her mouth to say something, but her eyes began to water, and she ran to hug him.

She knew she'd taken him by surprise.

Aiden hugged her tightly and stroked her hair. "Hey, it's okay," he said quietly. "I'm here."

Chapter 45

They were back in the library. The smell of books hovered in the air, mingling with the smell of candles and dust from magical artifacts that few had the courage to use. Even Ari didn't know what many of them were for, but she never had the courage to risk finding out. Maybe Sarah knew. She was the one who brought a lot of them here, out of the reach of the wrong people. Not to mention books with strange titles that whispered or screamed out of nowhere, without being touched in years.

"Tell me I wasn't the only one who saw what happened last night?" Ruby asked, looking down at her high-heeled boots, then looking at each one of them. Her eyes searching for information. Maybe something that could show her she wasn't crazy.

Everyone was staring at something, lost in thought. No one dared to move. No one, but Tom, who climbed the stairs in silence and disappeared between the bookshelves.

"I've never seen anything like it," Ari remarked. Her gaze was still fixed on the table in the centre. Her foot bounced up and down while she thought. "When I first saw her, she seemed so—"

"Helpless? Innocent? A non-threat?" Kay said. "I've watched her longer than you. I know exactly what you're thinking." He too had appeared for the emergency meeting, even after almost dying. His back was aching. His muscles contracted, trying to diminish the pain.

"I'm sorry, but … if you have forgotten, I wasn't there. What happened? What did Rosé do this time?" Skylar was confused. Everyone had been restless since Kay and Rosé's arrival from a mission, but no one had dared to speak clearly about what had happened.

"My daughter was able to drain the poison of a *Black Rosaceae,* without getting hurt and without any device, just with her hands. AND SHE WAS NOT EVEN TOUCHING THE WOUND," Tom shouted from somewhere, his tone indignant.

"And why is that bad?" she asked, frowning. It took someone a while to respond, and it was making her angry. Rosé was showing progress, what everyone was expecting her to do, and now they were complaining. She was the one who was getting outraged.

"It means she's more powerful than we thought. I've never seen Sarah do that or anyone in all my years of life," Ruby said, running her hand through her short, black hair. "If she didn't know how to control …" she stopped. "If she loses control …"

"She's a Lysion."

"She's too powerful, Sky," Gustav remarked coldly, looking at her. He was sitting on a table with his arms folded. His breathing was heavy. "I mean, drain a fucking poison like it was nothing, fuck, that is …" He didn't know what to say. All unfinished sentences.

Sky let out a mocking scoff. "And why are you troubled by her power? Is she too powerful for you? Are you surprised that someone who has arrived now can be more powerful than any of us who have been alive for years? You disgust me, proud old men. We're training her for it. We all knew she was powerful and yes, she changed, how come you didn't feel that? Her eyes have changed. How she acts, how she talks, how she handles things. Come on, she is trying," she said sullenly, throwing herself into one of the chairs, her braids swaying. "Oh, yeah, I am the only one able to see this progress … and Watson."

"Mr Watson, and … I agree with her," he corrected. "Black Rosaceae please," he asked the library and soon a black book appeared in front of him. He took it and started turning the pages.

Kay, who was once standing next to Gustav, pulled out a chair and sat down just like Skylar. She knew just by looking at him that his head was full of thoughts. He had observed Rosé for a long time and that was the only thing he could think of. He knew from the beginning what she was, but somehow it bothered him. As a demon she could feel his surprise, fear, jealousy, and something else.

Everybody was feeling something similar.

Tom had reappeared and was leaning against the handrail upstairs, tense.

"You called me here to discuss something, I'm here. If you're going to be quiet, then I'm going to retire," Skylar informed when once again the silence began to bother her.

"We're thinking," Ruby retorted with the same harsh, cold voice.

"What are you thinking? Come on." She clapped her hands. "Share your thoughts." She could discover it by herself, but reading minds was not an option right now, it was too much effort.

"She, technically, almost killed a sentimental without any effort, just through her mind, her voice made the ground tremble, she drained and practically healed Kay without realizing it. All, without having the right control of her powers. Imagine what else she can do," Tom informed her. "She almost killed. With. Magic."

"Well, that's what we're training her for, right?" Sky leaned forward.

"So, we know what she can do and use it. So, she could protect herself."

"I am afraid of continuing her training." Tom finally brought the topic to the table. "What if she hurts someone or herself?"

"Are you afraid your daughter will become a killer like you?" Kay said without thinking.

"You shut the fuck up, Dagon." Everyone had noticed the tension between the two from the moment they had arrived. The long-narrowed eye contact. The annoyance on speaking. "Come near my daughter again and I will …" he trails off, raising his finger at him, breathing hard.

"I'm not going to apologise for what I did. There's only one person in this world who deserves my apology and that is your daughter. I almost died protecting her. Wasn't that enough for you?" Kay commented, his fist forming on his lap. He was barely controlling his anger. "I can't stay away from her. I'm her guardian in case you forgot."

"This could have been avoided if you had gone alone," Tom said loudly. He straightened his glasses and stepped away from the handrails. "Your goal was to protect her, and it seems to me you're doing more than that."

Kay let out an ironic smile, looking away. "What are you talking about? I don't understand what you're getting at."

"You know very well. I trusted you to take care of my daughter, not to fuc—" Tom cut himself off. He ran his hands through his hair in frustration then disappeared again.

"What's he talking about?" Sky asked, looking at Kay.

"Nothing."

"What. Was. He. Talking. About?" she repeated. Kay didn't answer. "I don't accept silence as an answer so speak now or I'll cut you open and discover it in the worst way that you know," she said, approaching him.

"Rwvka."

"What did you call me?" she said, grabbing him by the ears and pulling. "I'll rip your skin off little by little and make a cover with it." He showed no reaction, which made Skylar even agriear. "I want to know," she said, gnashing her teeth.

"Hey, hey, hey, sweetie, calm down." Gustav tried to get closer to her and pulled her away carefully.

"You're going to be without yours if you call me sweetie again," she said, pulling Gustav's ear with her free hand. Kay was still expressionless, unlike Gustav who was on his toes complaining and asking her to let go, but she didn't let go that easily.

"Skylar Saten, that's enough," called out Mr Watson, flipping over one more page. She stopped kicking the chair where Kay was sitting and returned to where she was before.

"He and Rosé are having something," Ruby commented triumphantly, seeing Kay's angry face and smiling. "But he's afraid to get too involved, you know? Kay being Kay." Her smile grew.

Skylar's jaw fell to the ground. "Are you kidding me?"

"You could have spoken before she pulled my FUCKING EAR if that was your intention," Kay commented, casting a look of anger at Ruby.

"I don't know why I'm surprised actually; it was kind of obvious," she exclaimed, her expression now one of joy. She hugged Kay and kissed his cheek. "Oh, that is the extra thing I could sense on you. You will let me plan the wedding, right? Say yes!" She stopped again. "Have you ever asked her to date? How are you going to do that? Kay is in love again. Some of us had to be capable of it yet."

"Okay, I've heard too much. Sky, can you stop bothering Kay and sit down?" asked Ari. Sky removed herself from Kay's neck and sat in her chair again. He cast a 'thank you' look at Ari who reciprocated. "Let's talk about what really matters. Kay, what did he say?"

"They intend to invade during Tramocult when our alarms are not working. Little do they know, we haven't celebrated this in years. He also said they're recruiting more people and creatures. The Quintuples are on their side"

"We're going to need allies," Mr Watson finally said.

Ariady played two taps on the table and a notepad appeared. "I'm thinking we should get the people of Cantas to come, we're going to need the dragons." Kay agreed.

"We can't recruit too many people," began Gustav. "This fight is ours and Amondridia's. We can't trust many people. Rosé is still a Lysion and if they know she is one, if the Quintuple knows, we need to watch out."

"He's right too," remarked Kay.

"I have my contacts of trust. So, until then, we'll be ready to fight. We're going to have a great plan and everything's going to be fine," Ari said. "Let's be prepared. Everyone. Increase training. Reinforce protection enchantments."

"They want her alive," Kay announced, letting out a deep breath, getting comfortable on the chair. Ari made a choking noise, so surprised was she. The others just looked at him. Eyebrows up.

"Why?" Mr Watson asked.

"I don't know," he confessed. "Mental manipulation, torture …" He breathed hard. His jaw was so tight it could break. "Magic extraction."

Ari denied it. "No. They wouldn't, that is … there is a high price for that. They are not crazy."

Silence took hold again.

"Who's going to take care of Rosé?" Gustav asked.

"No one will take care of Rosé," replied Skylar. "We're going to train her so she can manage on her own," she said, groping at the table in front of her, impatiently. "She needs to learn to defend herself. I know I didn't get involved in her training. I'm not used to being on the surface, but I can help her in the dungeons. Double her training."

"I can help with that. I don't mind training her more," Kay hissed, trying to straighten his back.

"YOU ARE GOING TO STAY AWAY FR—" Tom shouted, until Mr Watson muttered something, and Tom fell to the floor, asleep.

"Thank you. My head was about to explode."

"Now, let's go over the plan. Ruby, you will train Rosé martially and with weapons," Ari paused. "Train her, not almost kill her, as you did last time. Am I clear?" She nodded. "Skylar, you and Aiden will intersperse this with training her powers—" Watson raised his hand, making them all turn to him. "You don't have to raise your hand to talk."

"I didn't want to interrupt," he commented, arranging his glasses. "I think I should help her with her powers since they are connected to her mind. It's just an opinion." He closed the book "Me and Skylar. Leave the poor boy alone for now."

“Fair. Skylar, you want to be a guinea pig?” Ari asked.

“Are you saying I’m going to be the person she trains her powers with and could possibly be killed?”

“Technically.”

“Of course. I’m in need of an adventure.” Everyone looked at her incredulously. “What?”

“What do you think, Mr Watson?”

“Good enough.”

Chapter 46

When Rosé woke up, she took a while to remember where she was.

She remembered that she had arrived yesterday from Rome with Kay. He had almost died. The kiss …

She stopped and put her fingers on her lips, she tried her best to remember the moment. His lips on her neck and lips. His hands on her body, pulling her into him. The possessiveness. The pleasure of his hands touching her body.

For a moment, she swore they tingled.

Aiden slept peacefully by her side, breathing heavily. She had come to him in the middle of the night, still in her red dress. She now wore a t-shirt and shorts.

She had never been in his room. There was a huge TV on the wall opposite the bed, and some computer monitors on the desk in the other corner, not to mention a rather large black wardrobe.

The walls of his room were different, they didn't look like stone, or a normal plaster wall. They were made of something Rosé could not quite identify. The room smelled like phosphorus and some parts of the furniture had black spots.

Rosé imagined that Aiden could have lost control and burned them unintentionally, which made her smile. The little flame and his temper.

There were countless clothes out of place and garbage scattered around the room. Rosé had never imagined Aiden was such a mess.

She needed to go to the bathroom to take care of her needs and, when she got up, she found Aiden in bed awake on his phone. "Did I wake you?" she asked, worried, stopping at the door. Aiden looked at her and denied it. He was still half asleep. "I'm sorry for what happened this morning, I couldn't sleep, and I was already wandering around, then I saw the cat and … I came here … when I saw you, I felt all my pain come—"

"It's alright. Breathe." He was smiling. Aiden didn't have Kay's dimples, but his smile was beautiful and comforting. She loved his smile. He got up from bed and came to hug her again. Bringing her to his thin and hard body. "Just please don't cry. I swear I'll throw you out of the window if you do that."

Rosé let a shy smile slip through her lips. She let herself rest on his chest, feeling his heartbeat.

"Prin?"

"Yes?"

"You stink." She looked at him confused and they both started laughing until Rosé pushed him.

"I thought you couldn't smell me?"

"I know, but yesterday you arrived with blood on your hands and your dress was wet and dirty," he said, passing his fingers through her hair. "Should I be concerned? Misty almost screamed at me when I called her to help me."

"You woke her up?"

"I had to."

She had forgotten to bathe after she returned from Rome. She contracted her nose when she remembered and went to the door, but Aiden stopped her. "I'm not implying anything. For love's sake, but like, if you want to take a bath here. There are some towels there and you can use my products and wear one of my t-shirts."

Aiden went to the wardrobe and handed over black t-shirt and sweatpants, but before Rosé could take it from him, Aiden pulled it back. "I just wanted to make it very clear that I'm offering because we're friends, no big deal." Rosé smiled.

"I know you idiot. No offense taken. You're not my type." *And I kissed Kay.*

"I'm glad we agree on this." Rosé took her hand to her chest and made a crying face. "Wait," he interrupted her once more. Aiden came into the bathroom and left with something behind his back. "Ready."

"What are you hiding?" Rosé asked, trying to see what was behind his back. "Tell me you didn't have a rubber dick in there. How didn't I see that when I came in?"

"I'm straight, Prin."

"Is that right? Sometimes straight people have strange customs too," she said, laughing and entering the bathroom, locking the door and rummaging through his products, but she only found shaving products, deodorant, and body creams, as well as shampoos and soaps.

"What the fuck are you doing in my bathroom?" he yelled behind the door. "Rosé, you are supposed to be taking a bath, not going through my things."

Rosé didn't think twice about the idea.

"Aidennn, what the fuck is this thing?"

"What?" he frantically shouts through the door, slamming it so hard and fiddling with the doorknob. Rosé began to laugh. "WHAT DID YOU FIND?" Rosé couldn't breathe. She had to sit on the floor to recover from laughing. "YOU'LL NEVER BATHE HERE AGAIN."

It took her a while to get her breath back.

"Aiden?"

"Yes?" He was still mad at her.

"I don't think we can be friends anymore." She sat on the floor with her back to the door and could hear him do the same. She needed to tell him. She couldn't hide it from him. Not from Aiden.

"Why?"

"I kissed the Walking Comic Book and I think I'm in love with him." To the point. Direct. No hiding from him.

Rosé never forgot the conversation they had when Aiden came to her room. The question about who they hated the most was what would make their friendship final and real. Now, she had fallen in love with him. She still had anger towards him, yet she had fallen in love with Kay.

Rosé held her breath, waiting for his answer. She knew he was there. She could hear his breath on the other side of the door. She expected him to yell at her. That he would burn the door and slap her in the face, telling her to go back to reality or ask her what Kay had done.

"I don't know what we are yet. A lot has happened, and I don't know what to think." She played with her fingers. "Just … thought you should know about it. You are my best friend. My 8." Silence.

"Where did you go and what happened?" That wasn't the question she expected.

She told him what had happened. At least a great part of it. She avoided some, like them together in bed, or the taste of her lips and the other kisses they had given each other. She avoided giving details about Kay because he wasn't there and she didn't a habit of talking and exposing people, especially the ones she cared about.

"Did he make you do something? Something you didn't want?" That question had also taken her by surprise.

"No, no, no. Of course not." Maybe, but no. Not technically.

"Good, I won't have to get my hands dirty today." *I love this man. I love Aiden.*

Rosé smiled and went to take her bath.

Chapter 47

Rosé and Ariady were in the greenhouse once again. It was strange to be back there after the event a week ago. It seemed like it was only an hour ago.

She hadn't seen Kay after that. *He needs to rest.*

She was scared and anxious at the same time. Thrilled. A lot had happened since she got here. Many revealed had been truths. She had met a side of her she had never seen before.

For years of her life, she thought her mother was Helena. She'd called her 'mother' countless time. She had loved her in an inexplicable way and that hadn't changed. Helena had treated her like a daughter. She had embraced her in the best and worst moments of her life. She had welcomed Rosé into her arms. She had given her advice. She had made her smile. She was there in her first steps and in her first words.

Helena was her mother. Her mother by heart, and the pain of longing was immense.

"Are you sure of that?" asked Ariady, holding Rosé's hands.

"I need it," she said, confidently. Her whole body was reacting to the anxiety. Her hands were sweating. "I need to see her. For once." Ariady nodded and held Rosé's hands harder.

She was shaking as well.

"You … you will see it through my eyes. From my memories. They may not be as clear as before and …" Her voice failed. "Just look me in the eye."

Rosé flinched and looked right into Ari's eyes. They were blue with a shade of pink. A colour that's hard to explain. They both took a deep breath. Ari closed her eyes. Her chest rose and fell. She opened her eyes again to find Rosé were as white as the marble in the castle and her heart was beating as though she had just run a marathon.

Rosé felt dizzy and weak.

<3

Ari's memories.

She was in a meeting room. A black table in the centre. A huge map on the table. Rosé/Ari was sitting in one of the chairs. She was singing something Rosé couldn't identify. Her vision was strange, as if it had been filmed on an old camera. It seemed a little blurry, as if the camera had lost focus.

The door opened. A woman with long brown hair walked through the door. Same as the portrait. Sarah. She wore a white fabric dress, adorned with flowers and butterflies. It danced with the movement of her body, as did her hair. There was a bump in her belly.

She was pregnant.

"Only a few days left," she said, smiling from ear to ear, running her hand over her belly. Behind her, a man had entered. The same hair, features, and glasses that Rosé knew very well. Tom. Sarah tried to sit in the chair, but she had difficulty. Tom held her hand and gradually managed to finally sit her down. "Thank you, love. Phew, she's getting heavier and heavier," she commented with a loving smile on her face. Tom was right, she looked pretty.

"We need a plan." Tom's voice was serious. Rough.

"Stop being an idiot," she remarked, laughing and slapping his chest. "We don't have to. She will be born, and we will protect her as we had planned. That is the plan." Rosé could see her own smile on her mother's face. "My princess. My wild rose," she said, stroking and looking at her belly.

The memory changed ...

"What dress do you think I should wear?" Sarah asked. They were in a room similar to Rosé's, if not the same. There were flowers on the white curtains and on the bed. She was younger. With less wrinkles and less affected than in the first memory. She held a light pink dress in front of her body.

"You shouldn't go out with him," remarked Ari.

"Why is that? Is he a ruthless killer?" she said, laughing. "He's changed. He's cute and I think I'm falling in love."

"Have you ever thought that he might be with you because of your magic?" warned Ariady, grabbing her. A warning. "You are not stupid, Sasa, but please open your eyes."

"He doesn't know and doesn't need to know." This time Sarah was the one to answer in a bad-mannered tone. "We're going out to eat, dance," she said, dancing out of Ari's hand, with the dress still stuck to her body, until the hanger got stuck in the curtain, tearing it. She ignored this. "And kiss and get drunk and ..." She fell into bed next to where Ari was sitting. "And who knows ..." she said, looking at Ariady who seemed to get the message. Sarah laughed.

Rosé could hear Ari laughing too.

There was someone crying in the last memory. They were in a huge bathroom covered in white marble. Live flowers everywhere. Sarah was in a white dress inside the bathtub, it was filled with a reddish liquid and a baby lying on her, being breastfed. Her hair was tied in a messy bun. She had a wreath in her hair.

Rosé observed her, looking at and memorizing every detail, desiring every gentle and loving kiss the baby received. Rosé, in that memory, was just a small helpless human being. As fragile as glass. Light and with so little worry in her head.

Her mother sang a song for her, a song she couldn't understand. It was another language. A language she'd never heard. Sarah sang and stroked the baby's head. Her hands passed, trembling, over her closed eyelids and fragile cheeks. She was careful she hardly touched the baby's skin.

Rosé could see tears run down her cheeks.

Sarah's eyes were swollen and deep.

Rosé wanted to touch her, hug her, and never let her go. She wanted her mother more than ever. She wanted to tell her she was fine. To say that everything would be fine and that she would be well taken care of. She wanted to say that she loved her very much and wanted her on her side forever. She wanted at least a minute with her. Just one.

To at least say goodbye.

There was one more person in the bathroom. Someone Rosé hadn't noticed.

Helena.

Sarah stopped singing but kept stroking the baby.

"You need to take her far away from here," she said to Helena. Her eyes don't leave her baby. "To protect her from this world. From our world." She finally looked at Helena who was sat, open-mouthed, in shock at the request Sarah had just made. "Take her to Brazil or wherever she needs to go. Helena? I know I'm asking too much, but that's my wish, you owe me. The debt you had to pay me."

"No." Helena was on her feet now. Hands next to her body. "You're going to raise her," said Helena, kneeling beside the bathtub. Her accent, strong. "Ask me anything else, but not this."

"I can't," she said, crying. Not failing to caress her baby. Her voice was a whisper. "I can't. They're going to come after me, and if they hear about

Rosélina … Take her away. Treat her like your daughter. Give her love, affection and normal life. Take care of her … for me"

Helena was crying. "Sarah, I'm not going to be able to take care of her alone. She—"

"Take Tom with you." Helena didn't say anything. "I know there's something between you. I've known that for a long time. Please take her somewhere else. They can't know about her. No one can."

"What about you?"

"I'm going to visit when possible." Rosé felt the lie in her voice. Sarah turned to the baby. To Rosé. "I love you. Of all the stars and roses in the universe, you are my favourite one and I hope you know that. My love for you cannot be measured"

Rosé was on the ground when she regained her sight. Ari was trying to help her get up and sit on one of the benches. She was panting, in a daze, yet Ariady was perfectly intact, as before. She watched Rosé, as if she were looking for something. She was worried. Her lips were contracted, and her gaze almost lost.

"I shouldn't have let that happen."

"You gave me an amazing gift." Ari's face softened, but not completely. She was still worried. It was all in her eyes. Rosé stood up and, without much thought, she hugged Ari, trying to show her gratitude for what she had done. They both started crying, but Rosé realized that Ari was crying over more than she was.

Rosé had to hold her so she wouldn't fall to the ground. She could feel Ari's tears wetting her shoulder. Her body trembled. Maybe she wasn't talking about letting Rosé see her, but about seeing her herself.

"I miss her so much," Ari cried between the sobs. "She was my best friend; she was my person. My 8. She was the only one who understood me. The only one who cared about me. She … Rosé, I'm sorry you didn't really know her and … every time … every damn time I look at you I remember her and there are moments I wish you were her." She would have been offended, but it wasn't the first time anyone had said that.

"I'm sorry." That was the only thing she could say. She really felt sorry for her mother, for Ari, and for herself.

She wanted things to be different.

It took Ari a while to stop crying and when it happened, they both sat silently on the floor. There was a lot to be said at the time. A lot to discuss. However, there was little courage on both sides. Rosé was afraid to ask things and Ari would collapse again. She didn't want to see her cry anymore. That was too much.

Ari was quiet too. She was looking at the floor. Breathing with difficulty. Her face was swollen. The only things she could say was to apologize for what had happened. Rosé had numerous questions but waited a while to ask.

"My room?" she began. "It—"

"It was your mother's," she remarked, playing with her hands. "After she married your father, she asked no one to touch it. She went there when she needed to be alone." She stopped and wiped her nose. "When I heard you were coming home, I thought it would be … it would be a good idea to leave it to you." *You were coming home.*

She was home.

"Did you pick those memories?"

"Yes. They were the most alive. I remember when she was talking to your father. She was so desperately in love with him," she mocked, laughing. "I was happy and worried for her. And jealous." Rosé looked confused. "I'm not in the mood to talk about it. Not right now. The meeting was a week before you were born. She was happy. I'd never seen her like that." More tears rolled down her face. "She always wanted to have a child and then you were born and … then she announced you had to leave." She was angry now.

"She just took you away from us. The whole Elite knew about you. They all did everything they could to hide it. The meeting was one of the only times she left her belly exposed. I … I spent her entire pregnancy wondering how I was going to be a good aunt and how I would spoil you so much." She smiled. "I imagined her and Tom fighting with me and me taking care of you. Then, overnight she …"

The light in her eyes went away. "She changed her mind."

"You showed up years later, much older than I expected." She got up, went to the sink, and threw some water in her face. "When I saw you arrive that day, I needed a second to get myself together. Not just because of your resemblance to Sarah, but because I didn't get to see you grow up."

"Did you know that—?"

"They were going to attack the palace and kill her? No. I didn't know, but something about me makes me think she did. They attacked, not even twelve hours after your birth. Tom and Helena were already at the airport, technically smuggling a baby." She would have laughed if she heard that under different circumstances, but not now.

Rosé got up and sat on the bench. "She was humming something in another tongue." Rosé could feel her hand tingle with anxiety.

"Latin. It's a song inspired in a poem she kept singing, *A Dance in the Dark:*

I see a girl

Dancing in the darkness

Where no one can see

Under the light of the moon and the stars

Singing a song

That no one

No one

Could hear

The flower I know

The risky touch

I see a beautiful girl

Being light in the darkness,

Lies dance in the rhythm of the melody

That guarded her heart That one day it broke." Ari sang.

"She's been singing this song ever since I met her. She said the song was a mixture of sadness and happiness. A perfect mix of the two. That's just a piece of the song, I don't remember the rest."

Rosé hummed it in her head until she managed to write it on her phone so she wouldn't forget it.

"It took me a while to understand that the girl was not dancing literally under the stars," Ari said, looking forward like she was lost in thought, aligning them so they could make any sense of it. "It is referring to things in secret. You can see the girl, but you can't at the same time. Like a shadow. How can you know she is singing if you cannot hear? How is she suddenly light when she was dark?" Ari looked at Rosé. "Sarah was this way … you could see her. Read her, but suddenly you realise that it was a lie. She had done so much under people's noses, only to appear later, like a dance in the dark."

"You see the shadow, but not the person itself." Ari nodded. "That is deep."

"You," Ariady pointed to Rosé. "Sarah fought for her pregnancy, and no one knew. She left a baby behind who grew up in the darkness." Ari raised herself from the floor. "You were a dance in the dark."

Chapter 48

Rosé decided to go back to her room. A conversation she had with Nikko at dinner time kept repeating itself in her head. She became so distracted that, when she came round, she didn't know where she was. Too immersed in her thoughts to pay attention to the world.

This was a part of the palace she'd never been to before and she had no idea how she was going to get back to her room. She had stopped taking her guide star with her a long time ago.

Conversations with Nikko sometimes ended up being intense, but innocent. He was too smart and too deep a thinker, which made Rosé burn too many neurons. Their conversations ranged from emotions and personal life to random and childish subjects, such as the best cartoons.

Rosé liked the conversations between them, they made her feel light. Nikko looked a lot like her in innumerable ways and she risked saying that he was her younger, male version.

He was not a child anymore but had the face of one. In which case, she didn't actually know his real age. He knew too much and when she said, 'too much', she meant it. In her day, her biggest concern was which toy she would take to toy day at school.

Rosé had already walked for a few minutes when she heard the most unwanted sound. The damn siren. It'd been a while since it had sounded, and she hadn't missed it. Some time ago she would have panicked. She would have started crying or become worried, but not this time. It was strange how in a short time she had changed so drastically.

She had no full control over her magic yet, but she had already learned a lot. She could take care of herself if she needed to, but she wasn't part of the Elite yet, or been cast to fight, and she knew that if she stayed out there too long and someone found out she would get scolded.

But …

Since when did she care about that?

The doors began to disappear, and the corridors had changed to black marble. Camouflage. At least, that's what they had told her.

Rosé tried to calm down and get ready. She'd never been out in a rad before by choice, so she didn't know what she was going to find. She decided she was going to stay where she was. She wouldn't go looking for trouble or anything like that.

Her hands were sweaty. She could hear some background noises, a world away from her. She took a deep breath, shook her hands, and warmed up as if preparing for a competition.

Besides, she was fighting to stay alive.

A noise at the end of the hall made her stop, paralysed with fear. *Okay, maybe I'm not ready for this.* Then she saw him. Rosé turned her head to the side, startled. *What the fuck was that?* The creature in front of her seemed to have been made of stones and human tissues, it had the body of one. Rosé was a little confused and wondered how she was going to kill it if she had no idea if it was alive or dead.

Was it too late to run?

No. She was going to fight, but how would she concentrate on that thing over there? "Are you human?" she asked. It probably wasn't what she was supposed to be doing, but she needed to know.

(Am I feeling stupid writing this scene? Yes, but it looks fine in my head. Just don't judge.)

The creature turned his face too, confused. "I don't know. Alive, I think." His voice was thick and demonic. Rosé thought about laughing. Was she really going to have a conversation with him? "Okay," she commented. "Do you intend to kill me?"

"Yes," he answered.

"And when do you intend to do that?"

"Now, I think."

"Why are you still over there then? Move, bitch."

"Laziness."

"Fuck, I know how that is."

"Don't even tell me."

Rosé saw this as an opportunity and wondered if that's what the Elite people fought with every time. Stupid asshole made of rocks..

"I like you." Who knows, she might convince him not to attack her. "You look cool"

"Thank you," he said, tilting his head. "You too."

"Are you going to attack me?"

"I am." That caught Rosé unprepared. He stabbed the ground, making everything tremble and sent a huge crack in the floor her way. Rosé moved to the side quickly, preventing him from getting on her right. In defence form now, she closed her eyes and concentrated. What kills stone? Paper, Rosé thought. Paper comes from trees (I said not to judge me, it is just a stupid book and a slightly drunk writer).

Rosé conjured branches that spread quickly, she pulled him to the ground, binding his hands and rising to his neck. She liked that power. Theo had taught her this trick and it was the easiest. He struggled against it, but eventually freed himself.

Shit.

She ran down two corridors with the creature following her.

Okay, maybe it wasn't a great idea to stay out. Rosé looked around and realised that she was not far from her room.

He started running towards her. She had a plan in mind. When they were near, Rosé slipped through his legs, as Gustav had taught her. Fast and agile.

The creature got angrier. "I WANT TO KILL YOU!" he cried.

"We have that in common," she said, turning to him, keeping an acceptable and safe distance from the creature. Rosé was breathing with difficulty, even though she hadn't really done much. She regained some composure. It shouldn't be hard to kill him. People probably do this all the time.

Rosé tried electrical impulses and everything she knew, but nothing helped. She always found some way to escape or bat him off. A lot of things didn't seem to affect him. "Open your eyes, girl," commented a voice. "Think of the details." The creature was now holding sword in his hand, Rosé had no idea where he had taken it from.

Details. Rosé looked across the entire length of the creature's body, but he was too fast, already running towards her. He jumped at her; the sword ready to attack. She was going to die there. Alone.

She closed her eyes and positioned herself for defence.

The attack never arrived and the same happened when the Olvs tried to attack her, but this time she saw it. The barrier field formed around Rosé. The ground shook and the shield trembled when it was hit. When he was close to her, she was able to see inside him. There was a bright red thing, like a heart.

She pushed the barrier out, shooting him away. Rosé stole a sword from a decorative suit of armour, probably the same place where he had found his sword. It was heavy and her body was not prepared for so much weight and that's when she decided she would not use it by hand, but with magic.

Without much thought, she threw the sword to the ground. Her hands were shaking. She had to try. Rosé's arm hurt, or maybe it was her whole body. The air was heavy, and sweat was running down her back.

She made the sword lift off from the ground and move; the next second the sword was pierced into the chest of the creature lying on the ground, his scream echoed in the corridor.

Rosé fell to her knees. She needed to rest.

A sinister voice reached her ears. "What a show. Too bad it took you too long to take down a creature so easy to kill." Rosé raised her head to search for the source. "I thought I wasn't going to see you again."

Montiero.

"I liked the track on your hand. Have you been masturbating lately?" praised Rosé, mocking him. "I should have killed you that day. I should have made you beg for it." Montiero let out a loud, sarcastic laugh. "You almost killed Kay." Rosé's blood was boiling. She could feel an electrical charge go through her body.

"You were the target, but as I was hit in the hand, my aim … it wasn't that good." He had approached her. "Why don't you kill me now?"

"I'd love to." She positioned herself. Revenge burning in her eyes.

Through the corner of her eyes, Rosé saw a door appear and something pushed her through it. It opened and closed and, in seconds, disappeared again. Rosé jumped up. There was a mattress under her that soon disappeared.

She went to the place where the door had been, but there was only stone. Rosé couldn't hear anything that was going on out there.

Rosé was in a dark room, not because of the lack of light from the windows, but because everything in it was black or grey. The bed was huge with thin columns. It had a large wardrobe and several bookshelves filled with books. It smelled familiar.

On one of the walls were numerous glued papers and arrows linking people to others. Taking one, she saw a man with light brown hair and greyish eyes.

Kay.

Rosé hadn't seen him in weeks and every time she asked someone, they said he was recovering. Rosé had spent these last few days wondering if anything had happened or if he was no longer interested in her. Multiple unanswered messages. Lies. What were they hiding from her this time? Hadn't he recovered properly?

She didn't dare touch his stuff, that would be an invasion of privacy, instead, she kept looking at the pictures.

Kay was beside a woman with the same shade of hair, but with chocolate-coloured eyes that Rosé guessed to be his mother. They were laughing. Kay's dimples caught her eye. They always did. In another photo he was with a man who looked like him, only older. An older brother.

In another photo, there were five people, Kay, and his parents. The man in the other photo and a young woman, Rosé deduced it was his sister. She was smiling. Her gaze resembled innocence and serenity.

Rosé's chest tightened. She had been abused. She recalled what Montiero said, and it killed her inside.

Among the numerous photos, Rosé saw another familiar face. Hers. There was a picture of her in the dark red dress in Rome. She had a sulky face; he had teased her when he took that picture.

As she tried to reach the photo, she noticed a horrible smell emanating from her own body. She was stinking. She needed a bath. Rosé went to look through Kay's clothes. Most of them were black. She took a t-shirt. She found some underwear that would definitely be loose on her.

Since she'd have to wait for them to kill people, she could take a shower.

She wasn't thinking much when she decided to do this, but when the hot water touched her body, all the fear and regret washed away with the water. His soap smelled like vanilla and something Rosé couldn't identify.

She put on his clothes and went to lie on the big bed. Maybe she was taking advantage, but she didn't care. He owed her that. The alarm had stopped when she got out of the bath, but she didn't notice until the door reappeared and opened itself.

Rosé wanted to spend more time there, but her hopes were dashed when she noticed the door slowly opening. She knew he was there.

Invisible.

She had reflected on this in the last few days. Kay was always with Gustav and in the last few weeks Gustav walked alone, but always muttering something.

She also figured this out when she stopped to think about how he was always around, but she only could see him when he wanted to talk to her. Rome, the library. Tourists without noting them.

"If you don't want to talk to me, that's fine. If you want to ignore me, it's okay too. You don't have to hide from me. Don't use your magic because of me. I'm sorry I kissed you. I know you don't feel anything for me." She wasn't really sure if he was there, but she had her theories. She thought about stepping out but turned around and lay down on the bed.

The door stayed open for a while until it closed.

Silence.

Rosé took a deep breath and the only thing she could smell was male perfume, mixed with the smell of books.

There was no one in the room. She was (supposedly) alone. Would something provocative have to happen for him to show up?

"Will you stay hidden?" Silence. "Okay."

She got up, took off her clothes, and went to the mirror. Her body was thinner, perhaps because of training and poor eating, and somehow it made her feel happy but guilty at the same time.

She saw herself from various angles and did some poses.

Men usually think with their 'down heads'.

Nothing.

She put the shirt back on. Anger coursed through her veins.

"Okay," she repeated. "I'm going to my room, but … I'm going to take this with me," she said, picking up her picture that was sticking to the wall. "Copyright," she commented, looking at the photo. She was kind of cute. "If you're going to have it, you're going to have to pay for it."

Rosé took another look at where the photo was and saw a copy of the picture had taken its place. Rosé removed it and within seconds another one was already there. She looked at her hand. It was empty. "Son of a bitch."

She tried a few more times, but no matter what she did, it always fell back into place. "Fuck you," she said, crossing her arms and throwing herself onto his bed. "I'm not leaving until you stop being a fucking son of a bitch and show up."

"Use your magic," he said from somewhere. Rosé got up from the bed and went to the middle of the room. The smell was stronger there. She felt like she was going crazy.

She went to the desk, letting herself be carried by the smell and this presence she couldn't explain. He was right there. She knew he was. Probably leaning against the table with his arms crossed.

She looked up, but the only things she saw were the countless papers he had on the wall. She lowered her head slightly and leaned forward until she hit something hard. "Stop it," she whispered. "Stop running away from me." This time she touched what would be his pectoral muscles. "It won't be funny to nail your invisible balls."

"Have I told you that I love it when you get mad at me, Smurf?" Rosé raised her gaze and there he was. Perfectly beautiful with a shy smile on his face and not nearly dead like Rosé had last seen him. Those damn dimples.

There was blood in his mouth and nose.

"How long have you been here?" she asked, trying to clean up the blood and remembering that she had been almost naked a short time ago. At that moment, it didn't seem that interesting anymore.

Kay looked at her and smiled again. A huge smile. "You know the answer to that question. Since before your amazing show in the mirror." Rosé felt a shiver go through her entire body, all the way to her flushed cheeks.

She hugged him and was surprised when he reciprocated the gesture, squeezing her against his chest. Rosé inhaled his smell. She had missed him, but this didn't last long, because she soon separated from him, pushing him away.

"You abandoned me." Relief had been exchanged for anger. "You disappeared. You took me on that fucking mission, you made me heal you, you said things, you did things, and then you disappeared. I …" She paused and pushed her index finger against his chest. "You ruin my moment of killing the son of a bitch out there, and that's all without talking about the other countless things." She started punching him until her hand started to hurt.

Kay had not protested to her punches, he barely registered them.

"Are you done?" he asked. Rosé looked him in the eye and threw another punch, regretting it because that had hurt more than the others. She pushed him, but he didn't budge.

Upon seeing her complaining of pain, he took both hands and kissed her fists. "I'm done," she announced, moving away and sitting on the bed again.

"You needed some time."

"I didn't need a break."

"Rosé, I … I lost control in Wysez, and I thought you needed time to think about us and well, I needed a break." She was angry because she wanted to kiss those lips. "Do you know how your father treated me when he found out what happened in Rome? About us?"

"I don't care what he said, I'm not a child." She got up again and went towards him. "You should have come to me, you should have given me an explanation and if you wanted time, should have come to ME and not to my father or to your little friends." She was angry. She didn't belong to anyone, and she was tired of saying that. Tired of having to keep reminding people. "And seriously, after all that time and everything that happened, is that what you tell me? And since when do you care about my father?"

"I was distracting you. You had to practice." Kay didn't move much. He was still, in the same position with his arms folded. Rosé avoided his eyes. They were too tempting, as were his lips.

"I liked the distractions." Regret came later.

"You like it?" he asked with a smile.

"Fuck you." Rosé tried to push him again when he approached her, but he pulled her along. She felt the impact of Kay's back hitting the wardrobe. "Why did you need some time? That's the truth, isn't it? It wasn't my father or the distractions." Her voice came out low and weak. Their faces were very close once more.

Kay looked to the side, but Rosé grabbed his face and turned it back to her, forcing him to look into her eyes. Their gazes met once more. Damn butterflies. Kill, kill, kill. It was like she had a dance school inside her stomach. "I needed to understand what was happening to me." Rosé kept looking at him in silence. "I needed to know how I was feeling about you. It's been a long time since … since I've known anyone, I'd be interested in. And every time that happened to me, I lost them. One by one." That hit Rosé in the heart; she had forgotten that he had had other women in his life. "I can't lose you and …"

He pushed her away. "I hate you," he stated. "I hate you so much you don't know … you … fuck." He ran his hands through her hair and turned to look at her. "I hate you because when I'm with you I don't remember who I am. I get lost and every time I'm with you I fell even harder and I never craved attention, but fuck, all I want is your fucking attention and your smile and your fucking seducing eyes on me… my life was so much easier without you, but after you appeared in it, I wondered how I spent all these years without you and your bipolarity and your threats against my balls."

Rosé approached him and took his face in her hands. She couldn't help but smile. "And did you find out how you feel about me?" She held her breath for a few seconds.

"I've spent my whole life avoiding this feeling as much as I could. Then you show up with your threats, anger, and sass and … fuck, fuck. I knew you were fucking trouble the moment you threw juice at me and rubbed that beautiful hand in my face and walked away with your hot ass like nothing happened. No one had ever challenged me like that and left without any punishment. You dominated my thoughts, and it was disgusting."

Kay grabbed her by the waist, knowing that she would try to escape, and he was not wrong. He turned her around and trapped her against the wardrobe. Rosé protested, but Kay's body weight was heavier. His thigh was between her legs. She wanted more. *Rosé, focus.* "I had to, otherwise you wouldn't let me finish the story. And don't you dare kick my balls again."

"And that neck of yours …" he remarked, coming up close and kissing it. "It's my total destruction and paradise at the same time." Rosé's head moved to give him more access. "I realised I was feeling something for you when the lack of your voice and your touch made me angry and, when I saw that man touching you, you don't know how much I held on so I wouldn't destroy this whole world. Every bit of it.

"You came here, all lost and angry at everyone. Destroyed. You'd fight and yell at people and it made me laugh and fall more and more in love with you. You have no idea how beautiful you look angry." Rosé didn't smile. "Then I started to annoy you, just to see you angry. Testing how far your boundaries went and some accidents happened and …" he said, moving closer to her "Fuck." He smiled. "You look so beautiful fighting and defending people. The only thing I wanted was to put you in a little pot, with your arms crossed and with this frowning face for me to admire.

"Then the training started, and things started to get hotter between us. Then you had the brilliant idea of playing with my feelings at the party in the dungeons. You have no idea how much I wanted to take you right there in front of everyone. Explore your body. Fuck it. You don't know how much I held on." Kay's hand ended up on Rosé's butt, pulling her closer. She had to bite her lips to retain the groan.

"Keep going."

"You're enjoying this, aren't you?"

"I'm loving it." His arms tightened around her. "In the hallway …"

"I killed him." The light in his eyes faded and his gaze moved away. "Honestly, this isn't a side of me I wanted you to meet." He closed the space between then. Feeling *him* against *her*. "See what you do to me? You make me too sentimental and horny." Rosé just smiled.

"What do you smell?" she asked. "When you are with me."

"At first, I was confused, because I didn't smell anything but your baby smell. Until I realised that I didn't smell a different thing because my favourite smell had become yours." Rosé blushed once again. "Can I keep you in a little pot?"

"I'm not mad."

"I've found out that I prefer you with a passionate face and blushing with the things I say to you, especially when I'm near you," he whispered in her ear, leaving a kiss below it. A shiver ran through her spine. "Imagine when I start saying more interesting things in your ear. Like what I want to do with your body right now." His leg moved between her thighs.

"Kay," a moan came out of her lips.

"You will be my destruction, Smurf. A good and disastrous one." he whispered.

Rosé stood on her tiptoes. "I want more." Kay laughed, his head still dipped in Rosé's neck.

"Magic word?" he asked, rubbing his nose against her neck.

"Fuck you."

"That's not the magic word."

"Please?"

"No."

"What is it?"

"*Por favor, meu homem gostoso*" Rosé laughed at his attempt to speak in Portuguese.

She repeated and he kissed her neck. His mouth was warm on her delicate skin. Rosé's whole body chilled, and Kay noticed it. "What would have happened if I didn't like you?" she asked in a whisper. Kay stopped what she was doing and looked at her. His face was close to Rosé's, sharing the same air.

"I would have let you move on with your life, but I'd always be there to protect you."

"I don't need protection."

"Then I would put myself in danger for you to come save me." Rosé laughed, then bit her lips. "Stop biting your lips or we'll have a serious problem here."

"I don't think I'd waste my time saving you."

"Evil." They both smiled. "I'm glad you love me."

"I didn't say I loved you."

"You said you did in Rome."

"I said I didn't know if was love."

"Do you love me?"

"I don't know. I need more information for that, so I can get a more accurate result."

"What kind of information?" Rosé smiled maliciously. "It's a little late to wake people up." But he didn't mind so he joined his lips with Rosé's. The kiss was not calm, but it was not needy either. It was like coming home. Until it became something else. His hand moving under her shirt, cupping her boob, squeezing it.

His phone beeping.

Kay reluctantly moved away from Rosé and looked at his phone, impatient after a few minutes. His face went from calm to worry. "What happened?"

"Emergency with the Elite."

Kay went to Rosé and kissed her one more time. It was a quick kiss, but deep. "Please I know you care and that you're worried, but just listen to me this time. I'll be back as soon as I know what's going on. Don't make me worry about you." He headed to the door, but Rosé was quicker, grabbing him by the arm. He turned to her.

"Can I come along?" Kay looked at her in silence. "Please, I'm tired of all this, but mostly of being left out."

Kay approached her and kissed her again. "I fall more in love with you every time you get stronger." Rosé changed clothes quickly and soon he took her by the hands, and they headed to the door.

Chapter 49

They arrived at one of the libraries Rosé used to frequent. "Wait, is where the meeting take place? I thought it was in a more interesting place." Kay did not answer. They headed into one of the areas that Rosé was not much of a fan of.

History.

It was full of maps of different kingdoms and Lyses. Including Wyzed and something called Quintuple. She had only read one book or two since most were written in old languages that Rosé had never seen or heard in her life.

What shocked her was the fact that her mother's name was in some of them, written in English.

Kay directed her to a particular bookshelf and took a book from it, he then put it back in place upside down. The bookcase began to move and make room for a circular staircase. Kay held her hand and they began to climb. "Some emergency meetings happen here."

She could already hear her father's voice and Ariady discussing something, she then heard Gustav. Kay let go of her hand to open the door and soon all eyes turned to her. It was the same room from Ari's memory.

Skylar was the closest and the first to break the silence her arrival had brought by hugging her and pulling her across the room. "It's so good to see you here," she said super excitedly. "Okay, now that we've got them all, we can start."

Silence prevailed. "Oh please, I think it's time she became part of the Elite," challenged Skylar, once again with an exasperated tone. "Everything we've done in the last twenty-something years has been about her. It's all about her. Rosé, Rosé, Rosé. What about Rosé? More lost than ever, seriously." She turned to Kay. "Thank you for having a little sense and bringing her." She joined hands with him.

Nobody said anything.

"Good …" she began, addressing the huge table in the centre where a hologram text message was displayed. "Kay and Rosé, Harry sent a message saying they have changed plans and intend to attack earlier." Rosé could feel the bile rising in her throat. Earlier?

"Earlier, when?" Kay asked, going to the hologram and fiddling with countless folders with more messages.

"We were not informed." Tom was in the corner of the room, leaning against the wall. "He says it's probably going to be a surprise. Blake's going to wake up and say they're going to attack, *yay!*" he said in a cracked pitch. "They want to be unpredictable."

"Can't we evacuate?" Rosé whispered to Skylar.

"You can't just run away from your problems," Sky whispered back.

"That's what I always do."

"Well, you have to stop doing that. Your mother took a long time to build this place, the way it is today. There's a lot more here than you can imagine. There's information in this palace that could end our world. You fight for Amondridia and it's going to fight with you," she whispered back, looking forward, trying to demonstrate that she was paying attention. "No matter where we go, they're going to come after you, so why not fight in a place you know well? Besides, we can't—" "Alright there, girls?" Ari asked. They were watching them.

Rosé's gaze stopped on her father, who did not take the trouble to hide his displeasure at having her there.

"All fine," Rosé was the one to answer. "I just asked a silly question and Sky answered me. Actually, answered me. Keep going." An uncomfortable silence took over the place. Ari looked at the hologram on the table, but the rest looked closely at them. "You can go on."

"Will you pay attention?" her father asked. He hadn't stopped watching her for a second.

"Yes, I'm sorry. They are planning to invade by surprise, what's the plan?" She tried to smile, but she knew it was just a fake one. She looked at Kay who was leaning on the table and wondered if he regretted bringing her. Not even five minutes had passed and something bad had already happened.

"Training," commented Mr Watson "We will all train. We need to be prepared for the possible things we're going to face."

"Gustav?"

"Josh and I went to Cante and we're going to have extra dragons and some trusted people have agreed to join us in compensation for what Josh, Chris,

William, and Poppy did in relation to the dragons when they were asked. Just get in touch and they'll send them as soon as possible."

Ruby remained in the chair, shaking one of her feet. "Harry's going to send the message and then what are we going to do?"

"We don't know how long in advance Harry will warn us, but I hope we take no more than one to two hours, who knows, hopefully more, so we can settle down and prepare. We need to make sure that all weapons are ready for use, and none are damaged. Gustav is responsible for this." Gustav nodded as Tom explained. "I need you to get someone to help you, there are many and we need your confirmation as soon as possible."

"Will text messages be sent to everyone?" Skylar asked.

"As always. It's the fastest way and everyone has access." Tom looked at Ruby. "I need you to have a text message prepared for this."

"How's Wysez's information penetration system?"

"They're in progress. I'm trying to do everything I can to access it, but it's very well protected. I wouldn't be surprised if they had more than a few groups of people taking care of the communication and protection networks. Their system is too safe. They are one of the Quintuple." She stopped and went to the monitors, dividing the projection into two.

"I can program the message now."

"I would appreciate it," Ari said.

Ruby started typing so fast Rosé couldn't hide her admiration. She didn't even have to look at the keyboard. The images moved so quickly that Rosé couldn't keep up with them.

Kay opened the 3D map of Amondridia. "We're going to have to split up. We can't just stay in the same place. The main areas to be covered and guarded will be the forest with the Olvs." Kay looked at Ruby. "Send a message to Joseph and Dandara about it. The main field, the skies, and obviously within the castle, in specific areas. We need to be strategic since there are not many of us."

"Who's going to stay where?" Gustav asked from the other corner of the room.

"This is something we will decide according to the information we receive on the day. We can't waste our time on this now, not when everything can go wrong. During this period, you need to be more on patrol. Let's divide who stays in the CR and hope that no other invasion happens so that we do not have a false alarm for when the real thing happens."

"Two of us on patrol every six hours or twelve hours?"

"I would say every six hours. That way we will be able to rest and relax and not lose much of our efforts when we are at work. I'll make the schedule and send it to you," declared Ari.

The conversation continued. They discussed the new security measures that would be implemented and new positions and, of course, Rosé was not included in that. Named of enchantments and code names to security systems she had never heard in her life.

She kept quiet for a long time, if not the first few hours of the meeting, as she didn't know about half the things they were discussing. Rosé couldn't just come in and stand up for herself. Skylar had continued to sit by her side. She felt that her presence there was not very welcome.

She was never welcome anywhere.

For a while, Rosé looked at Sky when she didn't understand, and Sky explained briefly and in a low voice so that she would not get lost. She was the only one who made Rosé feel welcome, but they were right, she shouldn't be there.

Her gaze from time to time met with Kay's and he would respond with a smile and then deflect eye contact, and it made her angry, but she accepted it. They still had a lot to discuss, and the emergency meeting interrupted their moment.

She imagined her mother there and how good she would be at planning things. How she stood up and gave the orders. Amondridia was hers. She had read and heard a lot about her and her talent in leadership and Rosé wondered if everyone there expected it from her or was disappointed by her silence and lack of knowledge, but. … it wasn't her fault. She's not the one who walked away from this world, forbidding herself from everything that had happened.

At times she imagined her mother there, leaning on the table, or sitting in the chair, listening and arguing.

If she were there if Rosé had had a few minutes with her, what would she have said to her? What would she have taught her about being an amazing and respected woman? Those were answers she would never have because her mother was dead and would never come back to her.

Kay's voice interrupted her thoughts.

"Let's follow the same scheme as any other invasion. The most vulnerable people, like children and the elderly, or anyone who is incapacitated from fighting, will be kept in their rooms and their doors will be removed and protected by stronger enchantments." And she couldn't even believe what she was hearing. "They will still train and be equipped with armaments in case of emergency and the new enchantments will cover the-"

"The children will be evacuated and taken elsewhere," Rosé said at last. This was the first time she had said something and everyone looked at her. "They will be kept as far away from this conflict as possible and there will be no discussion about it." They stared at her for a minute. There was no one better than her to make a poker face.

"We don't have anywhere else to take them, not to mention the time we're going to waste on it," Ari said. Her voice was calm.

"Another Lys?"

"We don't have allies that we can trust these children with," she added. She seemed to be the only one willing to answer Rosé's questions.

"Are you willing to risk their lives instead of wasting some of our time to save them?" she asked, confused. Anger was growing in her chest. Disgust emerged from what she'd just heard. "I've spent these last few months listening to how amazing Amondridia was and how my mother helped everyone and everything and you are telling me that we have no ally?"

"A lot is lost in someone's death, not just the person itself," commented Mr Watson.

"Our world is much more complicated than you might think, Rosé," Kay announced.

"They will fight, they have been trained—" began Tom.

"They have been trained to survive if they are in danger," interrupted Rosé. Ari had explained the education system in Amondridia. *We're not training to fight. They're not warriors yet. We train them in case anything happens. Protection. Our world is never at peace.*

"And what's going on now?" he asked, placing his hands on the table and leaning over it. "We are at war, *dear*. They grew up here, fed on this place. They slept here."

"We can prevent them from putting themselves in danger." Rosé's voice rose. "We can prevent them from being part of a conflict. Part of that war. They are—"

"They will fight," he interrupted her, his voice becoming louder than hers.

"Tom," cried Ari. "Let her speak."

Rosé thanked Ari. "They are children. They have no notion of the world. They're too young to suffer the consequences of a stupid conflict. Too young to be introduced to such a thing. I don't know what you went through as a child, but I'm not going to let these children's childhoods be affected by a war of mine and don't tell me it's not, because my name is the only one that's written on it. As far as I know, it is my mother's Lys and I'm the one who has her blood dripping through my veins." She stopped and took a deep breath, calming down. "Evacuate. This is a closed discussion."

"Do you really think you can come here and decide something? You don't know anything," reminded Tom.

"I would choose your next words very well, Tom," warned Kay.

"Who do you think you are, Dagon?" Kay went to open his mouth, but Rosé interrupted him. She didn't need to hear the two fighting now.

"Do not talk to him like that and yes, I think I can, in matters where I have the knowledge, and it is your fault that I do not know anything." She was now leaning on the table, across from her father.

"Immature."

She hit the table and sat down again, she stretched her legs out in the chair next to her and laughed. "I find it surprising the adjective you just used. Do you hear yourself?"

"Get out of here."

"No."

"I'm your father." (*Star Wars* vibe.)

"And you're going to do what? Send me to my room and ground me? Lock me in there? Yes, you're my dad and? What have you done to deserve this title other than putting your dic ..." She stopped and took a deep breath. "You only bring it up when it's convenient for you."

"You have no power in this place."

"Power?" She let out a smile. "Do you really want to talk about power with me?" Tom didn't answer. "Power is only dominated by fear or respect. And respect is the last thing you have for me right now. You're afraid. And you know what? I'm not afraid of death. I never have been, and you know that very well. If I die, I'll be sleeping peacefully while the world I left behind falls apart."

"Are you threatening us?"

"No, I'm just telling the truth. I'm the reason all this is happening. You want me out of here? You're going to have to take me out and, believe me, you don't want to. You lied to me, abandoned me, and now you want to request a title?"

She stopped. Rosé was now on her feet, squeezing the table so she wouldn't do something she'd regret. She was keeping her magic at bay. She was trying her best, but she could feel it struggling to get out of her body. "My blood is the beginning, the middle, and the end of this world. You depend on me. That's not in your control. Learn to live with it."

"You've changed," he said, lowering his voice.

"No. You just never really knew me."

"You are ungrateful. I've protected you my whole life."

"Did you protect me? Or did you send someone to do your job? They're very different things."

"You continue to be disrespectful. It has always been like this."

"Are you listening to yourself? I'm defending myself. Don't blame me for that, *Dad.* And next time don't insult me to feed your ego."

"Everything, every decision of my life has been made for you. Each. One. I did it for you and only for you. I lost the love of my life. The only woman who could see me behind the monster I had become and the only thing I had was you. But when I looked at Kay's back that day, I thought it might be you …" He had no words to express his feelings. "And then you two were …" He looked at Kay and then at her. "I was supposed to be the only man in your life and now that there's someone taking this place …" he stopped there. He was still for a while. "You are no longer my little baby. You're not the kind of person I can fool with a spell, or the girl I used to carry in my arms with your mouth full of chocolate. You were so pure. So innocent. The … I don't even know what else to say. I don't know how to get to you. I don't recognise you anymore, I don't know anything about you. Maybe Helena was right. We shouldn't have left Brazil."

They were too proud for this, and she knew this similarity between them. It was one of the flaws she carried in her blood – pride and ego. At that moment it was fire fighting fire. An eye for an eye.

They were the same.

Tom looked away and walked away from the table. "You look a lot like her." He found himself by the wall, his arms crossed. His voice showed his defeat, as well as his sadness. "In everything. In every bit of you I see her. The way you smile, how you get angry about something stupid, how you fight for what you believe in, your facial expressions, even how you fight." His words came out as if they were slitting his throat.

He let a long sigh out. "I shoot out countless sperm and your mother gets most of it. Unfair. I think mini Sarah's killed all the sperm I let go of and fertilized herself" After that, he left the room.

"Twenty minutes break and then we'll discuss this again. Kay, a minute with you," Ari commented, and Kay agreed. They both left the room.

(Go drink some water. Take a deep breath.)

"Well," said Skylar. "I'll go to the kitchen and get something to eat. I want to be prepared in case another dramatic fight happens. I almost spilled a tear and believe me, it's been a long time since that happened," she said. "Does anyone want anything?" Nobody said anything. Then she disappeared in a blink.

Rosé sat on one of the empty chairs, resting her head in her hands. Would she ever be able to have a normal conversation with her father? No shouting and insulting? She remembered her life in Brazil and how close they were. He was her superhero, the man she loved spending time with. The magic tricks he showed her that she now knew were real. The dances and the before-bed stories. She liked him when he was her father, not a murderer or a mage or whatever. Just her father.

Tom Johnson.

"So …" began Gustav, pulling his chair closer to Rosé. She didn't have to look at him to know he had a smile on his face. Gustav always had a smile on his face. Period. "You and Kay, hmm?" he asked, elbowing her lightly on her arm.

"What about us?" she asked.

"Ah Rosé, seriously?" he said, opening his arms and dropping himself on the chair. "You smell like him and the vice versa. You arrived together which meant that you were together and it's already almost four in the morning, my love. Don't try to hide it from me." His smile was so big that his eyes were small. "It was taking a while, don't you think? My little couple," he said, hugging her.

"You're an idiot," Rosé insulted, trying to hide the smile. "And well, I don't know what we are yet, because our conversation was cut short."

"Conversation?" Ruby asked. Rosé had forgotten she was there. Ruby wasn't looking at them, but at the phone in her hands. Rosé figured she had been paying attention from the start. "I thought you were doing more than that. How boring." Gustav's smile increased, if that were possible, exposing a gold fang.

"Honestly, I'm not going to talk about this with you."

"You don't have to." He let out a sigh. "Kay will tell me everything later anyway." He gave Rosé 'the look', giving her a slight pat on her arm. "I'm really happy for you guys," he said, seriously. "I haven't seen him like this in a long time"

She had already heard that love made people feel more alive and willing, but that's not how she was feeling. She was happy to have him there with her, but at the same time she felt guilty. They were about to go into a war, if they weren't already, and it could last a short time, which left her with a sense of guilt, but if she died, she didn't want to regret not doing anything.

Gustav returned to his chair where he was when Kay and Ari returned. Kay sat in an empty chair a few inches from Rosé's and within seconds her chair was pulled close to him.

Kay took Rosé's hand, resting on the arms of the chair, and kissed them. "Are you alright?" he whispered in her ear. Rosé nodded, her gaze on her lap. She was lying, but she wasn't in the mood to discuss it with him right now. "Do you want something?" She denied it. "I need you to talk to me. Look at me. I want to see your eyes. Admire them."

"You don't want to."

"I'm desperate to see them."

Rosé's gaze met his. He seemed worried. Her gaze went down to his lips, she wanted them now. "I have nothing to say at the momen—" A strong light interrupted her. As they looked up, they saw Gustav holding up his phone, pointing it at them.

"I'm sorry, you guys look so good together," he explained.

"Ready for one more?" Kay asked excitedly. Gustav waved. Rosé was confused and was ready to smile, but a slight touch on her chin made her turn to Kay, who was looking at her. She got lost in his greyish eyes, until he joined their lips and her eyes closed automatically.

She could feel the flesh.

Kay stroked her cheek and then left a kiss on her forehead. Rosé looked around and Skylar had already returned, her eyes were wide open, a strawberry in her mouth. Ruby kept looking at her phone while Ari stared at them with a smile on her face and Gustav was the same as before.

"I think I'm going to start planning your wedding," Sky commented, sitting down with her food.

"This is my job," protested Gustav.

"Your ass."

<3

They resumed the discussion which lasted a long time. They didn't know when Oldo and his Lys would attack or if other people would try to get in. There was a lot of stuff pending and to be planned, but everyone was already very tired, and their brains were no longer working right so they decided they would continue the conversation another time.

They left the library and said goodbye, Kay and Rosé started making their way to her room.

"Can I ask you one more thing?"

"Always. No, not always. It's dangerous to promise things to you," he said, laughing. Rosé punched him in the arm and he complained.

"Idiot." She stopped and looked at him. "Do you mind if I sleep in your room tonight?" Kay seemed surprised by the question. Rosé was nervous, her lower lip amid her teeth. "I'm not talking like that. I mean-" He laughed and put one of his arms around her waist, the other on her back, taking her into his arms. "We're becoming one of those soppy couples. I don't like it," she said.

"If you want, I can change that." he said "I can be mean, enough to not tolerate your jokes and punish you for them tied in my bed"

<3

Soon Rosé was back in the same dark room that they had left a few hours ago. Kay put her on the bed and headed to the wardrobe, picking up a baggy T-shirt and delivering it to Rosé. It smelled like him. Rosé didn't mind changing clothes in front of him. Maybe because she'd done it before.

Regardless, he went to the bathroom as she changed and returned shortly after she was dressed.

Kay stopped at the bathroom door. His look was different. Not malicious, but it wasn't normal either. "You missed the show," she said, heading to where he was.

"I didn't miss the show, I just thought you wouldn't feel comfortable with me there yet." She didn't know how to respond to that.

"I stripped for you already"

"I know" he smirked.

"You already forgot it, jeez"

"I didn't" he answered. "I will never"

Chapter 50

Rosé had stopped off at her room to pick up her training clothes and headed towards the canteen. What happened the night before was still going through her head. Kay, the Elite, her father, Kay again, and more Kay.

Shit.

Look at the emotional dependency going on.

Rosé arrived in the lively canteen when the dilemma arose. What table should she sit at? Kay was, as always, with Gustav and Ruby, sometimes Skylar came out of the dungeons to join them, but that was during dinner, and it was lunch now. Her gaze met with Kay's and butterflies danced in her stomach. She hated those butterflies.

The three Elementris had not noticed her presence yet.

Rosé stopped to think about pretending to be on her phone. It would be very rude not to sit with them.

She looked at Kay who was still watching her. She just wanted a way to communicate with him somehow. She looked down, feeling so stupid. She opened the message box and went to send a text, but an arm wrapped around her, pulling her close.

"Hey, what are you doing here?" Theo asked. "I thought I was the last one. Let's go to queue." Rosé agreed and followed him, keeping her phone in her pocket. The line for the food wasn't long. He started talking about how strange yesterday's invasion was, as if any raid was normal. Rosé was not paying much attention at first, but felt compelled to do so when he said that he and Aiden had been cast to be part of the fighting staff and was excited about it.

He felt important.

Rosé thought to describe how she had tried to fight too but realised she would have to explain that it took a long time to kill a quick creature, according to Montiero, and was not in the mood for humiliation. Not to mention that it would lead to Montiero and Kay and the Elite.

Rosé took her tray with not much food on it. She wasn't hungry and that should have worried her, but it didn't. There was a lot going on in her head. A lot she would need some alone time to process, but that wasn't now.

"You smell like him," he whispered in her ear, scaring her. "Anything to comment on?"

Rosé looked at him and tried to disguise it. "Who is he?" she asked innocently, grabbing a drink. She knew what 'he' Theo was referring to but decided to play dumb.

"Don't pretend to be innocent, Rosé … Big Kay. I know his smell very well and it's all over you. A little bird told me that today you left his room," he commented. Rosé cast a glance at him from, trying to figure out how Theo knew his smell so well. Theo recognised this. "Seriously?" he whispered. "Look at him. He's hot as fuck. Women aren't the only ones who fall at his feet. Don't tell Josh that." *Of course I'm won't.*

"We … Well, I don't really know what we are," she said, crestfallen. "A lot has happened recently, and he ignored me for a while and then came back and said things that … fuck, I can't even explain it, but I don't know if he feels the same way."

"But did something interesting happen last night?" That depended on what interesting meant to him. A lot of interesting stuff happened last night. Rosé cast him a glance and he kept quiet. No matter what he was thinking, she couldn't talk anyway.

"Nothing you need to know about at the moment, but … I fought last night. My magic is improving," she remarked, raising her shoulders and puffing out her chest. She was proud of herself. That was the first time she had fought for Amondridia in the palace, and she was happy. Theo congratulated her and together they sat at the table. She wasn't going to talk, but she needed to change the subject and thanked him when he didn't ask more than that.

Rosé greeted everyone and took out her phone. She knew they didn't like it; she recalled when she first came here, and they hadn't liked her for using her phone all the time instead of talking to them. 'It'll be quick,' she assured.

Rosé: I'm sorry I didn't sit there.

She left her phone on the table and started eating, she cast a glance at Kay who was looking down. She turned her gaze to the Elementris who were arguing about yesterday's invasion. Theo and Aiden seemed super proud of themselves. It was visible in their eyes, and she was happy for them.

Aiden had commented on wanting to be part of the Elite one day and that was a step forward to what he wanted. Rosé didn't know if it was the same for Theo.

Her phone buzzed on the table.

Kay: You don't have to apologise; you sit with whoever you want. Of course, I wanted you to be by my side, but it's okay for you to abandon me.

Rosé looked at Kay who made a fake sad face. Rosé showed him the middle finger, which was reciprocated, but deep down she felt bad about not being with him. She reread the message a few more times until she left it aside.

"Kay Kay, hmm?" Aiden asked. Rosé's eyes widened. Was everyone already aware about them? It had only happened last night. Rosé felt her cheeks blush and she began to eat.

"How does everyone know that? Was it you?" she asked with her mouth full. She had commented on the kiss with Kay, but nothing more.

"Theo just told us, when you were texting your walking comic." Everyone laughed, even Rosé. That nickname wouldn't go out of style so fast. "Gossip runs fast down the halls, so be aware of this." Josh had arrived at the table.

In the last few days, he sat with them before he and Theo went out together. They were very cute together and she couldn't help but notice that they were both much happier.

<3

The class with Skylar and Mr Watson was the same as when she trained with Aiden, but this time she was better. She had better control of her magic and could better follow instructions.

He tested countless spells and defences and tried others that no longer worked out too well or she lost complete control over.

She had already lost count of how many times Mr Watson had to fix that room. Sky, on the other hand, seemed to be having fun being attacked. She laughed even though her nose was bleeding and there was blood on her teeth.

Psychopath, that's what Rosé thought. Incredibly psychopathic and amazing.

Rosé didn't know if she admired her for not giving up. Rosé had hit, almost burned, almost drowned her many times. She had been cut by a blade, thrown around the room, and pulled up again by the neck. Skylar received countless injuries and punctures and still had the courage to smile and shout, "You can't kill me, so… have no mercy. The only thing that can happen is you send me to my father in a bad way, but then I come back again and pull you into the night."

Skylar was very good at keeping a secret, she could be tortured and still laugh in your face.

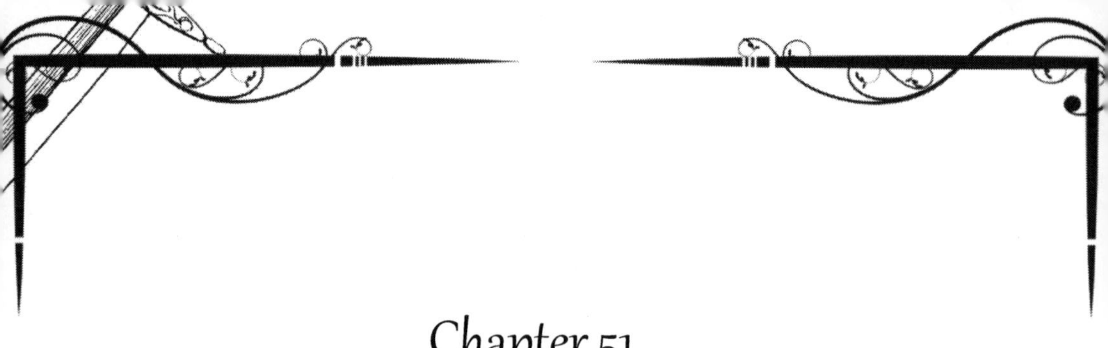

Chapter 51

"I promised I'd take care of her, and my word remains intact. She became my priority and if she dies, know that I will die first, protecting her."

"I don't doubt your word." Tom replied.

"Great."

Chapter 52

She had gone to the canteen again. She was starving.

She had skipped breakfast. Rosé was too sleepy and too lazy to get out of bed and get ready to go out in public. Having to change clothes and seem presentable to the world around her was too large an effort.

This was something she missed when she shared a house with Eliot, Hanna, and James – being able to go eat the same way you woke up: totally destroyed. The chance of them being up at the same time as her was low and even if they were, they wouldn't be much better off. Besides, it was only four people, except Jessi.

Living in a house shared with them was an adventure. Almost everyone studied art. One day Rosé woke up and found the head of a mannequin on the table and the body on the couch. She almost had a heart attack and Eliot appeared soon after and got scared. In the other rooms, there were costumes from horror movies or erotic clothes that he said were for a play.

She didn't care what exactly it was for.

James was the only one who studied something different, computer science, and from time to time he helped them hack some websites and profiles of people.

He was very good at it. But in return, he spent the day yelling at the computer.

Of course, there were odd times of intimacy around the house that weren't always pleasant. She had seen the boys walk around the house in just a towel or Hanna in a bikini on hot days without caring who saw her.

She had already had the experience of needing Eliot and him telling her to come into the room only to see him through an open door, pooping.

Hanna had brought another man into the house once and had sex on the couch but migrated to her room, leaving their clothes strewn across the living room floor, forcing Rosé to come back another time and all this with no warning.

The thought of having to get up and ready to leave had already been the reason she had skipped many meals since she arrived, but it was not the only reason.

Another problem was that today was Saturday, which meant that the canteen would be too full. No one was working or living life outside of Lys and she wasn't in the mood to socialise with people. But she had to eat. She ran her hand over her belly. She'd be sick if she didn't eat, she could already feel the headache starting.

She tried her invisibility magic and succeeded until a certain point, when, unexpectedly, Kay got her from behind, saying she could never fool his senses, especially when he too had this gift.

They sat on the grass close to the water's edge so she could eat in peace. She explained that she was using her magic to hide from others, so Kay became invisible, to give her a few moments of alone time, though it felt much longer.

It was a different feeling. She was alone, yet with him.

When discussing what they were to one another, they decided to use the phrase 'my person', instead of boyfriend and girlfriend, because it sounded so mundane and childish for them. Rosé also asked him to never give her flowers. She hated flowers as she associated it with death and funerals.

"I want you to know that I love you, for the way I treat you. For all my actions, attitudes, behaviour, I don't want you to doubt my love for you and I want you to know what I feel towards you, even when I am not around, or I do not say it. Love is not defined by the clichés. Know that Smurf. Love is felt and not said."

"Are you saying that you love me then?"

"This is something you should tell me. Do you think I am showing it enough?" He cupped her face. "There is something else I have to tell you. Love for us is different. It is cursed. When we love, we really do love. It is so intense it hurts. If I get too needy and overprotective and …" He shivered. "Please, slap my face when it happens."

Chapter 53

They were back in Kay’s room. The door lock clicked and before she realised what was happening, his mouth was on hers. his hands exploring her body, as if he wanted to memorise it. Every detail and curve. His hands passed all over her back, down to her ass, squeezing it mercilessly, until they passed her thighs, lifting her to him, forcing her to lock her legs around his waist.

Rosé could feel her body on fire, her blood seemed to burn in her veins.

The warmth of his body on hers was like heaven, making her melt in his arms.

The kiss got intense by the moment they reached the bed. Her chest rose and fell with a feeling of longing she had never imagined possible. The space between them was huge, even though they were glued to each other.

Rosé’s hand messed with his dark brown hair, soft between her fingers. Their mouths explored each other, not giving a fuck about the lack of breath. She didn’t know what was going on around her. She didn't care. She was lost in Kay. Her neurons were almost shutting down.

She felt something soft on her back. The sheet on her body that at that point seemed more sensitive than she imagined. Kay’s weight over hers felt so damn good.

Her hands wandered under his shirt. Her nails on his smooth, warm skin when he groaned in her mouth.

She tried to lift it up. There was a lot of fabric involved and she needed to eliminate it. Kay took it off easily and soon Rosé was looking at his exposed chest, the tattoos, and some scars he had left exposed. She ran her hand over them, feeling every texture of his skin, enjoying each reaction. His body contracting and relaxing under her touch as he closed his eyes.

She bit her lower lip to hide her amusement. "This is wrong" he mentioned before lowering himself again, holding her neck.

"What?" she asked.

"What you do to me" he kissed her cheek, moving to her neck and back to her lips. "What you do to me is so wrong and so fucking good" he whispered against her lips. "You don't know how much I craved for you. The thoughts I had about you. How you made me feel when you just looked at me" Kay took off her t-shirt, her breasts covered only by a black lace bra. "You're going to pay for those teasing" His eyes stopped there for a few seconds. They were no longer grey, they were black. His pupils dilated with pleasure. He ran his tongue over his lips, his lip piercing. He gave her a quick kiss and went down to her neck, sucking, and kissing her sensitive skin. Until he moved down to her breasts still coved by the bra.

Low but uncontrollable groans slipped from her mouth.

He ran his hands under her body, opening the clasp and taking off her bra. He looked at her for a few seconds again. To her exposed tits. And in a tempting and slow way, he went down to one of them. Kissing and sucking. His tongue making circles over her nipples. Grabbing them between his teeth.

“Kay,” she moaned. He held her tighter, holding her in place.

He left kisses and with every movement of his tongue, Rosé buried her nails more and more into his back, pulling him to her. With every touch on the tip of her breasts, her body reacted. She never thought they could be so sensitive to someone’s touch.

“You’re so fucking beautiful” Her body was ruling itself. She had lost control. She emerged into a world of pleasure for the first time. “All spread out and naked for me”

For the first time.

Not necessarily her first time, but her first time in a few years.

She hadn’t gone out with many men in her life, and it had never come to that. She was never ready for that. Every time she looked at them, she knew they were not worthy. She let herself be taken once by an idiot and that wouldn’t happen again. It wasn’t worth exposing herself and letting herself get so vulnerable in that way.

She felt safe with Kay.

That was the difference.

His hands were on her waist, gently pulling down her jeans. He kissed her stomach, right under her ribs. Fuck, she loved that. With a surprising amount of patience, he removed her jeans, looking Rosé in the eyes, until her jeans were somewhere on the floor.

He went up to kiss her. Kay was going slow, so slow it was killing her, until her back arched with his touch, his finger in the place she needed his touch. “Open your eyes,” he whispered in her ear. “I want you to look at me while I fuck you." She didn't open them. He was asking too much. Especially when he moved the fabric aside and introduced one and then two fingers inside her.

He was moving them slowly, she tried to talk to him, to open her mouth. "K-ka …" she tried.

"Talk to me, baby" he teased when a moan escaped her lips and he kissed her. He buried his finger even deeper in her core. Her hands holding the bed sheet.

He found a spot only her had even reached. Her legs shaking as he moved in and out, pressing her lower abs as his fingers moved in 'come here' movements.

She was vulnerable to him.

Until she came on his fingers.

"Good girl" his voice reached her ears while she was trying to recover. His hands around her neck.

"I want you" she said, reaching for his pants, removing them, only hearing his laugh as she rushed to get his pants out of the way with his boxers. Rosé looked at it. A shiny metal in the head of his thick cock. It took her a few seconds to assimilate things.

Kay pulled her back to bed moving on top of her as he hold her hands over her head. "Surprised?" he asked, but she didn't answer. Her head went blank. The image still wandering inside her brain. "You'll like it, baby" he got her hand placing on *him*.

His piercing between her fingers.

Kay was much older than her and had more experience. She? This was her first real-time and it scared her. Several 'what ifs' passed through her head, waking her from the trance she didn't want to leave.

She wanted to go back there. To that world of sensations, she was experiencing. To his touch. To his lips and his tongue. His strong hands on her body, squeezing her and pulling at him. She wanted to be flooded by his smell and affection. She wanted him so badly she couldn't breathe. Did he know that this was her (almost) first time? They've never talked about it before. What if something went wrong? What if she wasn't good enough and he broke up with her?

His hands went to her panties, ready to take them off, but he stopped, watching her. He didn't move for a few seconds then climbed up until they came face to face. Eye to eye. Exchanging a long look that said a lot.

Rosé didn't say anything. Her body was beginning to cool, being heated only by Kay's body. She wanted to cry. She had screwed up once more. She wanted this, but she couldn't do it. There was something there that prevented her, and she didn't know what it was. She felt disgusted and afraid he would see her the same way she sees herself.

Maybe it was her stupid mind.

"I'm sorry." That was the only thing that came out of her mouth. Low and almost failing. She covered her face with her hands. She couldn't look at him. "I—"

"It's alright," he said, running his hands through her hair. He took her hands off her face so he could observe her. "Don't worry. It's okay. I understand if you're not ready." He kissed her once more, calmly.

"I am, but I'm not." He smiled.

"I can wait."

"I don't want to keep you waiting."

"You shouldn't worry about me. This is about you, baby. Your body. Don't feel pressured. I'm not going anywhere," he said, leaving a kiss on her forehead.

"Sorry—"

"Don't apologise. There's nothing to apologise for." No dilated pupil of pleasure. "When you're ready, let me know," he said, kissing her agai then moving away. Rosé took a few seconds to get up from bed and went to his wardrobe, picking up one of his t-shirts.

(Before you kill me, this is better than nothing and I promise that in the next book things are going to get spicier. Besides, I just want to say that it is okay not to be ready.)

She took a simple black t-shirt as always. She looked at him and asked if she could borrow it. "What's mine is yours, beautiful thing." Rosé put on her blouse, ignoring her nickname.

His t-shirts were like a dress on her body.

Rosé went back to bed, finding Kay on his back and her bra cupping his eyes. "Are you really wearing my bra like an eye mask?" she asked, lying next to him.

"I'm in a re-run moment, don't get in the way."

"Re-run?"

"I'm reminiscing about what I just saw and what this piece of fabric holds every day." Rosé took his hand and placed it under her shirt. He had seen and kissed them; this wouldn't make much difference. He ran his hand over her, still with her bra in his eyes.

Rosé bit her lower lip when he passed over the sensitive tip of her breast. "I think I'm in love," he remarked.

"With me or with my breasts?" He took his hands off them and placed them on her waist, pulling her over him.

"With the full thing." His hands went down to her ass again, which was more exposed than before, realizing that her panties were a thong. He got serious. "Please, when you're ready, let me know as soon as possible."

"Don't rush."

"Never, my love. I would never do anything you weren't comfortable with." He was still serious. His jaw was in a straight and contracted line. They were silently looking at each other. At that moment she thought she wasn't at all sorry for kissing him. He gently put her back on the bed and returned to his side.

"Did you know?" Kay raised his eyebrows. Maybe she should stop asking vague questions "That it would be my first time in a while?" He nodded.

"You'd be surprised to know the number of things I know about you." Why wasn't she surprised? "But no. I had well imposed restrictions from your father and my own principles" She was relieved to hear it. Her hands touching this face and in this intimate moment that she was not falling in love, she was plummeting.

"I don't know much about you." She whispered.

"Ask me anything." Rosé stopped to think. There were so many things she wanted to ask him that she didn't know where to start. His favourite colour was black, she already knew his full name and what he had done. She had read this in one of the books in the library, but that's what everyone knew. But there was a question inside her that she couldn't help but ask.

"You can call me the Mood Killer," she remarked.

"Why?"

(Warning: sensible content)

"In Wysez with Montiero, he mentioned your sister and …" She stopped, analysing his face, trying to identify if it would be safe to continue. "You … she … I am sorry. Let me ask you something else. That was not my business. What—"

"Summer." Rosé stopped and looked at him. He was looking at the ceiling. "It's my little sister's name." Her picture ended up in his hands, the same one

Rosé had seen a few days ago. "I lived in Wysez for a while before it became the place it is today. It belonged to a man of trust who was very powerful. My father had passed away, so my mother and Summer had to come live with me for a while and my older brother was living a long way from here and … I … I should have imposed more rules on them. I did, but Summer was rebellious and often walked alone through the mansion and … it wasn't just once." He covered his face with his hands.

"It wasn't your fault, and it wasn't her fault for what happened. The person responsible has already been killed and it is over." But it wasn't over. It was a long way from that. Rosé couldn't imagine the pain Summer must feel. "Are they alright?"

"They are far away from Wysez. I visit them whenever possible, but things between us aren't the same." He paused. "Another question please."

Rosé thought of something lighter. Maybe she'd gone too far with that question. She got up from bed and began walking around the room, looking more attentively at things. "What do you like to do in your spare time and when you're alone? Not to train or kill, or whatever. Something personal." Rosé stopped to hear the answer.

"I like to read." Rosé went to the books.

"Anything?"

"Anything but those crap books of self-knowledge or cooking or things that say they help you, but actually make you more depressed than ever. I like the books of the Outer World. Things non-magical. It's funny and entertaining how you live your life without magic." He laughed.

She ran her hand over the books, recognising countless titles. He was the one who read classics. She wanted to vomit. How can someone does this?

Rosé walked a little further and noticed something hidden between a closet and the wall. She pulled it out and opened it. It was dusty.

Kay didn't seem to care since he didn't protest. Upon opening, she came across a shiny black guitar. "I'm not going to play it for you, I'm sorry." He was still lying in the bed.

"Why?" she asked, disappointed. Kay sat up on the bed and watched her.

"Don't make that face, it won't happen."

"You didn't answer me. Why?" Kay got up and went to her, taking Rosé in his arms and taking her back to bed with him. He put her there and lay on top of her, laying his head on her stomach. Rosé laughed at his attitude and began to make *cafuné* on him.

(I am going to teach you a word in Portuguese, because English does not have a word for that. *Cafuné*: act of caressing or running fingers through someone's hair. You are welcome.)

"Next question."

"What do you use on your hair?"

"Shampoo and conditioner. I don't know the brand. Just look in the bathroom."

"You don't know the brand of the shampoo?"

"It makes no difference in my life." Being a man was easier. She kept passing her hands through his hair and then lowered them to his back, stroking and lightly scratching the top of it. Silence took over once more. She could hear his breath.

How did this all happen? How did I get here? Rosé Lysion, not Rosé Johnson. No. Rosé Dagon one day? Shit, why am I thinking about it? Rosé Dagon doesn't sound good. Mrs Dagon. Okay, I'm already going too far. Rosé, questions, Rosé, the fucking questions.

"What's the dumbest, craziest thing you've ever done?" she asked. It took him a while to respond, and Rosé thought he had fallen asleep, but no.

"I went into the Down World and got out of it alive." He hugged her harder. "That's where me and Sky meet. We almost killed each other."

"What else takes up your time?"

"You." Rosé laughed. "It's amazing how you manage to take my time. I need to always be ready for whatever comes and goes. Tiring work, Smurf." Rosé stopped stroking his back which made him make a whimpering noise with his mouth.

"Insecurities?"

"My scars."

"Just that?" Rosé was outraged. She had many. "Defects?" "What are these questions?" he asked against her body.

"I want to meet the deep version of you, I warned you."

"I think I'm too selfish sometimes. Proud. Sometimes I'm a little arrogant too. I'm great at being fake with certain people." Rosé stopped messing with his hair. "That doesn't include you. Continue with the *cafuné*. I can be impulsive and irrational on occasions, especially when it involves you. There's been a lot of examples of that."

She lay still for a while, considering what he had just said, then refocused. *I can be impulsive and irrational on occasions, especially when it involves you.* That man was going to kill her from the heart at some point. She had already met his selfish and proud side, the sexy and provocative side.

"Fears?"

"None, but I've been afraid of losing the people I love."

"Dreams?" He also took a while to answer that. His hands were on Rosé's shoulders. His thumb rubbing them.

"Many."

"I want one of them. An innocent one," she commented. "No selfishness. Not involving killing anyone or taking over the world or whatever. Something personal. Sensitive. Something you never told anyone. I want you to be sensitive," she joked.

"This may sound stupid or whatever, I don't know, but ..." He stopped and took a deep breath. "I've always dreamed of having a family. To get home and listen to the kids. Sit down to eat and have mini-mess there and a lot of noise. Someone I can teach how to live. Someone to care for. A football team running around the house. And obviously with an amazing woman by my side." He stopped. "Maybe that's a fear. Fear of doesn't get it before burning in the Down World." They were silent.

(Calm down kids, no pregnancy trope coming. I just wanted to show a sensible side of Kaydan)

"Too sentimental? Are you disgusted with me?"

"I wish I could promise you that," Rosé whispered. Some tears escaped. She wasn't expecting that. "I'm sorry." She didn't know how long he'd been alive. But she couldn't get that image out of her head.

A family. It wasn't her wish right now. Before her world turned upside down, she dreamed of eventually having a family. Something further ahead. But her life became all about survival and she had forgotten a little of the future.

"I'd love it."

She hugged Kay. It was crazy how her life had changed in the last few months. How she had changed. She was no longer an antisocial girl with few friends. She had learned to tame magic she didn't even know existed. Control her emotions. Well, almost. That was something she had to do every day. Sometimes she'd fail but everything worked out fine.

Her relationship with Kay had changed. Aiden, Ari, even her father. She smiled. Kay moved up a little higher.

"You've changed since I met you," she remarked, returning to Kay's hair, leaving a kiss on top of his head.

"You too," he remarked, his breath on her neck.

And that's when the outbreak happened.

"This shouldn't have happened." A pain arose in her chest. None of this should have happened. Her and Kay, it was a mistake. She stopped again to touch his hair. She wanted him very much, in a way that she never thought she would want anyone in life. She was becoming emotionally dependent on him, and it scared her. The fact that she could lose him, scared her.

"What are you talking about?"

"Us." He rose slowly. He wasn't at all happy. His greyish eyes stared at her with anger and worry. He seemed to analyse every bit of her face, as if he were looking for something there.

"You really are a Mood Killer. I'm going to pretend you didn't say that." He wasn't lying on her anymore. Or touching her. He got up and sat on the edge of the bed. He sat still for a few seconds. He looked at her. His jaw flexed and eyes were deep. "Why?" he asked, keeping his cool. "Just answer me that. Why is that? Why do you think we shouldn't have happened? Rosé, I … shit … serious? I—"

"Of all the people in the world, you have been falling in love with someone who is being persecuted and who people want dead. I don't know if you've noticed, but you won't be able to protect me all the time for the rest of our lives and it's too early for that, don't you think? Think about the future. I don't even know if I have one." She sat up, looking in his eyes. That was a slap in his face.

"I promised to protect you until the last beat of my heart."

"Well, this problem is yours."

"Do you want to end it? That's it? You want that?"

They were about to start shouting at each other. She was still in bed, clinging to a pillow, while he was on his feet.

Did she want to? No. She didn't want to, but she should.

"No," she confessed. "I don't want to, but … Finish what? What exactly do we have? We started dating days ago, not even a month. We are making promises out of nowhere to a life we do not have yet." That hit them both hard.

"Of course we have something. I thought I made that clear just now. You think I go around kissing anyone? We have known each other for long enough. They are promises, Rosélina," he said, taking his hands to his messy hair and then looking at her again. His chest was raising and falling quickly. "As you said, we do not have eternity, but we have now."

"But—"

"Stop thinking about the future. It hasn't happened yet. Think about now." He was acting just like he said he wouldn't. Needy and protective, but how could she be mad at him? "You manage on your own, you don't need me, and I'll be a plus. I'm going to be right there next to you, in front of you, back, fuck, I'm going to be there, every moment by your side. That's what I promised and I'm going to do it, even if I have to spend the rest of my life here fighting on your side."

"Kay, you are acting—"

"I know," he interrupted her. His tone calmed down. "I am well aware of how I am acting, but I can't help it." He held her hand and kissed it. "It will get better, but now … do you not feel as I do?" They exchanged glances.

She did. She felt so fucking desperately in love with him, but she needed to learn how to control her mind. She wanted him all the time. "I do, but my fear of hurting you and putting you into danger is bigger." She went to him to kiss his cheek. "I think we both need time." She went to the door.

"Hey, please, come back." She looked at him.

"We will be fine, I promise," she said, leaving the room.

<3

She spent the rest of her day in her room, which seemed colder than ever, trying to tidy up and organise her life.

Chapter 54

Rosé was on her way to class with Gustav when she began to hear engine noises approaching and soon Gustav appeared by her side with an electric scooter, making turns around her. "Rosélina, we have a class now, don't we?" Rosé kept walking, trying to make things difficult for Gustav.

"We have and has anyone told you how random you are?" she commented without looking at him. "A scooter? Inside the palace? Are you serious about this?"

"More serious than Ruby," Gustav said, stopping in front of her and almost making her fall. "You've seen nothing. One day we did a Mario Kart race through the halls."

"Really? We're going to have to do that someday," she said, imagining the scene.

"Now …" he said, approaching her and whispering, "behind you is your beautiful man, staring at me with a look of anger." His gaze was focused on something behind Rosé. "And a little bird told me you had a fight." Rosé punched him. "Calm down, honey, don't make that face. Good … he's talking to someone whose name I don't know, and I don't care, looking at us here, arms folded, making his muscular arms look good in his black training shirt." Rosé felt a shiver just thinking about that image. "He was an asshole with me yesterday so we're going to be more of a motherfucker and make him very jealous. Laugh loudly."

For a moment Rosé thought about not doing this but remembering the fight they had she could not refuse the proposal, so she laughed. "Louder," he said, laughing too. "Lightly slap my arm." Rosé did but realised she had been too strong when Gustav complained. "I said light." Both shaved, still with a smile on their face. "Now get on the scooter."

She was glad she had her back to Kay, because, if she didn't, he would have seen her facial expression change. "What?"

"Come on, just jump on, we have a class and I'm too lazy to walk."

"Go alone."

"If you don't jump on, I'll make you do fifty push-ups."

"You wouldn't dare."

"I'm in charge," he teased. "I can."

"You're an idiot."

"Believe me, I've heard that a lot."

Regret struck when Gustav started the electric scooter. If he was already an idiot on foot, with the damn motor, he was worse.

<3

Classes with Gustav interspersed between struggle and parkour. According to him, it was very important to know how to fight and run if things got horrible and quickly travelling from certain heights without getting hurt was very important. Rosé was much better off since she had started taking classes with him, but not enough to beat him in certain competitions.

He complained, "Rosélina, you suck."

Of all her classes, the ones with Gustav were her favourite. After the last incident with Ruby, she hadn't been giving her classes for a long time and had only recently returned. She probably had just paused of her own will, or maybe Kay did something, but she didn't really believe that.

They finished their training and Rosé went up to her room, accompanied by Gustav who was sure they would find Kay in the corridor, and he was still angry with him. Supposedly, after their fight, Gustav had shown up to ask for something and Kay had insulted him. He did not go into detail, but the fight did not seem to be one with many words, because Gustav was complaining of pains in his ribs and he showed Rosé the bruises on his back.

"Believe me. We solve everything physically."

That made Rosé more pissed off with Kay and Gustav.

As predicted, they had passed Kay, who didn't even take the trouble to look them in the face. "Well, he ignored us, so you lost, friend," Rosé commented, giving Gustav a slight punch to his shoulder when they reached the door of her room.

But instead of him getting upset, he started laughing.

"Rosélina, are you serious? He was there for most of your training, and he must have passed us in the hallway at least twice," he said, smiling. His eyes almost closed so big was his smile.

"How do you know?"

"We've been friends for a long time, there comes a time when you can feel the presence of someone extra in the room, even invisible, Nugget," he commented, messing with her hair.

"Okay, this is crossing the line. He keeps watching me 24 hours a day. Seriously? Where does my privacy feature in this story? This situation is getting weird."

"Nooo, Rosa." Rosé looked angrily at him when he misspoke her name. "When we say we're watching you, it doesn't mean we're following you all the time. Don't feel so important because you are not." Was she supposed to be offended? "People know how, let's say … shit. Okay, you're important. They know how important you are, so when they're suspicious of something, they text us and we'll come to you and see if everything's okay. When we're close, we keep an eye out. Just because the alarm isn't ringing doesn't mean we aren't in danger. We need to make sure who walks around us. We can't go into people's minds and find out if they are evil." He was serious.

"But as far as Kay is concerned, you've fought and he's a proud bitch at times. He must be following you, trying to get the courage to talk to you. Is he an idiot? Yes. Asshole? For all the certainty of life. Are there times I want to kill him? Of course, but … People of your type … Love is a horrible feeling. Controlling and strong. He might get a little too sentimental and possessive with you so remember to put him in his place.

"Love is much stronger than he can control and it's a great weapon against him, because for anyone who wants to take him down, they now know exactly where to shoot. He fell in love long before he even knew it. Someone like Kay wouldn't spend a penny on you, nor let you insult him and get out alive. Someone like Kay wouldn't be so docile in his training. Remember Ruby and the dress training? Kay is even worse. He's feeling vulnerable at the moment." Rosé didn't know what to say.

"He's been acting weird since you got here. It's disgusting sometimes."

<3

A week had passed, and no invasion had happened. Everything seemed under control. Too quiet.

Rosé took a shower and changed her clothes. She had no more training that day, so she decided to go up to the library to finish one of the books she had started and never finished and train a little more with her magic this time.

Her life had gotten more complicated. She didn't have as much free time as she used to. She had classes to attend and sessions with Mr Watson. It had been a long time since she'd gone to the greenhouses to see and talk to Ariady.

Every time she went there, Ari was never there, so after a while, she stopped attending.

She had training with Elementris a few times.

She went to the library and sat in the same chair by the window and started reading but couldn't. Every time she started reading, her thoughts turned to Kay and by the time she came around she realised she had been on the same two pages without actually reading them.

Kay could have been there with her at that moment. He had previously admitted that he would visit when she was reading and kept her company, reading with her, and he loved to see her reactions when she was alone. He thought it was cute.

Mr Bebbols passed her one more time.

She had had lunch earlier in the day so she could go to the library during lunchtime, avoiding meeting anyone undesirable on the way, and it was a good idea because she didn't seem to meet a living soul on the way.

Mr Bebbols was in her armchair when she arrived and complained when he saw her, lifting his ass and rolling around with his tale up. She thought about asking him to stay with her, but she didn't know if he'd be able to keep his mouth shut for long.

Cats could see things beyond a normal human being. At least that's what they told her. She called out to him, he stopped to observe her and sat down. "Come here," she whispered.

"Why should I?" he asked, raising his paw as if he wanted to look at his nails.

"I need your help."

"I don't help," he remarked, getting up and walking away. "I work and it's not free." Rosé cursed. She hated that cat. But what did he want? Money?

"What do you want?" Mr Bebbols stopped and turned around, climbing up on her lap.

"Depends on what you want me to do?" he began.

"Information"

"Which kind of information?"

"I need the price first."

"A snack."

Rosé blinked. She couldn't believe she was negotiating with a talking cat.

Rosé focused once more and made five cat snacks appear in her hands. She was getting good at it. His eyes widened. "Uhh *me gusta,*" he commented and began to eat his snacks. "What information do you want, Heir of Lysions?"

Rosé approached his ears a little and whispered. She knew how sensitive cats' hearing was, so she barely made any sound when asking him. Mr Bebbols returned to eating his snacks and, when he was finished, he looked at her and went to leave the room.

Rosé was suspicious that she had just been tricked and manipulated by a fucking cat.

"I've heard that the books on Section B are very interesting, but being very honest with you, I'm not a big fan of them," he commented, already far away from her. Section B. Rosé waited a few seconds before looking at that bookshelf. It was filled with adult novels and anyone who looked through them would see nothing but harmless books. Little did people know what these pages were hiding.

She'd read almost half of them.

But …

There was something else there. As if it were a shadow, but totally invisible. Maybe it was just in her head. Something she imagined. But she knew he was there. *Fuck, I'm going to kill you.* He was really there. Rosé stood up and threw a book at him. How dare he spy on her again? He was irritating her on a level she couldn't explain.

As expected, the book did not hit the bookshelf before falling to the ground. She felt sorry for the book and regretted using it. It didn't deserve this; it was too good to hit someone like Kay. She laughed.

"Are you staying there?" No one answered.

She was tired. She had spent a great part of her free time in the library, training.

Rosé took a book about the different creatures in the magical world and examined their powers, trying to understand if she possessed them. She climbed some stairs that led onto a beautiful balcony, perhaps away from Kay.

Some magic she tried worked and some didn't. She had lost count of how many books she had read and knew she had exhausted a good part of her magic.

She did research on her phone too, desperate for more details.

She returned the book to the shelf, away from where Kay supposedly was. She was ignoring him. She went to sit in the armchair, but in doing so she felt her body sit on something warm and nothing soft like the armchair. She was wrapped up by what felt like arms. "Fuck you," Rosé remarked, adjusting in his lap. Too tired to protest.

"Hi, my love." He held her thigh. Whispering in her ear. "You look tired."

"Dead," she said, relaxing more in it. Kay began kissing her neck and her head automatically fell backward, exposing more of that region. His hot body beneath her and his mouth made her body react.

He kissed her neck for a while, brushing his nose. She took her hand back, touching his jaw and stroking his face.

She readjusted herself, fitting her ass between his legs and placing her head against his chest. He pulled her even closer and left a kiss on her forehead. "Do you mind if I get some rest here?" she asked with a yawn, half-drowsy.

"Stay as long as you want."

My love, she liked it when he called her that. She felt special and loved. She loved him. Shit.

She loved him and had admitted it.

She took her hands to his chin and jaw again and began caressing him. She knew Kay liked it.

"Did you miss me?"

"Every second of the day since our fight." His voice was soft and calm. Loving. He took her hand and held it, turning his head to kiss her palm. "Every moment I missed you and I hate you for that."

"I can't deny that either." She was right, she had fallen for him.

"But … we shouldn't—"

"I'm not going to discuss this with you again."

She sighed and raised her gaze. "You shouldn't have approached or promised, Kay …" She wasn't in his lap anymore.

"Why did you think I was avoiding this?" He was standing in front of her. "Why do you think I avoided this fucking feeling for decades? I didn't want to worry about anyone. You know how hard it is to feel so vulnerable. I can't breathe properly when you're not with me." He was horribly distant from her. "And it's disgusting to say that to you. It's disgusting to feel that way about someone. You've become my drug and I can't explain how stressed I am without you, but I gave you the space you asked for."

"I still need some time."

He took a step back and looked at her once more. Rosé went to the door. "That includes you not invisibly following me!" she cried.

"You know that's not going to happen." She stopped and looked at him, she came back and pushed him up against the wall. There was electricity in her hand, a few inches from his neck.

"Stop doing that." He just smiled at her. Electricity reflected off his skin. "I'm going to cut that smile of yours off." His smile just increased. She could feel his hands on her waist, pulling her towards him once more. The electricity was still close to his neck.

He looked at it amused. "Flirting with me?" he asked. "I love when you threaten me. You look so fucking sexy." He leaned over to her ears. He muttered something there, so only she could hear. Her heart sped up and he smiled and switched their positions against the wall. "I told you I wasn't the prince. I may be vulnerable, but I'm still the villain who steals the princess, beautiful thing. I already stole you once, I can do it again and again. As many times as it takes until you're entirely mine." He pressed her even more against the wall, in a pleasurable way. "You're playing with fire." He left a kiss on her hand that, at this point in the game, had no energy.

"I am the fire."

"Great. Together we will burn the world," he whispered in her ear before leaving the library.

Chapter 55

"Do you mind if I spend the night here?" Aiden had appeared at her door just as she had done before at his. His face was swollen. Deep dark circles had formed beneath his eyes. He was in pyjamas and slippers. Rosé could not turn him away, he had helped her when she needed it.

"Well, I … hmm," Rosé thought of Kay for a moment and then stopped. She couldn't care about him right now. Not because she didn't love him, but because she was angry and knew he could handle himself.

"It doesn't matter." He turned around to leave.

"Aiden." She wasn't with Kay now and even if she was, it wouldn't matter.

"You've got someone." Funny. She had countless people, but recently she was feeling so lonely that she wondered if the people around her weren't just in her head.

"There are a lot of people in my life and you're one of them. Stay."

"The walking comic?"

"I'm not talking to him at the moment and yet, I don't think he's going to care," she remarked, pulling him into the room and closing the door. "What happened?"

Aiden lay on her bed and began to look at the ceiling and Rosé did the same.

"I miss you."

"What? You are like this because you miss me?"

"You've been a little distant since you started dating Kay, or maybe before that. You sit with us every day, but … you are always far away." Rosé looked at him. She couldn't deny that. She and Kay had spent a lot of time together the last few days. "And I asked Misty out on a date, but she said no," he said, burring himself into Rosé's bed. "My heart broke, and I didn't want to cry alone. You are my 8." His voice was muffled by the mattress. Rosé jumped over him, hugging Aiden tight from behind.

"You know that it doesn't matter what happens, I will always be here for you," she whispered. "Heartbreak sucks, I am so sorry." Silence. She couldn't let him wallow like this.

"There's something I want to do before I die."

"Hm?"

"Don't judge me."

"I am already."

She got up on the bed, making Aiden sit up and stare.

"I want to walk around this place in a bathrobe, listening to loud music. Dance in the halls. Scream. Run around like there is no tomorrow. I want to stare at the stars until I can't take it anymore." The sound of rain hitting against the window began. Rosé ran to the window, opening it. "Perfect. We'll run out in the rain," she said with a huge smile.

She ran to Aiden who was still in bed, thinking about what she had said. She took him by the hand, pulling him. "Let's live. Do something crazy. Different. I dunno … Let's go," she screamed, their glances met.

Rosé made two robes appear.

"We can't make noise."

She passed him some earphones, connecting two pairs on her phone. The music began to play. Aiden began to shake his head and play an imaginary guitar.

Full Nappies.

They put on the robes and went out into the halls. They danced and lip-synced the songs they played. They played countless songs, from up-tempo to suffering and sad. They sang and danced until sweat began to run off their faces.

She didn't want to know how crazy they looked. Two microphones showed up. Glasses. Disco globes. She was losing control of how many things she had made appear. She was drunk from happiness. She looked at Aiden, they were joyous.

They started running until they were outside. The rain still falling on them. She took off her robe and started dancing there. She turned and fell to the ground. She fell on her ass. Aiden ran over to her to help her but ended up falling too.

She laughed. They laughed until they couldn't breathe. She hugged him tight, she could feel his bones, but she let him go, worried that he had stopped breathing. They laughed until their belly and cheeks ached. She shouted out and smiled. She looked up at the sky.

She tried at least.

She tried to look at the stars, but she didn't see any. She sat there looking for a while. Her smile was gone.

"I'm sorry," she whispered. "No. You know what? I'm not going to apologise. I'm tired of apologising. I know I shouldn't be here, being so careless, but I don't care. For a moment I am happy, Mum. For a moment in my life, I'm doing something I like and want to do." Her smile appeared again. "I know you fought to let me come into this world, so let me enjoy it. Don't hate me for that. I couldn't stand your hatred for me."

She closed her eyes, feeling the drops of rain on her face and the music still playing in her ear. She imagined her mother in the midst of the stars, smiling at her. Feeling proud. "Thank you."

Aiden fumbled and grabbed her by the arm, he pointed her to the front door.

Rosé stopped and looked. Kay was there watching them dance. She took a few steps back as Kay advanced. He was always there. She looked at him and smiled. Taking Aiden's hands, in a few seconds she felt the lightness in her body.

Invisible.

They were invisible.

"Run," she said, and together they ran, the music matching their movements.

Adrenaline in their veins.

Heart beating a thousand beats.

<3

"You're losing the notion of things."

Rosé was in a room with Tom and Ari and knew that, somewhere, Kay was there in invisible form, probably leaning against the wall with his arms folded.

Rosé remembered running down the halls holding Aiden's hands until she felt her body drop, and everything went dark. She woke up in this gathered office, with them all watching her.

She didn't know how much time had passed and where Aiden was, but she would take care of that later.

"What exactly are you talking about?" she asked, curious to know what he would blame her for this time. She crossed her arms, waiting for the answer she knew she would hate.

"You're risking your life in the middle of the night with fucking headphones. You might not have heard anything if something happened," Tom said.

"I think that would be my problem then," she remarked coldly. She could see the muscles tensing in Tom, his mouth was like a straight line, almost disappearing. "I was having fun. I was being happy." She ran her hands through her still wet hair from the rain and tied it in a bun.

"Having fun? Having fun? Our life depends on you."

"Well, I'm sorry about that." She laughed ironically. "'Ours'? It's always your life, you never refer to MY life. What I want. What makes me happy. MY happiness. I'm sorry if I'm trying to live MY life." He didn't say anything.

"You know what? I hate this place. I hate the people in it. I hate everything that has happened to me. I hate being who I am. I hate everything, because everything I love has been taken from me mercilessly, so I have nothing to love anymore. I just want to wake up in another body, live another life, with other people." She stopped to retrieve air. "No. I wish I was dead. Everything is based on my magic. Being a Lysion. Why don't you just kill me? Why don't you steal my magic and take that shit? Because I don't want it. And then," she said, getting up, "when you have it, you do whatever the fuck you want with it."

She left the room. She had one place in mind. The portal. She knew where it was. The only way to leave Amondridia undetected.

She arrived in the room and took one of the backpacks, picking up the necessary things. She was going to hide on her own. She'd go far from where they were, she'd go anywhere that wasn't here. She wanted her ordinary life. She wanted her mother. She wanted Helena.

She was going back to Brazil.

Rosé looked at her bookshelf and retrieved a little box from the top shelf. It was black and simple with a letter in it.

I should have given this to you a long time ago. It's the money I got when I supposedly betrayed you. You wanted money; I got some for you.

Rosé opened the box with her shaking hands. There was a wad of money. Several hundred-pound fastened with a rubber band. She didn't have time to count. She knew it was enough.

She threw it in the bag.

What would have happened if one of them were there? Helena or Sarah. It would be very different from the way it was now. She left the room. She didn't stop to say hello to anyone. She ignored any comments. Rosé didn't care about the whispers and gossip or the people stopping to look. She was tired.

She turned onto another hallway and, as she imagined, he was there.

"I'm not staying and don't try to stop me," she commented without stopping heading, towards Kay and the gate.

"I didn't come to stop you. I'll go with you," he informed, coming to meet her, preventing her from passing. He was much bigger than her.

"You won't," she said, looking into his eyes.

"That's my decision, don't you think?"

"You've made a lot of decisions for me, how about I make one for you?" She opened the bag and threw the money at him. "Take your dirty money and get out of my way." At that moment she put herself first. She didn't care about her feelings. Her brain was talking louder. She would deal with the pain afterward. She'd already lost a lot and survived. She could do that again, and again and again if she had to.

She could get over the pain.

"I'll stand by your side, whether you like it or not. Whether you want me or not," he said, putting himself in front of her one more time. He closed the distance that was left between them. "Rosé—"

"Don't call me that," she whispered, trying to maintain her posture, trying not to throw herself into his arms and give up everything. His body was like a magnet, pulling her to him.

"I thought that's what you wanted to be called." Not by him. Not by Kay.

"Get out of my way." She tried to get past him, but he was still there. He took her face. Forehead to forehead, breathing the same air. She kept her gaze down. She couldn't look. She couldn't do it. She just couldn't do that. She knew if she looked, she'd regret it. She tried to dumb him down, but she failed again. He just brought their mouths closer.

His smell was in her lungs. His perfume and old pages of books. She wanted more. She wanted to get lost in it, but she wouldn't surrender.

She had surrendered countless times and would not make that mistake again.

Breathe and keep your head in place.

She breathed and felt him.

Don't breathe and keep your head in place.

"Baby, look at me," he begged. "Please look me in the eye." She did it. *Shit.* He was close to her once more. His hands on her waist, pulling her into him. To his chest. His embrace. He took Rosé's hand carefully, as if she could break, and put it on his chest, on top of his heart, until she could feel his beats. "Every one of them is yours and yours only." He was trying to find the words. "You make me feel so wrong and vulnerable and I hate you for it, you know? You just needed weeks to end my life." He stopped and looked away a little. "Ugh that's disgusting. That statement was a little …" His grip became more aggressive, just the way she liked it.

Love is much stronger than he can control and it's a great weapon against him. He's feeling vulnerable right now.

She thought a little. She wanted to kiss him right there, she always wanted to kiss him. But if she did that, she'd lose. With her hands on his t-shirt, she clasped it, grabbing him. "I hate what you do to me." She dropped her hands and stepped back.

"I'll stay, but from now on I'll train myself. Whenever and wherever I want." She pointed her index finger to his chest. "I don't want anyone concerning themselves with my business. I'm going to make my own decisions about *my* life. I'm not going to live off the rules of this place." A huge smile popped up on his face. "I'm still mad at you," she warned him, pushing him. "And it's not going to be today that I'm going to settle this with you. One step out of line and I'm leaving, and if I leave, I'm not going to promise I'm going to stay alive. I'm curious what this world would turn out to be. I don't—"

Steps interrupted her. When she turned around the whole Elite was there, even Aiden and Theo. Everybody was looking at her. Ari came to meet her and hugged her. Rosé hugged her back without thinking. She would never disrespect Ariady. She was one of the few people who had shown her respect. "If you dare to leave this place with the intention of never coming back, I will hunt you to the end of the world and I will bring you back by the hair," she commented.

"You were going to run away?" Tom asked.

"Don't start," Kay warned.

"Fool."

Rosé dropped Ari and went towards him; in seconds he was in the air next to her. She loved it. That was her favourite power. Face to face. He couldn't talk, she had taken that gift from him.

"Disrespect me once more and you will suffer the consequences. I'm your daughter, you owe me respect. That's mutual. From one to the other and if you don't have it for me, don't expect me to respect you. I'm not going to put up with this anymore." He tried to retaliate but every attempt was futile. Rosé had taken his magic from him too. "Have you forgotten who I am? I'm a Lysion." Her voice was firm and authoritative. She let him fall in front of her. "I hope I was very clear about the new conditions for me in this place," she commented, turning to leave

They watched her go.

<3

"I never thought anyone could look as much like their mother as Rosé did now with Sarah," Tom hoarsely remarked, waiting for his lungs to work again. "They didn't even know each other properly."

"You miss Sarah threatening you, don't you?" Ari asked. "I swear that if you threaten this girl one more time, I am going to be the one to end your life."

"Psychopaths," Skyler commented.

"No. She's not like Sarah," began Mr Watson. "I'm sorry to say she has nothing to do with Sarah. Rosé is more powerful than her, I can see it in her mind." With his hands behind his back, he started walking. "You've been underestimating this girl from the beginning, but … be prepared. Rosé will do great things yet."

Chapter 56

It was past midnight when she walked into the training room. There were some people training there who watched her as she passed.

wasn't supposed to be there, and she knew it, but she didn't give a fuck.

She was tired of not being able to control her magic. And she could only do it if she practiced, so here she was.

She couldn't sleep and she wasn't going to waste her time in bed listening to the stupid voices in her head.

There were days when she lay in bed and could sleep peacefully. But she also had nights where she lay awake, destroyed, exhausted, but the brain more awake than ever.

The room was huge, surrounded by mirrors and filled with training objects with specific powers or magic. She didn't want to touch them.

She threw her purse in the corner and went to one of the mirrors and tied her hair back. Looking at her reflection, she noticed some new scars on her body. Her eyes were deep, with dark bags under them.

She desperately wanted to sleep, but every time her head touched the pillow, a thousand and one thoughts disturbed her and even when she could sleep, the same dream of being imprisoned haunted her.

She was angry. Her look wasn't friendly, but she didn't care.

She sat on the floor in the middle of the room, crossing her legs. "Negative emotions? Sure. Let's play with fire." She let her anger take hold. Rosé felt it course through her whole body, from her heart to her fingertips.

She felt something cold running through her veins. She could feel every part of her body connecting. She felt a river of emotions.

Her eyes narrowed, dominated by the pain that flurried within her.

She looked in the mirror, her eyes were as black as the starless sky, like the darkness that dominated her body. From the corner of her eyes, she could see that each object was in the air, touching the black cloud coming out of her.

Rosé's blood was like a poison inside her body, marking her from the inside, penetrating, but not hurting her. Occupying every vein in her body.

Her body was dominated by what looked like black veins. Drawn by brushes and paint.

All these years dominated by fear, insecurity, pain, anger, feeling inferior and excluded.

She came down from her own cloud, as a queen descends from her throne. Every step was as if the ground trembled around her until she came close to her reflection in the mirror.

Her eyes were unrecognizable, her mouth the colour of blood. The features of a perfectly designed face. She touched the icy glass, tracing every line and curve of her own face. She smiled from ear to ear.

She looked around. Everything was being controlled by her. She could feel a connection to each object as if they were physically attached to her. She smiled again, closing her eyes and feeling what she had never felt in her life.

Control.

Rosé lowered her hands, carrying with her each object, until the invisible lines were cut. Without having to conjure or move, she made the mirror in front of her crack. The noise was like music to her ears. Each crack created another and another. She headed over to it, watching her broken reflection.

The reflection of her heart after many years, represented by the mirror.

Who are you? asked a voice inside her head. "A Lysion, and people will have to deal with it."

Someone whistled, ripping her out of her moment. Looking around, she found a camera, with a flashing light.

They were looking. Watching her.

Rosé snapped her finger. In seconds there was glass scattered everywhere. She didn't even blink when they hit the ground. She looked at the camera and made an obscene gesture and walked away, stepping on the shards of glass she had left behind.

She didn't want them ogling her. She wouldn't stay to fix the mess she had made. She stepped on the shards, listening to the sound of them breaking more under her foot.

Broken glasses are made to be left and forgotten, not to be repaired, waiting for someone to gather them up for you. She was going to use what was left and from them make something greater. Stronger. Unbreakable.

Not like Rosé Johnson.

That girl had died.

Now she was a Lysion.

Chapter 57

The room was colder than usual. It got to the point that even her thick and warm blankets were not proving useless. She was in a thin slip at first because the day was hot. Then she added one more layer, and another, until eventually she covered herself with a heavy duvet. Still, her body was shaking.

She felt like she was stuck out in the middle of a snowstorm.

She curled up in the covers as much as she could, shrinking until she had it in a cocoon. Rosé could feel the weight of the many layers on top of her body.

After a while, it wasn't so bad. She felt comfortable.

Everything was okay. Her body was already warming up and was in a great position, until what she feared most happened.

Rosé needed to pee. She tried to ignore the urge to go to the bathroom. She asked herself if she could hold out until the next morning but remembered that it could do her harm, plus the fact that the feeling would hinder from falling asleep, torturing her.

Better now than later.

She threw aside all of the coverings that formed a mountain on her bed and went to the bathroom. She stopped by the window on her way back. The light of the moon entered through the almost transparent curtains of her room, illuminating it, and giving enough visibility for her to walk without stumbling over something.

Amondridia's grounds were deserted. The light breeze shook the trees and formed small waves in the sea. The lights at the training camp were on, showing that at this time of night there was still someone excited to train.

Rosé embraced her trembling body, trying to rid it of her goosebumps. She made sure all the windows were closed and she sat on the bed.

This wasn't normal.

She searched for her radiator and noticed it was turned off. She had never cared about it or turned it on because she had never found the button. She walked all over the room; any switch would be great. A button or something.

Nothing.

She grabbed a coat and opened the door.

She was going for a walk.

When she opened the door, hot air flooded her room. Her body relaxed. She could sleep with the door open if she wasn't afraid of someone coming in and killing her in her sleep. A second thought appeared: *That wouldn't be so bad. At least you'd be asleep.*

That was the way she had always thought of dying. Asleep. No pain. No notice. She would only leave this world in a state of tranquillity, doing something divine, something she loved.

She took off her coat and left her room. She knew exactly where to go.

The light of the moon followed her everywhere she went. She met a huge blue-haired woman sleepwalking around in her nightgown.

Rosé thought to wake her up, to warn her of what was going on. She couldn't cope if an invasion happened and this woman was left in danger, but for two reasons she just kept walking:

Never wake up a sleepwalker.

She'd be able to handle the danger. She probably had control of her powers.

She arrived at Kay's door and thought twice before knocking. She held her hand in the air, inches from the door.

They had been away from each other for over two weeks. Her life had become too complicated to enter into a relationship that would possibly end in the death of one or maybe both.

She said she wanted to live her life and she wasn't kidding, but that didn't involve hurting someone she cared about.

She also thought of Kay being too proud and the possibility of him breaking his promise and letting her die so he could survive. If they weren't together, this decision would be easier for him, to leave her behind and save himself.

A terrible thought to have, but possible.

She lowered her hand and gave up. She would try to get in and, if she couldn't, she'd go back to her room and try to sleep or go and stay with Aiden, like she had done before. It would be weird to do that now, but if it guaranteed a night's sleep in the warmth, then why not?

She took her hand to the doorknob and, with a deep breath, turned it.

It opened.

Kay hadn't taken that right from her yet.

She opened it lightly, avoiding any noise that could wake him up. Her goal was to get in, lie on the bed, fall asleep, and then, only then, the next day, she would deal with his ego.

She opened and closed the door carefully. He was breathing softly. Lucky for her he didn't snore or anything because that would be a huge problem. She couldn't sleep with a light on her face, or any loud noise, and Kay was perfect because he didn't make too many sounds when he slept peacefully by her side.

He was on the left side of the bed, which was perfect because she loved the right side. Carefully, on her tiptoes, she went to his bed.

She lifted the blanket to lie down, exposing some of his body. Kay was lying belly down and with his face turned away from her, but with the little she could see from his sculpted body, it was clear that he was completely naked.

She thought about turning around, but she stayed. Not because of his lack of underwear, but because she was sleepy, and his room was a great temperature.

She couldn't see anything more than his incredible round ass.

She lay down and snuggled in, pulling the covers close to her and closing her eyes. Now she'd be able to sleep. She let her body relax in his soft bed and be surrounded by the warmth of the coverings brushing against her body. She took a deep breath, but not loud enough to wake him up.

It was silent when she allowed herself to sleep.

Too silent.

She opened her eyes. The silence was too weird.

Kay was no longer asleep, his breathing was not consistent enough.

His body stiffened. "Don't even think of making any kind of comment, because you have no right but to stay on your side of the bed and sleep," she whispered clearly, but still low in case she was wrong, and Kay was actually asleep.

The bed began to tremble lightly. He was silently laughing. Rosé smiled and was thankful she had her back to him.

He moved on the bed until the spot next to her body sank and a heavy arm went over her waist and the other lifted her head lightly. Kay pulled her into him and styled her hair so it wouldn't be on his face.

His body was hot against hers. The pulsing between her legs was impossible to ignore.

"I thought I was clear."

"But you forgot that the bed is mine. Eventually, both sides of it are mine," he whispered against her neck and deposited a kiss there. A wave of hot air sailed all over her body. *Fuck,* she loved when he did that. His hand went up to her belly and began to caress her, making small circles around her navel.

"That doesn't mean anything," she remarked, closing her eyes and enjoying the affection. "I'm still mad"

"I know, but at least I'm close to you."

And that's when she suddenly realised the implications of coming here and felt extremely dumb about her decision. Because he knew she was coming. He was waiting for her. She thought she was smart or something, but she had fallen into his game so easily that she felt disgusted with herself.

"It was you," she said, incredulous, still with her back to him. "You left my room cold." He started laughing behind her.

"I don't know what you're talking about, love," he commented. "It's not good to go around accusing people."

She tried to get rid of his arms, but he was stronger and held her tightly against him, until she stopped and simply accepted it. She couldn't get out of there that easily. She had fallen for his bait so easily and quickly that it surprised her.

He approached her ear and in a hoarse voice whispered, "Our war is not over yet, you know that? We may have something extra here, but we're still at war, don't forget that, beautiful thing. I told you, you were playing with the wrong person." She almost lost her self-control and leaned against his voice to get closer to his lips. "I still know how to play, do you?"

"You will pay me for it," she whispered with difficulty. His hand went down to her thighs and gently stroked her.

"I will do what you want, my love." Realising the error in his comment, "No today, another day I will pay you."

"Did you know I was coming?"

"I smelled you when you got to the hallway," he remarked, stroking her thigh and raising his hand up to her hip and her waist, returning to her belly, leaving some caresses on the way. Rosé bit her lips to avoid groaning.

His hand on her body + whispers in her ear = her weakness.

"What made you think twice?"

"Ego."

"Mine or yours? Because I'm not the only one with a big ego," he said, climbing his hand a little further to where her bra was supposed to be, but it wasn't. She hadn't put her bra on to come here, and he noticed when he let a sound slip through his lips.

Rosé took her hand to his, preventing him from climbing further. "No. You can't touch them today. I'm still mad at you."

"Are you sure?" he whispered, going a little further and touching the tip of her tits. She wasn't sure anymore when his gesture pleased her body. *Fuck Kay, fuck his hands, oohhh shit, but* … It wasn't something she couldn't stop, but she didn't want him to stop. It was the relaxation she needed.

He continued playing there until she could feel his other hand going down another path.

He opened her legs slightly and placed his hand between her legs. Her body was burning. "For someone who was against it, you seem quite excited." She knew what he found there.

She had to shut her eyes. Her body was gently writhing in pleasure. "Kay," she moaned. She couldn't think properly. The pleasure had completely taken over her body. The feeling between her legs was …

"Ask me to stop and I will," he said. His finger was still over the thin fabric. She didn't want him to stop. "Be my good girl," he whispered.

Another moan. "Fuck." His words were not helping.

"Do you want me to stop?" Every movement and circle he made was paradise.

"I-I …"

"What? Use your words, love." She didn't answer, and he stopped. Leaving her without a climax. "I think I am winning this game."

He lowered his hand and took hers, he brought her hand up to his face and kissed it.

"I think I will have to get revenge out on your exposed friend down there." He knew she was coming.

"You've noticed. Interesting," he remarked, moving his hand to her belly. "And how exactly were you thinking of taking care of it? You know there are countless way—" Rosé moved her leg before he could finish the sentence but was prevented when he moved his leg over hers.

"Son of a bitch."

"Your children are in here," he remarked, laughing. "You should rethink your actions."

"No. Your children are there, my children are in my ovaries, and I may as well find someone else," she said in a rage, regretting her words immediately. Kay tensed behind her, and she knew she had made a big mistake.

Some time ago she would have been proud of that.

"You're definitely a Mood Killer," he remarked, turning around. She felt the heat leave her body in seconds.

"Don't use that against me."

"I hope you don't repeat what you said, or I'll throw you out of this bed and send you back to the north pole where you came from," he commented. His voice was distant.

"I doubt it."

Suddenly she could feel his foot on her, kicking her out of bed. The movement was so fast that she couldn't react, but before she hit the ground, something stopped her for a second and then she felt the hard ground on her body.

The laugh was inevitable. "I hate you."

"It probably hurt less than what you said to me." She relaxed when she could feel the humour in his voice.

She got up and went to the door, trying to open it, but couldn't. It was locked. "Sorry for hurting your feelings," she laughed again. She couldn't believe what had just happened. "I hope you are happy in your sauna."

Kay appeared suddenly and caught her from behind, taking Rosé back to bed. "Ahhh Rosélina, you are lucky I am a patient person with you," he said, returning to the same position they were in before she talked about their children. "One. You're making me miss my sleep. Two. I manipulated you to come here, yes, but with great intentions. Three. Please. Don't say, repeat, or think about that shit again. Four. It is too late for you to go wandering around and your room will take a while to get back to normal. Five," he stopped and left a kiss on her neck, "I want you here with me, by my side where I can keep my eyes on you, my arms around you, and my lips on you and I know you want it as well."

Not just her body, but everything in her wanted that. She relaxed and let his warmth wrap around her.

"I hate you," she whispered.

"I hate you more."

"Good night," she said, taking her hand out of his and moving it back to caress his face.

"Do you still need some time?"

She looked at him. Rosé stroked his face and soothed her thumb against his lips. "The time wasn't for me. I wanted you to understand the risks you will face staying with me. I don't want to hurt you. I don't want to die and leave you heartbroken. I am trying to save you and I was fucking mad you didn't understand that."

"I don't want to be saved," he whispered against her mouth and kissed her. They kissed as if they needed it to live, they fused their bodies until they needed to separate due to a lack of air and smiled. "I just want you."

"I can't promise you that we're going to age together, that I'll be with you until the end."

"Good, I don't want a grumpy old lady next to me, with wrinkles and amnesia and—" Rosé hit him slightly on his chest which made him turn to the other side of the bed again. "You're going to sleep alone tonight." She cuddled over to over him, stumbling into his body. "What the fuck, Rosé?" She forced him to wrap her back up in his arms.

"If you take those arms off me one more time I will—"

"I know what you're going to do." He rolled his eyes. She looked up at him once more. "Is there any possibility you can stop moving? Your foot is cold."

"I'm trying to get comfortable, I'm sorry." She got as close as she could to him and looked him in the eye. "I was serious about the two of us."

"Me too."

When she woke up the next day, Kay was no longer in bed.

Chapter 58

"What is Duellun?" asked Rosé from the bench while Ari moved around some plants.

"It's a competition and form of training at the same time. The participants put the prize in the middle and make a circle and speak *Ite nunc*, which means 'Go now' and fight to get to the object first. You have to stop the others from getting to the object, though … it happens inside a room and this room is programmed to stop you. Duellun's game."

"Where's the Duellun room?"

"In the training camp. That's how we train," she said, sitting in a chair. "The Elite use Duellun as a form of training because it tests our skills in many ways."

"Can I go?"

"Maybe one day." She looked at Rosé for a few seconds.

"Is there a problem?"

"I'm worried. You're growing up too fast. I don't know if I'm ready for this. It hasn't been a year since you first came here and look at you." She stopped. Two glasses appeared. She raised her glass, waiting for Rosé.

They toasted.

Ari drank a sip and wiped away a tear.

"Stop."

"You can't blame me for being worried about you." Rosé got up from the bench and pulled a chair over to face Ari. "You seem far away. From me at least."

"I do not want you to get hurt. I don't want anybody to get hurt because of me," she explained, taking a sip of her drink.

"I think that is our decision," Ariady countered. "If we want to stay or leave. But please do not leave. I will stay with you until the end." She took Rosé's hands in hers. "I swear, with my body and soul, I will be with you fighting."

"Ari, I will never leave you." Rosé held her hands tighter. "You are like a mum to me and for as long as I can, I will be next to you."

"Don't make me cry."

"You do not look like the emotional type."

"You bring out the worst side of me." Both women laughed.

<3

On the way to the canteen, she thought of her friends and how they would want her to sit with them, but she was with Kay, and she really wanted to be with him today.

When she arrived, she asked Kay to wait for her while she went to hug them. They seemed happy to see her after spending some time away.

When she returned to Kay, they went to get their food and sat at a table. Ruby hated the idea, it was clear from the look on her face, but Rosé didn't care.

She spent the whole dinner in silence with her red liquid in her glass and phone in her hand. Rosé wondered whose blood it was. Gustav was drinking the same. She couldn't ignore the smell of metal in the air, but it wasn't necessarily bothering her.

Sky came later and hugged her before sitting down with her food, she then placed a huge gun on the table, making it tremble.

Skylar launched into discussions as usual. During the conversation, Rosé put one of her legs on Kay's and expected some reaction from him, but nothing. After a while she decided to take it off, but she was stopped. He held her leg and rested his hand on her, stroking and squeezing her lightly.

That was a mistake. A huge mistake.

The subject of the invasion was put on the table but soon changed to the kitchen.

"I thought you were going to eat normal food today," Skylar said, taking a piece of meat to her mouth.

"I need to be well fed with blood. Food usually doesn't give me enough energy." Rosé observed her as she took another sip. "Is there something wrong?" Rosé denied it and went back to eating her food.

The silence came back, and it got to her.

At the other table what was most lacking, was a moment of silence.

Rosé looked at Kay who had not touched his food. When she asked, he simply said that he was not hungry and that he wanted to go to her room but was waiting for her. Rosé tried to get up to leave, but he stopped her, saying she shouldn't rush because of him.

"Gustav you are a terrible cook; you have no right to complain about the food here," Sky commented. Rosé returned to pay attention to a new conversation that had begun.

"You're a liar," he said, tapping his fist on the table.

"You burned three eggs and almost set fire to the hotel we were in."

"That was an attempted murder against you. It was on purpose."

"You burned noodles," Ruby commented, her expression neutral. "You don't deserve to be in the kitchen."

Silence dominated again. Ruby started leaving the table and Sky asked why she was leaving early, and her excuse was because she had to cut her hair and it took a while.

"I think women should keep their hair long," Gustav commented. Rosé didn't know if he was being honest or just trying to get Sky and Ruby angry, but Ruby showed him her middle finger and left the canteen. "It makes them sexier"

Sky tried to hit him with a plate, but Rosé managed to stop it. She didn't want a war now.

Not even ten minutes later, Rosé finished eating and looked at Kay, who looked extremely tired. "Hey," she said, caressing his hand that was on her thighs. "Do you want to go?" He nodded and began to get up but was stopped when the sound of heels made everyone turn to the entrance.

Ruby had shaved her head.

She came up to the table and stopped in front of Gustav. "Sorry dear, what did you say about hair and women? I think I stopped listening when you decided to open your fucking mouth to say shit," she said, taking his glass and drinking the rest of the blood in it. She smiled, showing her bloody fangs, and walked away.

Gustav watched her every move. "Oh, provoking her hits different"

Chapter 59

Two days later.

The training camp was packed. Everyone was preparing for what was coming. Rosé didn't know all these people lived here; she'd never seen half of them. Maybe because she only hung out with the same people or spent most of her day training alone or reading in the library.

Kay was behind her. She could feel him there. He greeted the people passing by.

In one of the rooms Rosé saw Nikko and Lux fighting with Ascelin and JJ. Ascelin was trying to help them prepare. Her face was neutral, but Rosé saw concern in her eyes when they exchanged glances.

It was all her fault. They were all going to fight because of her and her family. A knot was forming in her stomach as she looked around. This whole thing was happening because people wanted her magic.

"They won't fight, right? They're going to be evacuated as I ordered?" Rosé asked, stopping and turning to Kay. She had been very specific when she said that no child would fight. They were going to be evacuated somewhere else. That was no place for them here.

"Who?" he asked, slapping a man's back in greeting and then turning to her.

"The kids." Kay looked at them too. His gaze returned to Rosé's but he did not answer. She crossed her arms once more, not caring if he loved it or not. She thought about wrapping her hand around his neck, and not in a sexy way.

She didn't want anyone fighting and that's exactly what they seemed to be training for. All in black uniforms and with small guns in hand.

"About that …"

"About that, my ass. Do you need me to draw it out? Do I need a sheet of paper and a pen?" She was mad at them. Totally and indescribably furious. They didn't seem to take her seriously and it bothered her. She might not know about strategies or all the existing creatures or the possible plans of villains, but she had the right to speak and be heard. "I was clear with this, and they didn't—"

Nikko and Rosé exchanged glances before he returned his focus on Lux beside him, helping JJ, their little sister, with her blond long hair.

"Did you allow it?" She turned to Kay. "You should have said no."

He inhaled and exhaled loudly "The portals were interfered with in the middle of the plan. We couldn't risk sending more of them. Some have been evacuated. Others stayed. We prioritised the babies, those with deficiencies, and the elderly."

"They are children." she said "They won't fight," she crossed her arms. Kay ignored her and kept walking. They went through more rooms, more unknown and well-known people. Shit! Stupid portals.

When Rosé spotted the Elementris, she went towards them, but Kay pulled her by the waist, turning her so they were face to face and then threw her over his shoulders.

Rosé protested.

"You come with me and stop complaining for a minute, we're late." How dare he say she complained if he was worse?

"Complaining is part of my personality," she said. "Put me down."

"So you can slow us down? No. We have to find the Elite," he commented. "We do not have much time."

She could already feel the blood draining from her head.

"Besides you should stop complaining and enjoy the view, because honestly, I'm enjoying mine," Kay commented, slapping Rosé's ass. She could feel her face catch fire and it wasn't because she was upside down. She unintentionally put her hand on Kay's big ass.

Hard. His ass was hard. She took advantage and kept pinching it.

Upon arriving in the room Kay put her on the floor. There were countless guns scattered around the tables. Not only firearms that Rosé had already used with Ruby, but also swords and accessories and Rosé vowed to have seen a katana somewhere. Clothes were scattered everywhere. They all wore the same black uniform. As the wall changed colour, black would make them go unnoticed.

"The curse has arrived," remarked Gustav from the corner of the room. There were knives and weapons perfectly positioned in his trousers and jacket. Gustav didn't have many powers, so he needed the weapons to defend himself.

"You took your time," Ari commented. Her lips contracted. "I thought I'd been clear about you being quick," she said, directing this to Kay.

"I was doing my job, but you know that Miss I-want-to-know-of everything kept asking countless questions, besides delaying us with certain attitudes," Kay commented with a smile on his face, looking at Rosé who cast a furious look. "Don't look at me like that, honey, do you disagree with me?"

"What certain attitudes?" Tom asked, looking at Kay and Rosé, a pistol in one hand and a dagger in the other.

"Nothing," Rosé replied. "Where're my clothes?" She tried to change the subject. That wasn't something she wanted to discuss with him right now. Tom handed it to Rosé who headed to the locker room, smiling falsely, throwing the middle finger up at Kay.

Kay came up right behind her and, when they were away from prying eyes, he held her by the waist and whispered in her ear. "Why didn't you tell your father?" Love and hate. That's what she felt towards him.

"Tell him what, exactly?"

"That you tried to seduce me for information."

"Why didn't you say anything?"

"He would be pissed at me, and it would be more interesting if it came from you." Rosé took his hands off her and went to change. She was a fucking bitch with no feelings, she couldn't let a man get in the way.

Kay tried to enter the same changing room as Rosé but was stopped. "No distractions," she murmured. "We're late." Rosé put on the black suit. It was different from her training outfit. This was a turtleneck with sleeves. The pants were similar but contained zippered pockets on the side.

When she left the locker room, she found Kay waiting for her. He was already wearing his uniform. Rosé sat next to him and began to put on her boots but was prevented once again by him crouching at her feet, helping her. "I can do this on my own."

"I know you can, but I want to help you." His touches were subtle, he helped her as though she was a fragile doll that could be broken at any time. She watched him do it and a smile escaped.

No one had ever been as careful with her as Kay had. Although he wasn't careful in training, he always kept her from getting hurt badly.

"You need to stop doing this."

"What?" he asked.

"Doing everything for me," she said.

"I never had someone to take care of," he said, raising his gaze to meet hers. "I want to learn how to do this. Take care of you"

"I must be quite difficult to deal with."

"You have no fucking idea, but I love a challenge, Smurf." He winked at her, taking her hand to help her up. "Especially a sexy and powerful one."

<3

Together, they went into the main room. Kay pulled Rosé into a corner and helped her put gun bridges on both thighs, positioning two daggers on one side and a pistol on the other. She soon began to feel their weight.

"I thought I was going to use my magic to fight them."

"And you will, but if your magic fails or something, you have weapons to protect yourself. Magic does not kill," he said, finishing adjusting them. "The gun is already loaded. Six bullets. Don't waste them." Kay also handed over a pair of black gloves, saying it was important to protect her hands. "Feel free to pick something else from the table."

Kay pulled her lightly by the neck, without hurting her, kissed her, and went to another table to prepare.

The table was full of objects. Rings, English punch, daggers of numerous shapes, sets of chains, small axes, and other objects that Rosé did not know either what they were or what they were for.

Ruby appeared behind her and took one of the sets of rings from the table, it was pointed and connected by chains, and was worn like a glove. Her hair was almost all shaved like Gustav's and platinum with red flames painted across the side and back. "Great for causing a deep wound." She positioned it in her right hand and headed toward the wall and scratched it, leaving a deep trail of nails in the concrete. She winked at Rosé and left, exposing her jacket with countless thorns behind her.

They've all killed before, and I'm just a stupid girl.

"I don't quite agree with what you just thought, Rosé." It was Mr Watson. "You're just inexperienced, but not stupid." He approached her. "We are different from them," he said, pointing to the room. "It takes years to learn something that it takes us only days to learn. Their brains develop in the same slow manner as the rest of your body. They were surprised at how many things you learned in a small period."

"I thought you didn't read my thoughts," she argued, grabbing a ball in her hand.

"Sometimes they are too loud and impossible to ignore. Besides, I had to calm you down a little bit, your heart was too fast and it's a little irritating to both parties." He took the ball from Rosé's hand and returned it to the table, he pointed to a dagger with a cape over it. "That little ball will wipe out your lungs if it falls to the ground. This dagger has Fiore Nero's poison, but you know that I suppose." That was her mother's dagger. How did he get there?

"How do you do that?" she asked, taking the dagger and putting it on her thigh in the last empty space she had.

"The mind is the problem of everything and the solution to everything. Keep track of it and you'll have control of the world around you." And he left.

Looking around, everyone was ready. Weapons positioned. Ari was the one who was the least armed or at least looked the least armed. Gustav had daggers and weapons well-positioned all over his body and a cloth covered his nose and mouth. Skylar, who had just arrived, held a huge katana, and strapped a gun to her shoulder.

Mr Watson and Kay wore similar things.

Ruby had a mask on her face, plus a veil. Rosé questioned her about the veil. "We will attend several funerals, dear. We need to be ready to provide our non-condolences." Funeral reminded Rosé of the deaths that were going to happen that night. She could feel her stomach turning and a huge hole forming in the middle of her chest.

Ruby checked the ammunition on the gun and positioned it in the trough and grabbed a baton. "Time to play," she remarked, laughing before leaving the room.

"You don't know how long I've waited for this," remarked Skylar, hugging her gun and smiling, following her.

"Psychopaths," muttered Gustav, going after them. "And you gave them weapons. Congratulations!" he shouted from the palm-pounding hallway. Ari and Mr Watson followed them.

"Do you mind if I have a moment alone with my daughter?" Tom asked, approaching Rosé. Kay kissed Rosé's hand and left the room. Tom watched Kay leave and, when they were alone, he commented, "I don't remember having authorised any of this." He crossed his arms. Rosé just rolled her eyes. "Are you still a virgin?"

"Father!"

"I need to know."

"That's none of your business."

"One of the men I trusted most, with my daughter. Everything I ever expected," he said sarcastically.

"Better than someone you don't know."

"It would be better if you didn't have anyone." Tom held his daughter's hands. "Just don't forget to pay attention. Sometimes you think the man is worth it and he's just another good actor hiding his identity. I say that, because, well, you know?" Rosé just agreed.

"I don't know if I'm ready," she said. At that moment Rosé did not see her father as a cruel killer or someone who had magic but as her father. Her hero and caretaker.

"It's going to be alright and ..." His voice failed. "I know I shouldn't be saying goodbye or anything, but the last time this happened I lost your mother and ... And I could never say goodbye to her, so do me a huge favour and stay alive. Fight like a woman. There is nothing more powerful in this world than a strong-willed woman." Tom gave Rosé a kiss on the forehead.

"You did what you thought was right."

"And I failed."

"Everyone fails and there's nothing wrong with that. Although you failed a lot."

"I—"

Two knocks on the door interrupted the moment. "They're calling everyone out there," Kay warned.

Tom kissed Rosé on the cheek and passed Kay at the door, keeping eye contact with him. Kay watched him in the hallway and Rosé came to meet him.

"Are they really calling us?" she asked. Kay just denied it with his head and they both laughed, but not enough for the pain to leave her chest.

What if someone died? What if Kay died? She didn't want to say goodbye to his laughter, or to his greyish eyes, or to his smell. Rosé took her hands to his face, passing over his eyebrows, eyelids, cheek, jaw, until they reached his lips which were slightly open. Rosé could feel his hot breath on her fingertips.

Within seconds Rosé was sitting at one of the empty tables. Their mouth glued together. There was no delicacy in the kiss. His hands went from her waist to her thighs. He, like her, seemed determined to memorise every possible piece of her body.

A groan escaped. His mouth was hot and wet. Kay's tongue explored her mouth.

“Please don’t tell me that was a goodbye kiss?”

“It wasn’t,” he muttered, hoarse, still recovering from the kiss. “It was just a reminder that there’s someone waiting for you. Stay alive. I’ll find you and, if you are not alive, I am going to kill you.” They laughed together.

"We should go find them" she informs looking at the door.

"Five minutes" she raised her eyebrows questioning him but instead of answering he pulled her closer, so her inner thighs touched *him*. Hard against her.

Chapter 60

"Where is everybody?" Kay asked as they left to meet the rest. The place was empty, except for the people of the Elite.

"They're in their seats, now it's up to us to blend in," Ariady began. "Ruby, Gustav, Kay and Rosé, I want you inside. Skylar, Tom, Noah (Mr Watson) and I are going to stay here f—" Before Ari could finish, one of the three dragons appeared in the air above them. "Skylar, one of them is yours."

She grabbed her gun. "You know, I think the Down World is too empty today. It's time to send some motherfuckers over there. A little gift for my parents," she remarked, going towards them.

Josh came down from the red dragon and walked towards them.

"I need one more."

"I will do it," Mr Watson volunteered himself. "My magic is not that strong anymore. And remember, we're playing hide-and-seek. Either you hide so no one finds you, or you run after the one who's hiding." Josh came to her and hugged her.

"When it's all over, will you teach me how to tame one?" she asked. Dragons were fascinating and she thought it was essential to know how to tame one.

"Of course I will. For you I would do anything."

A huge roar behind them captured their attention. Dandara was there, followed by three others huge Olvs. The same ones Rosé had seen on her arrival.

One of them came towards Rosé and crouched, bowing his head. She stroked him. His hair was soft like velvet. He looked into her eyes and howled. "He asked you to stay alive," informed Dandara, with her strong accent. "Don't die, child, our world depends on you." Rosé nodded and she transformed.

Dandara crouched down and Ariady climbed on her back. "When this is over, I want you all alive. Amondridia needs you, fight with it, and it will fight with you," she announced. "Now!" "And always!" everyone shouted in a chorus.

Kay held Rosé's hand and together they began to run toward the palace. Her heart was beating a thousand times per minute. Her mouth was already dry and her hands were sweaty and tingling. *I have control over my powers and my mind.* She repeated this several times.

Upon arriving at one of the entrances, Kay drove her to one of the corridors.

"I thought we were going to split up."

"I changed my mind. Besides, eventually we're going to split up."

There were other people in the halls, in formation. "Where are we going?"

"To the hallway where the children are." Rosé could feel the bile in her throat. "you said you didn't want them to fight and they are not. Only in emergency, as it always was. They're inside the rooms. The doors will disappear as usual, but that doesn't mean they won't have to fight. Li Wang is among the people of Wysez, she knows perfectly how things work."

Rosé remembered her. She was the woman who wanted to expel Rosé from Amondridia. Her white hair always tied in a perfect bun.

"If you don't want to kill, just hurt them and let them die alone." He kissed her hand and her heart jumped. How could she live without his kisses? "Stay alive. Don't make me go to the Upper World to pick you up. I like an adventure, but not to the point of negotiating with the God who guards that world."

Rosé smiled lightly. "What makes you think I'm going to the Upper World?"

"Angels like you go to the Upper World because they would be too dangerous in the Down World. Too catastrophic." The siren sounded.

The walls changed colour.

The doors disappeared.

Silence.

"Time to play."

"Time to play," she repeated

She felt like she was in a survival game.

Kay was right. Soon enough, they were no longer together. Two non-humans in black had appeared. *Control your emotions, not the other way around.*

Within seconds she was fighting.

<3

Ruby put some gum in her mouth, the rifle over her shoulder. The alarm had already gone off and she had not been lucky enough to find any invaders around the palace. She could already hear the sound of gunshots. Each shot a spark of light. That was music to her ears, and she was betting it was Skylar shooting at the first thing she saw in front of her.

She remembered the first time they had seen each other a few decades ago. Gustav had turned her into a vampire, and she lived there until someone threw her out of this world, but … as always, the 'but' always exists … She had committed countless crimes in the past and the Upper and Lower World were looking for her. Angels and demons fighting each other to find her.

Her time on earth was over, but she couldn't leave it and had to make a deal.

Skylar was one of the demons.

Maybe 'demon' isn't the right word. The devil's daughter, who knows. They fought many times.

Both had already come close to killing each other.

People used to look at them, two people, but so different. They weren't friends, as people deduced. No one from the Elite was anybody's friend. Everyone just valued respect, but they weren't friends.

Back in the hallway, the heeled boots made noises on the ground. Her pocket was full of small, useful devices for people whose magic was limited or non-existent. She was more agile and fast, yet it wasn't enough when someone uses magic against you, she knew it more than anyone, but that was also an advantage.

A group of semi-humans appeared. Every corner a surprise. She felt like she was in a maze. Ruby pointed the rifle and started shooting, stopping just to reload, but that wasn't enough. She was good at aiming but couldn't work miracles at hitting everyone, so she dropped a small bomb and blew them up. *Boom!*

There were only three bullets left in her rifle. She left it on the floor and climbed one of the walls.

The shots had pricked the ears of more attackers. Ruby walked along the top of the walls, trying to make as little noise as possible, balancing her body so she wouldn't fall.

It wasn't something new, she had done it countless times.

It had become her trap.

And she wasn't wrong.

A group of people arrived in the hallway from both sides. Enemies.

She crouched down, waiting for them to pass through the bodies of the semi-humans, lifeless on the ground. They looked everywhere for her. Confused. Where could she be?

Look at the ceiling, bitches, and you're going to find what you're looking for.

One of them took the rifle she had left on the floor. "Hot," it murmured. *No, baby, it's going to be freezing. You heard gunshots a few minutes ago and have got countless dead people on the ground,* she thought. Ruby couldn't deny the fresh blood there, ready to be drunk. So juicy that her throat became dry and her head ached.

She passed her tongue over her lips and her teeth. Until she remembered that it was semi-human blood, probably full of disgusting things, but she did not care.

She was starving.

Her hand went into her pocket, picking up a cold ball. She blew a bubble that burst, making a *pop* noise. Eyes looked up, locking with hers. "Pikaboo," she murmured. The ball fell out of her hand and, upon contact with the floor, a gas began to take over the place. Ruby jumped to the floor.

The gas was only bad for human lungs.

With a knife she began to attack them, making their deaths less painful. Dying asphyxiated wasn't a pleasant thing. She stood up, satisfied with her work. Her posture straight. Her heels announcing her arrival. Warning that death was near.

She couldn't see them, but their blood was unmistakable.

The only thing she could hear was moans of pain and the sound of someone's final breaths. She arrived at the last man and brought him with her out of the smoke.

He was weak and a little disoriented. She approached his neck, searching for his jugular vein, and she penetrated him with her fangs.

He fell pale on the floor. Dead.

Ruby took a mirror from her pocket and wiped her mouth. The blood hadn't been bad, but if he was alive, she'd ask him to go on a better diet.

<3

Two men and three women set up in the huge hall of the palace. "We saw you come in, dear. At some point you're going to have to show up, or we're going to find you," said a long-haired blonde woman. Her high, cracked voice made Ruby want to really die.

She moved close, carefully.

"First of all, I don't like you calling me 'dear', and second, I would be running if I were you," said a voice from the ceiling. Ruby was on top once more. That's how she liked to play. In the dark of other people's eyes.

It was like a cat preparing to attack a little bird. Moving slowly, waiting to pounce. But sometimes she'd like to do it differently.

As they looked up, they saw Ruby sitting on one of the pillars. One of the men was struck in the head by a dagger. "Oops, I think I dropped it." Ruby jumped to the ground, in attack position. "What do you want to play?" she asked, turning a bat she had found and used on the way in her hand.

No one answered. "How rude. No one taught you manners?" she said with a tone of disappointment. "Well, with some I played piñata, as you can see." She showed the bloody bat. "With others I played 'target' and others," she said, gesturing to the air, "pikaboo."

Silence.

"Okay, I want to play baseball so I need a ball. Who has the bigger one?" she asked, looking at them with a smile on her face. They looked at each other, but they didn't say anything. "I thought you were men. Don't you get proud and fight about that? Come on." Her smile got bigger. "Okay, I think I'm going to have to figure it out on my own."

Before they could respond, Ruby had already started her attack. One shot in the heart, one shot in the head. A stab wound to the stomach a bullet in the heart. And so it continued until there was none standing. She cleaned her mouth and nose that bled after being hit in the face. "Hm what a pity, I just wanted to play." Ruby went to the door but was surprised to see more people assembling. "Okay, there's enough Ruby for everybody. Let's play."

And there she was, fighting once more. One gone. Torn neck. Two. Three. Four. Now there's only two left. They attacked Ruby at once. One of the men held her by the neck and lifted her up. His magic did it. She was fighting for air. He laughed loudly at her. "A vampire without powers, which will make—" Ruby was knocked to the ground, holding her neck, desperate to catch her breath.

"Did you miss me, sweetie?" Gustav asked her, helping her up.

"Not at all."

"Great. I'd be scared if you said yes," he said, kissing her hand. "You did a great job back there. I followed the trail, you could have left some blood for me." Quite sarcastic, his hands and mouth were covered in blood.

The man got up again and the metal was already in the air, flying towards them. Gustav was too distracted to notice when it came towards him and penetrated his chest.

The world stopped for a second. Just long enough for Ruby to see Gustav falling to the ground. Bumping into the hard marble floor. She looked at him one last time. The metal piercing his lifeless body.

Ruby screamed. They weren't friends, but they were partners. He had saved her at the worst moment of her life.

The man turned toward Ruby, feeling proud about what he had just done. He bragged about his act. Ruby began to fight the man again. Gustav's body lay on the ground, lifeless and pale.

Ruby was almost hit in the chest the same way but swerved. She tried to launch a dagger, but she missed. It was her last.

She tripped over Gustav's body, falling to the ground. She scrambled back up. Evident despair on her face. The black-eyed man ran over to her.

Ruby smiled at the man. "Okay drama queen, enough." The smile disappeared from the confused man's face. Ruby looked behind him and when he turned again, he came across Gustav, standing, smiling. The iron still in his chest.

"Darling, I'm already dead, you can't kill me again so easily. Try something different next time," he commented, removing the dagger and moving towards the man. "I'll tell you how I died. I got really sick, you know. My mother was desperate and—" The man fell into Gustav's arms, taking him by surprise. The man had been shot in the back. "Really? You've interrupted my story!"

"I'm sorry, weeping baby, but we're in a fucking war and I don't think it's the time for your stupid story."

Chapter 61

There came a time when she didn't have to think so much. Her body turned into an automatic mode that she never thought existed as if she had been doing this her whole life.

She not only used her magic, but she fought. Gustav had taught her many things including deviations and moves that would help paralyze her opponent. She used the air to her advantage, the fire of the lamps, and what the earth provided, not only to attack, but to create shields.

She lost count of how many times she was knocked down and hit by objects. Sometimes she thought she couldn't get up again.

At this point, she had been lightly burned on the arm and her nose was bleeding.

Sometimes she thought about giving up, but her mind wouldn't allow it.

She hadn't killed anyone.

Not directly. She had pierced people, cut them, and trapped people in materials. Taken the air out of the room so they became disoriented. She fought until they didn't have the strength anymore.

Over time things began to get quieter. Rosé could see bodies on the floor but avoided trying to identify them.

She was running aimlessly. Her chest burned. She took her hands to her cuts; the blood was hot in her hands. Nothing too serious to stop her.

Everything was very quiet. She could feel her face wet. Sweat was dripping off her. Her back was soaked. The cloth of the uniform seemed increasingly tight. It was heavy on her sensitive body which was covered with bruises and cuts.

She had injuries all over her body.

Rosé stopped for a second. She needed to breathe and find someone.

She began to hear some moans of pain. Someone needed her. She started paying attention to where she was going. After turning one of the corridors,

Rosé came across someone moving through some already burned lifeless bodies.

Aiden.

She hadn't had a chance to talk to him before they started. And now he was there. But there was something wrong. "Aiden," cried Rosé. "What happened? We need to get out of here. The war has barely begun, you idiot, and you're almost dying?"

"Rosé, it's good to see you too, but is that really what you want to tell me?" he retorted. His voice was weak. There was a piece of steel piercing into his belly and another in his leg. If it melts inside him …

His hands were black from using his powers. The part of the uniform near the wound was darker, but there wasn't much blood on the floor, which indicated he hadn't lost much blood.

Rosé helped him up and started walking. "They're stronger."

She heard footsteps behind them and didn't think much when she attacked the assailant, she propelled him into a suit of armor, and he was impaled on its spike.

"Do you know a safe place nearby?"

"No. The doors are gone, I don't know where we are." Neither did she. They started walking and luckily they didn't run into anyone. They kept going. Aiden was too heavy for her to carry alone which didn't help at all, especially with him moaning by her side. *The door, door. I need a door. Amondridia,* she cried out in her head. *Fight with me.*

Rosé stopped to get some rest. Through the window, she saw that there were more dragons than she imagined in the air and other strange creatures.

The sky was dark, but the fire lit up the flying black creatures.

"Prin." She turned to Aiden, but saw an open door and went towards it, taking him with her. The smell of old books took over. They were in the library. She helped Aiden sit in one of the nearest armchairs.

That definitely wasn't the library hallway. Rosé didn't know how that happened.

"Pri-n … What is thi-s …place?" asked Aiden. He was losing consciousness.

"Aiden, stay with me," she demanded. "Don't close your fucking eyes."

"I'm sleepy. I want to sleep."

"No, I need you to stay with me," begged Rosé, lifting his shirt. His body was hotter than a normal person's. A piece of metal was still stuck in him. She couldn't take it out. All the videos on how to survive if that happens to say not to take it out. *Shit. Shit. Shit. What should I do?*

"Rosé, what you doing? You *sees* me naked? I love you, not like that," he said, laughing. He could not form a correct sentence. Rosé started looking for something she could use to clean up his wounds, but found nothing. There was absolutely nothing in the immeasurable desk drawers.

"Mr Bebbols," Rosé shouted with the hope that the damn cat would appear.

"Who is Mr Beboll?"

"Shut up, Aiden," she cried impatiently. "Idiot cat where are you?"

"What the fuck is it? I WAS SLEEPING," the cat grumbled, coming down the stairs, his fur messy.

"We are in the middle of a fucking invasion out there and you were sleeping? What do I do? He's dying. What am I supposed to do? There's nothing here I know how to use. Help me, you useless cat."

"Rude."

"You are rude."

"Use your magic, stupid girl. Why do you have it for? As a Christmas ornament? The gods did not give it to you to shove up your ass," he grumbled.

"Am I dying? Why is this cat talking?" Aiden asked almost desperately, trying to get up, but Rosé pushed him into the chair again.

"There's an iron in him," she recalled.

"Take out the iron and then heal. I'm the smart cat and you're the girl who thinks like a normal cat." "I'm tired," remarked Aiden.

"Shut up," they both spoke together. "He'll die if I take it out."

"He's already dying, and the metal is going to melt. Stop questioning and do the fucking business. You didn't wake me up for help and not listen to me. Let's go! You're wasting time," Rosé held the iron and pulled it slowly. Aiden started screaming and more blood poured out of his wound. *Shit. Stop bleeding.* Rosé put her hands on the wound to stop the blood so she could heal it.

Hot. His blood was too hot, and she had to hold on so she wouldn't scream.

She closed her eyes and tried to focus, but she couldn't. Her heart was pounding harder and harder. The blood burned her hands. "I can't." Aiden was dying in front of her. She could see his eyelids getting heavier and heavier. "Aiden stay with me. Please, please, please." Tears flowed down her face. "Please, I'm sorry. I can't do this. Aiden, I need you. Fight." Her vision was blurred, and she couldn't see anything. She was crying.

"They said they would find you and take over the world," Aiden remarked, his lips bowing in a faint smile.

"Really? And what did you say?" asked Mr Bebbols, sitting at the table.

It took him a while to answer. He was smiling like a drunk person. "That they would have to do it over my corpse, they really listened to that." He stopped "That's what friends are for. We take care of each other, right? I wasn't going to let them do that to you."

The wound wasn't healing. Aiden took her face in his hands, forcing her to look at him. "It's alright, let me go." Rosé could feel more tears falling. "You're the important one."

"No, no, no. That's unfair," she whispered, looking into his chocolate-coloured eyes. "That's unfair. Losing you would be unfair to both of us."

"Rosélina, you'll always be my Prin, my 8." She shook her head frantically. No, she still expected him to call her that for many more years. She wanted to see his smile forever, deal with his hot temper.

"I'm done losing."

"So do not lose." He left a kiss on her forehead. "Control your emotions and you will manage to control your magic." Rosé took a deep breath. Once. Twice. Rosé, you can do it. Chaos flooded her vision. It looked like she was running through his veins. She could feel the blood wandering through her, the pain flooded her body.

Listen to him.

Chaos.

Blood.

His body was heavy.

When she opened her eyes, the wound was no longer there. There was blood on her hands, still warm. "I did it! Aiden. I did it!"

But when she looked at him, his eyes were closed. Aiden wouldn't move. "Aiden?" Her heart stopped beating for a second. Her face was neutral. She took her hands up to his face, but withdrew, leaving the mark of her hands there. They were dirty with his blood.

She took his wrist to check, but she couldn't feel a thing. She went up to his neck and found nothing.

She took two steps back, watching him.

Her legs were weak. Her hand went to his mouth, but she didn't touch it.

He was dead.

She had failed and now Aiden was dead. Her hands were smeared with the blood of the only person she had considered her best friend.

"I can't believe the cretin died in my favourite armchair," grumbled Mr Bebbols.

"You stupid cat!" Fire burned in Rosé veins. The cat was already on the wall when Rosé had risen completely. She had to hold on so she wouldn't fall.

A laugh sounded behind Rosé.

"I can't believe I heard this cat complain that I died in his chair." Aiden was still lying in the armchair. Weak and tired. "I love your cat, Prin." Relief took over Rosé's body. He still looked drunk. "I'm sorry, but I couldn't open my eyes and, for your information, I don't really have a natural pulse."

(Okay, I am done with fake death.)

"I'm not her cat." Rosé ignored what he said and ran to meet Aiden.

"I thought you were dead. Thank the angels." She must have been crushing him she was hugging him so tightly. "How? That doesn't make sense, you were dead." She looked at him.

"I heard your voice. Your scream," he commented, drying her tears. "You asked me to fight, and I tried. I tried a little more." They exchanged a long look.

"I don't want to lose you. I can't lose you."

"Neither did I." She stared at him. Memorising him. Admiring him. "Don't look at me like that. It's making me uncomfortable," he whispered. Rosé wanted to slap him, but she'd leave it for later.

"You're going to need to stay here. Until it's all over. Are you going to be okay?"

"Just go. I will stay talking to your cat."

"Oh no, you will not. I am going to sleep," Mr Bebbols muttered and left.

<3

The corridor was still empty. She took a deep breath. She needed air and a little rest. She couldn't do that around Aiden.

She collapsed on the floor. She could see the doors coming back to their normal place and the only thing she could do was think about the kids.

She was about to turn onto a corridor when Rosé heard someone stop at the end of it. They exchanged glances. A few seconds passed. "Bingo. I think I won," she said. She had yellowish eyes and her hair was tied in a bun.

"A lot of people before you said the same thing and well, they're not alive to tell you what happened afterward," Rosé commented. She didn't turn her head, she didn't wait for Li to respond.

She didn't want to waste her time on a stupid conversation. She didn't want to kill her, even though Li deserved it.

Rosé tried to mount an attack by throwing a wave of air her way, but she passed through it. Instead, it rebounded and hit Rosé, shooting her against the hard wall. She fell to the ground.

"Oh dear, you need to do more than that to kill me. A rune of reversal," Li Wang said, laughing and approaching Rosé. "For a Lysion, your powers are somewhat limited. Every magic you use will go against you. I don't think you studied the runes." Yes. She deserved to die.

No matter what Rosé did, Li was able to dodge her. "Poor thing. She thinks just because she has powers, she can kill me." With every word, she took one step closer. "Why did the gods give such great power to such a naïve person?" asked Li Wang. A circle of black fire formed around them.

Li brought their faces closer.

"Because you don't deserve it," Rosé said, spitting in her face. She walked away and wiped the spit off her face.

"You want to kill me, don't you?" she asked, looking at Rosé, keeping enough distance that she could escape any of Rosé's moves more easily. Rosé just agreed. Of course, at this point, she wanted to kill. "So? What's the difference between the two of us? We want the same thing.".

"The difference is, I'm protecting myself and you're killing me for wanting to." There was a pain in Rosé's words. Her whole body hurt, but she got up. If they could all get up, so could she. She leaned against the wall for support, but something hit her arm, causing her to falter, she held back a scream.

As she put her hand on her wound, she felt the warm blood on her fingers. More blood and metal.

Li laughed.

She took a few more steps back.

"I met your mother. Oh, of course I met her. She was the kind of woman you looked at and knew was powerful. She overflowed power." She smiled more as Rosé groaned in pain, her hand practically burned from Aiden's blood. "I'd always been jealous of her, of course. It's not every day you'd find a woman like her walking around. But I admired her, Rosé. I did. It would be hypocritical of me not to do that. Three months before you were born, she sent me to China.

I didn't know she was pregnant. She asked me to get something, and when I got back, I found out she was dead."

Rosé tore the dagger out of her arm.

"She was smart to send me away. She was suspicious of me, but she had too good a heart to directly send me away." Li was in front of Rosé now. A dagger pointed at her neck. "She knew she couldn't trust me. This shows that her power was no greater than her wisdom. Bu … when I look at you," she locked eyes with Rosé and she smiled more, "I can only see a silly, self-centred little girl who loves the attention."

Li squeezed the dagger over her neck. "What are you?" Rosé asked.

"Is that your question, right on the verge of death?"

"I suck at picking the right questions for the moment."

"I don't have powers like you, but I'm agile, I can read emotions and see in the dark. I have my gifts." She penetrated another dagger that Rosé had not seen in her belly. Rosé groaned. "And something curious about me, I don't like quick deaths, as you deal to other people. I could have hit you in the heart, but you'd be dead in seconds. Your stomach, but the bile would do all the work. Let's wait and see what happens to this cut on the belly." She turned the dagger.

"You won't be alive to know." *Something curious about me: I kill fast.*

Rosé took her mother's dagger and launched it directly at Li's neck. *'Our mind is our enemy and our source of magic, which controls all our movements,' they said, but what do you do when your source was pierced by a dagger?* Rosé found out in seconds.

Her body falling to the ground echoed in the empty hallway. Rosé pushed her to the side. She couldn't leave the feeling of satisfaction aside. She pulled the dagger out of herself.

She had to make sure Li was dead.

Fire wings came out of her back and were directed like two meteors to Li's body, burning it in seconds.

"Some witches need to be burnt," she whispered. The fire shone in her eyes. "Villains talk too much" she complained. "jeez"

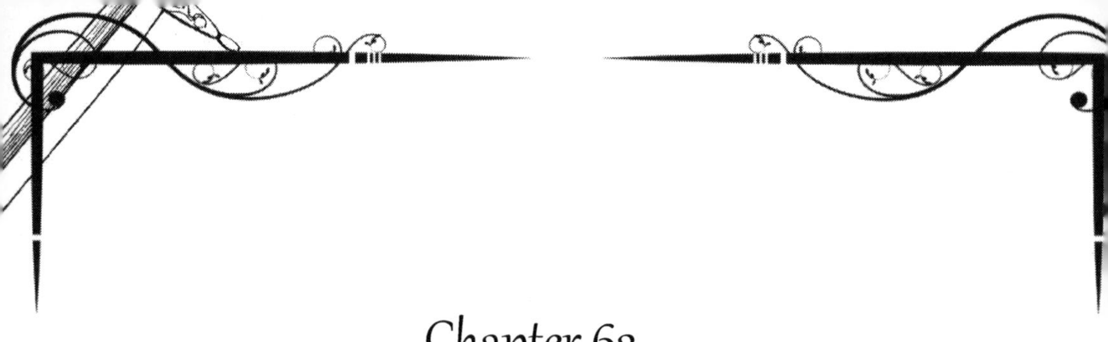

Chapter 62

The air was biting, and darkness took over. Skylar had already lost count of how many people she had killed during her battles with some of the most diverse flying animals she had encountered in the air.

It was too dark. She couldn't identify who was from Amondridia and who wasn't.

She looked at the palace and saw some lights were on. Some windows showed people locked in combat, fighting for their lives. Others were dominated by darkness.

At this point in the game, who would still be alive? Honestly, she wasn't very interested in that.

Few people had entered through flying portals. At least that's what she thought, but soon the sky became a battlefield. Fire, blue lights, green, red. Winds and tornadoes.

Dragons spitting fire, others with poisoned saliva. It was screams and dread, things Skylar had grown up hearing.

She was more than used to it.

The dragon she was using was amazing. She never thought she'd fall in love with one. They're very hard to dress up and she didn't have the patience.

Skylar spotted someone in a red tunic. It was no one she knew so it was someone she had to kill. She started following him. He seemed to be on a broom, which would make him an easy target. Shen was good at deflecting spells and jinxes. Even Skylar had to hold on tight so she would not lose her balance, and the huge human mounted in front of her didn't help.

She didn't know how she hadn't lost that shit yet.

She was nearby when Shen approached the target, she grabbed her gun and shot him, making a loud noise, hitting whoever was there. The scream was a sharp melody in the music of the war.

She smiled.

Screams.

She somehow knew that scream. It was masculine.

Skylar spotted Josh, it could only be him, fighting a black phoenix. While a normal phoenix had healing powers, the black phoenix caused destruction, its venom was worse than any existing animal. Its poison was known to make ammunition and was used in the ancient age in arrows against those guilty of treason.

It caused a slow and painful death.

It was like slowly burning, from the inside out.

Skylar went to meet him. Toxic liquid and fire, a deadly combination. Shen spat fire, hitting the black phoenix which began to fall, almost hitting Sky's leg with its claws.

If she hadn't moved her foot in time, she'd have a sore passage to the other world, but she didn't know to which one. None of them wanted her.

She smiled at the thought of it.

Shen spat fire again, scaring her and starting what looked like a free fall. "Hey, calm the fire in that ass down, boy." Then she understood why he had spat.

Josh and his dragon were falling.

Skylar held on, her goal was to reach Josh. She screamed for him and reached out, but she was not fast and strong enough, the four had hit the ground. Skylar went rolling. The hard ground had welcomed her harshly.

Everything was dark. Her vision was gradually returning. There were fireworks in the sky. She thought they had won and were celebrating, but that didn't make sense.

Her head hurt, and something hot pushed her to the side as if it wanted her to get up. It moaned in pain, just like her. He looked like a crying baby but was shaped like an animal. *A baby animal crying,* she thought and began to laugh, but her body protested.

With great difficulty, she rose. Shen was lying next to her. She didn't know how long she'd been unconscious. Her arm had several scratches and half of her uniform was no longer in place. There were tears and part of the fabric was loose.

At least there was nothing vulgar showing.

There was some creature crying beside her and it wasn't just Shen, there was something else. She turned around, limping. Her foot was aching and she could smell blood and taste it in her mouth.

She was bleeding, but she didn't care about it at the time.

Josh's dragon was crying like a little baby, emitting strange sounds. Sky went around him, trying to look for something and couldn't hide the shock when she saw the tear in his wings and black liquid dripping from it.

He had been hit by the black phoenix. Skylar stroked his face. She could see the weariness in his eyes. He was dying and she couldn't do much.

She went in search of her Katana, finding it a few feet away, and coming back. That was the only thing she could do for the poor dragon. She released the Katana from its cover and aimed it at the creature's heart. She closed her eyes and lunged.

One last noise came out of him before his eyes closed completely.

Skylar wiped her tears away and removed the blade. The blood was no longer red and that's how she was sure that what she had done was the right thing to do.

Skylar ran out to look for Josh. Maybe he was okay and fighting. She needed to help him. He was probably wounded, just like her, and they would have to fight together to combine their strengths. She couldn't see anything. Most of the ground was in darkness, the only light came from the fire in the sky.

She narrowed her eyes, trying to adjust her vision in the dark, until she saw something on the floor. Skylar approached and threw herself next to the body. She turned him over, she took her hand to his wrist.

"I am alive, demon," he cried. She could feel his pain in her own skin, but in a positive way and sometimes it bothered her, because it didn't matter how much she tried to be a good person, the pain of others was her pleasure.

"Unfortunately, you are, Dragon Tamer." She couldn't help him to get up. He was too injured. "We need Nina to help you."

"I know how to take care of myself. This is not the first time I have fallen from a dragon."

"Stay on the floor or I swear I am going to be the one to kill you."

She kneeled in the wet grass with the palms of her hands on the floor. She looked down, calling her servants. Even though she knew they wouldn't answer her fully, she had to try.

"Guardian of the Down World, I summon you. Obey your princess by darkness and ashes, bringing home every soul in the sky who doesn't come from Amondridia." Her voice was demonic. Her eyes were like fire.

<3

"What is your real name? Your daddy and mummy definitely didn't choose Skylar," Josh asked, looking at the sky. His pain floated through Skylar's body, feeding her.

Lying beside him, she closed her eyes and listened to the screaming. "Anubia. Anubia Saten."

"Why did you choose Skylar?"

She took some seconds to answer. "It's cute" she mentioned "You know, I'm able to like cute things too, idiot"

Chapter 63

"Can you stand?" That was the only phrase Rosé could fully understand. Kay was panting. Even with her vision blurred she could see the despair in his eyes. Before the world began to spin and a ringing sounded in her ears, she had tried to heal herself, but when Kay appeared, her thoughts focused on him.

She had seen that there was a lot of blood on his clothes.

Being on the verge of death, the only thing she could think of was how desolate and sexy he was at the same time if that were possible. There were new wounds on his face. His uniform was torn in countless places. Covered in blood, which Rosé desperately hoped was someone else's. His hair wasn't as neat as usual, it was messy, and a lock of hair fell into his eyes.

She tried to get it out of his face, but it came back, which make her laugh.

She didn't know if her laugh was internal or external. She wasn't sure if what she was seeing was real or just the fruit of her imagination. She hoped it was the latter.

Perhaps on the verge of death, the world would give you the opportunity to choose what happens or give you a final request in the form of an illusion that will make your life have a happy ending. Even for a minute.

Where at least, on the verge of death, you can be happy for a second, after a life full of disappointments and sadness.

Sometimes life likes to be funny and make everything a joke.

Sometimes it's hard to believe that life is vague and not a big coincidence.

'There is nothing more ours in this world than our own thoughts,' she had read somewhere.

The side of her navel hurt and with every move, she tried to make, the pain intensified. Her back seemed to be leaning against thorns, but she didn't feel as much pain there. It hurt, but it wasn't anything worse than the other injuries she had received.

And in answer to Kay's question, she just denied it with a shake of her head.

Rosé felt the warmth and strength of Kay's arms as he tried to lift her up. With effort, she passed one of her arms over his shoulders and he held her firmly. He must have been too tired, and yet, he was still carrying her.

She was in pain, but she wasn't. She knew she was hurt and could feel it, but at the same time her body seemed to have taken away her own pain because over time it wasn't as intense. She thought she had healed, but by placing her hand on the wound on her belly, her body seemed to carry an internal shock of pain until it stopped again.

Countless things crossed Rosé's mind, but her thoughts were interrupted by the pain when Kay moved sharply.

Rosé didn't know where he was taking her. Her eyelids were getting heavier and heavier. She wanted to close them, but Kay begged her not to. "Don't you dare close those fucking eyes. Stay with me, please." Pain. It was all she could feel in his words.

She had said the same words to Aiden a few minutes ago.

Stay with me.

Or maybe it was hours ago.

Kay had lost many people, and Rosé would be one more. One to add to the huge list. Rosé looked at his face, for a second their eyes met. One. Second. Enough for Rosé to find out that the damn butterflies were still alive inside her.

Don't kill them.

She wanted them there.

A moment of happiness in the midst of chaos.

If Rosé hadn't seen the tear come out of his eye, she would have confused it with Kay's sweat. She took one of her hands to his face and wiped it away.

Rosé had never seen him cry before. *Well, he wasn't necessarily crying,* she thought. There was only one tear, but then came another and another, and she dried each of them and, while doing so, Kay closed his eyes for a few seconds, enjoying, savouring her touch.

Kay was saying something, or at least it seemed he was. His mouth was moving, but the only thing Rosé could hear was the ringing in her ears. Her vision was a little blurred. Her body heavier, as if gravity was changing. But in the midst of all this, she could still feel Kay's hands on her back and legs.

Until he put her down.

Something was wrong.

Unluckily for them, someone was in the way. Kay left her in the corner to fight once more. She couldn't see who it was, but Kay had designed a shield around her and then a black cloud came out of her hands, as usual. He disappeared and someone fell. Rosé heard the sound of shots so low; they were almost inaudible.

Rocks flying.

A lot was going on.

Anger grew in Rosé's chest. Hate. Pain. She took her hands to the ground. She thought of numerous ways to kill the other man.

The ground started shaking and opening up in front of them.

Roots began to come out of the middle of the black marble, climbing up each leg, climbing up to his torso, and thus taking hold of his neck. Rosé closed her hands on the marble, feeling the small particles of stone scratching her hand. The man took his hands to the root of his neck, struggling to rip it off, but it didn't help, because it was in that position he stayed until his arms fell to the side of his lifeless body.

And from there he was pulled into a hole she had made in the ground until a piece of stone closed him, like a tomb.

Rosé tried to crawl to Kay who was still on the ground recovering. He got up with difficulty and picked her up again. How could he do that? Get attacked and then get up and still carry her?

She felt weak.

Kay began walking with her again until they arrived at a wall with a huge picture with strange symbols. It was another alphabet. An Asian dialect she didn't recognize.

The portal.

"Close your eyes." Rosé obeyed.

Everything went cold.

<3

They were in the Outer World, in the cold air of the night. Horns.

Laughing. Conversations mixing, becoming incomprehensible. Cars passing in the street. She was afraid, or at least someone was.

"What happened to her?" said a familiar voice.

"I don't know. When I found her, she was already like this." Rosé could have sworn that Kay was crying. No, he wouldn't be crying for her. He was still standing and intact. If he were crying, he wouldn't be acting like this. "We need to take her away. She can't stay, I can feel her magic on my hands."

Sky asked him numerous times to calm down, but it was useless. Kay was giving orders, asking her to open the car door and saying they had to go to the base.

Base? There was another base?

Kay put her in the back seat of the car. "It's going to be okay, baby, please hold on a little longer," and kissed the back of her hand. Rosé protested when he closed the car door. He wasn't going with her. She didn't know what was coming out of her mouth, but she heard Skylar say something about another vehicle.

Her body was reacting in slow motion. Her mouth moved, but her voice reached her ear a few seconds later, as her brain was having difficulty processing the sound waves that reached her.

"If she doesn't get there the way I left her, I will—" Kay began.

"You're going to kill me. I know. I know, Romeo." Rosé followed Kay's voice and saw that he was on a motorbike by their side, they exchanged glances once again. Sky started her car, abandoning him.

The path wasn't too long, or maybe she fainted on the way. She put her hand on her wound and raised her arm. She was still bleeding.

She could hear Skylar muttering something and cars honking. Someone was chasing them.

At that point, shouldn't she have died by now?

Soon she could feel Kay's arms on her body. "We're here." And that's when Rosé relaxed and lost consciousness.

<3

Kay was shaking. They arrived at what looked like an old, abandoned building. Sky was in front, opening the doors and leading them down the stairs. There were many rattled by their movement, as they seemed to have been there for many years.

Kay held Rosé in his arms, taking care that nothing, not a door or wall, dared touch her injured body.

After passing through numerous doors and corridors, all three of them made it to the base. There were tatami mats on the floor and a huge mirror on the wall. It looked like one of the training rooms, but a little smaller.

The base was the hidden training camp in London in case of emergencies or shelter. There was some tinned food and a tiny kitchen, plus some ingredients for the production of potions.

Sky had already begun preparing something that would help with healing when Kay put Rosé in a comfortable place.

"Tell me she's alive," Sky asked, panting, running from one side to another.

Like the others, part of her uniform was damaged and numerous injuries littered her body. She was shaking. With each attempt to measure some ingredient she ended up putting more or less than she should. Sky couldn't hold a spoon or pot in place.

There was oil on the floor, and other liquids that at the time of despair had fallen to the ground. She had knocked a glass bowl to the floor that broke into pieces and spilled a red liquid across the kitchen.

"Holy shit," she murmured.

Kay took his hand up to Rosé's neck and then to her wrist. "Alive." Kay was looking for something to put under Rosé's head. He searched through cabinets and drawers and found clothes, picking up all possible items and placing them under her head. "Is there any way you can hurry?"

"I'm trying to do it as fast as I can. Do you remember what you told me when we met?" asked Sky hopefully.

"I am going to kill you?" he remarked, confused.. "I don't know how convenient that is right now." He went to her and picked up some ingredients inside the small minibar.

"No, well yes …but you also told me, *'Stay out of my way'*, so stay away while I try to help you and Rosé," she announced, slapping him so that it moved out of her way.

"Tell me it won't be long?" he asked.

"No," she said, stirring the ingredients. "Almost finished. Distract your mind with something. Your despair is making me desperate. I can feel it from afar, and honestly, Kay, despair doesn't suit you. Put your fucking hand on your heart or whatever you do." Kay took his hand to Rosé's heart. Her heart rate was slowing down. It was weak in his palm. "I said on your stupid heart."

"The only heart that matters to me is hers." Kay looked at Rosé again. She was pale and so small. Kay passed his free hand over her forehead, leaving a kiss, then slid to her cheek, her chin, to her lips, and he remade the path on the other side.

Sky came to his side, lifting Rosé's t-shirt and depositing the mixture on her bruises. Her body contracted a little, but Kay returned it to the previous position. Sky poured the concoction on every wound they found on Rosé's body.

Rosé reacted instantly, trembling, and contracting lightly. Sky worked on closing every opening and wound until it was nothing more than a scar.

"There's just a little bit left," Sky informed, stirring the liquid in the pot.

"You can do more," Kay said, arranging Rosé's clothes.

"No more ingredients. It only had enough for one prescription."

"What about you?"

"I'll be fine." Sky got up and went to the bathroom and turned on the water while Kay pulled the clothes from under Rosé's head and handed some of them to Sky, along with the pot.

"I won't use it. Rosé closed some of my wounds while I was carrying her out of Lys. She used the rest of her strength to help me." Sky didn't respond, just waved and Kay went back to Rosé, sitting on the floor. He put her head on his thighs and his hand on her heart. It was beating faster than before, relief took over his body. It was only then that he realized his whole body was aching.

"Have I told you why I don't live in the Down World anymore?" Sky asked from the bathroom. She was without her shirt, just a bra. Cleaning up the wounds.

"No."

"You know who my parents are, right?"

"Impossible not to know," Kay commented, raising his eyebrows and smiling, his hands on Rosé's hair.

"There's a place there. A huge and beautiful building called Dreamland. I told Rosé about this place," she began, stopping to complain about the contact of the liquid with her wound and dropping a few swear words. "Where every person already existing in the world has a drawer with their lost dreams. Everyone. From the smallest dreams to the biggest dreams. The ones where people give up. One day I was walking there. I'd like to pick out a random drawer o and discover people's dreams. It was cool and depressing at the same time.

"For a good few century of my life, I thought only people on earth had a drawer there, but one day while I was wandering, I found my mother's." She sighed, writhing every moment that the liquid touched an injury. "She had innumerable dreams. More than I thought anyone could have, and between them, there was a dream of having a daughter who was crueller than her—"

"Why am I not surprised?"

"Shut up, let me finish." Kay raised both hands in surrender and then returned to Rosé's hair. "She wanted someone better than she ever was. Mercilessly. Psychopathic. I didn't understand why that dream was there. She didn't tell me she couldn't have other children. When I questioned her, she got pissed off at how I had the audacity to be snooping around her stuff. She said she was going to keep hers with my father's somewhere else so no one would know. She also told me that she couldn't have any more children and that she was being forced to settle with me and my two older brothers."

"Dade and Thanatus?"

"I wasn't enough for her. She said, when I was born, she saw something she never thought would come to someone like me. Someone born in the Down World. Someone born to kill and hate. Incapable of a sense of pity and sympathy. A demon. An underworlder." She looked at the cloth in her hands. It was soaked in blood. "She saw some kind of light. Something she couldn't explain—"

"Why are you telling me this?"

"For the whore who gave birth to you, Kaydan, let me finish the fucking story," she screamed.

Kay just laughed. "Sorry Princess of the Down World, proceed, Your Royal Highness."

"Thank you," she said, calmer. "I wanted to prove that I was cruel enough to be who she wanted. I've done things that have left me traumatised for years and that still weigh on me to this day, just for her to be proud of me. For my whole family to be proud of me. Dade and Thanatus were their favourites. They have brought countless people to suffer in our world. The pride in their eyes made me want to end my life, but … I couldn't do it. I was already in the world of the dead. When you went in there to steal Gloria's chalice, she ordered me to kill you in the worst possible way."

"Burned alive?" he murmured.

"There is a worse way to die than being burned alive. You tried to use the Ring of Repentance to get out, but it was fake, like everything in the Down World is. Everything is fake and wrong. Everything there is perfectly imperfect. The only thing that could get you out of there was me. I don't know why I saved you that day, burning you would make my mother proud of me, at least that's what I thought, but deep down in my heart, if I have one, I knew she wouldn't be proud." She let out a long sigh. "I don't regret what I did, not at all." Sky got up and went in search of something to eat.

"You didn't finish the story," protested Kay.

"When she found out, she kicked me out in the Down World. The end."

"You must be the first person I know who's been kicked out of there," Kay said, letting out a loud laugh before Sky put her index finger to her lips, she then pointed to Rosé on his lap.

"Crazy, right?" she asked, with a cereal bar in her hand. "I never saw them again, and that was, what? 1756?" She took a bite of the bar. "I can't even remember."

"Pretty crazy."

"You should clean up. When she wakes up, we're going to have to go back. We cannot simply abandon Amondridia." Kay didn't get up and didn't say anything.

"It's strange to see you like this," she remarked, leaning on the bench. "In love. Has your moment of shock passed?"

"If you're referring to the fact that I've already accepted and gotten used to loving someone, the answer is no." He placed his hands on Rosé's cheeks. "I can't explain what's going on inside my chest right now. I cannot say that I love her, because what I feel for her seems to be more than that."

Chapter 64

Sky continued to sleep in the corner while Rosé was in the bathroom, cleaning her body from the dry blood and minor injuries that Skyler had not found, or she had not taken the trouble to close. She changed into new clothes.

The new uniform was not black like the previous ones, but dark grey. It didn't have zippered pockets.

She had to adjust the gun supports on her body again.

She was wiping the blood from her arm until something grabbed her waist, turning and lifting her on the sink bench. "For a moment I thought I had lost you," he said, taking Rosé's cloth and wetting it in the water, passing over what was once injuries. The liquid only closed them, but they didn't cure it internally one hundred percent. "What happened?"

"I don't want to talk about it." It was still fresh in her head "Not now. So, you'll have to use force, because nothing is going to come out this way," she said.

Kay smiled, showing off his two dimples. Rosé looked at them and held back her own smile. "It doesn't take much to make you angry, you test my patience," he said without looking at her, putting more force in his grip. "I just don't want to hurt you."

"I know you do not, but I'm already hurt. Besides, we need to talk about something."

"Seriously?" He looked at her. "What?"

"Were you crying when you brought me here? I thought you never wept," she said, mocking him and smiling.

"Fuck you, Rosé. You can be bad sometimes." Rosé let out a laugh but stopped when their eyes met again, and he got serious. "Don't stop smiling, and … I wasn't crying. I had something in my eye."

"Okay, I'm going to pretend to believe that." Rosé got rid of Kay's hands and took her hands up to his cheeks. He hadn't cleaned himself up completely yet. There was dried blood on his face as she had seen before. She closed her eyes and concentrated. She felt his blood flow down her body and when she opened her eyes again there were no more injuries. She took his arms. His skin was smooth, as if nothing had happened, finishing the work she had not achieved before. She tried to get off the bench, but she was stopped by Kay.

"Why didn't you do this to yourself?" He looked mad. Rosé did not respond and tried to get out of his arms but failed. "Why?" They looked at each other for what seemed an age, until she tried to get away again. "Stop trying to escape and answer me." he grabbed her thigh so hard, it hurt.

"I tried before you got there, but then …" Kay looked away and ran one hand through his hair before turning his attention back to Rosé. "It was as if … I … then you came and I just … I didn't want to."

"What do you mean, *you didn't want to*?" His gaze showed hatred.

"Look at everything I've done. I've seen people dying. I don't even know who's alive or not anymore. I don't know anything else. I deserved to have died there. Slowly. I don't deserve anything my mother built. Nothing. I deserve every wound I have and more. I … I didn't deserve anything good. I hurt countless people. I almost saw Aiden die, I … I …" she stopped. She didn't know what else to say. She had nothing more to say. She tried to control herself, but the tears were already dripping and, just as she had done with him, Kay cleaned up every tear. "You have to clean yourself up, we need to go."

Rosé came down from the bench and Kay didn't stop her. She went towards Sky and woke her up. She got up and went to get her things without saying a word. "Are you hurt?" Rosé asked from the other side of the room. Sky turned to her. "I can cure you."

"You don't have to. I'm fine."

"Please. It's the least I can do. I can heal you internally too," she said, heading to Sky. "You saved me." Sky did not protest when Rosé took her hand and within seconds all the bruises, scratches, and cuts she still had on her body were exchanged for her normal skin.

"Thank you." Rosé reciprocated with a smile. "I'll wait for you outside. I'll make sure everything's alright and safe." For a moment Rosé thought of following her. She didn't want to be alone with Kay. She knew she was going to get a sermon or something, but she decided to stay. Rosé had to reload her weapons and position them again.

Rosé went to the corner where the guns were and dared not look at Kay. Why was she mad at him? She took her weapons and ammunition, placing them on her leg. Kay started doing the same.

They didn't even exchange a word.

She took new daggers since she had lost hers in Amondridia. She wondered if her mother's dagger had burned with Li and it flooded her heart with grief. She fastened her hair in a ponytail and looked in the mirror.

She was ready.

Some parts of her body still aching and when she touched the side of her navel, she released a low moan. She turned and went toward the door, still without looking at him.

"I still think you should finish healing yourself," he said from behind her. Rosé stopped and closed her eyes. She couldn't ignore him. Not after everything he'd done. She didn't even know why she was angry. She turned around. Their eyes met. "Don't look at me like that. You're going to break my heart," he said, pulling a mock sad face and taking his right hand to the centre of his chest. Kay came towards her, his movement was serious. Their faces were inches away. "What have I done to make you treat me like this?"

That was a great question, and the problem was he hadn't done anything wrong. As she looked into his eyes, she realised that the pain was not coming from him, but from her. She was angry at herself for letting all that happen. It wasn't his fault.

Rosé wanted to hug him and cry in his arms, but when she thought about it, it made her feel weak.

That's what she was, weak.

They had fought countless times in wars, risked their lives, and lost people. "Why aren't you talking to me?" *Because if I open my mouth I'm going to cry.* That's what she wanted to say. *Because if I touch you, I'm going to fall to pieces in your arms. We don't have time for this.*

Rosé turned and began to walk away. They didn't have time for emotions. They had no time for their weakness. He doesn't care about that, she thought, he's strong.

She took one, two, three steps before he grabbed her by the waist, causing the very thing that she feared.

The pain took over.

The feelings cut a hole in her chest and came pouring out.

The scream at the bottom of her throat escaped through her lips. Kay turned her around and hugged her, squeezing her against his chest. All the blood and bodies. The screams in the corridors. Her own blood in her hands.

He stroked her back and waited for her to stop crying. She cried until her whole body hurt. Until all the pain came to the surface and out of her body. "She took a while," remarked Sky from the door.

"I'm sorry, I'm sorry, I'm sorry."

"Shhh is alright, love."

"I tried to get … be strong. I've tried. You shouldn't have grabbed me. I'm just … I wanted the tears to stop, I wanted it to be over." Kay stroked her back until she calmed slightly and began cleaning her tears once more. "You must think I'm weak, that I'm not … I'm not like you."

Kay held Rosé's face between his hands. "Don't ever say that again, don't you dare think about it again." A few seconds passed.

"I must look horrible," she said, wiping her face.

"Rosé I'll beat you if you continue with these thoughts."

She was no longer crying. "Beat me and see what happens," she said, getting up. Kay started laughing and hugged her, something Rosé did not reciprocate.

He kissed her forehead, then her cheek, the other, her nose, until he descended to her lips. Warm and soft. The kiss was calm and home. Fuck! It felt like home. "I missed this," she remarked between kisses.

"I haven't." Rosé pushed him away and headed for the exit. "I was kidding, Grouchy Smurf," he said. Rosé passed Sky on the way. Relief passed throughout her body when the wind touched her face.

The day was dawning. Kay was behind her seconds later and he sat on the bike. "Come on," he said, hitting the back of the bike.

"I'm going with Sky," she said. Now she had a reason to hate it.

"I was joking." Rosé did not answer. Kay got off the bike and grabbed her by the legs, positioning her on the bike. Rosé crossed her arms and made an angry face at him.

Kay picked up his phone and took a picture of her, and then, moving his lips to her ears, with one hand in her hand and the other on her thigh stroking up and down, leaving light squeezes, he said, "Keep that angry face, I love it." Kay sat at the front but turned to Rosé and pulled her by the thighs, putting her legs on his.

Sky hadn't come back yet.

"Sometimes I hate you," she said, not looking at him.

"Sometimes? I'm glad it's just sometimes." She knew that if she looked at him, she would find a huge smile on his face and those damn dimples. "I'd be surprised if you told me, you didn't hate me."

"Do you hate me?" she asked, looking at him this time. A big mistake.

"I hate you until you get angry, then I fall in love again," he said, putting his hands on her thighs, which makes her blush, and her body ignites. Kay must have figured that out. He kissed her once more, this time more intensely. The kisses go down to her neck and her throat and shoulder. His finger passed over her lips while his mind seemed to be in another place. "Fuck!" was the only thing he said.

"Okay guys, not everyone is interested in this, plus we're in the middle of a war, dear. One we haven't won yet," Sky said, emerging from behind them and getting into the car, she lowered the window. "Any news?" Kay shook his head. "Great, I take it they may be dead." Kay cast a look of anger at Sky. "I'm just being realistic."

Kay's start on the bike scared Rosé, who quickly clung to him. He didn't stop to make fun of her.

<3

They arrived at a Chinese restaurant and entered. Rosé didn't protest or ask questions. "He's not here," remarked Kay, holding Rosé's hands. "Shit. Did they find out?" Sky and Kay exchanged glances and began to explore the place. Each to one side, abandoning Rosé.

She didn't know what exactly they were looking for.

"Kay?" cried Skylar, coming out of a double door that probably went into the kitchen.

"Yes?"

"He's dead." They exchanged glances.

"I thought so." Sky held a small note in her hands.

Give me the girl.

Chapter 65

"What the fuck just happened?" asked Rosé. "Is this the secret, untraceable portal of this Lys?" She knew that it was. She had been in that corridor a short time ago after a fight with her father when she decided she was going to leave Amondridia.

The idea crossed her mind once more. At first, it seemed the right thing to do. The solution to her problems, but thinking again, it seemed a little reckless. If she had had difficulty killing and defending herself, surrounded by people with experience, can you imagine her fate out in the world, alone and with no one around to help?

However, this idea had not fully left her head. If things got tense again and they treated her like a child, she probably wouldn't think twice before picking up her stuff and leaving.

"Exactly."

The smell of construction was in the air. "We have to move it," Skylar said on her side, but knew the message wasn't for her, but for Kay. He still held Rosé's hand tightly.

He always held her like this.

Skylar raised her hands and gestured something, muttering something so subtle that Rosé was not able to understand her. Skylar went up to the wall and hit it, demonstrating that what was once a passage to the Outer World was now a normal passage. "We're going to need to change both sides. Just one, it's going to continue to be a big risk for all of us." He agreed.

Rosé still felt guilty about not being able to argue about these things. War tactics, plans to keep Lys safe, magic in general. She knew little more than the facts she had read in books.

They were still in front of the white wall.

"He was too good for this world," Kay commented after a long uncomfortable silence.

"Good people don't stay in this world. And it's very selfish of us to wish them to stay." Skylar sighed deeply and slapped Rosé's arm, inviting them to move on because there was so much to do.

They started walking down the halls. She had already been in that hallway but had never imagined that it led to a Chinese restaurant. The walls had turned white, which highlighted the blood on the floor. There were some creatures and people clearing the corridors. Removing the bodies.

Others were tidying up what had been destroyed.

Bullet holes in the walls. Huge pieces of marble displaced. Destroyed frames and objects. There were countless guns on the ground as well. Burned things. Flooded. Branches of plants and plants themselves, others still floating.

For a moment she thought they had won.

He was waiting for her.

He was still alive.

"What did you do with his body?"

"What do you expect, Kay?" Her ponytail moved from side to side. Her gaze was low, looking at her feet as she walked. "I couldn't leave him there and I had no stars to deliver, without saying it was too early for that. I burned it. The fire will set off the alarm and the fire-fighters will decide what to do with the rest."

"They're going to open an investigation into this," Kay warned.

"Good luck to them finding the person responsible for this. None of us are on the record."

"Rosé is."

"No. Tom asked Ruby to erase them in time. Especially when she came into Amondridia. They have no record of her. It's like she never existed," Rosé had a slight smile on her face when Sky looked at her. "For your safety and so that anyone who wanted access to your data would not find anything. No one's going to be able to track where and who you've been with. Your allegiances and these businesses, all that can be used against you."

Rosé couldn't help but notice the angry looks on people's face and who was she to judge them? She had abandoned Lys in the middle of a war where she was needed. A war caused by her and responsible for the death of countless people. A lot of them are innocent.

At first, she looked at them, but then she began to look away. She felt like a criminal being hunted. She imagined a poster hanging with her picture on it and *Wanted* written underneath.

The air started to get heavy. The smell of sulphur and metal overwhelmed the place. She couldn't forget the faces of those she had attacked. Their last glances before their hearts stopped beating. The screams and gunshots echoed in her ears as if they were trapped in the air.

Each step was harder than the one before.

Kay shook her hand. She did not look at him, but from the corner of her eyes she knew that he too had not looked at her. The clothes on her body were still heavy. The ammunition, guns, daggers. She had lost her mother's dagger. Kay's hand also seemed heavier, holding her, rough and warm.

She looked at him but swerved. The silence was bothering her. It was leaving her with her own thoughts. A huge danger to everyone. What if she lost control?

She thought about what to say, but she didn't find anything fitting. Rosé had nothing to say and everything to say at the same time. But everything was too sensitive to be discussed. At least for her. This wasn't the time to cry.

She raised her head once more, taking a deep breath.

The memories of that night had come back to the fore in her mind. The screams, the crying, the people. Aiden was on the couch almost dead. The iron in his belly. Leg. Arms.

She tried to push the memories from her head.

She shook Kay's hand and this time he looked at her. "Is everything alright?" Sky looked at her too.

"Yes, I just don't know if I'm ready to know what happened while we were gone."

"The enemies vanished" that was the only thing Skyler said.

Upon arriving at the canteen, a huge hole opened in Rosé's chest.

There were innumerable people injured and healing. Sad and depressed.

The sun was already shining in the sky, penetrating the almost entire glass ceiling. It was the only thing entirely alive in that place. The air was heavy, more than before. Thick and dense, it made breathing difficult.

This was a place where Rosé had good memories, but now it seemed like a nightmare.

Looking at the side Rosé spotted Aiden and Misty at the table where they always ate. They were talking, but they weren't close to each other. He hadn't managed to conquer his feelings of rejection yet. "Rosé." A voice called her, before looking away she realised Aiden had heard.

Ariady came towards her and hugged her tightly and Rosé reciprocated. *She's alright. She's fine,* Rosé repeated to herself.

Ariady looked away. She was tired. Destroyed. Rosé had never seen her like this before. Her hands held Ari's arms and healed many of her wounds. She was getting good at it. "You didn't have to." It was the only thing she could do.

"Of course, I needed to. My way of thanking you for everything you've done."

She smiled. A faint smile covered up the pain.

Big smiles disguise great pain. Helena had told her that one day. If Ari couldn't hide it, she didn't want to know how broken she was inside.

Aiden came toward her and held her in a strong embrace. She could barely breathe, but she didn't care as long as he was alive. Her best friend was fine, she could feel him in her arms. He kissed her on the forehead and hugged her again. "I shouldn't have let you go at the time."

"How do you know?"

"Kay texted everyone," he said, releasing her. "It's all my fault. Again."

"No. For—" Rosé was interrupted by Misty hugging her. She was alive and well too. Rosé hugged her tightly until they parted ways. Theo and Nixie were not there, and Rosé began looking for them, but before she found them, her gaze found Gustav's and Ruby's side.

Gustav came running over and hugged her, lifting her from the ground. "Hey Rosélina, it's good to know you're alive," he said, putting her down again. Gustav was very strong and was surprised that none of her bones were broken. She checked to make sure she still had full movement of her body.

"It's good to know you're alive too," Rosé reported.

"It's difficult to take me down, dear. They've been trying for centuries and I'm here, alive. Well, technically I'm not, but …" he commented, and they both laughed. That was the reason Rosé loved Gustav, he was always happy.

Ruby was closer, but she didn't go near her.

"Hey child, good to see you alive."

"Not even a hug?" Ruby denied it. "A handshake?" She denied it again.

"The war isn't over yet, I don't know why they're so happy," she said. "We haven't won." She was right. They were still in conflict, but for a moment she had forgotten about that.

"Who did we lose?" Kay asked.

A dangerous question. Rosé looked at them. She knew she'd stopped breathing, waiting for the answer. No one spoke for a moment. Gustav looked away and took a step back. Ruby was drinking something from a glass. Misty and Aiden looked at each other.

"Kristina," Misty started the list and every name that came next was a punch to Rosé's body. Even though she didn't recognise any, the impact was great within her and she gradually lost control of her own body. "John, Marcellus, Casey, Jamie, Emm, Stacy, Kendrick, Harry." "Josh and Mr Lee," interrupted Skylar.

Her heart stopped as if it had been ripped from her chest and stepped on.

Josh

"Kidding, Josh is alive, Rosélina, you can start breathing again."

Rosé almost grabbed Sky's neck. "Well, he almost died."

She cannot deny that she felt more impacted by his almost death, but remorse hit her chest when she imagined that her mother would know every person in her own kingdom. She imagined that Sarah knew each person by name, while Rosé didn't know even a fifth of the people in that place.

Rosé had not had the opportunity to spend more time with Josh or get to know him better, but when he showed her the dragons, he was so kind and understanding.

For a moment she thought of Theo. Her eyes began to look for him and Josh until she saw him, along with Nina, near the table that his family always sat at. He was sitting looking at the floor.

Rosé was no longer paying attention to the list of names. Mr Watson was hugging Nina who was crying. Ascelin had JJ on her lap, asleep, and Lux was by their side. Nikko was missing. Maybe he was invisible, hiding his pain. Rosé didn't think twice before she started going toward them.

She almost knocked Aiden down when she pushed past him and walked away.

Theo raised his head to watch as she approached. She opened her arms and wrapped him in a tight embrace. He squeezed her hard and she did the same. Theo definitely had one of the best hugs.

He was about to fall on her, and she knew how he was feeling. The weight of the body was impossible to explain. There was so much information to process.

She helped Theo sit down again. He was too heavy, and her body was already weakened, but she did her best. She tried to wipe away some of her tears, but it was no use because more were coming behind.

"It is good to know you are alive," Josh said behind her. She hugged him as well. *They are okay. They are all fine.*

Nina raised her face. Her eyes were swollen. She had a huge cut on her chin and one above her eyes. Her uniform was still intact. "We are healing," her voice was weak and hoarse.

Rosé came to her and hugged her and healed her from there and Rosé could feel that she was doing the same for her.

"Where is Nikko?" Rosé asked. She needed to see him. She expected him to hug her from behind in surprise. With his smile and charisma.

No one answered. Nina started crying again. "Where's N-Nikko?" Rosé's voice failed.

She turned to Theo who was already standing again. Josh was by his side. Hands-on his shoulder.

"Rosé," Theo called. He was crying.

"No." *No. No. No. No. No.* "Where is N—" she stopped in the middle of the sentence and smiled. A faint smile. A form of defence. Resistance. She took a step back, tripping over her own feet.

"He b-became an angel," he said, forcing it out, as if the words couldn't get out of his lips. "He sacrificed himself and saved JJ"

Her heart stopped. She was speechless. It looked like her soul had come out of her body. Nikko couldn't have become an angel. Not right now. Never. She needed him. She needed Nikko. He was supported to be there now and for the rest of her life, besides her. With her. Hugging her and teaching sign language.

She didn't know where she was or where. What part of the world. What time. She'd lost that notion a long time ago.

She thought the unknown names were painful to hear. She tried to imagine every face and if she had found them in the middle of the invasion. But nothing compared to the pain in her heart when she realised what had happened to Nikko.

Her cursed angel.

<3

'You know what I'm going to do when I die?' Nikko had asked her.

Rosé took the pen and put the notebook on his leg. 'What?'

'I'll become your guardian angel.' Rosé looked at him. How could he be thinking about that? The sun shone on his face while the moon remained omitted, but with its unique brightness.

'I don't need a guardian angel,' Rosé wrote, adding a little smile.

'Everyone needs a guardian angel and I'll be yours and you will be mine.'

'I'm cursed. People like me don't have guardian angels.' She had no smile on her face anymore.

'So I'm going to be your cursed angel,' he wrote, getting comfortable at the bench. Rosé was holding the notebook so tightly and only noticed when she saw that her nails were leaving marks on the notebook.

'I don't want you as my cursed angel, I want you here with me. On my side. Don't ever think about it again. That is a horrible thing to think about, Nikko.' She was almost crying as she imagined Nikko leaving her. He was admiring the moon. One of his little hair locks almost got into his eyes. She pushed it away.

Nikko read and looked at her. Rosé couldn't smile. He took his little fingers to the corner of Rosé's lips and pulled it up so she would smile and let go. 'I'll always be with you,' he wrote. 'Death, for people like us, is just around the corner.'

Rosé wrote the same in response.

'I love you,' she gestured in sign language, something that Theo had taught her. Nikko smiled. A sincere smile that only he had. 'Of all the existing moons and suns, you are my favourite.'

'I love you,' he repeated.

It had been a long time since she'd told anyone that.

She looked at the skies one more time before writing. 'There are stories that could be infinite. Good people, books, films. Good stuff should not have an end.' Nikko looked at her for too long. Long enough to make her feel uncomfortable.

'What is the thing with the infinity? Good things are only good things because they do not last forever. Everything that lasts, gets boring and annoying, look at old people.' Nikko laughed with Rosé.

'Poor old people.'

'I don't want to live forever, just enough.'

'Just enough.'

<3

Aiden didn't let go of her for a second.

<3

"Where does he want to find me?" Rosé asked.

There were many things Rosé hated. Getting flowers. Body contact with someone she didn't have much intimacy with. Lies. Very hot days. She hated people who chewed loudly by her side or breathed with their mouths open. She hated people who felt sorry for her. Failure.

A lot of things.

People who marked books or folded the tip. She hated it when she smelled or when someone else smelled. She hated her uterus on those days of the month. She hated a lot of things, but nothing compared to the fact that someone hurt someone she loved.

They could beat her, swear, torture her, and she wouldn't mind. She'd deal with that. She'd find a way to survive. She always did.

But …

If someone touched, looked wrong, spoke ill of someone she loved … that was a whole different story. It hit her in a different way. It messed with her in a different way.

They had done much more than touched him. More than cast an ugly look at him. Much more than saying things about him. She didn't ask who it was, or where or when it happened. *There are things in this world that should not be said or heard,* Mr Bebbols had said something like that. She wanted to, but she didn't need to know.

"You're not thinking of going, are you?" Ari asked. She grabbed Rosé by the arms, squeezing her. She was looking for her gaze, but Rosé refused to look at her almost rosy eyes. "Are you crazy? You … No. No. I can't let you do that."

"Ariady. Where. Is. He?" she repeated. Still not looking at Ari.

Pain.

A feeling is often strong, even for those with a very well-disciplined mind. A feeling that manipulates, controls your actions and your body in such a sneaky and mischievous way.

In the imperfect world we live in, we are the ones who decide what to do with the pain that is brought to us. A feeling that can kill you is a great fuel for revenge.

She could grieve for everything that had happened and nothing would change. Not even a cell would move. Time wouldn't go back to prevent all of this from happening.

"In the d—"

"Are you serious about this? Are you really going to tell the place?" Kay said, taking a step toward Ariady.

"You know what? I don't want to be boring or anything, far from it, but Kay, stay out of it," protested Rosé, pushing his chest slowly so that he would walk away.

"Don't talk to me like that and *stay out of it?*" he said, turning to her and laughing sarcastically. "Are you listening to yourself?" he asked, pointing to his own ear and taking another step toward her to the point where she had to look up to find his eyes.

"Don't you think this is my decision?" She used his words against him.

He caught her face, bringing it closer to his. "You don't have an ethical reason to go there."

"Where have you been all this time? Didn't you hear what happened? Didn't you hear the list of people we lost for a war that was mine? I've spent my whole life afraid of everything. People, my decisions, what I've done or failed to do. I've lived my life for other people. Being quiet and putting up with all this shit. I'm tired. I've been afraid to fight this whole time and look at what happened," she said, looking around. "I let people do it for me."

"I can't let you go," he said, leaning closer to her, his mouth near her ear. "I can't," he whispered, but before his mouth could touch her skin, she pushed him lightly, grabbing his uniform.

"Don't you dare. I'm not kidding," she said. "I have nothing to lose."

"Yes, you have. You have a lot. You have me. You have all of us. We all care about you."

"You just care because if I die, you're all screwed," she said. "Because if I die and they take my power, you will live in a world more fucked up than this one."

"Yes, okay. If you die, we're all fucked, but you're still one of us. You're still my person, a friend, a partner. You're still Rosé. You're still someone important to us. Love … my life …" he said. "Stop being selfish."

"Selfish?"

"That's not what I meant," he said. "I—" He tried to say something else, but she closed her hand in front of him and no more sound escaped him. Any of them.

She had taken it from them.

"I'm sorry," she whispered. A tear fell from her eye and Kay wiped it, even though she left him mute, he looked after her. "But selfish?" She looked him in the eye. Her hand still held their voices in the air. "Maybe I am. Maybe I'm more than that. I let people die in a fight that is mine. This war was mine and mine only and for fear of fighting alone, I allowed you all to fight with me. I was selfish because I put my fear above everyone else. I let innocent people die for me. To protect me. This is my fight and I've done enough damage here." She wasn't yelling. Her mind was aching. Her tone was calm and subtle, in a perfect tone for all of them to hear.

"I'm tired of being afraid and yes, now I'm going to be selfish again. This is my fight, and I won't share it with anyone else. I'm going to go on this suicide mission alone and I'm going to fight for my future. I'm sorry, but I don't need to explain my decisions. And I shouldn't even be apologising for it. I think people have decided too much for me."

She took a deep breath and kissed him. He pulled her into it like he'd never done before. She returned their voices.

She looked at Ari. "Where the fuck is he?"

"Dungeons." Her face was so pale that Rosé could see her veins.

"Great."

"Don't die, please." He held her arm.

"And who said I'm going there to die?" Rosé turned around and started walking out of the canteen. She didn't say goodbye to anyone and no one came after her. She didn't care about the looks.

Sometimes the princess can't just sit in the tower waiting for a prince and her 'happily ever after'. Sometimes she must break down the door, dominate the dragon, and kill the king on his throne.

<3

"She didn't look back," remarked Gus.

"I raised her like that," Tom said.

Ari went to him, lifting him up by his collar. "And you didn't stop her."

"She was very clear in the corridor of the portal. Don't you remember? She took your voices away just by closing her hand. Wake up, Ariady Prinze."

Chapter 66

"Pay attention. Never. Never put your head down to life. It is too cruel, and if you lower it, things are only going to get worse. Even though the crown is heavy, a princess never drops it."

There's no way you can avoid the crown falling. Sometimes it's not the crown that weighs, but the head. Tears weigh. The eyes get heavy, and the pain pulls it down. *She was right,* Rosé thought. Life is cruel and it only gets worse. Life will never get better. It destroys you. It sucks you and pulls you into an abyss that you have to fight to get out of, with countless hands grabbing you all the time and pulling you down one more time. Bus she was wrong. "*A princess never drops her crown.*" We all drop the crown, but few are brave enough to grab it from the floor and place it back on the top of the head.

<3

She walked through the door and followed the path she had walked with Kay a few times. Every step made her heart race more and more until it was nearly leaping out of her chest. Everything she had gone through in her life came to the fore in her head once more.

It was cold and dark. Lifeless, just like her.

She stopped at the last doorknob, ready to go in. She took a deep breath on one, two, three, four. Stopped.

Her heart in her hand and death in her eyes.

Upon entering, Rosé came across the strong smell of alcohol in the air. Bottles that once contained drinks were broken into thousands of pieces everywhere. It looked like someone had taken advantage of the moment alone to throw a glass party.

Take out your anger on all the breakable things that existed.

The lights were on. The graffiti was ruined with red paint. It wasn't just simple drawings. The dungeons were covered in graffiti and incredibly well-made and often realistic designs.

From the top she could see all the damage. Anguish took hold and she felt pain for all that had been destroyed. She was so focused on destruction that she forgot what she was doing there. She took the sword. She glowed in black flames.

She positioned herself. She trusted her powers, but not enough to put the sword aside.

She was looking everywhere she could. Everything her eye had a right to see. Positioned. She reminded herself of the position of each of her guns, in case everything fell apart.

She went up the stairs.

The space was very open. He didn't have many places to hide.

One step.

Two.

She stopped and watched the perimeter. Trying to see beyond what an ordinary eye could see. Something invisible. A detail she was forgetting.

Another step.

One more.

The glass had been a great move. Depending on the way you fall, it could do a lot of damage to your body. It could cause an injury that would stop you from doing whatever it took to protect yourself.

Five steps.

Six.

The air was cold. It had never been like this before. Maybe it's the lack of human warmth in it. Her breath left a slightly visible smoke in the air. Why was it so cold?

Seven steps.

Eight.

There was no sound.

Nine steps.

She looked at the ceiling, nothing there. The only noise that existed was from her boots on the dark stone floor, which she cautiously crossed.

There was only one place he could be. Behind the curtains, that's where her focus turned. The curtains danced in a wind that had no noticeable source. She was waiting for them to open up, finally revealing Oldo.

Oldo.

She remembered him very well. His careless blond hair. His strange old robes. His snare smile and clumsiness. She remembered him at the underground station and especially in her room. Eliot. Oldo. From his disgusting hands on her to his voice, it made Rosé's stomach turn.

She went to the curtain. Not so close in case something happened, but close enough to listen to what was there.

The curtain opened.

She positioned herself. Her hands went to the base of her dagger, but it did not put her anxiety at ease.

Some old dolls started moving. A princess. A dragon and her prince. It was the typical story of the maiden, trapped in the tower until the prince saved her. He would kill the dragon and take her with him to the palace and make her queen.

Well, that was the original story.

Little did the princess know that when she became queen, her life would be worse than when she was inside the tower. There she was alone, she used to do what she pleased. She got food in some mysterious way that no one knew. There she was happy. After she got married, she was trapped inside a castle. Stuck in a cycle of events and meetings, bound by conduct and rules, and the only interesting thing she would do was fuck the prince with the obligation to have heirs.

However, this story was different. The prince entered the tower, reached the princess, and when they were about to leave when he was about to finally save her, she locked the prince inside the tower. She pulled out a gun, tore the dress, climbed on the dragon, and escaped.

If she hadn't been at war, she would have laughed and laughed about the story, but instead, she clapped her hands. "My congratulations, I didn't know that someone like you had creativity."

"It's sad, isn't it? You fight for something. Risk your life for someone who betrays you," a very familiar voice whispered behind her. "So depressing. A true story. It is what happens in our society and proves to us that our own self-preservation is much more important than other people."

Rosé gradually turned around. She knew that voice too well. More than she wanted.

Chapter 67

(WARNING: I see a clown and he/she is reading this)

"Smurf," Kay said, approaching her, his hands on her waist, pulling her to him.

Rosé frowned, confused. "I asked you—"

"Let you fight alone? I know. But I just couldn't," he said against her neck, pulling her even closer to him. To his hard body. "I couldn't let you." She closed her eyes, enjoying every second of that moment. His mouth moved over her neck. His hands were on her waist, squeezing and pulling her.

The kiss rose to her jaw and was about to come to her lips when she stopped and walked away from him. A move that cost her a lot of effort because she really wanted to be with him. She wanted more than his lips.

"How did you get here before me? Where's Oldo?" She looked around for him. To the old man with dirty-blond hair. The glass cracking on the floor with every move. "Ari said he'd be here waiting for me."

"You took too long doing your dramatic walk," he said, swinging one hand in the air, "and well, Oldo is here."

"Where?" she asked, looking around. Kay's hands passed over the entire length of his body. Rosé thought for a second until it all suddenly made sense. After several months in Amondridia, Rosé had completely forgotten what had happened before her arrival in this Lys.

Oldo had turned into Eliot.

A very similar version of him.

She stepped away.

Kay was no longer there, but the figure she was waiting for. Oldo Blake. He wasn't underdressed like she had seen him in the underground but wearing a black suit. Perfectly fitting his body. His hair stuck in a high bun.

It took her a few seconds to react. Her brain now had to work very fast. Assimilating the last few months of her life and be prepared for every sudden movement. The disgust came as she thought of all the moments she had lived with Kay. Their short story.

Every intimate moment was corrupted.

She had let him play her.

"I told you I was the villain, all this fucking time" he commented, standing with his back to her and walking away. More cracks in the floor "I believe you have a lot of questions, right? I want you to die knowing everything," he said, sitting with difficulty in a chair, one of his hands on his back. She said nothing. "As you can see, I'm getting old, and my magic is weak. I need to renew myself and you …" he said, pointing to Rosé. "You are my passage to greatness. Salvation." He opened his arms. "Be kind, darling. Turn yourself in."

Silence.

Rosé had so many questions and none at the same time.

She could have killed him there. Ended. Her magic burning inside her chest. In her veins. Every cell of her body but she felt miserable. She thought that she was clever and somehow in the stupidity of her mind, she imagined being a step forward.

She had fallen into the commodity of being safe when her enemy was right beside her.

"Come on, we don't have much time." He said "Ask me, kid"

She didn't know what to think. What to feel. She had been used this whole time. Played like a poppet in a show.

She looked down, "Since when?"

"Since your visit to your father's house, do you remember?" The man who opened the door inviting her to wait for her father inside. Little she knew that that address was fake "I've always turned into him. He appeared to save you from me, but he failed"

Bile rose in Rosé's throat.

He's been acting like this ever since you got here, Gustav had informed her.

"The real—"

Oldo didn't let her finish her sentence. It was almost like he knew what she was going to ask.

"The real Kay failed to protect you and he never fell in love with you. Never! You never talked to him. You've never really met him. You never touched him. You never trained with him. He barely knows you." He made a glass filled with a brownish drink appear and had a sip. "And I don't know how you could be so foolish to believe that someone like Kaydan Dagon would be able to fall in love with someone like you." That pity voice of him, was not helping. She never met him. How could she, after years of stone heart, allowed herself to love? Knowing this world was fucked up. "He already has a woman in his life. Very pretty, by the way. Blonde, model body. Eyes greener than an emerald. Powerful and who knows how to have complete control of her magic. Penelope is her name."

Penelope.

She kept her expression neutral. Her tears waiting for a signal to leave. One of them fell, but Rosé cleaned it up. She analysed his every move. Every move of his mouth. His look. His hands and his foot, which was moving up and down very fast. Anxious.

Could he be telling the truth?

Before the world collapses, Rosé: questions and answers.

It wasn't easy to keep calm. She found strength she never thought existed.

He already has a woman in his life.

"Where is he?"

"In a place far away from here. From you. Penelope has been helping me to keep him away. Nothing that magic could not resolve," he said, satisfied. "Hmm, I think I'd rather talk to you like this." Kay was right there in front of her again. "Love makes people weak, I told you that. I tried to warn you. I needed you weak. I needed your trust, I needed to break you into a thousand pieces and ... Look where you are. I can feel you," he said with a smile. The same damn smile that made the butterflies in her stomach dance. The same damn smile that made her want to live.

It was all a lie. A trick.

She shuddered at the icy air that caressed her skin. They were still looking at each other. Kay/Oldo drank a sip of his drink and left it on the floor.

"The false despair, *I can't let you go.*" He let out a laugh. "I told you my life depended on you, *vida.* Only someone who lived in the Outer World would know the Smurfs. Childish film" He uncrossed his legs. Kay. Kay was right there in front of her. The same Kay she had loved. Kissed. She had let him touch her, to see her vulnerable.

It was a lie.

A fucking lie.

"The training. Our beautiful trip to Rome. The expensive dress I bought for you and the shoes. I … honestly, Rosé, I was trying my best to impress you. Kay would never do that. He's a hard ass. He spends a lot of money on himself, because of his ego." Gustav had also mentioned this. Kay would never spend money on her. "Ah yes, his ego is too big. Montiero," Rosé is disgusted to hear his name. "That's why I didn't kill him. Why I didn't let you fight him. One of mine. I told him to go there, Lorenzo … Betrayer." He drank another sip, making a sound with his mouth as if he had not drunk for a long time Rosé remained silent. Gathering strength. "Summer? A trick to get your sympathy." She was still watching him. Incredulous.

"You don't need my magic. You took it from my mother."

"From your mother?" he asked, confused, taking his hand to his chin, thinking. "Oh yes. That was a lie, too. I'm not the one who killed your mother. By the time I got there, she was already dead. Lying on the ground. Dead, dead. A hole in her chest. Poor woman. A great woman, Sarah. But I lied and told everyone it was me. The power of conquest through fear. My daughter helped me with illusions. How do you think I managed to overpower Wysez? How do you think I got everyone together?" Still no answer from her. "I threatened them, I said I would kill them otherwise because everyone believes I'm powerful." He leaned over. "What's the point of being powerful, but being stupid?"

"Come on, Rosé, think of everyone involved in this. Your father, who's been lying to you all these years. Your mother, who died, not to protect her own daughter, but to protect her legacy. She never loved you enough to fight and be with you. It's all about power. Helena who never dared come after you, she never risked coming to see you, not even in the Outer World." He was laughing and then stopped, making a sad face.

"Aiden and Misty, the almost couple, right? Where are you going to fit in? Kay doesn't love you. Theo hates you now, Nixie doesn't even talk to you. Ariady …" He laughed. "Just helped you to protect the world from me, the same as Noah Watson, Gustav, Ruby, Li … You let Nikko die, it's all your fault. JJ's traumatized. Ascelin is broken. The unspeakable twin. You killed an innocent Sentiment. You don't deserve what you have.

"Nikko, you little angel. The child you should have taken care of. The child that mirrored you. Little did he know you were more broken than he was. Think of the girls at school. In solitude. Think of all the times you looked at a new internet post from a party or something you weren't invited to. From the times you looked in the mirror and saw nothing less than a monster." He stood in front of her, smiling at her.

He's manipulating you. That's what she said to herself, but ... there was no way to be manipulated when what he was doing was telling the truth. Why was she feeling so miserable? So vulnerable and depressed.

He was using her past. He knew about her past.

She looked at him once more. She could feel the icy dagger in her chest, and he wasn't the one holding it. She felt empty and so fucking lonely. There was no one to help her, because one more time she decided to fight alone. One more she lost.

Rosé admired him once more. One last time. That perfect, well-designed face. His light grey eyes. His mouth and smile. "Poor thing," he said, his smile widening. "I can feel his such strong feeling on my bones" He reached for the dagger and threw it away. "Have you forgotten? I want you alive. And I'm not done yet." He wasn't Kay anymore.

Aiden.

His light brown hair and chocolate eyes. He stood up and walked away from her. "One of the things in the world worse than a heart broken by unrequited love is the betrayal of a friend. From someone you trusted," he said, turning around, making the glass crack. She was on the floor, on her knees, not knowing how she ended up there.

He raised her with magic and threw her into the chair he was sitting on before. Her head raised to look at him. An object covered her mouth.

Pure iron.

"An act of manipulation," he said with his back to her. "I was not him, though but...Manipulating a child's mind like Aiden was the easiest thing there is. A naïve boy with a hot temper who one day hated you and the next appears in your room with food and the biggest smile on his face." He laughed, turning to her and kicking some shards of glass. She closed her eyes, but she could feel one of them stick in her cheek. "Come on, Rosé, I thought you were smarter. that child was afraid of you. Fear of your magic. The guiding star wasn't for you exactly. It was a way to get to his mind." Oldo informed. "A touch in the fabric a spell on control" he whispered, explaining all his games.

Aiden. Oldo. It approached her face. The only thing she could see was her best friend. Her 8. "Do you know how hard it was to keep him close to you when what he hated most in the world was you and then ..." he paused. "It turned into fear. He thought it was you manipulating him." His voice. His face. His movement. His smell. Aiden, but not Aiden.

"I hate you. You were never my best friend. You were never going to be. You disgust me," he said in her face. "You are nothing less than selfish. Look at the number of people you let die, Prin."

"S-OP," she tried to scream. That was the best she could do. She screamed desperately. Her lips shaking. Her eyes could barely stay open. Her body begged him to stop. Her mind was full and confused. Weaken and tired. She was mentally and physically exhausted.

She now knew about the manipulation. The lie. But it's different when you're in front of the person you loved, and he tells you the truth to your face. That was all so real.

Aiden. Oldo laughed. Aiden's laugh. "No, no, no. It's not over yet." Not Aiden.

Sarah.

She shifted into her mother.

Her chocolate and wavy hair fell on her shoulders. Her face was serene, hands together above her belly button. Rosé could see her own reflection on her mother's face, understanding why people kept comparing her.

Rosé looked at her without believing what she was seeing. No. No. No. That's a lie. She approached Rosé and knelt before the chair.

It was easy to say that it was a lie. A mental manipulation. She knew it. Rosé knew perfectly, but … when you are there – looking and hearing – it is just … it seemed so real, and her desperations and fragility were just another key locking the rational door inside her brain. The exhaustion. She felt like hallucinating.

And Kay? It just perfectly fits.

Sarah seemed sad and worried. She put her delicate hands-on Rosé's cheek and dried up the countless tears that fell. Her touch was delicate. She was smiling. It was shy, almost non-existent. She was stroking Rosé's face.

The air was heavy. She couldn't breathe.

Rosé body was trapped in the chair. Not by ropes, but by magic. The damn magic.

"Mum?" This was what she meant to say, but her mouth was blocked.

Sarah's thumb stroked her cheek. "Hi dear." Her voice was more beautiful than she could have imagined when heard in real life, more than when she heard it in Ariady's memories. She looked at her, memorising every detail. Every dot. Every wrinkle. Every sparkle in the eyes. Every little movement of it. She paid attention to everything she could get before it was over. "You look so beautiful and so much like me. I wanted to be here with you. I wish I'd taught you everything about your magic. I wanted to …" She let a tear slip. "Oh dear, I'm sorry." *He* stopped. *He* left a kiss on her cheeks. "I'm sorry for everything that's going on and for leaving you." She dried another tear.

Real. Too real to be one of the purest lies.

A great actor. But she knew more than anything in life that that woman wasn't her. Her mother was dead, and she wouldn't get her back.

Rosé's face became neutral.

Sarah laughed and walked away. Her/his laugh was … she had no words.

She had desired this moment numerous times. Imagined her mother by her side. Her hug and kiss. The warmth of her body. The comfort of her embrace. She's imagined it over and over again.

Kay was back. "Why not let your man take you to Wysez? Maybe it'll make you more comfortable."

Looking at him and knowing that everything they lived through was a big lie, it was like a knife tearing at her heart little by little. Like the air being ripped away by force.

She looked at him and did the same to her mother. She didn't know where the real Kay was and maybe she would never see him. She looked at him and memorised his face so that in the middle of the night she could imagine the two of them together. Even if this was true, she was going to lose today.

His smell. His look. His lips. His dimples when he smiled …

His dimples? There was no dimples when Oldo smiled. She observed and smiled ironically. Maliciously. Even with the object in her mouth, she smiled, like a villain or a psychopath.

So many sweet lies.

You don't play with my feeling without get injured in return. Tell truth is one thing, even for manipulation, but lies? Little fucking lies?

The sword rose, as did every piece of shattered glass, and before he could notice, the sword was embedded in his abdomen. Glass covering every inch of his body, now coloured red.

Rosé broke free without much effort and freed her mouth. Throwing the metal far away. Her jaw clenched so hard it hurt.

Warm blood flowed down her hands, but there was no pain, no scream.

The greyish eyes widened. The only pain that could be heard was Oldo's. "You almost killed me. Maybe if you had tried a little harder you would have succeeded." Rosé started smiling. "Almost." Rosé looked into his eyes. The eyes of someone she loved so much. Her face inches from Oldo's/Kay's. "You disgust me, and I feel sorry for you, despite your greatest effort to bring me down, you failed. One. More. Time." Rosé spun the sword in his chest. "You forgot a very important detail. Magic leave traces. Even I know that"

Rosé squeezed the sword more into Oldo's chest. His lips were open, blood dripping from them. He was still in Kaydan's body and that … that scene, broke her into countless pieces. He might not be Kay, but he still looked like him.

Rosé released the sword.

He changed to Aiden and then to Sarah and stayed that way until his eyes closed and he went back to being Oldo Blake.

But it was too late.

She'd seen the scene before. Three people she loved, dead and lifeless on the ground. Lies dancing in the melody of her pain.

The ground shuddered.

Everything became bright and then dark.

<3

Dream

She was back between the concrete walls.

Something wet her exposed body and it wasn't the rain.

It was darker than a night without stars.

She leaned against the cold wall and pulled her legs up to her chest, raising her face.

She closed her eyes, feeling the liquid form a pool around her. Her hair stuck to the side of her face. She let the liquid take care of her. It flooded her. Covered her, until her entire fragile body was completely immersed in it.

She screamed.

A water bubble went to the surface.

She opened her eyes and the concrete walls turned to dust.

She freed herself from the tower of her mind by becoming friends with her own pain, so that she could kill the most beautiful lie: happiness does not come on a white horse to save you. So don't wait anxiously for THE DAY because it doesn't exist.

Get out of the tower and conquer what the world tried to take from you, telling you beautiful lies, disguised as stories.

Epilogue

Amondridia was the last memory she had. The white palace. The gardens. The ocean. Every piece of Amondridia was passing in front of her eyes like a movie. How she failed that place, until it got small, and air disappeared.

<3

Rosé woke up as if she had woken up from a nightmare. Her chest frantically raising and falling. Her lungs looking for air. She slapped her chest, coughing.

Her hands touched something soft and warm.

When Rosé opened her eyes, she was in a room. Not in Amondridia. Not at the University. Somewhere different. She didn't recognise it. She had never been there before. It was small and cosy.

She tried to get up. The memories came back gradually.

Someone opened the door. Rosé looked at her and soon she disappeared.

A while later a woman came back. Very familiar.

"Welcome dear! Make yourself at home."

"What happened?"

"I don't know. Why don't you tell me?"

Characters' list with quick descriptions.

Rosélina Johnson Lysion – The main character. She has honey eyes and light brown hair. Too stressed for her size.

Helena Johnson - 'Mother' of the main character. Tanned skin. Light brown curly hair and blue eyes.

Tom Johnson - Father of the main character. Black hair and brown eyes. Wears black glasses. Probably hated by everyone.

Sarah Lysion – Mother of the main character. Honey eyes and light brown hair.

Ordinary flat mates (appear only at the beginning.)

Eliot – MC's favourite flat mate. Ginger. Tall and skinny man. The dramatic friend.

Hanna – Blond hair and blue eyes. The crazy bad bitch friend.

James – Dark skin, shaved head and dark brown eyes. The computer master guy.

Jessi – Never appears, but I imagine her as having black hair and dark brown eyes. The always-parting-and-out-of-the-house friend.

Elementris:

Aiden Moore (fire): AKA her 8. Brown eyes and hair. Skinny, but with build-up muscle. He matched Rosé's weirdness.

Theo Watson (earth): Two coloured hair and skin (due to his vitiligo). Blue eyes. The sweet, happy, calm man. The one who is always in peace with the world.

Nixie Watson (Water): Blue eyes and dark blond hair. Hates attention but loves a good drama.

Misty Ortiz (Air): A curvy black woman. Dark eyes and amazing curly hair. The fashion Queen. The happy, humble woman with a badass personality.

Vampire:

Ruby Browen: As white as snow. Hair always changing, brown reddish eyes. Tattooed. The I-don't-have-time-to-your-shit kind of person. Don't like people.

Gustav Maximilian: Dark skin. Shaved head. Gold fang. Build-up tattooed body. Dark eyes. The human comedy.

More:

Skyler Saten: Demon's daughter. Dark black-bluish hair with reddish ends. Brown reddish eyes. The freak that everyone loves. Kind of crazy sometimes.

Kaydan Dagon: Dark mage. Her enemy that became lover. Dark brown hair. Greyish eyes. Tattooed build-up body. AKA walking comic and, the guy you might fall in love with. (or not)

Ariady Prinze: Mage. Her mother's best friend. Pink long hair and faded pink eyes. Petite. So cute and adorable until you provoke her. Always worried, but a badass.

Mr. Watson: Sorcerer with mind gifts. Nixie, Theo and Nikko's grandad. Grey hair. Dark eyes and grasses. A huge scar from his left eyes till the corner of his lips. The patient-impatient man.

*Mr. Watson is Nina' dad and have other grandchildren: Ascelin, JJ and Lux.

Nikko Watson: Sorcerer with mind gifts. Tall skin boy. Dark hair. Honey and white eyes. THE NIKKO.

Oldo Blake – Villain. Blue eyes and blond hair. The son of a bitch. Lier.

Mr. Bebbols/Mr. B – the ginger sassy cat.

Author's notes

You can breathe now. Kay and Rosé are still a couple, and you might be "Wtf happened?". Well, answers will come in the next book.

I really hope you didn't doubt me. Because no, that wasn't a dream. That would be very cliché and stupid.

The story of this princess (or not) is just starting. This book was just an introduction (That it might not have been that good. Not 'gonna' lie).

But...

Be ready because shit is about to get real.

We haven't reached the "end" yet.

Until our next journey, a spicy kiss <3

Acknowledgements

(*If someone actually read this*)

Honestly, I believe that *A Dance in the Dark* was written for myself (If that is not too stupid to be written *nervous laught*). During this process, I started to understand more about my own pain and mind. For a long time, I thought I was lost in this world and this novel help me find myself again. How? Well ... that is too complicated to explain. Sorry!

This was the place I used to run to on bad days.

Writing this novel made me realise how this world is complicated, but most of all it showed me that what is not real can save lives. It showed a different alternative to things, of being a refuge, and I know that, as a reader myself, many people find refuge in books. Find comfort in fictional characters and their fictional world.

I believe that the purpose of this book is not only to entertain but maybe to save lives. I do not know if this book is going to help someone, but I really hope it does, as it helped me.

I hope you enjoyed the beginning of this journey and I hope that I didn't offend anyone. If I did, I am REALLY, REALLY sorry. It wasn't my intention.

It is my first book. It probably sucks, but I am learning.

Of all the people in this world, I really wanted to thank my family for all the support they constantly gave to me. Especially when this book was just a stupid idea and I looked at them and said, 'I want to be an author. I want to write books for the rest of my life.'

I want to thank my mom for being the first person to read my work and my cousin for designing that amazing map at the beginning.

Also, I want to thank all my friends who showed support.

And (yeah, there is more) I want to thank God, for always giving me strength, resilience, and patience to keep writing and not give up, even when I looked at the document on my laptop screen and wanted to delete it and give up everything.

Being my first novel, writing it basically alone, with no experience, I do not have many people to thank. But I want to make it clear that anyone who helped me make this dream come true has a special place in my heart. (Right side of it 'btw')

In addition, I want to thank you, the reader, who got to this point and didn't give up on it. Sorry if It boring at some point. I know this book is not perfect or well-written, but it is something.

I really appreciate everyone who gave my novel a chance.

Thank you so much!

About the author

(First of all, it is pronounced Julie. Portuguese phonetics and parents' decisions. What can I do?)

Jhuly is an Italian-Brazilian writer who lives in England. Passionate about fantasy and romance stories, she decided, after reading tons and tons of novels, competition entries, short stories, and poetry - to deal with her feelings and write her own novel and finally make her dream come true.

She describes herself as a dreamy and passionate person, who can be kind of crazy sometimes. (Nothing you should worry about). She doesn't have a degree, but she lived in three countries and speaks almost four languages fluently (I call that genius. Kidding!).

She is definitely not a serious person, as you can see.

Printed in Great Britain
by Amazon

86896438R00237